Kate Aylesford
A Story Of The Refugees

by

Charles J. Peterson

Double9
BOOKS

Kate Aylesford
A Story Of The Refugees
by Charles J. Peterson

Copyright © 2024

All Rights reserved.

ISBN: 978-93-62762-64-1

Published by

DOUBLE 9 BOOKS

2/13-B, Ansari Road
Daryaganj, New Delhi – 110002
info@double9books.com
www.double9books.com
Tel. 011-40042856

This book is under public domain

ABOUT THE AUTHOR

Charles Jacobs Peterson was an American editor, publisher, and author. He was an editor at Graham's Magazine, co-owner and partner in The Saturday Evening Post, and the founder of Peterson's Magazine. He wrote several fiction and nonfiction historical works under his own name, as well as the anti-Tom literary novel The Cabin and Parlor; or, Slaves and Masters under the pseudonym J. Thornton Randolph. He belonged to the Peterson publishing family, which also included his relatives Robert Evans Peterson and Henry Peterson. Thomas P. Peterson and Elizabeth Snelling Jacobs gave birth to Peterson on July 20, 1819, in Philadelphia, Pennsylvania. He earned a law degree from the University of Pennsylvania in 1838. He was admitted to the bar before graduation but never practiced law. He went on to become the owner and partner of The Saturday Evening Post, as well as the editor of Graham's magazine. He shared an editorial desk with Edgar Allen Poe, who later named him one of the "journalistic ninnies" of Graham's. In 1842, he established Ladies' National Magazine to compete with the successful Godey's Lady Book. Peterson's Ladies' National Magazine was renamed in 1848, and from 1858 until 1898, it was just Peterson's Magazine.

CONTENTS

CHAPTER I
THE NIGHT AT SEA

"Beautiful!
I linger yet with nature, for the night
Hath been to me a more familiar face
Than that of man." — Byron.

"The silver light, with quivering glance,
Play'd on the water's still expanse." — Scott.

It was out on the broad Atlantic. The sun had just set, red and colossal, behind a bank of clouds, leaving the whole firmament around him in a blaze of glory. Far along the western horizon, where the hollow dome of the sky cut the level plain of waters, a streak of vivid gold was seen, which grew less and less luminous, however, as it curved around to north and south, until finally it faded off, at either extremity, into the misty shadows of approaching night. Above this were piled, in gorgeous confusion, purple and crimson clouds, the warmer colors becoming fainter as they ascended, until a gold apple green prevailed. This itself subsided, towards the zenith, into a pure, transparent blue, in whose fathomless depths appeared a solitary silver star, that shone there like the altar light, which twinkles alone in the profound obscurity of some vast and silent cathedral.

Two persons, on the quarter-deck of an armed merchant man, were gazing at this scene. One was an elderly lady, precise in dress and look, the very type of a conventional and somewhat pompous old dowager. Her companion was a young girl just budding into womanhood, and of a beauty as peculiar as it was dazzling. The attitude in which she stood, though assumed without a thought, was just that which an artist would have chosen for her. The tiny left foot, with its high instep and slender ankle, peeped from beneath her petticoat as she leaned on her right arm to watch the sunset; the round shoulder, white as milk, yet with a warm tint like rich Carrara marble, was slightly elevated; while the shapely set of the swan-like neck, the trim waist, and the undulating outline of her whole person were more than ordinarily conspicuous. As she stood, her head was partially turned, so that one could see that her complexion was brilliantly clear; that she had a small, red and pouting mouth; that her eyes were so darkly blue as to seem almost purple; and that her hair, which swept in rippling masses from her forehead, as in a Greek statue, was of that rare color, which, though brown in shadow, flashes into fleeting gold whenever a sunbeam strikes it.

"How beautiful!" she said, after a long silence, drawing a deep breath that seemed almost a sigh.

The words, though rather a soliloquy than a remark intended for her companion, nevertheless drew a reply from the latter.

"Yes! niece," answered the dame, briskly, "I wish our cousin, Lord Danville, could see this sunset. He won't believe that we have skies, in America, equal to those of Italy."

"We must be near the coast," said the niece, after another long pause. "We don't find such sunsets up on the Banks."

"In about two days we shall be at New York, the captain says."

There was a third silence. The clouds in the west had now lost most of their gorgeous tints. They were generally of a deep purple, almost approaching to black, with only their edges tinged here and there with gold or crimson. Instead of lying, in fleecy piles, or hanging like thick curtains drawn partially aside, as they had awhile before, they were broken up into all sorts of fantastic shapes: castles and battlements, mountains and deep valleys, towers and spires, vast elephantine forms and figures, gigantic and weird as the Brocken: airy dissolving views that were every moment changing.

One mass of these clouds the two persons we have introduced continued to watch for some time. At first it had attracted their attention by its striking similarity to Gibraltar, as it stretched darkly along the horizon, like a colossal sleeping lion. Gradually the vapors spread horizontally, and became almost shapeless. Then, suddenly, they assumed form again, and there, plain to even the most unimaginative, was an old woman in a short-gown, with one foot angrily uplifted, a pipe in her mouth, and the most grotesque of all caps upon her head.

A light, silvery laugh broke from the young girl, and clapping her hands, gleefully, she cried,

"Aunt, aunt, see!"

Even the stately dame smiled, but only for a moment, when she looked more prim than ever, as if fearing she had lowered her dignity.

"The moon will rise directly," she said, crossing to the opposite side of the ship, whither her niece soon followed her.

In the eastern sky, the clouds were now of the richest amber, while under them the ocean was suffused with a delicate rosy hue. These tints slowly faded from both the firmament and sea, and darkness began to accumulate upon the prospect. In the course of a quarter of an hour, night had settled down. And now there appeared above a bank of cloud, that lay like a range of dark hills on the seaboard, the upper edge of the moon's disc. Instantaneously a bit of moonlight glimmered on the waters close under the side of the ship. As the planet gradually rose from behind the cloud, like some huge burnished ball of copper, the line of light extended itself to the eastern horizon, a tremulous bridge of silver.

It was but a little while, however, that the bright orb shone unclouded. The whole firmament, indeed, was fast becoming flecked by vapory masses: and one of these soon floated between the moon and the spectators. In a few moments the planet was entirely concealed. But far away, almost on the utmost verge of the horizon, her light, still shining from behind the cloud, lay on the waters beneath, like a silver lake on a blue and solitary plain. Gradually this began to contract, lessening and lessening until it seemed a mere thread of light along the seaboard; and then a low, white sand-bank: after which it vanished altogether. Simultaneously the upper edge of the obscuring cloud showed a faint pearly lining, which the instant after brightened into silver. Soon the tip of the moon's disc appeared; and once more the waves beneath the spectators began to glitter with the planet's wake, which directly bridged the undulating deep again; the crests of the dark waves, and even their higher sides, sparkling and shining as if discharging electricity.

"It is like a scene in the Arabian Nights," enthusiastically exclaimed the younger female. "But see," she added, shortly after, "see again!" The animated speaker caught her aunt's arm, as she spoke, while she pointed to a new variation in the brilliant scene before them.

Another cloud was now approaching the moon, and in such a way, that its shadow fell like a bridge of ebony, right across her wake. In a few minutes, the planet had vanished a second time; a second time the lake of silver shone on the far-off plain of blue; the white coast-line followed; the momentary darkness recurred again; and the moon again emerging, walked up the firmament, in cloudless majesty, like some majestic, white-robed virgin.

For nearly an hour the two females remained watching the changes of this lovely night. Not the least beautiful spectacle were the moonbeams shining on the snowy sails, which rose above the beholders, cloud on cloud, until the upper ones almost seemed lost in the sky. The single star still twinkled over head, swinging backwards and forwards past the mainmast, as the ship careened and rose in the freshening breeze.

Few words were spoken. The younger of the two passengers, absorbed completely in the loveliness of the night, had lost herself in a succession of those bewitching dreams which haunt the imagination in youth. The dim obscurity of the scene, when the moon was hidden for any considerable period, affected her with a sense as of the presence of eternity; and when her relative, complaining that the air grew cool, proposed an adjournment to the cabin, she was astonished to see her niece's eyes full of tears.

"I think it will rain," said the aunt, scarcely knowing what to say, yet wishing to dissipate what she supposed must be sad thoughts of the past.

"The wind sighs mournfully," answered her companion, vacantly, as if pursuing some secret train of thought, "mournfully as a lost child, alone on a moor, calling for its mother."

Again the dame looked at her. But there were often thoughts and feelings in the imaginative niece, which the good prosaic lady could not comprehend; and so she wisely made no reply, but called the captain, who stood not far off.

"Will we continue to have clear weather, captain?" she said. "It would be a pity, after so fine a voyage, to meet a storm at the end."

"A night like this is no sign of the morrow, ma'am," was the reply. "I shouldn't be a bit surprised if it was to blow great guns before morning. The wind has a treacherous feel about it."

"Dear me, you frighten us," exclaimed the good lady, with a slight scream, and visibly turning paler.

"Your niece does not look scared, at any rate, Mrs. Warren," said the captain, laughingly, as the young girl raised herself, proud and self-collected, at her aunt's remark. "I confess that I almost regret we have had no storm," he added, "for I would like to see Miss Aylesford's courage put to the test. She looks as if nothing would make her afraid."

"Oh! she'll be the death of me yet," replied the aunt, "she's so reckless. You'd tremble to see her ride, captain, leaping fences and galloping like a wild huntsman. She'll get thrown and killed yet: she has, all the time, such fractious horses; I never had a minute's peace in England, and I'm sure I shan't have any here either."

"Never fear, aunty," said the niece, affectionately, putting her arm around the other's waist, and yet with something of the manner with which one would soothe a timorous child. "I'll not be so lucky as to be thrown romantically from my horse, like heroines in novels, and rescued by some handsome cavalier—"

"Nonsense, child."

"Whom I shall marry, of course—"

"How foolish you talk."

"Even if I run away with him—"

"Pshaw!" said the aunt, quite vexed, not noticing the laughing glance which her niece directed towards the captain.

"Well, come then, I was wrong," said the gay girl, kissing her, "I won't keep you out in this chill night air. See, I'll wrap your shawl close about you. Captain Powell will take good care of us even if it does storm."

With these words, they bade the captain good night and descended to their cabin. The skipper continued walking the deck, for some time, listening to the rising wind, and occasionally looking up to the clouds that now began to scud swiftly across the sky.

"I was foolish to say even a word to alarm the good old soul," he remarked at last, as if conversing to himself. "I've seen worse nights than this turn into a clear morning. Besides, we have a stout ship and a good offing."

So speaking, he dismissed all idea of possible danger.

CHAPTER II
KATE AYLESFORD

"I love that dear old house! my mother lived there
*Her first sweet marriage years. * * * ***
The sunlight there seems to me brighter far
Than wheresoever else. I know the forms
Of every tree and mountain, hill and dell:
Its waters jingle like a tongue I know:
It is my home." —Mrs. Frances K. Butler.

Kate Aylesford was an only child and an orphan. It had been her misfortune to lose her mother, at so early a period of life, that she retained no distinct remembrance of her, and could only recall a mild, sweet face, which, as in a dream, seemed to have looked down on her, far away in the past, like a Madonna in a picture.

Eighty years ago, when our story opens, the facilities for female education were small anywhere, for it was a generation when Hannah More was considered a prodigy and when to be able to write grammatically was regarded as all-sufficient, even for a gentlewoman. There were few good schools for girls in England, and none at all in America. Mr. Aylesford, the father of Kate, held a different, and as would be said in this day, a worthier estimate of woman, from that which was popular among his generation. He looked back with regret to the time when ladies studied Greek and read Virgil in the original. The story told of Lady Jane Grey, that she preferred to stay with her tutor, Ascham, and read Plato, rather than join the chase, was one of his favorites. He early resolved, accordingly, that his daughter should be educated in a better manner than was the fashion of the day. He declared she should be capable, as he phrased it, of being a companion for a husband, instead of a mere plaything: that is, he added, with the reverent piety which, without being Pharisaical, formed a main ingredient of his character, "if God willed she should be so blessed." For, among his other old-fashioned notions, Mr. Aylesford held that a woman is never so fortunate as when a happy wife and mother.

Hence it was, that though he desired his daughter's intellect to be cultivated, he took care that her moral qualities, using that word in its widest sense, should not run to waste. In order to have her properly educated, he had determined that she should go to England; but unwilling to trust her to a public school, he had sent out with her his sister, an elderly widow lady, the relict of an officer in the army. It was a hard trial for him to separate from his only child, and one so winning as Kate; for not only the fond father, but every one who knew her, declared her to be the life of the house. To the sweetness of her mother's disposition, she added the gay heart which had distinguished her surviving parent when young. Fearless by nature, the life which she necessarily led, in a then comparatively wild district of the province of New Jersey, had given to her a courage and self-reliance above her sex and years: for not only at an age when girls generally are still in the nursery, had she learned to ride, so as to often accompany her father, but frequently, with no attendant but one or two stag-hounds, she galloped for half a morning through the woods. It was, perhaps, to her having spent her early years in this manner, that she owed her present blooming health and elastic step. Beauty is oftener the result of fresh air and exercise than of cosmetics.

Three years after her arrival in England, Mr. Aylesford died, leaving Kate one of the richest heiresses in the colonies. In part, her property consisted of houses and stores in the city of Philadelphia, and in part of vast tracts of land in the middle counties of West Jersey. The war between the colonies and mother country soon after broke out, and, for a while, it seemed as if the heiress was destined never to see her native land again. Her guardians were averse to her return to a country distracted by war, and her aunt, who, in spite of being an officer's widow, was timorous to the last degree, seconded them. But Kate inherited the resolute spirit of her father, and had early resolved to return, as soon as she became mistress of herself. Her fixed determination at last influenced her guardians, so that, after she had left school and been presented at court, a favorable opportunity offering, they had consented to her wish. They were the more willing to concede the point, because, at that time, the royal arms seemed about to triumph; New York was in undisturbed possession of Sir Henry Clinton; and the portion of New Jersey, where her estates lay, was, according to the current reports in London, free from the presence of the enemy. We need not add that these guardians, as well as her aunt, were warm friends of the king. It was on this return voyage, after a successful run of thirty days, and when, as the captain calculated, forty-eight hours would bring them within sight of Neversink, that we have introduced Miss Aylesford to the reader.

A long time elapsed, even after she had retired to her berth, before Kate could sleep. A vague presentiment seemed to oppress her. In vain she closed her eyes. The gradually increasing wind, and the rush of the waters alongside, prevented slumber. Once or twice she forgot herself in a doze, but a louder shriek of the rising gale, or a sudden dash of some huge billow against the timbers at her head, roused her with a start. Still, as there was nothing of fear in her nature, these things did not agitate her. She never even thought that anything serious impended, for she had heard such sounds often before during the voyage. Finally, long after her aunt was lost in slumber, she fell asleep.

She was roused suddenly, some hours after, by the noise of her relative.

"Wake up, my child, wake, wake," cried the good lady in accents of terror. "We are all going to the bottom. Oh! what shall we do?"

Kate sat up in bed and looked around. She and her aunt occupied the after cabin of the ship, which had been engaged exclusively for them; and this apartment was now lighted by a swinging lamp, which threw a faint yellowish hue on the surrounding objects. The floor of the cabin, rising almost perpendicularly, and then sinking again, showed that the ship pitched and rolled with unusual severity. Kate had never seen anything like it. Her aunt was dressing as rapidly as a person could, who had always to hold on to something with one hand, and often with two.

On deck, the hurrying of feet, the rattling of blocks, the creaking of yards, the sharp whistling of wind through the cordage, the quick, loud word of command, and other noisy and tumultuous sounds, betokened some important crisis. The roar of the sea had become almost deafening. It was, however, occasionally exceeded by the thunder of the gale, which now dying partially away, swelled again into a volume that overpowered everything else. At rare intervals, when other noises partially subsided, Kate fancied she could distinguish the rushing sound of rain.

The terror of her aunt called up all the courage of Miss Aylesford. Hastily attiring herself, she staggered across the cabin floor to her relative, and began to assist the latter's shaking hands.

"They have fastened us down here, too, I suppose," cried Mrs. Warren, in a tremulous voice. "We shall be drowned, without having a chance to get on deck."

Kate herself knew not but that, in another moment, the ship might sink. Certainly, all she had ever read, or imagined, of a storm at sea, was nothing to this. She felt that if there was something tangible to meet, if she could only get on deck and see what was going on, she would be better able to face the peril.

"We are in God's hands, you know, aunt. If you are not afraid of being left alone, I will try to reach the deck, and learn what is the matter—"

"Don't, for mercy's sake, leave me," cried Mrs. Warren, clinging to her niece. "What shall I do down here alone?" But a tremendous surge, almost heaving the ship on her beam ends, a new terror overcame the dread of being left for a moment, and she cried, suddenly, "Yes, yes, go, go, and see what is the matter. Tell the captain we are in no hurry. Perhaps it's his carrying so much sail, as he calls it, that makes the ship lean over so. Dear me, if I once get on dry land, I'll never trust myself at sea again."

Kate did not wait for a second permission. She crept along towards the forward cabin, which served for the dining room, reached the stairs, and clambered up with difficulty. A moment after she stood upon the deck.

The night was now pitch dark. A cold, heavy rain was falling, hissing and dancing as it struck the deck, and occasionally driving wildly past in an almost horizontal direction. But Kate did not for a while even know that it rained. Her entire energies were demanded to keep her feet, for between the violent motion of the ship, and the fury of the wind, she was nearly prostrated. When at last she had gained a slightly sheltered position, and found something to hold on by, she looked anxiously around.

The wide expanse of waters was black as ink, except where, here and there, the white caps flashed up. Miss Aylesford, in that first impressive moment, forgot all thought of possible peril, so overpowered was she by the dread majesty of the scene before her. She could liken it to nothing but the abyss of woe, surging its black waters from depths that no plummet could ever sound, impiously against heaven, which frowned in awful anger back; and the illusion was sustained by the white and ghastly objects which flitted across the vision, like spectres cast up from the profound below, and driven remorselessly past by inexorable fates.

But this feeling of awe and admiration lasted only for a moment. She remembered her terror-struck aunt below, and looked around to see if there was any person of whom she could inquire. But everybody seemed engaged in a struggle for life or death. A dim figure, in which she fancied she recognized the captain, stood at the helm, with a speaking trumpet at its mouth; while two stalwart forms grasped the spokes of the wheel; and other vague shapes hurried hither and thither across the deck through the darkness and storm. There was a wild confusion of orders, given so rapidly that she could distinguish no words, and of noises compounded of the wind and sea, so that she was almost stunned.

This rapid survey consumed but a moment. Looking down the sloping deck, she saw close under the lee of the ship what seemed a vortex of foaming water; and now, for the first time, she recognized a dull, sullen roar, which she knew to be that of breakers. At once the whole peril of their situation flashed upon her. Instead of being a hundred miles at sea, as Captain Powell had supposed, they were close upon the coast; and these superhuman exertions, which she saw master and crew making, were designed to get an offing for the vessel.

Suddenly a loud report was heard, like the discharge of a cannon in the air, and looking up, Kate saw what seemed a white cloud flying down to leeward.

"God have mercy on us," she heard a voice cry, its sharp tone of agony rising over all the roar of wind and waters, "the main-topsail is gone. Look out, she strikes!"

At the same instant, Kate felt a shock, which precipitated her on her face, and instantaneously what appeared an ocean of water rushed over and submerged her.

CHAPTER III
THE SHIPWRECK

"To hear
The roaring of the raging elements,
To know all human skill, all human strength,
Avail not; to look around, and only see
The mountain wave incumbent with its weight,
Of bursting waters o'er the reeling bark,—
Oh! God, this is indeed a dreadful thing." —*Southey.*

"In breeze, or gale, or storm,
Icing the pole, or in the torrid clime
Dark-heaving; boundless, endless and sublime.
Each zone Obeys thee, thou goest forth, dread, fathomless, alone."
—*Byron.*

In a moment, however, the brave girl struggled to her feet. Her first thought was of her aunt. She was about groping her way down to the cabin, for the purpose of seeking Mrs. Warren, when the latter's voice was heard, faint with terror, calling on her name.

"Here I am, aunt," answered Kate, as cheerfully as she could. She held out her hand, which Mrs. Warren eagerly caught.

At any other time Kate's sense of the ludicrous would have overcome her at the figure of her aunt. The good lady had only had time to huddle on the most necessary garments, and some of these were even awry; while the elegancies of the toilet, about which the stately dame was so particular, were totally neglected for once. It was the fashion in those days, for elderly matrons, to wear a cushion on the top of the head, over which to comb the hair; but this was now wholly wanting to Mrs. Warren, and her hair, usually so precisely arranged, and so carefully powdered, hung in tangled elf-locks about her face. The whole of her person and dress, moreover, was dripping, like that of some Triton just risen from the sea. Could the excellent old creature have seen her image reflected in a glass, she would have fainted outright from shame and outraged propriety. But mortal fear had now so conquered every other sensation, that when she rushed into her niece's arms, it was with the paramount feeling that in Kate's heroic character was the only hope at this frightful juncture.

"Hold fast under the lee of this bulwark," said the niece. "It's the safest place I can find."

Her aunt mechanically obeyed, without reply, for her increasing fear had now deprived her of the power of speech.

The tremendous shock with which the ship struck, had snapped off the masts as if they had been pipe-stems, and Kate's next thought, after having temporarily provided for the safety of her aunt, was what was to be done with the wreck of spars and rigging, which, beating against the vessel's sides, threatened to crush them like egg-shells. Suddenly, through the gloom, she saw a figure, armed with an axe, creep along by the larboard bulwarks, until it had attained a favorable position, when it began cutting away with rapid strokes at the hamper. In this person she had no difficulty in recognizing the captain, who continued skillfully and rapidly dealing his blows, though often half submerged in water, until the confused mass began to give way, and rushing into the boiling vortex, was swept down to leeward. Other strokes from other axes were heard simultaneously, and a moment after the remaining masts, with their complicated yards and canvass, went off also into the wild maelstrom.

While some of the officers and men had been thus engaged in freeing the wreck, others had turned their attention to giving warning of their situation, in case assistance was near. Accordingly, the masts had scarcely been whirled away by the tumultous surge, when a bright jet of flame shot out from the starboard side of the ship; and the solemn boom of a signal gun went forth across the night. Discharge followed discharge, at regular periods, the crew listening eagerly, during the interval, to detect an answering sound, if any should be made. The profound darkness in which the vessel was enveloped was dissipated, for an instant, at each discharge; and the anxious faces of the crew, the desolate decks, and the vexed ocean, stood out, as if revealed by a lightning-flash; but the sudden gleam passed as quickly as it came, a darkness followed, apparently the deeper from the blaze of light; and horror, gloom, and dread fell again on all.

For a considerable time the signal-guns continued to be fired, but when the sailors found that no answer came, a recklessness seized them, the offspring of despair acting on brutal, animal natures. They first began to murmur in undertones; then to refuse doing duty; and finally they left the gun in a body, swearing that there was no use in further efforts. In vain the captain, rushing among them, endeavored to bring them back to discipline;

they either sullenly slunk away or openly defied him; and he soon found that he could not even count on his mates, but would probably be murdered if he persisted in his endeavor. In a little while everything was in confusion. The crew, breaking into the spirit-room, speedily became intoxicated, and all semblance even of order was now lost.

While some of the seamen were still lingering in the spirit-room, a cry arose that the ship was breaking up; and immediately a rush was made for the boats by the intoxicated crew. Here again the captain attempted to interpose his authority; but he was knocked down, trampled on, and indeed came near losing his life. It was soon found that but one boat remained fit to use, the others having been stove. Into this the rebellious crew tumbled pell-mell, the mates following; and such was the hurry of the affrighted fugitives, that they forgot to secure either water or provisions.

The whole of these events, from the ceasing to fire signal-guns up to the present period, had followed each other in the quickest succession. Indeed they appeared to have consumed less time than we have taken to describe them.

The boat had been filled and manned, but just as it was pushing off, a voice cried—

"Captain Powell, you may come aboard, if you like"

"No," was the prompt answer; "I'll stick by the ship, you mutinous rascals."

"As you please," answered the speaker. "But there are the passengers. Ladies, will *you* come aboard? Make up your minds quick."

At this the captain rushed to where Kate was standing.

"Don't go," he cried, eagerly. "They'll all be drowned. No boat can live five minutes."

Kate hesitated. She was inexperienced, and knew not what to do. On the one hand it seemed inconceivable that so many persons would rush to what they ought to be aware would be certain destruction. On the other, the tone of absolute conviction in which the captain spoke, added to the high opinion she had formed of his seamanship and good judgment, inclined her to follow the advice.

"Quick!" cried the speaker from the boat, while other voices murmured impatiently.

She still hesitated, though her aunt pulled her arm, as if to go. Any further decision, however, was not permitted to her, for, the next instant, another voice from the boat cried, sharply—

"We can't wait all night; push off, push off."

Other voices, almost simultaneously, seconded this impatient cry, and the boat, on the instant, sunk away from the side of the ship, to be seen, the moment after, rising on a wave a good pistol-shot distant.

"Madmen!" muttered the captain between his teeth.

He had scarcely spoken, when a gigantic roller overtook the boat, still dimly visible as she floated broadside on, for in the haste and confusion of putting off all the men had not yet got out their oars, and consequently her head had not been pulled around.

A cry from the captain, and a stifled shriek from Kate burst forth, for the wave, rising like a moving hill, was now seen overtopping the boat for one brief moment, while a crowd of horror-struck countenances, whose looks Kate never forgot to her dying day, gazed up at it from below; and then, with a roar as of a hungry lion descending upon its prey, the enormous billow plunged headlong upon the miserable wretches. In that roar were mingled shrieks such as made the blood of the listeners curdle, the last wild cries, and the agonizing prayers of dying men. A whirlpool of foam was all that could be seen at first, after the boat had disappeared, out soon an oar floated to the surface, then a hat, then a struggling figure or two, and then faces upturned wildly in the death-struggle. But the next surge that swept over the spot carried them under again, or bore them out of sight into the gloom ahead.

A solemn silence prevailed for a while, broken at last by the captain, who said—

"God pity them!" And after a while, he added. "It is strange that men will be so foolhardy! But when presence of mind is lost, even the bravest become crazed."

"Is there any hope even for us!" said Kate, after a pause. "Where are we?"

The captain looked down on her with admiration, at the firm tone in which she spoke.

"While there is life there is hope," he answered. "If these old timbers last till morning, we'll be able to see where we are; and, if near the coast, perhaps help may be had."

"You are ignorant, then, exactly where we've struck?"

"Yes. My reckoning must have been false. I thought myself more than a day's sail from the coast, and was thunderstruck when the lookout cried, in the middle of the night, that there were breakers ahead."

"You were on deck?"

"I never go below, when near the end of a voyage, even if I think everything safe. As soon as he spoke, I leaped into the rigging, and there sure enough, I saw the white water flashing near at hand. I hauled the ship close on a wind at once, and began to crowd the canvass upon her."

"It was the hurry and noise of making more sail that woke us."

"It was of no use, however," continued the captain, acknowledging the interruption by an affirmative nod. "Do all we could, we could just hold our own; and very soon the main-topsail, on which I had placed my chief reliance, split and went to leeward. She fell off instantly, striking with force enough, one would have thought, to shiver her into atoms. The masts went overboard, and you know the rest. Poor thing!" he added, mournfully, apostrophizing the vessel, "she's carried me across the Atlantic, this is now the tenth time, but she'll never do it again. Ah!" he continued, with natural emotion, "I little fancied we'd part so."

"It was just as the sail went to ribbons," said Kate, after a pause, for she respected the feelings of the master too much to proceed at once, "that I came on deck. You said that, when day broke, succor perhaps might be found. But we may be some distance from land; for, if I recollect—I was born in New Jersey—there are bars far out at sea."

"You are right," answered the captain. "The shore, too, is but a sand-bank, all along that coast; and one separated, by miles of shallow lagoons, from the fast land. If we've struck anywhere below Squam, we'll not be likely to get aid, even if the high tide has carried us over the outer bars and landed us right on the shore. Few, or none of the beaches, if I've heard rightly, are inhabited. But let us hope we're nigher the Hook, for, in that case, we must be close in, and there are farmhouses and fishing-cabins there, in sight of the sea."

He did not add, that, even if this should prove to be the case, it was extremely problematical whether assistance could be rendered to them, while the waves ran so high. His secret opinion was, that the chance of escape was the very slightest, for he had no faith in the ship's timbers holding together till the gale subsided, even if they did till morning. But, brave as Kate was, he shrank from acquainting one so young, and who had every prospect of a happy life before her, that a speedy death was almost inevitable. Besides, he noticed the extreme terror of her aunt, who could, indeed, scarcely hold to her support, so unnerved was she by the peril of their situation.

For, even during this conversation, both the speakers had occasionally been almost carried from their feet. Nearly every surge swept more or less over the ship. Twice the master had to interpose to save Kate from being prostrated; and still more frequently his services were required in behalf of her aunt. Occupying a position between the two women, he was fortunately able to afford instant aid to either. Meantime, the storm showed no symptoms of subsiding. The rain still fell in sheets, often stinging the bare hands of the victims like hail. The wind shrieked as if the sea had temporarily given up its wicked dead, who gibbered as they rushed past in the gloom.

The seas also seemed to run still higher. They came trooping on, fast and thick as hungry wolves; rushed by with a howl that fairly appalled the listeners; or leaped and snarled about the ship, as if eager for their prey, and grudging every moment of delay. Now and then a roller, more colossal than its predecessors, would sweep the whole length of the deck, making a breach completely over the vessel, whose every timber quivered as if she was about to part.

The darkness, all this time, was palpable. Often it seemed as if the low sky and the upheaved waves were about to commingle above the doomed ship; and always, in looking seaward, the boundary line between the two was lost in a chaos of obscurity scarcely a hundred feet off.

CHAPTER IV
MORNING

Environ'd with a wilderness of sea;
Who marks the waxing tide grow wave by wave,
Expecting ever when some envious surge
Will in his brinish bowels swallow him. —Shakespeare.

It is, methinks, a morning full of fate!
It riseth slowly, as her sullen car,
Had all the weight of sleep and death hung at it!
She is not rosy-fingered, but swollen black. —Jonson.

"We shall be more sheltered," continued the captain, "if we change our places. The waves, I see, don't sweep the deck further aft on the starboard side. Shall we try to get there? I doubt if you could hold out till morning here. Certainly your aunt could not. She is already more dead than alive."

Kate saw, at once, the wisdom of the suggestion. The ship, before going on the bar, had been running nearly parallel to the breakers, her head being slightly inclined seaward; but when the main-topsail went, she had whirled around, and struck bard on, heeling to larboard: consequently she now lay almost at right angles with the surf. Along the inclined deck the waves continually washed. The stern, however, protected the after portion, especially the higher side; for the waters, even when they made a clean breach over the ship, parted right and left around this sheltered spot.

"But can we get there?" said Kate, in a whisper, glancing at her aunt, who, through fear and wet, was now almost incapable of moving.

"I think I can manage her," was the reply, in the same low tone, "if you can hold on here till I return."

"We will go, then?"

Captain Powell did not lose a moment. Putting one stalwart arm around Mrs. Warren, and holding on by the other, he watched his opportunity, and started on his perilous enterprise. Kate gazed upon them breathlessly. Once she feared that they would lose their footing, for a large billow, rushing in over the lower side, swept the decks through their whole length; but the captain fortunately had seen it coming, and had hurriedly told his companion to hold on with all her strength. When, therefore, the waters had subsided, Kate saw that the captain was already advancing again across the slippery decks; and the moment after she had the satisfaction of beholding him safely deposit his companion in the sheltered nook, under the high stern.

Kate had never intended that the captain should return for her, because she knew how much her aunt's terror would be increased by being left alone; but she had said nothing of this purpose, in order to spare remonstrances. As it would not do to wait, she set out at once.

When Captain Powell, therefore, having arranged a seat for Mrs. Warren, turned to go for Kate, he saw the brave girl already more than half way on her route. He shouted to her to stop till he could come up, especially as he saw a roller advancing; but she paid no heed to his words; and the next moment, as he had feared, she was hurried from sight under the huge wave as it swept the deck.

Striking the ship a little to the larboard of where he stood, this mass of dark water, that glistened like solid glass, went rushing up the sloping deck, in front of him, till it struck the bulwarks on the higher side, when dashing to pieces, a part flew crackling over in shattered fragments and clouds of spray, while the remaining portion, now churned to a milk-white color, rushed forward with irresistible force, carrying everything before it, till it precipitated itself in cataracts over the bow, or found escape by spouting from the hawse-holes, as if driven through them by a force-pump.

Under this enormous volume of water Kate disappeared entirely from sight. Captain Powell feared that she had not seen the approaching peril, and that, having no firm hold, she had been swept from her feet. Mrs. Warren, even in her half exhausted state, uttered a faint scream, and would have rushed forward, if she could have broken away. The captain looked eagerly to see Kate's white garments amid the foam, as the wave swept onward. It seemed, meantime, as if the waters would never subside from the deck. What was in reality not more than a few seconds, appeared to him interminable.

At last, the sight so eagerly desired greeted his eyes; and Kate was seen comparatively unharmed. Pausing only to recover breath, and watch that no more such surges were coming in, she darted forward with the swiftness of a deer, and reached his side, panting so that she could not, for a moment, answer his eager inquiries.

"Did I see it rolling in?" she said, at last. "Yes, and took a firm hold; but I thought it would never pass over me; I seemed to be an age beneath the water."

"It was fortunate it was no worse. I would not have taken one to a thousand pounds on your escape."

"Oh! you don't know what a sailor I can be," answered Kate, cheerfully. "Thank you," she said, as Captain Powell arranged a seat for her. "We shall get along nicely till morning now. How fortunate it's not winter, isn't it, aunt?"

Seating herself at these words, she put her arm around her aunt, and drawing the head of the latter to her shoulder, began affectionately stroking the water from her aged relative's head. The poor creature could only answer this caress by tears, which flowed heavily down her cheeks, and by grateful looks.

"Are you cold, aunt? You shake your head. Yet you must be chilly, wet through as you are."

"If you please, Miss Aylesford," said the captain, "I think I can make my way into the cabin, and bring up some cloaks and shawls for you and your aunt." And without waiting for a reply, he left them.

In a few minutes he returned. The warmth of the dry over garments, gradually revived Mrs. Warren. But even when she regained the command of words, she could only deplore their situation, and repeat, again and again, that she knew they never would reach the shore alive.

Kate, in the meanwhile, did all she could to reassure her aunt, though far from feeling confident herself. Much of the time, when they were silent, she spent in inward prayer. And surely, if ever petitions could avert evil, those of that pure-minded, brave girl ought.

Slowly the night wore on. To those lonely watchers for the morning, the hours appeared almost an eternity. A hundred times they turned their longing eyes seaward, in hopes to see the horizon lighting up. Sometimes they were deceived into thinking the dawn at hand, by a temporary lifting of the clouds in the east; but the darkness soon closed in as profound as ever; and the disappointment was then all the more poignant from that momentary gleam of hope.

Low and wild the clouds continued to drift past; but the rain had now slackened. On the other hand, the waves ran higher than ever, so that the captain's fear that the ship would break up before morning, increased momentarily. Already the wreck was badly logged, as even Kate could see;

and at any instant the hull might be expected to part into two pieces, under the blow of some new roller, as powerful as the one which had so nearly carried her off.

"She holds together bravely," said the captain, when several hours had passed. "The good craft is as tough as old junk. I begin to feel now that she'll not go to pieces till next tide, at any rate. Have you noticed, Miss Aylesford, that the water is falling?"

"I had not," answered Kate. "How can you tell in the darkness and storm?"

"Leave an old salt alone for that," was the reply, with something of that professional pride which even peril cannot entirely subdue. "You see, Miss, the gale's as high as ever, and the waves run as wild, yet the decks are not swept as often, or as deep, as they were. We haven't had a surge to reach us since we changed our places. The ship heels over also more, which she would naturally do as the tide went out."

"I understand," said Kate. "But look," she cried, suddenly, "isn't that morning? Surely, we cannot be mistaken this time."

She pointed to the east as she spoke, where indeed no streak of light was to be seen, as on ordinary dawns, but where a thinning away of the heavy vapors was quite perceptible. Overhead all was yet blank, and the forms of the clouds were undistinguishable; but in the eastern seaboard, the sky had a fleecy look, as when mists begin to break away on a mountain side.

"You are right," answered Captain Powell; "it is morning, God be praised."

"Didn't I tell you so, aunt?" said Kate, cheerfully, turning to her relative. "You hear what the captain says. It is really daybreak. We shall soon be able to see the shore, and no doubt be succored."

Oh! the blessed dawn! It comes to the weary invalid, and gives new life to his veins. It comes to the watchers by the bed of death, and inspires them with momentary hope. But never comes it more welcome than to those, who, like our shipwrecked group, expect it as their only reliance. It made even Mrs. Warren feel strong, almost gay again.

Gradually the darkness vanished. It was not by any sudden influx of light, but by an imperceptible growth, which could only be noticed by the changes which long intervals produced. The black curtains of gloom, which had hung like a pall close around, slowly receded, the light diffusing itself, as it were, reluctantly and warily.

All eyes were turned in the direction of the land, long before it was possible to distinguish objects, at a distance, with certainty. At first, nothing but a waste of white waters, of billows racing after each other into a boundless space ahead, could be discerned. But finally, what seemed a long, low sand-bank, was made out, a short cable's length off. It was a mere bar, elevated a few feet above the ocean, which, in many places, appeared to be actually making breaches over it. Not a house, nor even tree was distinguishable, on this barren and inhospitable shore; but here and there a few bushes, around which the drifting sand had collected, offered some slight opposition to the advancing waters.

For some time no one spoke. Kate's heart swelled within her, and she could not frame words; once or twice she attempted it, and choked. She saw that the ship had struck on one of those uninhabited beaches, which the captain had described in the night; and that there was no longer any hope, for probably not a farmhouse, or human being existed within miles. As for Mrs. Warren, she gazed from the captain to her niece in speechless horror, wringing her hands, for she read in the face of each the despair that had succeeded to the momentary exhilaration produced by the dawn.

At last the master spoke. He had waited until the prospect brightened sufficiently landward to observe objects at some distance. But when he found that nothing was discernible, for miles on miles in that direction, through the drizzling mist—except salt marshes, against which even the partially protected waters inside the beach dashed fiercely, and over which the leaden-colored clouds swiftly drove,—he turned to Kate, and said, in a hoarse whisper.

"God help us, for there is none in man!"

Then, his thoughts reverting to his family, he ejaculated, "my poor wife!" and, completely unmanned, covered his face with his hands.

CHAPTER V
THE COUNTRY TAVERN

The night drav' on wi' songs and clatter,
But aye the ale was growing better. —Burns.

We must now go back a few hours in our story, and introduce the reader to a different scene and personages.

The southern half of New Jersey is almost a dead level, covered with pine and oak forests, growing on a sandy soil. A slightly elevated ridge, however, runs in a southwesterly direction between Delaware Bay and the Atlantic, though much nearer the former than the latter, and divides the waters that flow westward from those that run toward the east.

One of the most considerable of the rivers, descending from this watershed toward the Atlantic, empties into a wide, deep bay, almost shut in from the ocean by low beaches in its front. Notoriously the best anchoring ground between Sandy Hook and Cape May, it is a place of constant resort for coasters. At the time of which we write, it was, for similar reasons, a rendezvous for American privateers; and, in fact, their prizes usually discharged their cargoes on the neck of land where the river first swelled into the bay. Others, ascending higher up the stream, unloaded at the head of navigation, from which point the goods were carried across the country to Philadelphia by teams, the blockade of the Delaware, by the British fleet, preventing access often in a more direct way. It was not uncommon to find a dozen or two armed vessels lying in this river, waiting for a chance to sail.

Five and seventy years ago, when our story commences, this bay was even more shut out from the Atlantic than it is at present; for while now there is an inlet directly in its front, at that period the entrance was further to the south. Where, at present, vessels of considerable draught pass under full sail, was then a beach, elevated some distance above the water.

On an arm of this bay, or to speak more accurately, on an inconsiderable stream jutting into an arm of the bay, there stood, at the time of which we write, a small settlement, which, though its first beginnings dated back scarcely more than ten or fifteen years, already gave promise of becoming a thriving place. In the rude tavern of this incipient village, on the evening preceding the events detailed in the last chapter, quite a number of persons were gathered.

Most of the company appeared to belong to the various privateers then lying in the bay, and were merely boisterous tars; but there was one individual, whose bearing, not less than his dress, bespoke him of a higher rank. He was a man apparently about eight-and-twenty years of age, handsome in person, and with a face which, though by no means homely, was principally remarkable for the indications it gave of frankness, decision, a good heart, and a superior intellect. It was impossible, indeed, to look on that countenance, without feeling that, while its possessor was born to rule in public affairs, his destiny was to be equally fortunate in winning esteem and affection in private life. He wore the buff and blue of the American army. Sitting in one corner, where he was busily engaged in writing, he seemed to be entirely unconscious of what was going on around him, except when he occasionally intermitted the busy motion of his pen, and leaning his head on one hand, gazed with an abstracted smile on the sports of the crowd.

For, night having closed in, and the seamen being ashore on leave till morning, a black fiddler had been procured, and a dance begun. It is true there were none of the fairer sex present to participate in the amusement, but this, so far from checking the merriment, only gave it more freedom and boisterousness. Several countrymen, from small farms in the interior, who had come down with produce in the afternoon, and whom the exhilarating sounds of the violin had tempted to linger behind, when their sturdy dames were expecting them at home, joined heartily in the fun. Utterly heedless of the black looks awaiting them, when, repentant on the morrow, they should slink into the chimney corner, they laughed, and joked, and danced, and drank whiskey with Jack Tar, as if there had been, and never would be, a "gudewife" angry at neglect, and "nursing her wrath to keep it warm."

As the hours wore on, and the wind outside began to rise, the mirth waxed louder and more contagious. Perhaps the landlord's old whiskey contributed its mite also; but be this as it may, long before midnight the uproar was terrible. The floor shook under the feet of the performers; the rafters of the ceiling trembled with the shouts and laughter: and the shrill notes of the Cremona rose over all. The few tallow candles, which, from tin sconces, threw at best but a faint yellow radiance around, were almost obscured by the dust that rose from the floor and the smoke that ascended from innumerable pipes. The landlord, with a boy for an assistant, stood within the quadrant shaped bar, that occupied one corner of the apartment, looking out, from between the upright rails, with a well-pleased smile, for he knew that the louder the merriment, the greater would be his profits. Indeed, he had little leisure even to look, so frequent were the calls from his thirsty customers.

It may seem strange that the officer should select this apartment for the purpose of writing, or that he could abstract himself sufficiently to write at all in such a din. But, in truth, the inn afforded no place whither he might retreat. In the primitive fashion of that age and district, it had but one huge room, unless the loft overhead, where the guests slept in rows, could be dignified by that name. It was a matter of necessity for him, therefore, to turn this apartment, which alternately served for ball-room, bar-room, dining-saloon and town-hall, into a library. Fortunately, circumstances had early taught him that valuable discipline of mind, which enables the possessor to concentrate his thoughts on the subject before him, regardless of the confusion and noise around.

Toward midnight rain began to fall. Occasionally, in pauses of the merriment, the storm would be heard beating wildly against the window panes, while now and then, when the door was temporarily opened, the wind would dash the cold drops into the faces of those near the entrance. The trees, which overshadowed the house, moaned in the gale. Down the village street the tempest went howling wildly, till in the distance it sank to a low wail. The water in the neighboring bay, driven fiercely against the meadows, roared with an ever-increasing sound, as if threatening to inundate the low tongue of land whereon the hamlet was built.

But little cared the crowd of guests for the storm. A spirited contest was going on between two dancers, who, after having often been engaged in temporary trials of skill during the evening, had now apparently entered on a decisive struggle. One was a short, square-built sailor, in a pair of canvass trowsers thickly besprinkled with tar. He wore a tarpaulin on his head, and sported, in the fashion of the day, an immense queue behind, which, as he danced, worked up and down on his back like an iron pump-handle. His antagonist was a tall, lank countryman, with a body disproportionately small, legs that looked like a pair of stilts, and arms that, swinging in tune to his double-shuffle, resembled those of a windmill revolving without their sails. His yellow hair hung down lank all around his face. He had thrown off his coat, and now stood in his original shirtsleeves, with a deep waistcoat that reached almost to his knees. A pair of pinch-beck seals, attached to an enormous watch that was his especial pride, being almost the only one in his neighborhood, bobbed heavily up and down against his baggy breeches; while a few copper farthings jingled ostentatiously in his pockets, as he went vigorously through the figures of that time-honored dance, which is known to the initiated as a "Jersey Four."

"Keep it up, Jack," shouted the friends of the tar, and "Go it, Lively!" answered the backers of the other party; while the spectators laughed, clapped their hands, and kept time to the music; the fiddler nodded his head in sympathy with the motion; and the two rivals did their best to satisfy their patrons and win the laurels they coveted. The sailor danced away as stoutly as if worked by machinery, his feet, hands, limbs and portly paunch moving neither faster nor slower: it seemed for a while, as if he could continue to dance in the same impassive way forever, if necessary. The countryman, however, was less phlegmatic. Occasionally, the vigor of his saltatory action would fall perceptibly off, but becoming aware of this by some observation from the crowd, or through his own consciousness, he would suddenly give himself a jerk, as if his whole body had been moved, all at once, by pulling a string; and then away he would go, in and out, around and back, dancing to his partner as if life and death depended on his agility, his arms swinging, his legs going, and the perspiration rolling from his face.

"Jack's got enough; he's giving out," cried one of the landsmen, triumphantly calling attention to the tar, after the countryman had, with another jerk, started off apparently as fresh as ever. "He's blowing like a porpoise. Hoe it down right smart, Jim, and you have him. Hurrah for *Jarsey!*"

It was plain that the pursy seaman was beginning to be exhausted at last. He still danced away as imperturbably as ever; but there was a perceptible anxiety in his countenance; and at last, after fresh attempts, on the part of his comrades, to encourage him, had failed, he gave in, completely exhausted.

"You're too much for me, shipmate," he said, panting, good-humoredly addressing the victor. "I've seen the day, though," he added, turning to the crowd, "when I could dance anybody down, but Portsmouth Peggy. But this chap, I own up, is my match. Give us your hand, my hearty, I bear no ill will."

The countryman, on seeing his antagonist retire, had uttered a shrill cry of exultation, and cut a pigeon-wing, which latter he had just concluded, as the seaman tendered his hand. He clutched this between his horny palms, returning the good-fellowship with hearty accord.

"Let's liquor," he said, magnanimously, throwing his arms around his late adversary, and pulling him, nothing loath, towards the bar. "It's my treat. Bring up your shipmates. I'm as dry as if my mouth was gunpowder. Hillo, Major," he said, turning to the officer, "won't yon drink? You'd rather not! No offence, I hope; for I meant none. Here's to 'Old Jarsey: small but spunky.'"

The toast was drank with all the honors, and then nothing would satisfy the exhilarated victor, but that the fiddler should also partake of a libation. Accordingly the sable performer was summoned to "stop that infernal caterwauling," as his tuning up was elegantly termed by the speaker, and "walk up like a gentleman, to drink with the landlord and him."

For a moment, after these words were spoken, and while the negro was grinning as the landlord handed out his glass, there was one of those moments of temporary silence which will happen even at the noisiest entertainments. Simultaneously there came a lull in the driving rain and howling wind without.

Suddenly, in this unexpected hush, there was heard what seemed a gun fired out at sea. The officer had just ceased writing, and was putting away his implements, when his attention was attracted by the sound. Few, if any others, heard it; and the merriment was beginning again, when he raised his hand and cried, in an authoritative voice, "Hark!"

His gesture, tone, and look, silenced every voice immediately. On the instant the sound was repeated. It was a low, sullen, stifled roar, apparently miles away.

"It's a ship in distress," said one of the group, whose dress bespoke him a waterman native to the region. "Hark: there it is again!"

"You must be mistaken, Mullen," interposed the landlord, who saw that the words threw a damp over the company. "You couldn't hear a gun so far off."

"What else can it be, I'd like to know?" answered the man who had been called Mullen. "It's a cannon, isn't it, Major Gordon?"

"It's a gun, certainly, and must be fired out at sea—a signal of distress. Recollect, the wind is favorable for bringing the sound this way. Listen, there it is again!"

There could be no mistaking it. As if to gratify the anxiety of the now excited group, the tempest had lulled almost entirely for the time, and the deep boom of a cannon, fired at intervals of about a minute, was heard distinctly. A sudden solemnity fell upon the listeners. The fiddler mechanically began replacing his instrument in its green bag; the landlord looked ruefully towards his assistant, as much as to say that he might close the bar, for there would be no more drinking that night; while the sailors, and indeed most of the company, crowded to the door, where they stood eagerly waiting for the reports, in spite of the rain that dripped from the roof just overhead, or drove occasionally into their faces when a gust of wind swept by.

"We must do something for them," said Major Gordon, breaking the silence.

"It's impossible to do anything tonight," answered Mullen. "But I'll go off with you at dawn, as far as the beach, anyhow. I've a good boat, and we can easily get volunteers. You'll go, Newell, and you, Muncy," he said, turning to various young men, all acquaintances, whom he saw standing around, "and you, and you, and you."

"We'll follow the Major, and yon," said the one he had called Newell, "wherever you may lead." "Thanks, my lads," answered the officer, "and now to rest, so that we may be all the fresher in the morning, when God grant that we may not be too late."

The suggestion was followed. In a few minutes, those who had been so fortunate as to obtain beds, had retired to the loft above; while the remainder stretched themselves indiscriminately on the floor, and were soon buried in profound repose.

By this time the tempest had increased again, so that the signal guns could not be distinguished. But Major Gordon, who had never heard similar sounds before, was long haunted in his sleep by the report of cannon booming solemnly across the night.

CHAPTER VI
MAJOR GORDON

The morning comes, but brings no sun.
The sky with clouds is overrun. —T. Buchanan Read.

A piteous fearful sight,
A noble vessel laboring with the storm. —Maturin.

It is time that we should say something of the young officer, who, as the reader has suspected, is destined to play no inconsiderable part in our story.

Major Gordon had been left an orphan at an early age, with but a small competence, most of which had been exhausted on his education, so that, on his attaining his majority, his whole property consisted of little more than sufficient to purchase a library and support himself for a couple of years. By assiduity in his profession, however, which was that of the law, assisted by a natural gift of eloquence, he rapidly rose to ease and distinction; and was fast taking rank, indeed, among the eminent advocates of whom Philadelphia boasted then, as now, when the war of Independence broke out. Like most other generous and heroic spirits, he threw himself with ardor into the patriotic cause. Abandoning his practice and the tempting offers it held out, he joined the troops raised by the colony of Pennsylvania, in which he speedily attained the rank of Major. Subsequently he had been attached to the staff of General Wayne, and afterwards had been employed on several delicate missions, where judgment and discretion were required as well as courage. It was one of these latter tasks which had brought him to the coast now. A cargo of powder was expected to be landed in the river, and as it was much wanted at camp, he had been despatched to receive and forward it to head-quarters.

There were as yet no signs of daybreak, when Major Gordon, who had slept but indifferently, awoke and looked at his watch. By the dim light of the solitary candle, he saw that morning would dawn by the time they could get their craft ready; and accordingly, picking his way between the rows of beds, he descended into the lower apartment, and proceeded to arouse Mullen. The latter individual was awoke with some difficulty.

"Morning, is it, Major?" he said, sitting up and rubbing his eyes. "Why the night's as black as a wolf's mouth yet. Look at the window and see for yourself."

"But it will be daylight before we are ready. I'd trust my watch sooner than my eyes, especially on a morning like this."

"Well, I'm your man," said Mullen, who, being now thoroughly awake, sprang up with alacrity and proceeded to arouse his comrades, one by one; carefully avoiding, however, disturbing the other sleepers, who all slumbered heavily after their debauch.

In a short while the little band came forth and took their way, by the light of a lantern, to the spot where Mullen's craft was moored.

"What a storm it has been," said Major Gordon. "I heard the rain beating, the wind roaring, and the waters dashing, all through the night. Sometimes I also fancied I distinguished signal-guns; but that, I began to fear, was only a dream, since there's no sign of them now."

"It's sartain none have been fired since we came out," answered Mullen, "for we'd have been sure to hear 'em. The wind has lulled, but the gale's not over. There'll maybe not much more rain fall; but I shouldn't be surprised to hear it blow great guns the better part of the day."

"I suppose the schooner would not be apt to come in, on such a morning," said Major Gordon, alluding to the vessel whose arrival he was expecting.

"No, she'd keep an offing, while she has it. Her skipper is a good sailor, and he'll turn up, right and tight, though not till the gale's over."

"Unless he's been captured," said the Major. "He should have been here two days ago, and his delay makes me think, sometimes, that he has been taken by the British."

"Give yourself no consarn on that p'int, Major," retorted Mullen. "The schooner's a clipper of a craft; none of your scows, made by the cord and cut off in lengths to suit customers; but a ra'al beauty, sharp as a nor'wester on a winter mornin', and that can go into the wind's eye like a duck. The skipper, too, knows every inlet on the coast, and all the shallows, so that if a cruiser was to follow him, he'd lead the fellow aground in no time, and then giving him a shot, to make fun of him like, set everything drawing on the opposite tack, and leave him to get off as he could."

By this time they had reached their craft, which was a half-decked boat, with a single mast, of a description still frequent in those waters. There was some delay in getting her ready for a start, and still more in tracking her out of the small creek where she lay; but at last the adventurers succeeded in gaining open water just as the gloom of night was giving way to the dim, stormy day. The high wind compelled the crew to close-reef their mainsail, and even with this mere shred of canvass, the boat staggered along like a drunken man, laboring heavily in the rough, cross sea.

"Heaven grant we may be in time," said Major Gordon. "But this long silence of the alarm guns, and this fierce wind, are ominous of disaster."

"It's four chances to one that we're goin' on a fool's errand," answered Mullen. "First, the ship's probably gone down before this; and second, if she hasn't, her people are most likely drowned; for, if neither of these had happened, we would have heard her guns off and on through the night. Third, if she's struck, it's probably on the outer bar, a mile from shore, where nobody can get at her. Fourth, if even she's in the very breakers, she'll probably go to pieces before we can do anything to help 'em."

"Surely," said Major Gordon, "if she's in the breakers, we can save her people in some way."

"There's small chance of that," was the answer. "You don't know this coast like I do, Major, or you'd hardly have insisted on coming out. No boat could live a moment in the surf that must now be beating on the shore. I've seen many a poor fellow hang in the shrouds, in my time, for a matter of twenty-four hours or so; and that, too, with a dozen or more looking at him all the while—yet he's been forced to drop into the sea at last, because no one could get to him. It was only last January, that one of King George's transports struck and bilged in a snow-storm, on the beach right ahead of us; and not a soul was saved. The coast was strewed, for miles, with dead bodies, some of officers in uniforms, and others of common soldiers; and there were women, too, among 'em. I wasn't on the beach myself, but from all accounts it was dreadful to see. Once, howsomever, I knew three men to cling to the cross-trees of a sloop, which had sunk in some twelve feet water, and there they held fast, like dying men will, for two days and a night. I could hear their cries all the while, for the wind blew strong on shore; but they got weaker and faint-like, 'specially towards the first night; and on the second morning there was only one could be heard."

He paused, moved by the mere recollection, and then proceeded.

"His voice, too, as the day went on, got weaker, till about an hour before sunset, and when at last the surf was beginning to go down, he dropped quietly into the sea. The others had died hours before. So I doubt if we can do any good, even if we find a wreck. It's a bad thing, too, Major, to see poor creatures in mortal agony, yet not be able to help 'em. You'll wish you'd never come. But as you say go, go we do."

"Thank you," answered Major Gordon, with a husky voice, deeply moved by the sad narratives of the speaker, and almost convinced that he was only conducting them to the threshold of another drama of the same character. "But I could never again rest in my bed, if I didn't make an effort, at least, to see if there's a wreck, and try what can be done. I should be always hearing the boom of the alarm gun in my dreams."

The rain had now ceased, but a drizzling mist had set in, through whose folds the dreary landscape looked more desolate than ever. The slate-colored clouds, flying just overhead, drifted rapidly in from the sea, and sweeping past, like the wings of gigantic birds seen in the dusk of night, disappeared in the vague haze inland. As the boat beat across the bay, the water flew crackling over her forecastle, often even wetting Major Gordon and Mullen in the stern; while the parted waves, bubbling and hissing by, whirled off behind in creamy eddies.

After awhile the southern edge of the open water was attained, when the craft entered a labyrinth of comparatively narrow channels, winding between salt-marshes. The black, saline mud of these marshes emitted a pungent smell, as the waves washed along the banks; while the long grass, which thickly covered their surface, whistled or rattled in the gale. Occasionally, a gull was seen, screaming aloft, in spite of the storm, now swept swiftly down the wind, and now slowly battling his way up against the tempest.

"There it is," suddenly cried one of the crew, and, as he spoke, he pointed across the beach, along whose inner side the boat was now coasting.

They were opposite where, at its narrowest part, sea. and bay approached within a few hundred yards of each other; and, following the direction of the man's finger, Major Gordon saw a large ship, lying some distance from the shore, with her masts gone and apparently deserted.

She lay, careened towards the south, at a right angle to the coast, so that nearly every wave swept her for the entire length of her decks. At first, as we have said, she seemed deserted. But, looking more closely, Major Gordon discovered, under the lee of her weather side, and sheltered by the high stern, two female figures, attended by a solitary companion of the other sex.

"Luff, luff," he cried to Mullen, who was steering. "She'll lay close alongside the bank, won't she? Let go everything with a run."

In a moment the craft rasped against the steep mud bank, and in another Major Gordon had leaped ashore, and was moving towards the surf, leaving the others to follow more at leisure.

CHAPTER VII
THE ABORTIVE ATTEMPT

Shout to them in the pauses of the storm,
And tell them there is hope.
* * * It is too late;
No help of human hand can reach them there;
One hour will hush their cries. —*Maturin.*

All sat mute,
Pondering the danger with deep thoughts. —*Milton.*

At this sight, the three persons on the wreck, who, when first seen, had seemed as inanimate as stone, started up, and while the females clasped their hands, their companion began to wave a handkerchief as a signal.

In a lull of the gale, Major Gordon shouted to them, making an impromptu speaking-trumpet of his hands. Only a faint sound, however, came back, proving that the strangers had replied; its purport was undistinguishable.

"They can't hear a word you say," remarked Mullen, coming up. "But they saw you were speaking to them, by your actions. If we can't hear them," he pertinently added, "with the wind towards us, how can they hear us?"

"Hark!" answered Major Gordon, "I thought I made out a word or two then. Didn't he say that all on board were lost except themselves?"

"Likely enough. But see, he's got a speaking-trumpet."

As he spoke, Captain Powell raised that instrument to his mouth, and shouted, in broken intervals, that all on board had been lost except three; that they had no boats, nor anybody to man them if they had; and that the ladies could never reach shore alive, if they jumped overboard, even lashed to a spar. He concluded by saying—

"Haven't you a whale-boat?"

Again Major Gordon attempted to make himself audible. But though he shouted again and again, and with a Stentor's voice, it was evident that his accents were not heard on the wreck. Two or three of the others made a similar essay, but with no better success.

"We can't hear a word," shouted Captain Powell. "The ship won't hold together much longer. Get a whale-boat, for the love of God, or we are lost."

"Alas!" said Major Gordon, turning to Mullen, "there's no such thing within ten miles—is there?" "No," interrupted Mullen, shaking his head.

"But something must be done. I think a strong man might swim out to the wreck with a rope." "Swim out with a rope!"

"Yes!"

"What good would that do?"

"If," replied the Major, "we had a line out to the ship, it might be used to draw a cable from her ashore; and if there was a cable hauled taut, I'm sure I could rig a sort of sliding hammock, by which to land the ladies: for the hammock could be made to travel to and fro by lines attached to either end."

Mullen regarded the speaker in mute admiration for a full minute before he spoke.

"I always said," he replied, at last, "that it was everything to be a scollard. Now I might have puzzled over this matter for a week, yet never have thought of such a way as that. It would do, sartainly, if we only had the line out."

"If I had a mortar here, and tools, I could fix it so as to throw a line over the wreck at once."

"A musket wouldn't do," said Mullen, musingly; "even one with so big a bore as a 'Queen Anne.' I've a capital one in the boat."

"It couldn't throw a line strong enough. The strain of the cable, when the latter came to be dragged through the water, would snap it immediately."

"More's the pity," answered Mullen, as if reluctantly abandoning a scheme, which he would have liked to have seen tried for its novelty, at least, "for I see we'll have to give the thing up."

"Give it up!" cried the Major.

"Yes!"

"Can't a man swim off, as I proposed?"

Mullen shook his head.

"I'm not so sure," stoutly said Major Gordon.

"It would be tempting death."

The men had been eagerly listening to this conversation. The scheme of Major Gordon, to judge by the expression of their faces, had filled them with not less admiration than it had Mullen. The Major now turned to each countenance in succession, to see if any listener thought more favorably than Mullen of the feasibility of swimming off with a line. But the scrutiny was in vain.

"Think of the women," he said, addressing the group, and hoping yet to move some one. "Have you no wives or daughters? Have none of you mothers? There is one lady there whose gray hairs ought to remind you of a mother. Would you stand idly here if your own was in such extremity? Have none of you sisters? That young, delicate-looking creature there should appeal to your hearts."

As he spoke, he pointed vehemently to the wreck; but no one moved. Suddenly, he began to disencumber himself of his superfluous clothing.

"I, at least," he said, "will not see them perish without an effort to save them. A strong man, I am sure, might swim out, by taking advantage of the breakers. He can't run any great risk, either; for, if he fails, he can be drawn ashore again by the rope. Run, some one, to the boat, and bring the halyards. I will tie one end about my waist; the other can be held fast here; if we splice it, we can make it long enough." By this time he had thrown off his coat and waistcoat, and was proceeding to disencumber himself of his boots, when suddenly one of the men spoke up. It was Newell, the one whom Mullen had asked to volunteer. He was a youth about nineteen, powerfully built, and deep-chested like a bull, who had been watching his leader and listening to his words, with a face whose agitated working showed the tumult in his heart. His honest nature could now endure it no longer.

"Stop that," he cried, stepping forward, and laying his hand on Major Gordon's arm. "You're not agoing. I say, you're not agoing, sir," he added, determinedly, "for I'm going myself." And he began doggedly to strip at the words. "I'm the best swimmer here, and therefore the properest man to undertake the job. I can do it, when you'd drown."

"But—" began Major Gordon.

"Look here, Major," interposed the youth, fiercely. "Don't you think other men's got feelings as well as you? Don't you 'spose I can pity 'em," and he jerked his finger over his shoulder in the direction of the wreck, "as much as some others? I only waited till I saw you were in real earnest; for it's more than an even chance the man drowns that tries it, and that's enough to make any one hold back a bit; but since you're fixed to go, I'll go instead."

"I have a right to throw away my own life, but not to ask you to throw away yours," said Major Gordon, putting his hand on the youth, as if to stop his further disrobing. "No, I shall go."

The youth looked fiercely on the speaker, as if he would have liked to knock him down, provided their relations in life had been more equal; but he contented himself with shaking off the Major's hand, and continuing, with rude directness —

"My life's my own, and yours is your country's. If I drown, there's no one to cry over it, not even my poor old mother; for she died last winter, God pity her, after the refugees robbed her." And he brushed a tear hastily from his eye.

"Let him go, Major," said Mullen, "for he will go, now that he's said it; and he's the most fitting, too, by odds. Charley Newell can, after all, swim like a duck, and knows these breakers from a child; I doubt if the porpoises can tumble about as safely in them as he can. I had forgotten him, or I wouldn't have said it was so mad a thing to try to swim off. He'll do it, if man can do it. Here come the ropes from the boat. At the worst we won't let him drown. We can haul him in, hand over hand, at the first sign of his giving out."

The youth had, by this time, stripped himself of every article of clothing not absolutely necessary, and now stood before the group the model of a modern Hercules. Major Gordon, as he looked at the brawny arms, and the volume of muscle knotted on the ample chest, could not but acknowledge that his opponent, even without his greater skill in the surf, would be able to contend twice as long in the waters as himself, from sheer superiority of muscle. He, therefore, ceased to object to the substitution. What would have been duty, if no other person had volunteered, became foolhardiness when a more suitable one offered.

"Go, then," he said, fervently clasping the youth's hand, "and God be with you. I shall not forget your heroism."

"I'll do it, if it's in the sinoos of a man," said he, returning the grasp, till the Major's fingers crunched as if in a vice. And measuring the distance between the beach and the wreck with his eye, he continued — "Many's the time I've swum ten times as far for fun, and though never in quite such a surf, yet often in one a'most as bad."

By this time his comrades were engaged in fixing one end of the rope around his waist. He felt of it, to see that it held firm, and hitching himself up, he said, with an attempt at jocularity not unusual at such times with men of his class —

"It's rather a long tail for a man to go to sea with, and beat's a Chinaman's dead hollow; but I guess a fellow can manage it. So here goes."

As he spoke, he ran gayly down into the undertow. For an instant, his comrades looked upon him in silence, but when he turned, on the very edge of the surf, to wave a last farewell, they broke simultaneously into a cheer.

The youth did not wait till the huzza subsided, but, watching his opportunity, plunged into a wave that was just then about to break, and while the tons of water, overwhelming him, rushed roaring and churning up the sands, vanished from sight.

For what seemed an age, the spectators watched and waited, in vain, for his reappearance.

"He is gone already," said Major Gordon, drawing a deep breath, after this interval. "No, there he is. He comes up buoyant as a cork. See how he takes that second roller!"

It would have excited even the most phlegmatic had they witnessed the gallant manner in which the youth battled his way against that terrible sea. For, during a time, he actually seemed to be about effecting his purpose. It is true that, when forced by temporary exhaustion to ride the incoming billows, he was often swept almost ashore again: but by a few skillful plunges he would regain the ground which he had lost, and even more. Now an intervening billow, towering far towards the sky, would hide him completely from the gaze of his anxious comrades; and often his disappearance would be so prolonged, that the spectators would tremble again for his safety. Now, just when all gave him up for lost, he would shoot into sight once more, rising on the side of another approaching billow, and shaking, as he rose, the water from his hair, like a Newfoundland emerging after a dive. One moment his form would be seen, standing out in bold relief against the polished side of a wave, and the next it would be half concealed amid a whirlwind of foam that rushed over the crest of the breaker.

At one time nearly half the distance between the shore and wreck had been conquered. The worst was apparently over.

"He'll do it," cried Mullen, excitedly. "What a brave fellow he is! I never could have believed it, if I hadn't seen it with my own eyes."

"Ah!" suddenly interrupted Major Gordon, as a tremendous billow was seen approaching the swimmer, and forgetting that his warning could not be heard, and would have been useless if it could, he shouted— "Look out, look out!"

For one instant it came on, heaping its mass of waters up continually higher, towering and towering until the spectators fairly ran cold with horror. Then, curling majestically over, away up against the sky, it poured downwards like some huge cataract in one vast mountain of foam, a pistol shot out beyond where the waves usually broke. The swimmer had seen it coming, and had plunged through it with steadfast courage, but apparently in vain; for the shattered waters rolled past him, yet he remained still invisible. Another gigantic wave was seen rising close in the wake of its predecessor, yet he did not emerge. The minutes appeared hours. Then the second wave broke and came on, racing after the other, covering the sea with its whitened fragments.

"It's the rope that's dragging him down," cried Mullen.

"He could have done it alone, but the weight of the line, and the strain on it shorewards, are too much for him. He'll drown, if we don't pull him in, and that at once."

"Hold," cried Major Gordon, authoritatively, as several sprang to aid Mullen with the rope. "There he comes again. Don't you see him? He's alive and safe. But he's lost way terribly," he added, "in those two surges."

"He's alive, sir," replied Mullen, "but his strength's gone. You can see that by the way he swims. He'll never do it now, sir. The seas are coming in, too, as if they knew what he's after, and were not going to lose their prey out yonder. What monsters! Every one of 'em rollers, and chasing each other as if they were wild Indians. The very beach shakes as they break. He swims bravely, but it's no use. I can see he blows hard. Ha! he goes under; his arms fly up over his head. Pull now, my lads," he shouted quickly, "pull away, or your comrade will be dead before you get him in."

Mullen had not exaggerated the peril. It was apparent that the prisoner had struggled long after every rational prospect of success was gone; and that he had succumbed at last only by overtasked nature giving way all at once. Major Gordon, who had watched the struggle for the last five minutes, as if his own life depended on the issue, cheered the men by his example, and taking his station in the very midst of the breakers, stood there, hauling in on the line, and watching for the first indication of the exhausted swimmer.

It required but little more time than we have taken to describe all this, when the apparently lifeless form of Newell made its appearance. Major Gordon grasped it eagerly, but being prostrated at that moment by a breaker, would have been drowned himself, if the two had not been dragged ashore together by those on the beach. He recovered his feet even then with difficulty, and quite breathless; but the swimmer was seemingly dead.

"Turn him over on his face," cried Mullen, quickly. "Lift up his feet. Now rub him with sand. Every moment is precious."

But these, as well as the other restorative measures usually adopted on such occasions, utterly failed. The spirit seemed to have fled forever from the bruised and beaten body.

"It can't be," said Major Gordon, kneeling in an agony by the prostrate form. "But for me, too, he had not died. Charley! Charley! look up!"

Whether the mortal anguish with which these words were spoken had power to stop the spirit when about to wing its flight, or whether nature was already resuscitating, the eyes opened faintly, at this crisis, with a shudder, closed, opened again, and then steadily regarded the kneeling officer, while a faint smile stole over his face.

"He's coming to," said Mullen, in a voice tremulous with joyful emotion. "You know us, Charley, don't you? There's no fear, Major; he'll do well enough now."

In five minutes, indeed, he was able to sit up on the sand, though still too weak to speak, except a word or two at a time.

"He's worth a dozen dead men," said Mullen, gayly, at this, the spirits of the party recovering with a rebound.

"It most fotched you that time," said a negro, who was among the volunteers, as he paused from rubbing. "I thought you a gone coon, Charley, when I saw you rolled over and over, like a kitten that's got a dab from its mammy's paw. But you dodged the devil; them that's born to be hanged can't be drowned. Ha! ha!" and as the recovered mariner made a weak, playful attempt to strike him, the dapper little fellow fell over in the sand, in convulsions of laughter at what he thought his wit.

CHAPTER VIII
THE RESCUE

I saw him beat the surges under him,
And ride upon their backs — Shakespeare.

With head upraised, and look intent,
And eye and ear attentive bent,
And locks flung back, and lips apart. — Scott.

During the period that Newell had been in such imminent peril, the persons on the wreck had been wholly forgotten. Major Gordon was the first to remember the sufferers. Looking up, he saw that the companion of the ladies had left their side, and was slowly working his way out on the bowsprit, which impended far over the boiling surge. At the same moment, Mullen also raised his eyes.

"Does he mean to leave the wimmen?" he said, indignantly.

"I think not," answered Major Gordon. "He could scarcely be such a craven."

"And yet," musingly returned Mullen, "it's only throwing away another life if he stays. He can't save the wimmen; yet," he added, dubiously, "perhaps he might save himself."

Major Gordon, however, could not thus excuse the desertion. He made no reply, therefore, to Mullen.

"The ship seems to be breaking up," remarked Mullen, "which, I take it, is the reason of that fellow's hurry. The wind, since the vessel came ashore, has hauled towards sou'east, and the waves, as you see, instead of striking her plump aft, rush quartering over her sides. They begin to reach the place where the wimmen have sheltered themselves, and will wash it, every other surge, before long. No timber can stand such tremendous racking, and you'll see the craft split in two directly. But what can't be cured," he added, with homely philosophy, "must be endured. I feared this, when you wanted to come, for I don't like to see such sights; but we can't do 'em any good; and they're not the first, you know, that have died in this way. If your plan could have been carried out, we might have got 'em off safely; and it's a pity, for it was a good notion, that of yourn."

To much of this, however, Major Gordon had not even listened. He had been intently watching the proceedings of Captain Powell.

"Ha!" cried the Major, now, "I thought the man could not be such a villain. He'll try to swim ashore with a rope. He has taken the hint from us."

As Major Gordon said, Captain Powell, divining the plan of those on shore, had resolved to attempt reaching shore with a line, when he saw Newell's failure. Accordingly he had crept forward to the bow of the ship, where hastily fastening a light rope to a cable, and arranging both so that they would run out freely, he dropped himself into the sea, from the end of the bowsprit, just as the Major spoke his last words. "Well, he's a ten-spot anyhow," said Mullen, taking a figure from his favorite game of cards. "See, he comes to the surface. He strikes out bravely. As you say, Major, he'll maybe do it, for he has the current to help him. But if he fails, there'll not be a bit of hope left for those behind. Look how they watch him. The young one has actually clambered up the starboard bulwark, and is looking over to see him, and the old one's praying."

Kate, as the speaker said, was leaning over the side of the ship, at no little peril to herself, in order to watch the progress of Captain Powell. She it was who had first unriddled what seemed to the captain the unaccountable movements of those on shore, her fertile intellect having suggested the possibility of the proposed mode of rescue, and mentioned it to her companions. It may be supposed that she watched with intense interest the gallant effort of the young swimmer to reach them. When that attempt failed, she had resigned herself to death, until Captain Powell declared his intention of making an endeavor to carry a line ashore himself.

"It's our only chance. Without people on land to help afterwards, it would be of no use; and it's an even chance whether it succeeds now. All that I have in my favor is the current, and that may prove treacherous. You are both lashed fast, and can't be well washed overboard. But, in any event, this suspense won't last much longer; for the ship must soon go to pieces. God grant that I may not be too late, even if I reach the shore."

"She's a brave girl, whoever she is," the Major answered to Mullen. "Most of her sex, at such times, I'm told, lose all presence of mind, and I don't wonder at it. But she seems as courageous as Joan of Arc."

"Jane Arc," said Mullen, innocently. "I don't know her. Some soldier girl in the army, Major, like Captain Molly, at Monmouth battle?"

Major Gordon did not reply; in fact he did not hear the remark, for his faculties were absorbed in watching the crisis of Captain Powell's fate. Now the swimmer would be hurried on, a hundred feet or more, by a single wave. Now he would be caught by a counter current and drifted obliquely out to sea again. Here a roller would submerge him. There he would succeed in riding an enormous wave, which the spectators had feared would carry him under. For awhile he appeared neither to gain nor to lose. At last, a fortunate billow, exactly such another as had frustrated Newell going in an opposite direction, caught the swimmer, and hurried him towards the beach, like a stone sent from a sling.

Instantaneously everybody rushed to the edge of the breaker.

"Join hands! form a line!" cried Mullen; "we must catch him as he comes in, or the undertow may carry him off again. And even if it don't," he added, "the breakers will pummel the life out of him directly." Mullen himself took the advanced post, thrusting Major Gordon behind, saying, "I'm more used to it!" and the rest placed themselves as accident permitted. A few moments of eager expectation followed. Then the form of the now senseless mariner was seen rushing towards them, on the crest of a breaker; the waters descended; the two leaders of the line seized the body; and then all went under together, most of them being struck flat on the strand.

It was only for a second, however. Still holding fast to each other, they struggled to their feet, and when the wave receded, stood there triumphantly, Mullen and the Major having the Captain in their arms, and the rest of the party already seizing the line which communicated with the ship.

Captain Powell, though temporarily stunned, revived almost as soon as they bore him out of the water. But his accents were broken and faint. He trembled also like a child. He had wound up his entire energies to his late terrible struggle, and the revulsion left him, nervously as well as muscularly, as helpless as an infant.

"Haul on the line!" he said, feebly. "I made it fast to a stout cable. Thank God! Thank God!"

Never did men pull on a rope more lustily than his hearers. Mullen himself timed them, with a "Yo, heave o', merrily, lads, merrily," so that in a little while, the cable had reached half way to the shore. All at once, however, it refused to advance. In vain they pulled; not an inch would it give; and at last Mullen ordered them to desist lest they should break the rope.

Ever since Captain Powell had been brought so successfully to land, the spirits of the party had risen to the highest pitch, for they regarded the deliverance of the ladies as now certain. But at this check their feelings underwent a change. Whatever it was that stopped the cable, all hope of succoring those on the wreck must be abandoned, unless a way could be found to remove the impediment.

"The line won't hold out long, either," said Mullen; "for the force of the waves, with the dead weight of the cable attached to it, will snap it in two."

"It must have caught on the ship," added Major Gordon. Then suddenly, he continued in excited tones, "That brave girl sees it. She leaves her companion. She is coming forward, clinging to the starboard bulwarks. Heavens! the wave will reach her. No, it dashes to her feet, and then recedes, as if awed by her high courage. She has gained the bow. She stoops to examine the cable. She waves her hand to us. Pull away. It yields. It comes. Merrily in with it, lads."

The excitement of this scene had not been confined to Major Gordon. The spectators followed every movement of Kate, with an absorption of feeling it would be impossible to describe; and when finally the cable began to move again, they burst simultaneously into a huzza. Even the two swimmers, exhausted as they were, and still unable to stand, had raised themselves on their elbows to watch the progress of Kate, and now joined feebly in the shouts at her success.

The cable was hauled in without further obstruction. Once secured, and made taut, the men proceeded, under the directions of Major Gordon, to rig the traveling hammock. Two of the mainsail hoops were first taken from the mast of the boat, however, and passed over the cable. The hammock was then soon rigged. A long line was attached to one end of this hammock, in order to be used for the ship, while a similar one was fastened to the other end.

Two of the most agile of the party were now selected to go off to the vessel. This they effected by traversing the cable, which they did with an agility that only sailors possess. It would have made any other description of person giddy to have crossed that awful abyss on a support so slender and vibratory.

We will not detain the reader by a tiresome recital of the rest of that eventful history. For, after the impromptu apparatus had been once securely rigged, the deliverance of Kate and her aunt was merely an affair of time.

Kate insisted on being left till the last. There was some difficulty in getting her still terrified aunt to the bow of the ship, and more in placing her safely in the hammock; but as her assistants had the precaution to lash her tightly in, so that she should not, in a moment of frenzied panic, leap from her frail couch, she reached the land without further hindrance. Kate followed. With unmoved nerve she stepped into the frail car, disposed herself so as to preserve its equilibrium, and holding firmly to it, was borne ashore with a rapidity that seemed almost like flying.

The two watermen now lost no time in abandoning the vessel. It was wise that they made such haste, for, in less than half an hour, and before the party had been able to prepare their boat for making sail again, the stout old craft, succumbing at last to the angry surges, parted in the middle, and rapidly broke into fragments.

CHAPTER IX
SWEETWATER

Sweet Auburn! loveliest village of the plain,
Where health and plenty cheered the laboring swain,
Where smiling Spring its earliest visit paid,
And parting Summer's lingering blooms delay'd,
Dear, lovely bowers of innocence and ease,
Seats of my youth, where every sport could please. —*Goldsmith.*

Near one of the affluents of the river, off whose mouth occurred the transactions recorded in the preceding chapters, stands the village, or rather hamlet, of Sweetwater. It is one of those quiet, solitary spots, nestled by lake and wood, which makes visitors from cities so passionately in love with the country. Situated about half way between the Delaware and the Atlantic, and surrounded for miles on miles by an almost unbroken forest, it is effectually shut out from the roar and tumult of the great world. The very atmosphere breathes of peace and happiness. The stars seem to shine there more gently than anywhere else. A dreamy languor pervades the place, as if amid the drowsy hum of bees and the low gurgle of cool waters, life would pass like one long, delicious, summer afternoon.

The few dwellings which Sweetwater boasts—and more would destroy the magical quiet of the place—are ranged around one end of the pond, which forms the chief beauty of the location. An open space, something like a village green, lies between them and the water, only here, instead of being covered with sward, it is of the whitest and purest sand; and no one, who has not visited it, can imagine the fine effect of this snowy bit of landscape, relieved on one side by the translucent lake, and on the other by the dark pine woods.

At the northern end of the hamlet stands an old mill, whose waste-gate is raised for most of the year, so that, look over the little bridge when you will, the water will be seen gliding darkly underneath, as it shoots roaring and flashing to meet the stream below. Full many a time, when we were a boy, have we leaned over the wooden rail which formed the parapet, and watched by the hour the white foam go whirling off down the creek, leaving a thousand glistening eddies under the gravelly banks. Beautiful Sweetwater! shall we ever again in this world experience the sweet calm which used to descend, dove-like, upon our spirit, as we sat musing by thee, listening to the pine-woods sigh in the evening breeze, while the moon walked up the heavens, or the stars twinkled in thy mirrored depths?

After passing the hamlet and bridge, the road winds in front of a picturesque white mansion, situated in the rear of a garden built out into the pond. From the back of the edifice a flight of steps leads down into the water, where, when we knew the place, a light pinnace always lay, like a Venitian gondola. Embowered in green trees, and surrounded on three sides by the lake, that white mansion seems, with but little stretch of the imagination, like a swan nestling among green rushes.

A few hundred rods further on, the road gains the head of the lake. Looking back from this point, the scene is one of rare loveliness. Before you stretches the pond, still, glassy, quiet, dream-like. Half way down its eastern side the mansion rises amid its shrubbery, as if on a fairy island about to float off into the lake. On the other side the tall pines cast their sombre shadows into the water. In the distance whole fields of white water-lilies cover the surface of the pond. Still further off, and at the very extremity of the vista in that direction, two or three blasted trees raise their tall, bleached skeletons, like grim sentinels guarding the pathless swamp in their rear, where, if tradition errs not, more than one wayfarer has lost his path and perished.

Close by the head of the pond, in the centre of a grove of oaks thinned out from the original forest, is a white church edifice. Here, every Sunday, assemble the few inhabitants of Sweetwater, as well as those of a neighboring village, where, in the days of which we write, a foundry existed, at which cannon balls were cast for the patriot army. Beside the church is a grave-yard, surrounded by a rude fence, and shaded by oak trees. The birds build their nests undisturbed here, and the grass and wild flowers bloom and fade in peace.

A few paces in the rear of the church runs a deep but narrow stream. This creek, flowing from a cedar-swamp near at hand, pours its rich, chocolate-colored waters between tortuous wooded banks; now slumbering in the deep shadows of some gigantic tree, whose half-bared roots stretch forth, talon-like, as if to grasp the ebbing tide; and now whirling around an abrupt corner, its polished surface glistening like burnished gold as it shoots into the sunshine. Here the long branch of some bush sways to and fro in the tide, and there the old trees arch greenly overhead. A delicious coolness hangs ever about that stream. On the hottest of summer days one may sit on the old gnarled root, at the end of the path leading down to the water, and listening to the purling of the quiet current, almost fancy himself far off among the gardens and fountains of Damascus.

In the summer parlor of the mansion at Sweetwater, about a fortnight after the events narrated in the preceding chapters, sat Kate and her aunt. The windows were up, admitting the cool breeze from the water, and presenting an uninterrupted view of the pond in the direction of the little church, whose white walls, gleaming out from behind the trees, afforded a pleasant repose for the eye in the distance. Mrs. Warren sat, so far as dress could make her, in all the dignity and state of a dowager. Not a ruffle could be seen in her stomacher. Every hair in her powdered toupee was in its exact place, as firm and stiff as the clipped box trees in the garden. Her robe was spread majestically around her; and her hands lay crossed in her lap, on top of an open book, as if she had just ceased reading. Truth compels us to add that the good lady was drowsy, a condition not a little assisted by the hum of insects without, and by the almost inaudible plash of the water, as the faint breeze gently dashed it against the garden wall. Yet, even in this crisis, Mrs. Warren was not unmindful of what might be expected from her. Bravely did she struggle against the weakness of the flesh, waking up continually and looking fiercely around, as if to show that she was not sleepy in the least. But soon the lulling sounds would prove too much for her; her eyes would close languidly; her mouth would gradually open; and perhaps a sacrilegious snore would be heard, to Kate's infinite amusement. Then, all at once, her head would pitch forward, when, waking up with a start, she would renew her defiant glance, but only to subside again into a doze immediately.

All this while Kate sat sewing, by a little table, on which stood a bouquet of fresh flowers, the choicest the season could afford. She wore a pretty morning dress of white cambric, which, fitting close to the bust, as was the mode, yet opening in front, revealed a stomacher of illusion, and then swept off in full and ample folds below the waist, parting on each side before the elaborately worked petticoat. In the changes of fashion, an approximation has been made to the same style in our own day. Kate also wore a short sleeve, reaching to the elbow, with a fall of deep lace around it. One little foot peeped out from beneath her skirt, just revealing the silk stocking and the daintily-made high-heeled shoe. Her rich masses of hair fell curling over her shoulders in a style still to be seen in some of Sir Joshua Reynolds' pictures: for, with natural taste, she generally eschewed powder. Her brilliant complexion contrasting with this simple white dress, made her look like a fresh white rose-bud—one of those which has a blush in the heart, while all the rest is of snowy whiteness. The very room seemed to be more fragrant for her being there.

It is needless to say that she never looked lovelier. But this was not entirely owing to her attire, but was partly the consequence of her employment, which always throws such an atmosphere of home around a highbred woman. He is a hopeless bachelor, indeed, who can watch a graceful girl, engaged on some pretty piece of needle-work, without thinking how beautiful she would look as his wife, plying that small gold thimble with those delicate fingers, by the same fireside with him, on a cold, wintry night, chatting gayly as she nimbly worked, and continually looking up at him with the sweet, dear smile of confidence and love. Ah! miserable man, whoever you are, whose life is spent in hotels; who know nothing of the quiet overflowing bliss of domestic happiness; and whose only knowledge of women is obtained from belles at balls, or flirts at watering places;—we wish you could have seen Kate then. In our time, alas! the needle is almost obsolete, so that you have small chance of being conquered. Young ladies would scream now-a-days, if caught sewing, whose grandmothers won scores of hearts by this bewitching feminine art. The world is thought to be improving in every respect, but we are old-fashioned enough to think that the grandmothers understood our sex the best, and that they slew thousands with their pretty household graces, while their fair descendants, with all their Italian music, slay but tens.

Those good old times have gone forever. It is the cant of the present day to abuse them as stiff and formal. But when again shall we behold such highbred courtesy among men, such a sense of personal dignity, or such chivalrous deference to the fair? Our *gentlemen*—where are they? And the change is almost as much the fault of women as it is of her companion sex. In that day, ladies were known by their domestic virtues, quite as much as by their erect carriage, their swan-like movements, their robes of rich brocade, or their stomachers of lace. But now, while we have silly girls, or heartless coquettes, or artful establishment-hunters, or rampant woman's rights agitators, we have few *ladies* like our grandmothers, highbred both in parlor and in kitchen. Men have lost reverence for women, because woman ceases to be true to herself. Lovers no longer count themselves in heaven if they are allowed to kiss the tips of their charmer's fingers, or sue on bended knees, like Sir Charles Grandison, for the sweet affirmative; but thinking themselves very condescending to have the dear creatures at all, solicit them in a nonchalant manner, as much as to say, "It's a bore anyhow, and I'd quite as lief you'd decline." Young America has more sentiment for a fast trotter than for a fine woman. We have seen enthusiasm in bargaining for a "two-forty," but never heard of it in asking a lady for her heart. "Oh!" cried Mrs. Warren, waking up with a little scream at the noise made by her book slipping to the floor, "I haven't been asleep—have I?" And she got up and rubbed her eyes.

"About half an hour, this last time," said Kate, laughing.

"This last time!" indignantly exclaimed her aunt. "I wasn't asleep at all, but merely forgot myself for a moment, and only this once."

Kate pulled out her watch.

"It's just an hour and a half since we came in, and you've been nodding for more than an hour of that time. But hark! Didn't the knocker sound?" And, as she spoke, a charming blush suffused her cheek and even neck.

"Yes; it's some visitor. Who can it be? Dear me, it must be Major Gordon, for he hasn't been here yet, though we've been expecting him every day; and there's no one else to call. It's considerate of him, I must say," continued Mrs. Warren, sitting down, smoothing her dress, and otherwise putting herself into company trim, "to have deferred his visit till we had time to get up something of a wardrobe. What would our cousin, Lord Danville, have said, if he had known in what dishabille we've had to dine. Such shocking creatures as we've been till within a day never did exist, I suppose."

"I don't think Major Gordon judges people by their dress merely," said Kate, softly, with another blush.

"Tut, child, what do you know about it? You've scarcely exchanged a dozen words with him. He's a gentleman, however, and can make allowances; what a pity he's a rebel."

"Hush, aunt," said Kate, raising her finger, her heart beating so that her boddice visibly throbbed, for the firm tread, which she fancied she recognized, was heard approaching the parlor.

Almost at the same instant the door flew open, and a servant announced Major Gordon.

CHAPTER X
ARAB

Oh! spirits gay and kindly heart,
Precious the blessings ye impart. —Joanna Baillie.

There's little of the melancholy element in her, my lord:
for she is never sad, but when she sleeps;
and not over sad then; for I have heard my daughter say
she hath often dreamed of unhappiness, and waked herself
with laughing. —Shakespeare.

It would be difficult to explain the cause of Kate's flutter of spirits at this visit. Certainly, she could not have analyzed her own feelings, even if she had tried. Her agitation both surprised and annoyed her. Never before had she been thus affected on any similar occasion, and she mentally pronounced it a bit of weakness unworthy of her.

It is true that Major Gordon had occupied no inconsiderable portion of her thoughts during the last fortnight. Nor is this surprising. His almost exclusive agency in the rescue of herself and aunt could not be concealed from her, in spite of the modesty on his part which would have represented it as a deed equally shared by many others. Indeed, the deportment of Major Gordon in reference to the affair, heightened the estimate which Kate had been predisposed to form of him. Though the words he had exchanged with our heroine had been few, she still seemed to hear the mellow tones of his rich, manly voice. Not that Kate was what is called a romantic girl. She was very far from supposing that, because a handsome young officer had been instrumental in saving her life, she must fall in love with him, irrespective of other and higher claims to her notice. Imaginative as she was, she had too much strong sense to be so weak. She had often detected herself speculating at the causes which kept Major Gordon from visiting them, as he had been formally solicited to do by her aunt, and by herself more reservedly, though not less earnestly; but she had not felt it as a personal slight, like an ordinary heroine of romance would have been expected to do, under similar circumstances.

The emotion of Kate, from whatever cause it sprung, was but temporary. Before the door was fairly opened, much less before she was called on to return Major Gordon's bow, she had schooled her face and manner into that highbred ease, which, in combination with the natural force of her character, made her so bewitching as a woman.

Major Gordon, attired carefully in the full uniform of his rank, had a striking personal appearance. He looked every inch a gentleman, even as gentlemen were in those, their palmy days. Bowing gracefully, with a calm, self-collected air, first to Mrs. Warren and then to Kate, he took the seat offered to him by the servant, and glided gracefully into conversation.

"We have been expecting you before, Major," said Mrs. Warren. "Especially since we heard you were stationed at the Forks, which is so nigh to Sweetwater."

"I have been delayed by important public business," was the answer. "The powder, for which I was on the lookout, having arrived, I had personally to see to its safety and subsequent transmission to head-quarters. I made daily inquiries after your health and that of Miss Aylesford, however," he continued, "and had the pleasure of hearing that you were slowly but surely recovering from your fatigues."

"We have been told," said Mrs. Warren, still taking the lead in the conversation, "that you have been appointed to the command at the Forks, which has been created a military post."

"It is so. There is so much valuable merchandize there, that it has been thought best to station a few soldiers at the place. Allow me, ladies," he politely continued, "to tender you their protection, though I trust no occasion may arise for claiming it."

"And you really will assist," said Kate, archly, "such horrible tories as ourselves."

"Not such inveterate ones, I hope," answered Major Gordon, in the same gay spirit, "as you would have me suppose. Had that been so, you would not have remained at Sweetwater, but have gone to New York; for General Washington is always ready to give ladies a pass, especially frightened ones."

"Oh! I could never think of deserting Sweetwater, my beautiful Sweetwater, which I have not seen for so many years."

As she spoke, she involuntarily glanced out of the window, in the direction of the church. The Major followed her eyes.

"I do not wonder at your love for it," he said, with undisguised admiration. "It is certainly the most charming spot in all West Jersey. You live here," he added, "like a queen; for England, in all her breadth, has not a park as boundless as those vast woods: I am told the tract embraces a hundred thousand acres."

"All which," continued Kate, in the same gay tone, "makes me seriously think of turning whig; for if your General Washington wins at last, some greedy patriot might have my estate confiscated. Aunt is to remain a tory, red-hot for King George, tea and stamp-duties, so that, if you rebels—that's the word for her, you know—get the ascendency, she can keep the property for me in her name. I believe it was in some such fashion—wasn't it?— that the rebels in Mother England used to keep the lands in a family. Isn't his grace of Hamilton only a younger branch of the exiled peer!"

Mrs. Warren, who could never understand a jest, had vainly tried to interrupt Kate, as the latter thus rattled on. Now, raising her hands, she cried—

"Niece, niece, how you talk. Major Gordon," she continued, turning in real distress to the American officer, "you mustn't mind what the silly child says. I know you are too much of a gentleman to take advantage of such wild talk. We are two inoffensive ladies, who wish to have no part in the unhappy controversy which is now distracting this land, except to render what assistance we can to those who suffer, and to disburse our hospitalities to all who may visit the neighborhood."

Major Gordon could not but acknowledge this last pointed reference to himself with a profound bow, but it was with difficulty he refrained from a smile, especially when, glancing at Kate, he saw the suppressed mirth which laughed in her eyes.

"Well, aunt," demurely said the niece, "Major Gordon will be so good, I hope, as to consider what I said to be unsaid—"

"Certainly," gravely replied the Major.

"Nevertheless, I may say," continued Kate, in the same tone, "that he won't misinterpret me, when I add that I, at least, am not a bit afraid. Our family has been so long in this part of the country, and has labored so sincerely for the good of the people," she added, more seriously, "that no one but an outlaw, and a villain of the worst kind at that, would harm us."

"You must not be too sure, Miss Aylesford," answered their guest. "These refugees, or pine robbers, as we call them in Monmouth county, are becoming very daring over the whole extent of territory, from this and even further east and north, to Maurice river and the Delaware. It was principally to guard the stores at the Forks from their attacks, that my little detachment has been stationed there."

"So I tell this willful girl," interposed Mrs. Warren. "I say to her continually, say I, that it isn't safe for her to ride out alone, as she used to do, and wishes to do now."

"You are fond of riding?" said the Major, his eye lighting up as he turned to Kate; for he thought a woman never looked more beautiful than in the saddle.

"Passionately," answered Kate. Then, coloring at her enthusiasm, she continued— "That is, I like it, when I have a good horse."

"An article in which, I presume, you must be deficient at present, not having expected, as I understand, to reside here, but in New York."

"I always designed living here, if it was practicable," replied Kate. "And as for a horse, I am not so unprovided as might be thought; for the stables were kept up, in some degree at least, notwithstanding our absence; and I find a six-year old here, which I am sure I could ride."

"Has he been broken?"

"By the stable-boys."

"Is he wild?"

"Only gay."

"Has he blood?"

"As Mr. Herman says, 'where's the horse without it?'" answered Kate, laughingly. "But, to reply in the language of the turf, he is a lineal descendant of Flying Childers."

"Ah! I scarcely imagined there was such a one in America," said the Major, with increased interest.

"My father was very choice in his stock, and imported several highbred racers himself. There are excellent stables in Virginia also, and he purchased a good deal there. Mr. Herman says that Arab could be ridden easier by a lady than by a gentleman; I suppose it's because, like all well-born cavaliers, he is chivalrous to the weaker sex."

"Pray," said the Major, smiling, and turning to Mrs. Warren, "who is the Mr. Herman that your niece has mentioned thus twice in the space of five minutes? I suppose," he continued, glancing at Kate, "I dare not ask herself."

"Mr. Herman?" replied the aunt, slowly. "O! that's the old farmer who was such a friend of my late brother. An excellent man, Major Gordon, though not blessed with many of this world's goods."

"He's a dear love of a man," said Kate, with a pretty pout, for somehow, she would have liked to have mystified her guest, "If I ever marry, it will be him—"

"Niece!" As she spoke, Mrs. Warren uplifted her hands in horror. "Why, Mr. Herman is married, and has children as old as yourself."

"But I expect him to become a widower," wickedly continued Kate. Then, with a serious air, she resumed, addressing Major Gordon. "I must really introduce you to Mr. Herman. He's the best man we have in the county, and quite a philosopher in his way. He's of the old Swedish stock, which, as you know, is famous for sterling honesty, straight-forward common sense, and a just estimate of life. When I wish to hear wisdom, I go over to his little clearing. But, if you are fond of horses, as most officers are, would you look at Arab, and give me your opinion?"

"Do, Major," anxiously said Mrs. Warren, "and tell her that the horse will kill her, if she attempts to ride him." "I should like to see Arab very much," answered Major Gordon.

"James," said Kate, summoning a servant, "have Arab brought out in front of the house. We will accompany you as far as the porch, Major," she said, addressing her guest, and bowing for him to lead the way.

Arab deserved the enthusiasm which Kate evidently felt for him. He was a dark chestnut horse, about fifteen hands high, with a head, neck and shoulder that were perfection. He came dancing up to the gate, with elevated crest and arched neck, the very beau-ideal of high breeding. As he turned his head toward the porch, on hearing voices, the expression of his large, dark eye, showed that he recognized Kate, who had already, by feeding him from her hand, established an intimacy with him.

She could not resist the mute appeal, but impulsively running toward him, patted him on the neck and face, while he turned his head, as gently as a child, to lay it caressingly in her small palm.

"Mr. Herman is right," said the Major, turning to Mrs. Warren. "Miss Aylesford could ride Arab when nobody else could."

"Do you really think so? You take a load from my mind by saying it. But, indeed, the dear child is so rash."

"Your niece appears to have excellent judgment; and courage is not rashness."

Then observing that Kate was looking his way, as she held one arm affectionately around her horse's neck, he moved towards the gate, saying.

"I think Miss Aylesford would like me to try Arab."

"Will you canter him for a few minutes?" Kate whispered. "Aunt is really too timorous. Perhaps she'd have more confidence if she could see how gently Arab will go, when ridden properly."

A saddle was placed on Arab's back, when the Major, vaulting into the seat, cantered as far as the church and back, Arab going to the admiration alike of Kate and of her aunt, his fine action pleasing the one, and the readiness with which he obeyed his rider gratifying the other.

"He moves beautifully," said the Major. "If I may presume, Miss Aylesford, will you ride with me to-morrow? I can assure you, Mrs. Warren," he said, turning to her aunt, "there is no danger."

Kate assented with secret pleasure, and directly after wards Major Gordon took his leave.

CHAPTER XI
THE RIDE

I wish I were as I have been,
Hunting the hart in forest green.
With bended bow and bloodhound free,
For that's the life is meet for me. —*Scott.*

Gather the rose-buds while you may,
Old Time is still a-flying. —*Herrick.*

If Major Gordon had thought Kate charming, in her simple morning dress, he considered her transcendently beautiful on horseback. The easy, graceful seat; the light bridle hand; the erect figure; and the animation which the pastime kindled in eye and cheek, rendered her doubly lovely to his mind. She seemed to fulfill every requirement for that beau-ideal which he had long sighed after as unattainable, and which should unite in one person a Rosalind, an Imogen, and a Portia.

The day was sultry, so, after proceeding a short distance, Kate said—

"I think I can find a cooler road, if you will permit me to be the guide. There used to be an old one, somewhere near here, which had become quite deserted before I went to Europe; it was grass-grown in many places, and must now present an unbroken sward, which will be a relief to the horses after toiling through these hot sands. For half a mile or more, the way leads through a cedar-swamp, where what we call a corduroy road had been laid down. We shall find it deliciously cool. Here is the very place."

So saying, she turned her horse into an opening between the trees, where, in spite of the obliterated wheel-tracks, it was apparent a road had once run. Tall pines rose on either hand, stretching far away in a vista that seemed interminable, like pillars in a gothic colonnade. The air was full of the sweet aroma they shed. Their fallen tassels, faded to a rich brown color, carpeted the road.

"What a bit of ground for a canter," said the Major, who was eager to test Kate's horsemanship. "Shall we give our steeds a brush?"

"Willingly," said Kate; and away they went.

It was a beautiful sight to see the two spirited animals cantering side by side, so that a blanket would have covered both. Arab was full of play, and turned continually to snap at his companion, which Kate laughingly permitted him to do occasionally, while at other times she wheeled him off with a dexterous turn of her wrist, which elicited the open admiration of Major Gordon.

Very soon, the natural emulation between the two mettled steeds began to tell on their pace, which gradually increased from a canter to a gallop. They went snorting along now, their necks arching at the strain upon the bit; their hoofs crackling the pine splinters that strewed the road; the foam flecking their glossy coats as they tossed their heads; and now one, and then another, momentarily succeeding in passing his antagonist, only however to be passed in turn.

"They are determined to try each other's mettle," said Kate, laughingly. "It's as much as I can do to keep Arab in. Suppose we let them out and have a race in earnest."

"Agreed," said the Major, entering into the spirit of the thing as fully as his fair companion.

"You see yonder thunder-riven pine," said Kate, pointing with her riding-whip. "It is probably half a mile off. The best one gets there first. Are you ready?"

"Ready," answered the Major.

"Go," cried Kate, giving her horse his head.

Away they went, like twin arrows from a bow: the riders laughing in the very abandon of fun; the horses, with outstretched necks, straining every nerve. The Major's steed, though a superior one, was somewhat too heavily built, and this quickly began to affect his speed. Arab, on the contrary, was in his element. With his neck extended almost in a straight line, his nostrils expanded, and his fine eyes a-blaze, he soon sprang far ahead of his adversary. Kate, as she left the Major's side, merrily looked over her shoulder, waving her hand in triumph. In a few moments she drew in at the blasted pine, walking Arab slowly until Major Gordon came up.

"Your horse runs like a deer," said that gentleman. "Yet, from his looks, I should think a child might ride him, when he's at full speed; he doesn't seem to move his body at all; it is only his limbs; but they are drawn up as beautifully as a greyhound's."

"He's a darling," said Kate, enthusiastically, leaning over and patting his neck; at which Arab looked around gratified. "I wouldn't exchange him for half of England."

Major Gordon smiled a little at this enthusiasm, though he could not but think that it became Kate charmingly.

"Poor Selim," said the Major, patting his horse in turn, "you did not win, and it's not often you're beaten. But never mind, old fellow, you can carry your master in battle, if need be, as gallantly as the best."

"To confess the truth," answered Kate, "I had no idea Selim could run so well. He's a noble fellow," she continued, leaning over and patting him also. "Ha! you like it, do you, my brave Selim? But I declare if Arab isn't jealous. See, he is ready to bite both you and your horse, Major. I must draw him off," she added, laughingly, as she turned his head, striking him at the same time with her heel, so that he sprang to one side. "Fie, fie, Arab!" and she patted him anew, "you should be ashamed of yourself, sir. You are first in the heart of your mistress, and might allow her at least to be civil to others."

By this time they had reached the edge of the cedar-swamp, which Kate had described. The road was much decayed, so that it would have been necessary to walk the horses, even if there had been no race. Kate was in high spirits, and rattled on gayly. To the Major, unaccustomed for several years to female society, except at rare intervals, her conversation was perfectly bewitching; and indeed it would not have been without its spell even to the most ennuied *habitue* of the choicest circles; for it exhibited that rare union of refinement and wit, intellect and sentiment, which, when combined in woman, renders her so irresistible.

"Ah! here we are at the spring," she said, at last, drawing up Arab at the side of the road, where a pool of dark, amber-colored water, limpid as flint glass, lay slumbering under the mossy roots of an enormous red cedar. Slowly the rich, aromatic water welled out from the impenetrable recesses of the swamp, into this natural basin, ebbing away from it, at the other side, as imperceptibly, and flowing off over silver-white sand, till it lost itself beneath the rude bridge crossing the road. Gigantic trees, laden with dark foliage, fairly met overhead, obscuring the sunshine, and filling the air around with spicy odors. To add to the fairy-like charm of the spot, the atmosphere was as cool as that of a cave.

"This is delicious," said the Major, lifting his hat from his heated brow. "It is Greenland at our very doors. The water looks so tempting that I must have a drink," he continued, dismounting. "Will you permit me, Miss Aylesford, to be your cup-bearer?"

"I haven't the heart to refuse," said Kate, fanning herself, with her broad-leafed hat, "for the water is the best in the whole region. Besides, to be frank, I'm half dead with thirst. But will your horse stand?" "Like a lamb, generally, but as he is also thirsty, and might drink, I'll fasten him thus," and with these words the Major threw the bridle over the limb of a tree.

"Yonder you'll find a leaf large enough for an impromptu cup," said Kate, observing that he was looking about as if for one. "I used to come here frequently, before I went abroad, and always knew where to find materials for a woodland goblet." And she directed him with a wave of her hat, still fanning herself.

The Major was not long in profiting by the hint, and skillfully arranging the leaf, filled it with water, and bore it to his lovely companion in triumph.

"Handsomely done," said Kate. "Yon must once have been the wood-nymphs' Ganymede, if the doctrine of transmigration of souls be true. Ah!" she continued, with a sigh, "what a world of poetry went out with the Greeks, who peopled every object in the landscape with life, so that a wood, or a tree, was an actual dryad or hamadryad. How I drank in those pages of Tasso, when I was still quite a child, where the Christian knight hews down the tree, which, a beautiful nymph, bleeds at every stroke. I cried over the poor lady, imprisoned in the cruel bark, as if my heart would break."

"It's the most alluring feature of the old Pantheism, that beautiful fiction of tutelary spirits of the woods and streams," said Major Gordon, as he took the emptied cup; and filling it, in the spirit of the thought he poured the water out again, saying, "A pious Greek would have propitiated, in this way, the deities of the place by a libation."

"They don't seem to be in an especially good humor now, at any rate," said Kate, who happened to glance up at the sky at that moment. "As well as I can see, through the leaves overhead, a thunder storm is coming up. We have been so long in the cool forest aisle, that we have noticed neither the increasing darkness, nor the fall in the temperature. The day has been sultry enough for a tempest, and, if we don't make haste, we may get drenched through."

Major Gordon was in the saddle before she had ceased speaking. Cantering a short space ahead, where the verdant vault parted partially above, he confirmed Kate's opinion. In a moment she was at his side.

"Hadn't we better return?" he said, surprised to see her following him.

"We should be too late to escape the storm," she replied. "Mr. Herman's farm is the nearest place of shelter I remember; it is only a mile off; but we can reach it before the rain comes on, if we lose no time. Follow me."

As she spoke, she gave Arab his head again, and dashed forwards. She did not, however, permit him to distance Selim, as he might easily have done; but held him back sufficiently to allow Major Gordon to keep at her side.

In a couple of minutes the riders emerged from the swamp, on a comparatively clear space, where the forest had just been cut away: and here the grandeur of the approaching storm broke upon them in all its terrific majesty. Colossal clouds, as black as ink, were rolling up from the west, piling one on top of the other, and making the lately azure heaven as dark as the day of doom. The trees moaned ominously. All at once a dead calm fell upon everything. Nature seemed panting for breath. Then, suddenly, a hurricane arose, which rushed through the woods, stripping off the leaves, and tore along the now sandy road, driving before it huge columns of lurid dust.

Kate wheeled her horse, at this crisis, into a by-road at full speed, merely looking around at Major Gordon as a signal for him to follow.

A few strides carried them within the shelter of the forest again. A few more, and they emerged on a small clearing. Major Gordon had only time to observe that it contained about fifty or sixty acres, and boasted a thriving apple-orchard, when they dashed up to a comfortable looking, though primitive dwelling, constructed of hewn logs, a story and a half high.

The house stood a few rods back from the road, and was approached by a lane guarded by a gate. This entrance was now closed, and Major Gordon was about to press forward, in order to open it, when Kate, rushing her horse at it, and skillfully lifting him, gallantly cleared it. The Major had just time to raise Selim for the leap, when Kate reached the door of the house, throwing Arab back nearly on his haunches, as she reined him suddenly in.

A patriarchal old man was standing in the open entrance, with two lads at his side. As Kate sprang nimbly to the ground, he advanced, and, seizing her hand, drew her in, for the big drops were now beginning to descend, heavy as miniature bullets.

At the same time he said, as Major Gordon alighted,

"Lads, take the horses, quick, and put them in the barn. Be lively now, or the saddles will get wet. But walk in, walk in, Miss Katie; and welcome to the old man's hearth again; it's been many a year since you were here."

With these words he fairly pushed her in, signing for Major Gordon to follow.

CHAPTER XII
UNCLE LAWRENCE

A wit's a feather, and a chief a rod,
An honest man's the noblest work of God. —Pove.

Along the cool, sequestered vale of life,
They kept the noiseless tenor of their way. —Gray.

The rank is but the guinea stamp,
A man's a man for a' that. —Burns.

The room into which Mr. Herman ushered his guests apparently occupied about half of the lower floor, and was employed indiscriminately for a kitchen, sitting-room and parlor. A huge fire-place, with a high-backed settle inside, occupied a considerable portion of one side of the apartment, the rest of the space being filled up with a cupboard to the right and a staircase to the left. There was no carpet on the floor, but the boards were scrubbed to a snowy whiteness; and a pine dough-trough which stood under one of the windows, was also as white as rubbing could make it. The whole aspect of the place indicated, in fact, the most scrupulous neatness. The good wife herself was a pattern of tidiness. Although it was not yet noon, and her day's work, therefore, was but half over, she advanced to receive her visitors in a clean apron and cap, which, in the single minute left her for preparation, she had managed to snatch from their repose in one of her lavender-scented drawers. A cheerful, motherly face was that of Mrs. Herman, such a one as made a visitor feel at home immediately.

Her husband was of medium height and strongly built, but looked smaller than he really was, in consequence of a slight stoop which he had contracted. In sitting, however, this partial deformity added to the habitual thoughtfulness of his aspect. The head, covered with thin, patriarchal gray hair, in which a few threads of a darker color still remained, was large and squarely shaped, with a jaw indicative of a great decision of character, and expanding above into a square, solid brow, in which the reflective faculties were largely developed. It was not without meaning, so Major Gordon thought, that Kate had called him a natural-born philosopher. His face in repose looked severe to sternness, especially as age had begun to wrinkle it; but when he spoke, his blue eye brightened, and a pleasant cheerfulness, which yet rarely amounted to a smile, diffused itself over his countenance. His manner, in acknowledging his introduction to the Major, partook something of shyness. But before the interview was over, his guest decided that, though a man of reserved habits, he was nevertheless quick to observe and reflect, and that a warm heart beat within his bosom, full of genial benevolence to his race, and glowing with sweet domestic affections.

"I declare," said his good dame, dusting a split-bottomed chair, which Major Gordon thought already clean to a miracle, and looking apologetically towards Kate, while she tendered it to the handsome officer, "if I had known anybody had been coming, I'd a had things more in sorts."

"There, mother," said the husband, quizzically, "Miss Katie knows you well enough not to need an apology. It's true," he continued, with dry humor, glancing about the scrupulously neat apartment, "if we had a shovel here, we might pitch some of the dirt out; but since that can't be done, our friends will make the best of things, I hope, and not be too severe on us."

"Father will talk," said the dame, apologetically, a little disconcerted; "he's no better, Miss Katie, than when yon left, you see."

"No, I really come into my own house sometimes," rejoined Mr. Herman, his eye twinkling with laughter, though still good-humoredly, "without taking off my shoes. I'd like to see the boys do it, however," he added, with a pleasant laugh.

"Mrs. Herman makes me always ashamed of our housekeeping at Sweetwater," said Kate, with tact.

"Don't say that now," replied the gratified housekeeper, whose whole face glowed with delight at the compliment, than which Kate knew no other could possibly have been more agreeable.

The conversation now became more general. After awhile, Kate said, addressing Mr. Herman by the familiar name she had been accustomed to use when a child—

"How are the deer now, Uncle Lawrence? I think I remember something of having heard, when in England, that a very severe winter had destroyed large numbers. Mr. Herman," she continued, turning to the Major, "is the best hunter we have in all West Jersey."

"They are getting pretty plenty again," answered her host. "That is, for one who knows where to look for 'em. But for others, they're as scarce as ever. I took several loads of venison to town last winter, and got good prices—the war don't seem to make much difference," he added, slyly, "to the nabobs."

"You farm this place also?" said Major Gordon, interrogatively.

"Yes! we farm a little. Enough for our own use, raising a bit of rye, a few potatoes, and some corn. The boys do most of it, though, to give them justice. We don't want much, we simple folk," he continued, "so that we easily manage to live on what I bring from the woods and what the boys raise. Mother there keeps us pretty well supplied with linsey-wolsey. Whenever I go to town with venison, I bring back a few nice things for her in return; and I shouldn't wonder now, if we could look into some dark corner of her closet, if we wouldn't find even some tea, whigs as we all are. How is it, mother? Is the tea there? And did I buy it for you, or did it come from this saucy tory, Katie.

"We get along, too, as well as the rest, so far as I can see," continued Mr. Herman; "At least I often think so when I'm in Philadelphy. We haven't as much money, to be sure; but then we've no vessels at sea, like Mr. Morris and others there I know, and can sleep soundly, in spite of storms and British frigates. Then we've fresher air than they can have, let them build as big houses as they will. I never cross the ferry but I don't for awhile think the air's pisened, for what with the vegetables rotting in the market, and the sewers that empty on the river front, the whole place smells dreadfully, leastways to a man from the woods. Before the war broke out, some of my acquaintances there, rich men, you know, used to come down here to hunt awhile, once a year. It was a sight to see 'em eat," he continued, with a low, chuckling laugh. "I've known 'em, after a tramp in the woods all day, when there's been no luck, sit down to a piece of cold pork, that they wouldn't look on at home, and eat it as if it had been the best saddle that was ever sarved up. Then, to see 'em drink our water! When they've had a hot run in the woods, they'd kneel right down by the side of the road, and lap up like a dog the water running from a cedar-swamp; and they've told me they never drank Madeery, not Port, that was half as good."

"Yours is the true philosophy," said Major Gordon, "and the world would be all the better if there were more who followed it. I confess," he continued, turning to Kate, "that there is an independence and content about it, which strongly tempts a soldier."

"Yet yours is a grand profession," said Uncle Lawrence, "at least in times like these. The trade of a soldier is the meanest alive; think of the

Hessians coming over to murder at so much a day; but when a man takes up arms for his country, and to drive out an invader, he's doing a brave deed." And the old man's eye gleamed. "I was out in the Trenton campaign myself, for that was a time when even age couldn't excuse staying at home, unless to them as were tired of liberty. I've one son now in the army, and another will 'list as soon as he's big enough, if it's the Lord's will," and he looked up reverently, "that the war should last that long."

In similar conversation nearly an hour passed, by which time the rain ceased, and the sun shone out again brightly: and Kate now rose to go. As she stood at the door, while the horses were being brought around, the birds sang merrily in the orchard, and the rain-drops sparkled in the grass.

"That's a music I never get tired of," said Uncle Lawrence. "It beats the best playing I ever heerd on the spinet, even Katie's here," and his face relaxed as he looked at her. "Then those spangles in the grass are handsomer than any diamonds. I've heerd that, after one of them grand parties in town, where the music plays and jewels sparkle, that people go home worn out and often ill-humored; but I thank God that I never listen to the birds, or see the rain-drops shine in this way, without feeling glad."

When Major Gordon, having placed Kate in the saddle, offered his hand to the old man, preparatory to mounting, Uncle Lawrence said—

"If you stay in our parts long, Major, and would like to hunt, I'll go out with you a'most any time. I think we may be certain of a fine doe, or even a buck, if you'd rather."

Thanking his host heartily for the offer, which was evidently a sincere one, Major Gordon bowed to the good dame, and cantered after Kate.

"What a grand specimen of an honest, simple-hearted old Nestor that is," he said, addressing his companion, as soon as they were out of hearing.

"I knew you would like him," answered Kate, highly pleased. "And he has taken a fancy to you, or he wouldn't have asked you to hunt with him. Father always said, in any difficulty, 'I wonder what Uncle Lawrence thinks,' for though he has read few books, except his Bible, he has ten times the wisdom of many a lettered man. I don't know what the neighborhood would do without Uncle Lawrence. He is the general peace-maker; yet no man can be firmer, when a great principle is at stake."

"He has the air of one who could become a martyr, if need were, even to dying at the stake."

"And he would," said Kate, her fine eyes glistening with enthusiasm, for in this her own character sympathized with that of the old man. "He told you he was out in the Trenton campaign, but he was too modest to add that he walked to head-quarters in little more than twenty-four hours. There are few men over sixty years of age, who could or would have done that."

The conversation continued till they parted at Sweetwater, for Major Gordon had to return to the Forks to dinner, and could not accept Mrs. Warren's invitation to alight.

CHAPTER XIII
KATE

With thee conversing, I forget all time;
All seasons and their change. —Milton.

This was the beginning of an acquaintance between Major Gordon and the heiress of Sweetwater, which soon ripened into intimacy. Of the dangers of such a friendship, to the gentleman at least, he was in part ignorantly, in part willfully blind. Bewitched by the grace, wit and beauty of Kate, not less than by the sweetness of her disposition as displayed in a thousand home ways, Major Gordon abandoned himself to the pleasure of her society, forgetting the barrier which fortune had placed between them, in making him poor and a patriot, but Kate an heiress and a royalist. Yet, to do him full justice, he did not think of the passion that was overmastering him, or the probabilities of its success. Love was a new thing to him. The law first, and the camp afterwards, had been his mistress hitherto. He little suspected, therefore, how necessary Kate was becoming to his happiness. He did not know he was in love. But an irresistible fascination drew him to Sweetwater, at first almost daily, and finally punctually every morning. Often, indeed, he left the Forks, intending to ride elsewhere; but invariably he found himself in Kate's presence; and at last he ceased even to invent excuses, such as bringing her a bunch of wild-flowers, a book, or a bit of news, as originally had been his custom. When away from her he felt a void, which only her presence satisfied. He rode, walked, boated on the lake, chatted or read with her, accordingly, as the weather permitted, or circumstances allowed.

Mrs. Warren was almost invariably present when these interviews took place at Sweetwater. She generally sat knitting, in a corner, occasionally joining in the conversation, and always managing on such occasions, to bring in her cousin, Lord Danville. Her connexion with that nobleman was a source of pride indescribable to her. It elevated her and the whole Aylesford family, in her opinion, into an entirely different sphere from that of the provincials about her. She felt annoyed, therefore, at the frequency of Major Gordon's visits, which promised an intimacy that, some day, she thought might become troublesome. He was very pleasant as a temporary acquaintance, she reasoned, but having no peer for a cousin, quite too plebeian for a friend. Her manner accordingly grew less cordial daily to their visitor, though it never ceased to be civil; nor did the good dame neglect to attire herself in all her state—she "owed it to her family," she said, "even when not to her guests." Meantime, also, she studiously avoided making a parade of her royalist sympathies, professing, as at the first interview, to be entirely neutral, and little dreaming that her guest saw through her poorly acted part, and amused himself secretly at her weakness and self-confidence.

Kate, all this while, was as gay, as frank, and as bewitching as ever. Sometimes she was so full of spirits, that serious conversation was impossible. On such occasions, she made a jest of everything, especially of love; for often, in reading the poets with her guest, that fertile theme came up. As merry and willful girls will, she delighted to play at fence with this mysterious passion, which she secretly felt would some day be her master. How she made sport of the meekness of Desdemona; of the fainting of Rosalind; of poor, deserted Imogen's melancholy. "She would never break her heart for a man, not she," she would say, glancing roguishly at her guest. "There must be a latent weakness in the women who had furnished the types of these characters to Shakespeare; for she supposed some women were so foolish, as everybody said Shakespeare never violated nature." As for Amelia, the heroine of the novel she was reading, and about which she and Major Gordon had daily battles, "never was there such a silly little thing." "Why," she said, "that good for nothing husband wasn't worth a single one of poor Amelia's tears. Booth was a brute; and if men were like him, she wondered women didn't—" But here she stopped with a blush, on seeing her guest's wondering look; and, with a pretty little laugh, added, "Heigho! wasn't it ridiculous, anyhow, for her to be talking of love, of which she knew nothing, and never cared to."

At other times she would be quite serious. On these occasions Major Gordon would secretly admire the sound sense of her father's views on female education. For Kate could converse on subjects of which few women, at that day, knew anything: and many an animated discussion took place between her and her guest. In truth, her visitor liked to engage her in debate, for he loved, at such times, to watch the animation of her eye, the heightened color of her cheek, and the dexterity with which she defended her cause, often forcing him to a positive capitulation.

Kate's real opinion as to the war remained, all this time, a puzzle to Major Gordon. Her face, indeed, glowed with enthusiasm, whenever a gallant deed was mentioned, whether the actors were Americans or royalists; but she never expressed any sympathy for the cause for which he had drawn his sword, except sometimes in jest, when she wished to tease her aunt. In the pride of birth, which so eminently distinguished Mrs. Warren, Kate confessed that she shared. "Let philosophers say what they will about the rights of man," were her words, "I feel that it is something to be descended from heroes who fought with Richard at Askalon, and withstood the chivalry of France at Agincourt."

Yet, in her demeanor to those more lowly born, there was nothing of the hauteur which might have been supposed to accompany such opinions. There was an old negro woman who had once been a slave in the family, and who, in that capacity, had often assisted to take care of Kate when an infant. To this poor creature, who now lived alone in a small cabin about a mile from Sweetwater, our heroine was as affable and kind as if she had been her own flesh and blood.

"Yonder is Aunt Chloe's cabin," said Kate, one day, when riding with Major Gordon, "and I must stop awhile. The poor thing will fancy I have grown proud, since I went abroad, if I don't draw rein and ask her how she does. She was at the house the other day, and would have amused you, I am sure. The paper-hangings on the drawing-room seemed to strike her fancy particularly. She had never before seen wall paper, for when she lived with us the rooms were painted. But where can she be?"

As Kate spoke, they drew up in front of a small clearing, about two acres in extent, with a log hut in front. A few cabbages, a bean-vine or two, a mock orange, and half a dozen gaudy sun-flowers, constituted the garden. As no signs of the occupant appeared, Kate nimbly jumped to the ground, and throwing her bridle over one of the gate-posts, entered, beckoning to her companion to follow.

The door stood wide open, and on reaching it, the aged dame was seen inside, holding her dog in her hands, intently occupied in alternately dipping his paw into a bucket of some kind of colored dye and making marks with it in regular order, on the white-washed wall of square-trimmed logs.

We have said that the crone, already nearly deaf with age, did not hear the guests. Kate watched her with a puzzled look, for a while, and then going close up to her, she put her light-gloved hand on the old woman's shoulder, and said, in her musical voice, but with something of astonishment—

"What are you doing, aunty? Have you lost your wits?"

The dame, thus apostrophized, turned, and, after disdainfully regarding her visitors as if scorning their ignorance, answered tartly, turning to her work,

"Chile, I'se paperin' de wall. Dis makes a fus-rate lion's claw. Don't yer see? Dar!"

And, giving a finishing touch to her work, she stepped back admiringly, as a Landseer may be supposed to do, when he has completed a masterpiece.

The first instinct of Kate was to laugh heartily. But regard for the feelings of her poor old nurse, who would have been mortified inexpressibly, induced her to restrain herself, though her eyes literally ran over with suppressed glee, as she glanced at her companion, who, in turn, could scarcely keep his merriment under control. The visit, after a few kind inquiries from Kate, terminated by our heroine slipping a dollar into the hands of the crone, a gratuity which Major Gordon secretly doubled as the fair girl rode off ahead.

When the cabin was fairly out of hearing, however, the woods rung with the silvery laughter of Kate. At last, her merriment subsided, and she said—

"It's hardly fair to laugh at poor old Chloe. She only does what all the world's doing. Her poke-berry juice and dog's paw are but an humbler way of aping the luxuries of the great."

Major Gordon made no answer, but said to himself— "Her heart is right, even where her education is wrong."

CHAPTER XIV
THE MARCH ON TRENTON

The old Continentals
In their ragged regimentals. —Knickerbocker.

That Spartan step without their flutes. —Brainard.

Another day, the conversation, when Uncle Lawrence was present, happened to turn on the battle of Trenton, and the famous winter campaign of Washington in the Jerseys. The veteran had brought some rye to mill, and while it was being ground, stepped over to the "big house," as it was called, where Kate, obeying the hospitable custom of the day, had him immediately into the parlor, to drink a glass of wine. Mrs. Warren was absent in the kitchen, scolding the cook.

Never before had Major Gordon heard our heroine exhibit so much interest in behalf of the Americans as on this occasion. Her eyes sparkled, her cheeks glowed, and she really seemed at last to sympathize with the patriots.

"Do you know," she said, turning to Uncle Lawrence, "that the great Frederic has declared that battle to be one of the most brilliant strokes of the century?"

"Did he, indeed?" said Uncle Lawrence, his face glowing with gratification. "Did the great King of Prussia, the hero of Rosbach, really say that?"

A century ago, Frederic the Great, it must be remembered, filled something of the same place in military history which Napoleon does now. He was especially the idol of the English and Americans; quoted, strange to say, as the "Protestant Champion;" and considered a marvellous captain, as indeed he was, at least in many respects. Thus even Uncle Lawrence, little as he knew of the doings of the great world across the water, was familiar with the exploits of the Prussian monarch.

"Did the great Frederic," repeated the old man, putting down his glass only half drained, his whole countenance irradiated with pleasure, "really say that?" And he looked from Kate to Major Gordon, as if half doubting whether the latter, whom he secretly considered a better authority on military matters, would confirm the assertion.

"He is said to have used substantially those words," said the Major, thus appealed to. "I have no doubt of the truth of the report either, for the movement on Trenton was certainly masterly. The results show that. In ten days, the enemy, though twenty-five thousand strong, and though holding all the principal posts in this state, from the Raritan to the Delaware inclusive, were forced back on New Brunswick, and the whole region rescued from their hands. It is one of my greatest griefs as a soldier that I could not participate in that campaign, being at that time still ill of a wound I had received at Long Island."

Kate, who heard of this circumstance for the first time, looked with interest at the speaker; for a woman, even if an enemy, regards a soldier who has suffered with something of tender pity.

"You not at Trenton!" exclaimed Uncle Lawrence; and he shook his head, as he added, "Ah, I can understand your grief!"

He paused a moment, and then said, as the memory of that day rose more vividly before him,

"I've heerd better men than I can ever hope to be say that we saved the country then; and if so be it turns out to be true, I shall be prouder to have my children say their father fought at Trenton, than if King George had made me a lord."

Major Gordon instinctively looked at Kate, whose countenance was lighted up with enthusiasm at the words and aspect of the speaker; at least our hero thought so.

"You are right in asserting that the victory at Trenton saved the country," he replied, with animation. "Miss Aylesford will excuse me, if I speak too boldly. But I know she honors bravery wherever it may be found." And he bowed respectfully to her.

"Don't let me be a check on you," she replied, blushing. "I know that both you and Uncle Lawrence are conscientious in your opinions".

"Well, then," resumed the Major, his blood quickening at this acknowledgement, "if our cause triumphs, it will be because Trenton was the turning point in the struggle. Up to that time, with the exception of the evacuation of Boston, everything had gone against us. This was especially true of the period immediately preceding it; I mean the period following the defeat at Long Island. The terms for which most of the soldiers had enlisted were expiring; and but few were willing to renew their engagements. Meantime new recruits came in slowly. The force of Washington, the only one at that time left," he continued, addressing Kate, "was reduced by loss in battle, by the capture at Fort Washington, and by the expiration of enlistments, to but little over two thousand men. A general panic seized all except the most resolute patriots. The Congress was preparing to fly, for there was no barrier between the capital where it met, and the victorious enemy, but the comparatively feeble one of the Delaware; and the British, twenty thousand strong, were rapidly advancing on that river. Lord Howe considered the revolution virtually at an end, and issued his proclamation, offering pardon to all who, within sixty days, would lay down their arms and take the oath of allegiance. You do not know, Miss Aylesford, you could not, living in England, as you then did, the temptations and terrors which beset men in that awful crisis, especially those who had families. The axe and scaffold, I should rather say the gallows-tree, loomed up before the eyes of every patriot. Many gave way. This was especially true of those who had property. Crowds took the required oath of allegiance. The liberties of the country, the future of mankind, quivered in the balance."

He paused for a moment for breath, for he had spoken rapidly and impetuously. Uncle Lawrence nodded assent approvingly. Kate, with downcast eyes, but heightened color, sat, playing with a rose, which she had just taken from a vase beside her.

More composedly, the Major resumed—

"In that crisis, if Washington had given way, all would have been lost. But he was like Atlas, who upheld our world. Firm as a rock, when night, tempest, and angry surges combine against it, he stood up, not only unshaken, but unappalled. 'If we are driven from Philadelphia,' said he, 'we will retire beyond the Alleghanies.' Never, even for an instant, did he think of surrender. And then it was," added Major Gordon, kindling again, "that he conceived that daring night attack, to strike at all the posts of the enemy on the Delaware, from Trenton to Burlington, which, even though it but partially succeeded, resulted in throwing the royal forces back on Brunswick, and recovering, in ten days, all which the foe had gained during the entire autumn."

"Only partially succeeded?" interposed Kate, with real surprise. "Why I thought it was a complete victory. It was so considered in private circles in England."

"The intention was to cross below, as well as at Trenton, and so cut off the whole series of posts," replied the Major; "but the driving ice prevented

Cadwallader, at Bristol, from achieving his part of the task. Above Trenton, however, Washington succeeded in crossing, and carried all before him, as you say."

Uncle Lawrence, while the Major was speaking, would have been a study for an unconcerned spectator. His usual calmness of manner had given place to intense, but suppressed excitement; and now, as the Major's last words recalled the whole scene of that eventful night, he could control himself no longer. The color rose in his aged cheeks, and his eye flashed with youthful fire. In general, he was the last person to speak of events in which he had been himself engaged. But now he seemed to lose his own personality in the magnitude of the transaction he described.

"Such a night as that was," he said. "The weather had been warm afore, for the season—kind o' spring-like—but all at once it set in cold, and when we reached the place where we had to cross, the river was full of ice, driving like mad in the dark. At first I thought all was up, for with the great cakes grinding together, it seemed to me as if we'd never get over, leastways with the cannon—we had twenty small brass pieces, you know. Along shore, in many places, the ice was piled ten feet high, where it had jammed, and one bit slid up over another. Often, in the middle of the river, whole fields would come together, so that, for a while, you'd think you might walk across. Then, with a low growl, like thunder miles away, it would split apart, and the whole begin to move agin. The Gin'ral, howsomever, determined to try; the boats were filled, and we set off. It was a hard fight to push 'em through, a'most as hard as the battle in the morning; and more than once I said, said I, 'we'll have to give it up.' Sometimes a boat would be carried a mile away from the one it started with, in spite of all the rowers could do to make it keep its place. Once our batteau was crushed by getting where several fields of ice met. If we pushed her off from one she ran agin a second; and soon they began to slide over each other; all the time moaning as if in pain, like the great leviathin that we read of in Scriptur'. At last we had to give up, and just wait what the Lord would send, but expecting every minute to be ground to powder. All this time there were twenty others, some with horses on board, as bad off as ourselves; the horses snortin' and plungin', frightened mad, poor things! The wind was cutting cold. Our hands got 'numb, and the water froze on us.

"Howsomever," continued the old man, "we made the shore at last, but not till four o'clock in the morning, when we ought to have got over by the middle of the night. Washington had crossed among the first, and there he sat, for hours, on a bee-hive, on the shore, watching the rest of us. You may guess how he must have felt! We had nine miles to go, and every minute was precious; for there wasn't much time wasted, after the cannon was landed. But now the weather, which had been threatening-like all day, set in stormy, snow and sleet mixed together, and the wind sharper than ever. The hail stung our faces; the cold went to the marrow, and some of us were thin enough dressed. Many a poor fellow, who had no shoes, marked the road with his blood. Not a soul met us, to bid us God speed! But I've often thought since, that people, asleep in the farmhouses, must have heard us as we went by; but they but half woke up, perhaps, and saying to themselves it was only the Storm, dozed again, little knowing that the fate of America was being decided.

"Well," continued the veteran, "it was nigh eight o'clock afore we reached Trenton. Long afore, when they told Washington that the wet would spoil our powder, he had said that 'then we must fight with the baggonet;' so we all knew that it was to be for life or death. Two of our men had dropped out of the ranks and died; but that only made the rest of us more eager. Not a fife was heard, nor a drum beat, as we marched along; the rumble of the cannon, and the tread of our men was the only sound; but the roar of the gale through the woods was often louder. At last, as I've said, we reached Trenton, just as daylight began to break. Washington rode down our line, and pointing with his sword ahead, said, 'Now or never, my lads!' He may have said more, but that was all I heerd; and that was enough; for I felt, after it, as if I could fight like a dozen men. I shall never forget how he looked. He seemed as big as a giant through the sleet and fog; and his face, oh! such a face, it said a thousand things."

Uncle Lawrence paused for a moment, as if compelled by emotion. His listeners hung eagerly on his words, Kate quite as interested as Major Gordon. Directly the old man resumed.

"The Gin'ral had hardly got out of sight, when there was a flash ahead, and patter, patter, came the sound of musket-shots. It was the picket, at the end of the town, which had just found out that an enemy was upon 'em. We dashed forward, the cannon jolting and leaping past us, the horses at full gallop. Of what came after, I don't remember much. The fight didn't seem to me to last five minutes, though I'm told it was five times that at least. I s'pose a hound, when he's been long held in, and is at last let loose on a deer, feels something like I did, after marching all night to get at the Hessians, and fearing often that we'd come up too late.

"You both know how we whipped 'em," said the veteran, resuming in a less excited tone. "They were dancing, and feasting, and drinking, just like Belshazzar, when the Lord sent the Persians agin him; and Col. Rohl, who was killed, was act'lly playing cards, we were told, when we rushed into the town. They wouldn't believe it in Philadelphy, though, till we marched the Hessians through the streets," concluded Uncle Lawrence, with a chuckle.

CHAPTER XV
THE FIRE IN THE WOODS

Here flying loosely as the mane
Of a young war-horse in the blast;
There, roll'd in masses dark and swelling,
As proud to be the thunder's dwelling. —Moore.

I'll read you matter deep and dangerous.
As full of peril and adventurous spirit,
As to o'erwalk a current, roaring loud,
On the unsteadfast footing of a spear. —Shakespeare.

"What! mounted already?" said Major Gordon, as he rode up to the gate of Sweetwater, and saw Kate in the saddle. "I had no idea even that you intended to ride today. I thought, in fact, that we were to read Milton."

It had come to be as much of a habit for the Major to appear at Sweetwater every morning, as it was for his men to report themselves to him at roll-call. Kate, moreover, always had a smile for him, even if Mrs. Warren had not; and often, before he left, the manner in which the next morning should be spent, whether in riding, reading, or otherwise, was determined.

"Haven't you heard!" answered Kate, as she arranged her dress, giving a brief nod, her whole demeanor full of excitement.

"I have heard nothing."

"Not heard it? The woods are on fire. See!"

As she spoke, she pointed with her riding-whip in the opposite direction to that from which her guest had come.

The Major, looking where she indicated, observed, far off, hovering over the distant swamp, a thick, black cloud, which, if the day had been more sultry, he would have supposed to be an approaching thunder storm.

"But why should you go?" he said.

"It is my duty," was the reply. "The population is thin at best in this wild district, but thinner than ever since the war broke out. But few men can turn out, and I thought"—she hesitated, and then added, frankly, "that my presence, perhaps, would stimulate them to exertion. For, you know," she added, changing her tone suddenly to a light and jesting one, "that my poor wealth is in timber almost entirely, as that of the patriarchs was in herds and camels; and one doesn't like to have whole acres burned up, even though caring for riches as little as your humble servant."

"But you ought not to have thought of going alone. You should have waited for me," said Major Gordon, impulsively. "It may be fraught with danger."

"Thank you!" saucily replied Kate, bowing with mock gravity. "You must excuse the curtsey," she added, "for you see I am on horseback. Oh! don't explain. I say again, I'm a thousand times obliged to you, for thinking I'm not able to manage myself, or look after my own property; but am just like the hundred and one silly, weak creatures, whom you men would keep in glass cases, as a pretty toy for the mantel-piece."

"Indeed, Miss Aylesford," began the Major. "I beg you—"

"Nay, not another word, as you would be restored to favor," she said, playfully lifting her right hand, from the wrist of which her whip dangled by a silken cord. "Or rather be put on trial for good behaviour. The truth, sir, always comes first. I see now what all your pretty compliments mean. Nay! not a word." And she shook her head, a pout on her lip, but her eyes dancing with merriment; for the Major was looking quite disconcerted. "You and aunt both agree in having the most sovereign contempt for my capacity for taking care of myself; I will not add the most supreme confidence in your own powers of advice, if not guardianship."

"I cry your mercy," said Major Gordon, when, after this wild rattle, she suddenly gave her horse his head; and as he spoke, he cantered on beside her. "I haven't a word to say for myself. But, as I have never seen a fire in the woods, you'll be, I hope, my cavalier, so that I may gratify my curiosity." His tone, as he uttered these words, was demureness itself.

The gay creature he was attending laughed outright. It was a light, silvery laugh, and with all its abandon, lady-like. It was a laugh running over with happiness and glee. She turned her head over her left shoulder, and looked the Major frankly in the face.

"Well done," was her reply. "You have beat me at my own weapons. But enough of such nonsense." And in a tone of real seriousness, she asked, "Have you, indeed, never seen a fire in the woods?" "Never. Are they not dangerous sometimes?"

"Often. If the wind shifts, the flames come roaring down on the workmen, frequently faster than a man can run. These pines, in a dry season, burn like tinder. It is a common thing for the conflagration to rage till a heavy rain extinguishes it. Sometimes miles of forest are devastated before the fire goes out."

All this time, the Major and his fair companion had been pressing forward, at a hand gallop. Before long, the smell of the burning woods, as well as the increasing clouds of smoke, betokened their near approach to the scene of the conflagration; and in a few minutes, turning an angle of the road, they came in full sight of it, and checked their horses.

Directly in front of the equestrians, appeared a space from which the trees had been cut off by the charcoal-burners employed in providing fuel for the neighboring iron-furnace. Here and there about this clearing, which was nearly a mile long and a half a mile deep, stood various smoking, semi-circular mounds, like huge black ovens; while scattered around, were to be seen cubical piles of pine-wood, some partially covered with earth, and some as yet entirely bare. Though Major Gordon had never seen the process of charcoal making before, its different stages, as thus revealed, explained the whole to him. A log-hut, the rudest in construction he had ever seen, located in the midst of this desolate tract, showed that the charcoal burners temporarily resided here. But, at present, no signs of human life were visible about the cabin. Indeed, the eye of the Major did not rest on it, or on the smoking mounds, for more than a second, the spectacle beyond being such as to fix his attention immediately.

Back of the charcoal-clearing stretched the pine forest, like a wall of enormous reeds, sombre and gloomy as death. Just as the Major and Kate arrived at the turn of the road, the fire, racing before a brisk wind, had come into sight at the further end of the clearing. In little more than a minute, it swept across a tract of woodland nearly a furlong in extent. The flames had scarcely caught the lower part of a tree before they had run to its very top. Distance seemed to be no impediment to them, for, reaching a side-road, they did not perceptibly pause, but crossed it at once. Indeed, the dry, resinous trees appeared often to take fire without the contact of the elements, flashing into conflagration from the heat alone.

As the ocean of flame advanced, it tossed billows of pitchy smoke up into the sky, while red forky tongues shot continually forth, and lapping the air for a moment, went out forever. Where the undergrowth had been left standing along the edge of the wood, or where there was a tract of wild grass, the fire, catching to it, whistled along with a rapidity the eye could scarcely follow. It was a melancholy sight to see the tall pines, the growth of a century, standing one moment green to the top; and the next, after writhing helplessly in the lurid fire, left blackened and shrivelled wrecks. The roar of the conflagration, meantime, was awful, the sound of it seeming to pervade all space. Every instant it grew louder and deeper, for the flames had now skirted along almost the entire side of the clearing, and were consequently directly opposite to our equestrians, within only half a mile.

For the first time it now occurred to the Major that their situation might possibly become perilous. He censured himself for not suspecting this before, but as less than five minutes had elapsed since their arrival, perhaps less than half that time, and as, in that brief interval, his whole attention had been engrossed by the novel spectacle, his error was natural. He turned immediately to Kate.

She had not been less absorbed than himself, and was still eagerly regarding the conflagration, her whole attitude and air betraying intense abstraction. The quick, earnest words of her companion aroused her, however, at once. She started with a blush, at the first sound of his deep voice.

"We shall be cut off by the fire," he said, "if we don't fly for our lives. As soon as the flames reach this end of the clearing, they will extend laterally in our direction; for that is the course of the wind. Not a minute must be lost."

Kate scarcely waited to hear him out. At once she saw the truth of what he said, and recognizing the imminency of their peril even better than he did, for she was more familiar with the treacherous rapidity of these conflagrations, she turned her steed, and, with no answer but a look, galloped back along the road they had come.

The horses had, for some time, been restless. But their riders, engrossed by the scene, had not observed this, though mechanically quieting them, from unconscious habit. The moment the animals felt the rein relax, and found their backs turned on the nameless horror which had oppressed them, they gave way to their affright, and rushed onward with terror, the sweat starting on their glossy coats, and their distended nostrils reddening with blood. Neither the Major nor Kate made any effort to check them. For both now recollected that the road they were following curved in towards the line of the fire, and that for a considerable time at least, they would be approaching the conflagration, instead of increasing their distance from it. In this extremity the same thought occurred to both. It was whether it would not be wiser to return, for, even in the event of being surrounded by the flames, the clearing would afford comparative safety. But each felt that already it was doubtful if they could regain the clearing, and that nothing was left but to press on at the most rapid pace of which Arab and Selim were capable. They looked at each other but did not speak, for looks supply the place of words in great emergencies. Both read each other's thoughts, and both said mentally that their lives now depended on the mettle of their horses.

The air, meantime, was becoming so oppressive, that breathing grew difficult. The smoke and heat filled the whole atmosphere, and the terrified animals, now more unnerved than ever, were bathed completely in sweat, and began to exhibit a disposition to bolt aside. It was with the utmost difficulty that Kate could keep Arab's head facing the approaching fire, the alarmed beast swerving continually. Selim, from having been trained to the battle field, was less affrighted at the smoke, though, as terror is infectious, he also commenced to be unmanageable.

Precious moments were thus lost. Suddenly the conflagration made its appearance, about two hundred yards in front of them, and crossing the road almost immediately, blocked up the passage with a solid wall of fire; while rapidly spreading laterally, it threatened, in a few instants more, to engulf our equestrians. Blazing fragments of bark were already falling around them; the flames crackled sharper, and the roar deepened.

Heretofore, in seasons of danger, Major Gordon had invariably known what to do. There had always been some possibility of escape, something which, if tried, might perhaps avert death. But now he saw no chance, however remote. He was like the miserable victim, who, bound hand and foot, is laid down in the path of the hideous Juggernaut, and who beholds, with chill horror, the terrible machine advancing continually nigher and nigher. Yet he thought less of himself than of Kate. To see her perish before his eyes, and of a death so awful, he being powerless to assist her, was the pang that wrung his soul. But his agony was not unmixed with a certain pleasure. From the deep recesses of his heart, surprising even himself, there thrilled, in this crisis, a wild joy. He could not pause to analyze it, but it seemed to say that death was sweet, with Kate to share it. Instinctively he looked at her, something of all this finding expression in his glance. Her eyes met his, in a long, full gaze, as if her whole soul was in it, a gaze which raised this sensation of joy to one of absolute bliss. For a moment he almost thanked heaven for the calamity which had broken down the barriers of conventionalism and sex between them. The near approach of death had revealed to him how much he loved Kate; and that look, did it not, he said, betray that she loved him as well?

All this occupied but an instant. But the conflagration, in that brief interval, had diminished its distance one-half.

CHAPTER XVI
THE MISUNDERSTANDING

Trifles, light as air,
Are to the jealous, confirmation strong
As proofs of holy writ — Shakespeare.

'Tis than delightful misery no more,
But agony unmixed. — Thornson.

Suddenly Kate cried, in a voice almost inaudible from eagerness,

"I see a bridle path, I remember. Follow me."

As she spoke, she struck Arab with all her strength, so that he shot forward like a bolt from a cross-bow, entering the forest, on the right, where the tracks of an old road were dimly visible. The trees had so overgrown the way, indeed, that Kate had to stoop to his neck, in order to avoid striking the branches. Her companion darted after her, burying both rowels into his steed.

There was no sign, as yet, to what point the path would lead. It was evidently a temporary road, made by the wood-choppers long before, at some period when they were cutting rails or timber in the forest. There were scores of such tracks traversing the woods, but their course was never direct, and often they led back quite near to the place where they started. A person, unfamiliar with the particular road, might lose himself speedily in its labyrinths. But the positiveness with which Kate spoke convinced Major Gordon that she had used the path before, and that it held out a possibility, at least, of escape.

In confirmation of this, he observed that the conflagration, though pressing close on their left, moved in a parallel line with them. For several seconds it was a race for life and death between the advancing fire and the fugitives. On sped the horses, their muscles starting out like whip-cord, and the ground fairly flying beneath their hoofs. But close and hot in pursuit, like a troop of hungry wolves, whose breath already burns the flying hunter, the conflagration came leaping and roaring behind. Not once, however, did Kate look around after the first hurried glance, which ascertained that her companion had understood her and followed.

Rushing through the forest in this way, they regained, after a while, a spot where the path widened, the road not being here so much overgrown. They were now able to see that the way opened ahead into a broad, well-beaten highway, with several parallel wheel tracks, which crossed nearly at right angles to the horse path they were in. Never was harbor a more grateful sight to the mariner than that white, glaring, sandy road to the Major and Kate. The latter glanced back over her shoulder, waving her hand as she dashed on; while, the former, in his excitement, found himself almost bursting into a huzza. The cheer, however, would have been checked on his lips, if he had yielded to the impulse; for a second glance revealed a tree, lying right across their path, its branches forming a chevaux de frieze, while the thickness of the wood on either side forbade the hope of turning it. Meantime, the forest was shaking in the eddy which ran immediately before the fire; and looking back eagerly over his shoulder, he beheld the flames, only about a pistol shot behind, careering fiercely after them.

But what was his amazement, and an amazement coupled with the wildest delight, when he saw Kate rushing Arab at the tremendous obstacle before them. The leap was one, which, except in such an emergency, he would have thought it suicidal, even for the best horseman, mounted on the finest of hunters, to attempt; but Kate, not hesitating an instant, lifted her horse with a sudden cry of encouragement, and went flying over the impediment, just brushing its top as she passed. Quick as lightning the Major followed, driving his spurs deep into Selim's flanks, and cheering him on.

They had escaped, by what seemed a miracle; for directly after the conflagration reached the fallen tree. There, checked by the width of the highway, temporarily, it seemed to rage more furiously than ever, roaring and leaping like baffled wolves that howl along the shore from which their prey has escaped.

They galloped forward in silence, for some time, Kate leading the way. A swampy bit of ground being crossed, they reached the head of a pond, around which Kate made a short circuit, when she drew in her rein.

"We are safe now," she said; "this is the pond of Waldo furnace, and is between us and the fire, so we can take our time."

She was scarcely audible, and Major Gordon, looking into her face, saw that it was pale as death. High-spirited as Kate was, the reaction had been too great for her, and she seemed, for a space, as if she would actually fall from her saddle.

"Let me help you to dismount—you are fainting," cried Major Gordon, springing to the ground.

But she shook her head, smiling her thanks.

"At least rest a while," he urged, "*dear* Miss Aylesford."

It was the first time he had ever used this mode of address, and his whole frame thrilled as he tremulously uttered it. Kate made no reply. She was plainly too weak, for the time, to speak. But her eyes drooped, the color mounted to her face, and the delicate hand which held the rein shook perceptibly. She did not, however, check her horse; and her companion seeing, by this, that she preferred not to stop, ceased to urge her, but vaulting into the saddle, followed her slowly.

The last half hour had opened Major Gordon's eyes. He had yielded, for more than a fortnight, to the fascination of Kate's society, without inquiring what was the nature of the spell which bound him; but that moment, when he thought death inevitable, had suddenly, as if by a lightning-flash, revealed the truth. He knew that he loved Kate with all the ardor of his soul. Nor, if he had interpreted her look aright, was he indifferent to her. At any other time, he would at once have urged his daring suit. But the agitation of Kate forbade it now.

He followed her in silence, therefore, until they reached the vicinity of the church near Sweetwater, when, just as they were crossing the old bridge in its rear, Kate drew Arab in.

"I never pass this spot without wishing to stop," she said. "Running water and its musical sound always fascinates me."

The old bridge fascinated Major Gordon also, as he looked at the dark waters, some twenty feet below, swirling and rushing from under it. Almost completely shaded by the sombre cedars, which here entirely overarched it, the river swept swiftly onwards, the color of dark walnut, except when a stray sunbeam, penetrating the thick canopy, and falling in broken gleams on its surface, burnished it momentarily into gold. Insects skimmed to and fro on the water, now darting out into mid-current to be borne rapidly downwards, and now dozing on the very edge of the rushing tide, or circling in the eddies that revolved under the mossy banks. An almost undistinguishable hum pervaded the atmosphere, from the thousands that buzzed on busy wing about. Occasionally a low sound, as if the cedars audibly sighed, rose up when some faint breeze stirred through their ancient boughs. The scene was the more lovely and absorbing, for its contrast to the conflagration they had just witnessed.

Suddenly a horse's hoofs were heard striking the bridge. Kate and her companion looked up, the former with perceptible embarrassment; a circumstance which induced Major Gordon to examine the new comer narrowly.

This person was a young man apparently about eight and twenty years of age, and attired in an elegant riding-dress, such as only gentlemen of birth and fortune wore in that day. Slender and tall, though not disproportionally so, and with a haughty yet graceful carriage, he had that peculiar air which the world is accustomed to call aristocratic. He sat his steed with careless ease, managing him principally by the heel. To the Major's practiced eye he was plainly an adept in horsemanship; though his skill was that of the *manege* rather than of the field; in short, he was evidently no military man, though so finished a rider. His face was of the high Norman cast, and would have been strikingly handsome, if less cold and supercilious in expression. In his fiery eye were traces of a daring, if not passionate will. But either care, or late hours, or excessive dissipation, had given to his countenance a worn and exhausted look, not generally seen out of great cities, nor often even there in persons so young.

A perceptible scowl gathered on the face of the stranger at sight of the Major. But without noticing him further, he checked his horse, and addressing Kate, said, authoritatively—

"Your aunt has sent me for you. She became alarmed at your long absence, and the woods on fire, too. So, the moment a horse could be saddled, I galloped in search of you, without even stopping to change my dusty coat."

Kate colored, but, to Major Gordon's surprise, she showed no signs of resentment, though the Major felt as if he would have liked to punish the speaker for his insolent tone. In fact, she turned Arab's head immediately homeward, as if obedience to the mandate so surlily delivered was a matter of course.

"Who can the fellow be?" said Major Gordon to himself.

But his curiosity was not destined to annoy him. Kate directly remembered that the gentlemen were strangers to each other, and proceeded to introduce them.

"Cousin, this is Major Gordon," she said, turning to the new comer. "Major Gordon," she said, turning to the latter, "my cousin Charles;" then correcting herself, she added, "Mr. Aylesford."

The gentlemen bowed distantly. Kate's cousin, with a supercilious air he did not attempt to conceal. Major Gordon, with a look, at first of surprise, and then of marked resentment.

"A cousin," said the latter to himself, his whole feelings taking a sudden revulsion, "and I never even so much as heard one mentioned before! Strange! He seems to exercise more than a cousin's authority over her." And a jealous pang shot through his heart.

A constrained silence followed, which was first broken by the lady.

"When did you leave town, Charles?" she said.

"At daybreak this morning," was the reply. Then, as if he could no longer contain himself, he said, emphasizing her name formally, "Really, Catharine, you do wrong in worrying your aunt in this way. She insists that you will come to harm, riding out in these troubled times." And he looked as if he echoed the opinion. "But, above all, what or who induced you to go out to-day?"

"Oh! you forget," answered Kate lightly, affecting not to notice this last remark, "that Major Gordon attends me."

"I beg Major Gordon's pardon," said the cousin, without even an attempt to conceal a sneer. "I had quite overlooked that circumstance, which of course insures your safety, though unfortunately it does not, it seems, prevent your aunt's alarm."

Kate's face was crimson at these words. But she said nothing, and did not even look to Major Gordon to implore his forbearance, as the latter, with a lover's exacting nature, thought she ought. The consequence was that the Major, already jealous of the cousin, became irritated at Kate herself; and insensibly drawing his horse to one side, left Mr. Aylesford and lady to ride together; for, during this conversation, the speakers had set off slowly towards Sweetwater.

"What a fool I would have made of myself," soliloquized Major Gordon, angrily, "if I had told her, five minutes ago, I loved her, as I was tempted to do. She is evidently plighted to this cousin, for in no other way can his cool assumption of authority over her be explained; and she has been only amusing herself with me; her look I misinterpreted, or, which is probably truer, she is the most arrant of coquettes." An angry lover is rarely just or logical. "Why did I not see whither I was being led? Yes; if she had not been trifling with me, she would have mentioned her cousin at some time or another," he continued, getting more enraged, "but it was necessary to her success to keep me ignorant of him, and so his name was studiously avoided. All she seems to think of now is the possibility of a collision between us, for he has probably returned sooner than she expected; and she dreads his haughty insolence. Well, my pretty lady, it would give me a pleasure, if the gentleman and I were alone, to make him taste my sword."

In this way he rode on, sullen and apart, till they reached the gate of Sweetwater, where courtesy compelled him to approach to make his adieus.

"Won't you come in?" said Kate, in her old, frank way, though in a lower, perhaps softer tone than usual.

In an instant he forgot his indignation. But recollecting that he could not be mistaken, and saying to himself that this was only another of her wiles, he answered, coldly—

"No, I thank you," and, replacing his hat ceremoniously, he rode stiffly on, internally cursing the whole sex, from Kate back to mother Eve, as irritated lovers will.

CHAPTER XVII
JEALOUSY

I care not for her, I. —Shakespeare.

It is a quarrel most unnatural,
To be revenged on him that loveth thee. —Shakespeare.

The instant Major Gordon was out of sight of Sweetwater, and had plunged into the forest that lay between it and his quarters, he gave vent to the angry emotions that had raged, like a suppressed volcano, in his bosom.

His first ebullition was directed against Aylesford. The insolent tone of the cousin, in recalling, galled him to the quick; and his hand instinctively sought the hilt of his sword, when he remembered that supercilious and confident look. A savage, almost murderous feeling took possession of him. He muttered between his teeth. "If I had him alone, here in the forest, with a clearing of but a dozen yards or so, he should answer for his conduct with his life."

The angry lover felt that he could not return to the Forks as yet, where prying eyes might read his mortification, so he turned into a cross-road, which led into the heart of the wilderness, and, giving the rein to Selim, galloped till the panting beast was covered once more with foam. In this rapid motion the turbulence of his soul gradually found a partial vent. The first blind impulse of outraged love passed away, and he began to scrutinize the facts with comparative calmness.

He went over, mentally, the whole of the last fortnight. He recalled every word, gesture and look of Kate. Something almost like a groan burst from him, as he admitted to himself, after this review, that she had never given him cause to indulge the wild hopes he had entertained that morning. She had invariably been affable. But a woman in love, he had heard, was shy and timorous. She had boldly controverted his opinions, when they differed from her own. But if she had secretly loved him, she would have implicitly adopted them. Major Gordon reasoned in this way, not from experience, for he had never before been in love, and had enjoyed comparatively little female society, but from what he had read of the passion, in its effect on the sex, in the romances of the day: Clarissa Harlowe, Amelia, Tom Jones, and Sir Charles Grandison. It is no demerit, we hope, even in these days, for an honest man to be practically ignorant about such matters, when there is no way in which he can be informed, except by trifling with the happiness of trusting innocence.

Nor was this all. Kate's social position, her large fortune, and the hereditary loyalty of her family, now rose before him, the barriers they really were to a union with a rebel officer, who had no income but that derived from his sword. Instead of repeating the charge of coquetry against Kate, he owned to himself that she had been frank throughout; for a new light was thrown upon him, in reference to their conversations respecting rank and descent. She had evidently intended, he saw, to put him upon his guard. "Into what a bit of folly has not my vanity led me," he cried.

The day was drawing to its close before he returned to the Forks. As he emerged from the denser forest, he discovered that the obscuration in the sky, which he had noticed for some time, and which he had thought was smoke from the conflagration, was in reality a thunder-storm coming up. He quickened his pace at this, and reached his quarters just in time to escape a drenching.

For half the night he walked his chamber, his mood of mind alternating, as that of lovers will under similar circumstances. Now the first angry impulse against Kate would return. Now he would exonerate her from all intentional coquetry. Now he would recall her glance in the forest, when both considered death inevitable, and decide that there was some mystery, which, if understood, would explain satisfactorily her subsequent conduct.

In this mood he retired to bed. The rain still continued. It had been falling in torrents the whole evening, the huge drops rattling on the roof like shot. The water splashed like a small cataract, as it ran off from the eaves. The great buttonwoods about the house creaked in the gale; and the river, which ran close by, surged along with a wild, mournful sound, at times rising to a sullen roar, as if threatening a freshet. Amid such noises our hero fell asleep.

When he woke, the storm had ceased, the sun was shining brightly, and the birds sang as merrily as on a morning in spring. It was Sunday. The usual busy hum of the Forks was hushed, and everything breathed a Sabbath silence, made more eloquent by contrast with the tumult and rage of the preceding night. Not a leaf stirred; a thousand diamonds sparkled in the grass; the air was full of balm; and all was still, save the sound of a hymn that rose from a neighboring cottage, whose family was at morning worship. The sweet influences of the hour, combined with his late sleep, made Major Gordon heartily ashamed of his angry mood of yesterday. "What if Mr. Aylesford is preferred to me," he said. "Is that a reason why I should seek his blood? It is nobler to forgive than to resent."

In this mood he prepared to attend church. It was the first Sunday that services had been held since his arrival at the Forks; for, at that time, Sweetwater had no regular minister, but was compelled to rely on chance itinerants. The Methodist connexion, always a missionary church, but never more so than at that period, was then just beginning the great work, which has made it since such a bulwark of morality and religion in this republic. A new preacher, who had never visited the district, was to conduct the services.

The Major reached the edifice early. But the excitement of a strange minister and of the conflagration of yesterday had already collected an unusual crowd, at least for the period; for half the male population was absent in consequence of the war. Having tied his horse, as the rest had done, to the bough of a tree, our hero joined the principal group. He heard, as he had expected, that the storm had extinguished the fire, which otherwise, it was declared, might have swept the whole region, "down to Waldo itself," as one of the men said.

While they were talking, Uncle Lawrence came up. It gratified Major Gordon to see the respect, almost reverence, in which the veteran was held. The conversation still continued to turn on the fire.

"I've often wondered," said Uncle Lawrence, with quick sagacity, divining a scientific truth which has since been demonstrated, "if there wasn't a connection between these great fires and the rains which nigh a'most always follow 'em. I've observed, neighbors, nine times out of ten, that a fire in the woods brought a deluge of rain close on its heels."

"That's a fact, anyhow," said one of his hearers, with a puzzled look, "though I never thought of it afore."

"The Lord is always merciful," continued Uncle Lawrence. "If he didn't send these rains, I don't know what would become of us, for mortal man couldn't put out such a fire. It's skeered the deer clear off their old haunts, for I met one at the crossing of the branch in the main road, as I came to meetin'."

After awhile, Major Gordon left the group conversing and turned aside into the grave-yard, on the right of the church. It was a spot that might have been selected for an elegy as fittingly as that of Stoke-Pogis. There were few headstones in that humble cemetery; no pompous heraldic emblems; nothing of the usual vanities of life, that seem, in similar places, such a mockery of death. Good and true men, who, in their lowly walk, had lived more nobly than Pharaohs who now slumber beneath pyramids, or conquerors who repose under marble mausoleums, slept there unheralded, and forgotten by all, except by the descendants who still reverenced their virtues, and by that Omniscience in whose eyes the sainted poor are "beyond all price." As the Major stood, thoughtfully regarding the graves, he heard a step behind him, and turning was accosted by Uncle Lawrence.

"A sweet, quiet spot, sir," said the old man. "Just such a place as seems fit to lay this mortal body in, to await the resurrection. Some day, I shall sleep here myself. Yonder," he continued, pointing to the right hand, close to the fence, and about half way down the little cemetery, "is the corner I should choose of all others. I have thought of it so often that I have got a sort of home feeling for the spot. I never could understand," he added, "how folks can have grave-yards in cities; it seems kind of natural like, however, to be buried where the birds can sing, and the grass grows above you."

"You view the grave with no horror, I see," said his companion. "It is a noble state of feeling, and eminently Christian, for the old Pagans had nothing like it."

"I bless God," said the patriarch, "that I have no fear of death. It is but casting off this old garment of the flesh, and, when a little while has past, in the twinkling of an eye, at the last trump, I shall be raised again." And, leaning on his staff, he looked above, reminding his hearer, for the moment, of Elijah, when the prophet saw the chariot of fire.

If Major Gordon had retained any of his yesterday's anger, its last traces vanished now. His mind was attuned by the calm yet elevated conversation of his companion to the services of the day, and the solemn thoughts they merited. In this mood he followed the veteran into the church.

CHAPTER XVIII
THE COUNTRY CHURCH

You raised these hallowed walls; the desert smil'd,
And Paradise was opened in the wild.
No weeping orphan saw his father's stores
Our shrines irradiate, or emblaze our floors;
No silver saints, by dying misers given,
Here bribe the rage of ill-requited Heaven;
But such plain roofs as piety could raise,
And only vocal with the Maker's praise. —Pope.

The bustle of the arrivals had reached its climax at this moment. For nearly half an hour the congregation had been collecting, some on foot, others on horseback, and still others in antiquated, worn out carriages. The last, however, were very few. Generally the conveyance was nothing better than a common hay wagon, with temporary seats placed for the good dame and her children; while the harness was of the most primitive description. The horses were tied about, under the shade of the trees, and were busy whisking the flies off with their tails, and occasionally glancing around with a knowing look at the groups of people. The women generally entered the church as soon as they arrived, but the men stood talking about the crops, the war, or other matters of interest. Now and then a rustic beauty would create a buzz of remarks, as she tripped coquettishly by the young bachelors, glancing askance at them; and now some elderly person would step out from the throng to assist a poor, ancient dame, who came hobbling along on crutches.

A murmur of voices without, and of rustling fans within, filled the air.

Suddenly a handsome carriage dashed up from the direction of Sweetwater, drawn by two spirited horses, and was checked in front of the church. In the driver Major Gordon recognized his rival, who, throwing the lines to a servant that rode beside him, leaped out, and hastened to assist the ladies to alight. But Kate was too quick for him, for already she had opened the door and stepped nimbly to the ground, much to her cousin's discomfiture, as Major Gordon thought.

When Kate turned, after her aunt had descended, to enter the church, her eye met that of Major Gordon. The latter bowed with all his old cordiality. Her recognition was instantaneous and frank, and was accompanied with a bright blush, and a sudden lighting up of the whole countenance, as if with gratified surprise. This little incident was not, however, observed by her cousin, who had preceded Kate, Mrs. Warren leaning heavily on his arm, with more than her usual assumption of dignity.

"I declare," said Uncle Lawrence, "if that ain't Charles Aylesford come back. I thought he'd gone to Philadelphy for a month or two." And, shaking his head, he added, "Strange, that two such near relations as Miss Katie and he should be so different. But their fathers were so before them, and there's a good deal, Major, in blood."

In what this difference consisted, Major Gordon had not time to inquire, even if he felt so disposed, for as he finished speaking, Uncle Lawrence led the way into the church.

It was, as we have stated, a small edifice. A single block of benches, with an aisle on each side, afforded room for a few score of people only; but these were quite as many as the neighborhood supplied, even in better times. The pulpit was high, approached by a staircase, and surmounted by a sounding-board. On each side it had a window, half obscured outside by waving oaks; and through this casement the summer air stole in, laden with sweet fragrance from the cedars that overhung the stream. In either corner of the edifice, to the right and left of the pulpit, was a deep square pew, reserved for the proprietors of Sweetwater and Waldo, who together had built the church. One of these young Mr. Aylesford now occupied, in solitary state; while the other was tenanted by Kate and her aunt. The sexes, throughout the congregation, sat apart, in like manner, the women to the right of the preacher, and the men to the left. Uncle Lawrence, advancing to the head of the church, took his seat, evidently an accustomed one, on the front bench, dragging with him the Major, who would have shrank, if alone, from such a conspicuous position. The old man evidently expected Mr. Aylesford to rise and invite Major Gordon to enter the pew, a civility usually tendered to strangers in the Major's rank of life; but as Kate's cousin sat still, and only noticed the officer by a civil stare, Mr. Herman signed to his companion to occupy the bench at his side.

Our hero could not avoid, after a while, glancing in the direction of Kate. She sat, with eyes downcast, and her hands folded meekly before her, looking, in her spotless white, like some virgin saint. The deep love for her, which already filled the heart of Major Gordon, welled up warmer and more gushing than ever at this sight. For true manhood reverences woman all the more for those religious instincts which, implanted in her by her Maker, can never be obliterated without defacing her fair image. Her lover thought as he looked, that Raphael, when painting his Madonna, must have had a vision of such a face.

The preacher ascended the pulpit, and at once the shuffling of feet subsided, the preparatory coughs ceased, and a profound silence fell on the audience. For a few moments, with his head leaning on the Bible, the man of God engaged in silent prayer. The hum of insects without, and the light rustle of leaves, gave audible meaning to this deep stillness. In at the east windows, the sunshine, glimmering through the grave-yard oaks, slanted downwards into the church, and dappled the white, sanded floor with shifting light and shade. The murmur of the stream, like the solemn undertone of a distant organ, swelled softly on the ear, filling the whole atmosphere with sacred quiet.

The hymn was given out. It was that one of Charles Wesley's, beginning, "Lo! on a narrow neck of land." After a slight pause, a manly tenor struck up. The solitary voice was soon joined by a treble; a deep bass followed; and directly the whole congregation, women and men, adults and children, had joined in the singing. Rude as the music was, it had an earnestness, which placed it, in Major Gordon's opinion, far ahead of the meretricious vocalization he had often heard in fashionable churches. At the end of every stanza, the preacher read the next, when the singing commenced again. It seemed to our hero that he could distinguish Kate's voice, rising melodiously above all the rest, like that of some fair seraph, soaring high up over the choirs of Heaven.

The text was suited to the hymn. At first the preacher labored perceptibly, and the attention of the audience slackened. The disappointment was great. Near Major Gordon sat a pompous, self-satisfied looking man, occupying a corner of the bench, who was notorious for his noise in meeting, his sharp bargains out of it, and his opposition to all new preachers. He had publicly declared he would not like this one, and now, after listening awhile, he quietly leaned his head back, covered his shining bald pate and face with a bandanna handkerchief to keep off the flies, and surrendered himself to sleep. But as the preacher warmed in his discourse, the opinion of the congregation began to change. The orator, though what is called illiterate, was evidently deeply read in the Bible; and no man can be that, yet remain really ignorant; for he will know the human heart, if he knows nothing else, and will have at his command the most sublime imagery in all ancient or modern poetry. The preacher soon showed that he was also terribly in earnest. Heaven and hell, God and Satan, were awful realities in his eyes; and he labored to impress them as such on his hearers. He described a conscience-struck sinner, seeking to flee from the wrath to come; and described him with a glow of language and a fervor of eloquence which went directly to the heart. Cries of "Amen!" became frequent in the congregation. Even the comfortable old sleeper, disturbed in his slumbers, began to respond occasionally also, though still retaining the bandanna over his face, and making a vigorous effort to doze on. But now the warnings of the orator became more earnest than ever. The conflagration of the preceding day was introduced. "Where will the sinner be," he cried, "when, at the last judgment, the whole world will be wrapt in flame? No providential rain will then put out the fire of an angry God." The effect was electric. The women sobbed aloud, and some even shrieked. "If eloquence means the adaptation of style to an audience," reasoned Major Gordon, "this man is a Christian Demosthenes." Even the captious sleeper could endure it no longer, but, half starting to his feet, he snatched the handkerchief from his face, and shouted stentoriously, "Amen!"

Towards the close, the sermon became a fervid appeal, in which the most majestic Bible imagery was employed with startling power. Tears rolled down the speaker's face, while emotion often choked his utterance. The effect, when the preacher sat down, was evidently deep. For some minutes not a listener stirred. Even the noisy critic was now melted into heartfelt and silent emotion. Indeed, it was only when the minister, apparently too exhausted to conclude the services, leaned over the pulpit, requesting the well-known patriarch of the neighborhood to conclude with prayer, that the spell seemed even partially dissolved. Then, for an instant or two, there were deep drawn breaths, as of relief, and a slight movement through the audience, as of persons shifting from uncomfortable postures.

The prayer of Uncle Lawrence was simple, but fervent, and while Major Gordon listened to it, he could not help saying to himself, "this is the religion of the primitive Christians."

A doxology and benediction concluded the services, after which the congregation streamed out, the boys snatching their hats before the blessing was over, and rushing from the church, pell-mell.

Major Gordon lingered behind, not wishing to be jostled in the crowd, so that, when he reached the doorway, the Aylesfords were just driving off with the preacher, whom they were entertaining as was the patriarchal custom of Sweetwater. He remained a few moments, watching the congregation disperse. Here a good dame was climbing into a rude vehicle, there a small farmer was untying his plough-horse from a tree; here a group of damsels were glancing aside at the young men, and there the young men were sheepishly returning the glances. Finally, Major Gordon, mounting his horse, and bowing to the crowd, rode off.

CHAPTER XIX
THE MEETING

My bloody thoughts, with violent pace,
Shall ne'er look back, ne'er ebb to human love,
Till that a capable and wide revenge
Swallow them up. —Shakespeare.

In this
You satisfy your anger and revenge;
Suppose this, it will not
Repair your loss; and there was never yet
But shame and scandal in a victory,
When, rebels unto reason, passion fought it. —Massinger.

The next morning Major Gordon was early in the saddle. Like a brave man and a soldier, he resolved to see Kate at once, and know his fate.

But he was destined to meet with a disappointment. He had ridden about half a mile, when he was startled from a revery, in which she took a leading part, by the soft sound of hoofs advancing through the same path. He looked up, and recognized Kate's cousin.

The influence of the preceding day had not yet left Major Gordon. He was no longer eager for a quarrel with his rival, but on the contrary was resolved, if Kate refused him, to withdraw entirely from the contest, and even to avoid Mr. Aylesford, in order to prevent the possibility of a collision. He bowed, therefore, civilly, though distantly, and was passing on, when the other stopped him by placing his horse across the narrow road.

"Excuse me, Major Gordon," said Mr. Aylesford, haughtily, "but, as I was on my way to visit you, I would thank you to give me your attention for awhile.

"Certainly," said the Major, politely, endeavoring to look calm, though inwardly chafed by the manner of his rival: "I wait your commands," he added, seeing that Mr. Aylesford did not speak; and he backed his horse, so as to widen the space between himself and the other.

"I was astonished," said Mr. Aylesford, looking up with a frown, "to find, sir, on my return from the city, that you were paying attention to a lady engaged to myself," and he paused for a reply.

Major Gordon felt his color change at this confirmation of his worst fears; but the eye of his rival was on him, and he strove to seem composed. He could not trust himself to speak, however; so he only bowed, as if for the other to proceed.

"I presume, however," resumed Mr. Aylesford, "that you were not aware of the circumstance; at least such is the conclusion I have arrived at on second thoughts. I have made it my business, in consequence, to seek you, in order to state the fact, and to suggest to you, what your own sense and honor doubtless will hint also, that, for the future, your visits at Sweetwater should be made fewer, if not altogether dispensed with. For the services rendered to the ladies, my aunt, and cousin, by the party with which you were in company, when they had the misfortune to shipwrecked, I thank you, in their name."

It was not possible, perhaps, to frame a speech more galling to one of his disposition than was this to Major Gordon. The taunt in regard to his honor, the sneer at his conduct at the wreck, and the supercilious tone in which Mr. Aylesford thanked him, as if he had been a mere lackey, made his blood boil. Nevertheless he endeavored to retain command of himself. He saw that a brawl between him and Kate's cousin could not but be disreputable.

"I thank you, sir, for your courtesy," said the Major, at last breaking the silence, and looking his rival steadily in the face; "but as for your advice, I shall take the liberty of declining that—"

The hot blood mounted to the forehead of Aylesford, as, interrupting the speaker at this point, he stammered, half insane with rage—

"Sir, sir, do you know who you are talking to?" I am a gentleman, and not a mere adventurer—

"What do you mean, sir?" said Major Gordon, temporarily losing control of himself, at this crowning piece of insolence: and he pushed Selim close to Aylesford.

"I mean what I say, sir," answered the latter, drawing back his horse, and putting his hand on his sword.

But a moment's reflection recalled our hero to himself.

"Put up your sword," he said, contemptuously; "I have no quarrel with you. I was on my way," he continued, "to call on Miss Aylesford, and from her, if from anybody, must I receive notice that my visits are disagreeable."

"Do you question my word?" fiercely said Aylesford, again interposing his horse across the road.

"I merely deny your right to prescribe who shall, and who shall not visit her."

"That is the same thing." And he stuttered, white with rage, "sir, sir—"

"Permit me to pass," said Major Gordon sternly

"Never."

The temptation was strong to rush Selim at his antagonist, ride him down, and pass on. But Major Gordon was still unwilling to be driven into a brawl; and therefore, after a moment's pause, during which he was conquering his anger, he wheeled his horse about in order to seek another road.

His irritated antagonist, however, was not thus to be baulked. He seemed determined to fix a quarrel on Major Gordon, now that the latter had expressed his resolution to visit Kate, if he had not indeed determined on it from the beginning. He, therefore, followed our hero, saying contemptuously—

"Coward!"

Under any other circumstances, that word would have been enough. Observing, however, after going a few paces, that Aylesford still followed him, he sternly said.

"Enough of this, sir. You must see that I won't quarrel with you. Permit me, therefore, to take my way, and you take yours." And, as he spoke, he checked his horse again.

But the rage of Aylesford had now become ungovernable. Nothing, indeed, maddens a temper such as his so much as cool conduct like that of Major Gordon. Taking his sword by the hilt, he suddenly raised it, and striking our hero across the face, before the latter could parry the blow, said, with an oath,

"Take that, sir. It's the first time that I ever saw even a rebel officer disgrace his cloth by poltroonery."

Natures that are slow to anger, or that give way to it only after strenuous attempts at self-control, are always the most terrible in their wrath. The countenance of Major Gordon grew livid as he reeled from this insulting blow. It was a considerable interval before he spoke, for at first the words choked in his throat; and afterwards he could not trust himself to speak, lest he should, in the first moments of passion, utter something unworthy of himself.

"Dismount," he said silently, in a low, concentrated voice. "Your blood be on your own head."

Aylesford, with a mocking laugh, leaped from the saddle, threw his bridle over a convenient bough, and stepped into the middle of the smooth, shaded road. Then drawing his sword he stood on guard.

Major Gordon did not keep him waiting. Disposing of his horse in a similar manner, he unsheathed his blade and placed himself in front of his antagonist.

Nearly a minute elapsed before the duel commenced, the combatants measuring each other, meantime, with their eyes. Our hero saw at once, from the easy position of his opponent, that all his skill and caution would be required to disarm Aylesford; for already he had cooled sufficiently to come to the resolve not to shed his adversary's blood.

On his part Aylesford was secretly admiring the fine person and practised air of our hero. But no charitable feelings found place in the bosom of the insulter. He had determined to take his opponent's life, and he had few misgivings as to success, for he was not only an expert swordsman, in a day when every gentleman thought it a necessary part of his education to have skill in fence, but he had been considered, by his teacher, the most adroit of scores of pupils. As yet, indeed, he had never met his match, except in his old master. "It will be easy work with this militia officer, and quondam attorney," he said to himself, scornfully beginning the contest.

But Aylesford was not long in discovering that he had underrated his adversary's skill. He quickly saw, by the style of his opponent's fence, that it was the intention of Major Gordon to disarm him: and irritated at what he believed to be a contemptuous forbearance, in one of whom he had just been expecting to make an easy victim, he began to throw more vehemence into the combat than was altogether prudent. He soon, in consequence, laid himself open to a lunge from his antagonist; but, as we have seen, it did not suit Major Gordon's purpose to take advantage of this; and Aylesford, taught a lesson, fought for awhile with more caution.

We will not weary the reader with a catalogue of terms, of whose meaning he is probably ignorant, in order to describe, in accurate detail, the progress of the duel. But if he had been a spectator, he would have held his breath in horror at the rapid flashing of the blades and the rattling of the steel, whose lightning-like movements his eye would have vainly tried to follow. Every moment he would have expected one or both of the antagonists to fall, and would have wondered, as the struggle went on, why this did not happen.

The reason was, that never, perhaps, were two combatants more equally matched. Aylesford was really superior in skill, but Major Gordon was more cool; the first was ready to take every advantage, the latter fought only to disarm his adversary. For some time, therefore, the chances hung equally balanced. At last Aylesford, impatient to terminate this protracted strife, began again to be more vehement in his assault. But though pressing his opponent severely, he took care not to expose himself a second time. His attack was so rapid and fierce, that Major Gordon was compelled to give ground, at which Aylesford, now confident of a speedy victory, rushed on more relentlessly than ever, though still covering himself with so much skill, that his antagonist could not but admire, even as he reluctantly fell back. Had the assault been less splendid, Major Gordon might have reserved his own strength, while Aylesford was expending his; but it demanded our hero's whole energies to save his life, so that he soon became as exhausted as his opponent. The assailer perceived this, and continued his vigorous assault, knitting his teeth, and inwardly vowing, in the savageness of his passion, to run his rival through to the very hilt. At last, when he had pressed Major Gordon a considerable distance, the foot of the latter struck against an inequality in the ground; he made a slight stumble backwards; and, for an instant, lost his guard. Quick as thought, Aylesford took advantage of it, and lunged desperately, regardless of caution, which he thought no longer necessary.

But what was his astonishment, instead of seeing his blade enter the defenceless front of his antagonist, to observe Major Gordon recover himself, and avert the thrust by a dexterous twist, which he thought was known only to himself and his master. It was all the work of an instant, demanding less time than it has taken the reader to peruse the description.

"Ha!" hissed Aylesford to himself, with a curse, now fairly frantic with rage and baffled revenge, "he must have had lessons from my old teacher. From no one but him, or the devil, could he have learned that trick of fence. But he is blown; he is less practised than I am; and I'll have his heart's blood yet."

It must not be supposed that there was any pause, while he thus soliloquized. On the contrary, the attack went forward as desperately as before. Major Gordon at last began to acknowledge to himself it would be impossible for him to disarm his adversary, and that he must either lose his own life, or take that of the vindictive young man. The last alternative was only less objectionable than the first, since it would incontestibly banish him forever from Kate. But the liberty of choice was not left to him. He felt himself so hard pressed that he could count on nothing with certainty. All he could do was to defend himself, and watch for his opportunity, if fortunately it should come, or to die, if another and more serious stumble should be his lot.

CHAPTER XX
THE INTERRUPTION

There needs no ghost, my lord, come from the grave,
To tell us this. —*Shakespeare.*

Do not insult calamity,
It is a barbarous grossness. —*Daniel.*

But at this crisis, and when another instant would have dismissed one, if not both of the combatants, to death, a gun-barrel was thrust between them, striking up their blades, and simultaneously Uncle Lawrence stepped out into the road, having approached unperceived and unheard, through the woods.

"For shame," he said. "Put up your swords, young men. I thought better of you, Major Gordon," he continued, addressing the latter, "for your blood belongs to your country, and you've no right to waste it in a private quarrel."

Somewhat abashed, the Major dropped the point of his weapon.

Uncle Lawrence, turning to Aylesford, went on.

"Put up yours also, sir. I've no doubt this brawl is of your making. You needn't scowl at me; it will do no good; I was respected by your father before you was born, and I shan't allow you to murder, or get murdered. Now mount your horse, young man, and go home. You needn't look at the Major. He's coming with me, for I have business with him: and I know he'll promise me there shall be no more of this."

Sullenly Aylesford, after a vain attempt to bluster, sheathed his sword, and telling his late antagonist, with an oath, that they would meet again, got into the saddle, and moved away as he was directed. When he had turned a corner of the road, a few rods distant, and was out of hearing, Uncle Lawrence said to Major Gordon:

"Now tell me how all this happened. He insulted you, of course, for I know him of old, and I marked his rudeness yesterday in church."

There was a tone of authority in the speaker, yet one entirely free from assumption, which there was no resisting. With his blood still boiling, the Major put up his sword and prepared to obey the old man. He could not tell everything; Kate's name was studiously avoided: but he gave otherwise a fair account of the interview. When he had concluded, Uncle Lawrence said:

"It is just as I expected. Now it's strange," he continued, "how one brother'll differ from another. This young man's father wasn't the same man at all that Kate's father was; and the son's worse even. The old one spent half his fortune on wine and women, and the son has sent the helve arter the hatchet. He leads a wild life, when he's in town, where he can get company of the same sort; and did the same here, for awhile, when his cousin was in Europe. You can see that, though, in his face."

Uncle Lawrence paused, but as Major Gordon was silent he went on.

"His family, even Miss Katie, are in fear from his temper. You've had a taste of that yourself, and they say its sometimes awful: he'd as lief kill a person, if he was angry, as look at 'em. Miss Katie, too, pities him, as is natural, for they were children together. I have heerd it was a plan of their fathers to marry 'em, when they grew up." His listener winced. "How that'll be now, however, I can't tell. Miss Katie worships the very name of her father, and would do a'most anything that she knew he wished: but I'm sartain, if he was alive, he'd sooner see her dead than married to her cousin. Her aunt, I hear, don't think so, and is a great friend of the young man's, which is the more odd, because she married just such another, who spent all her money and nigh broke her heart. But they do say, she went a'most crazy with grief, in spite of it all. Women, Major, are queer critters."

"I suppose it's this old compact," said the Major, endeavoring to assume a composure he was far from feeling, "which has brought Mr. Aylesford down to Sweetwater."

"Most likely. Though there may be something else afloat, as other sarcumstances make me suspect. He's a tory at heart, I'm sartain. He was always high, and thought nobody good enough for him, talking of his cousin, Lord somebody, just as Mrs. Warren does," and he laughed that low chuckling laugh, which was all his mirth ever rose to. "Such a man, Major, is naturally a tory; and tories are always on the watch, with their cunning ready, for this youngster's as cunning as a fox; so I don't know but there's mischief afoot. That brings me, too, to my business, which is public, and to that private affairs must always give way, you know. But you'll go back to the Forks?"

In manly bosoms, love, though the master-passion, is not the selfish and all-engrossing one, which mere romancers would have their readers to believe. Though Major Gordon was as anxious as ever to learn his fate from Kate, he saw that the present was not the time for it, and therefore declared his readiness to return to the Forks, and meanwhile, to hear what Uncle Lawrence had to say.

"It's about the refugees, Major, that I've come to see you," he said, walking by Selim's side, as the latter proceeded homeward at a slow pace. "Yesterday, when we were all at meeting, widow Bates' house was robbed and fired; and it could have been by none but them thieving vagabonds. Poor thing! she has a hard time to get along anyhow. Her husband was killed at Brandywine; and both her oldest sons are 'listed for the war; so that she had nobody at home but her youngest, a boy of only twelve, and her little darter, who's still younger. Among us, we manage to plow her little bit of land, so as to give her corn and rye enough to eat; but how she picks up the rest of her living, it's hard to tell. Yesterday she walked into meeting with her children, though it's a matter of five miles or more; and when she was away, somebody robbed her, taking everything that was worth carrying off, and then burning down her house."

"The villains!" exclaimed the listener.

"You may well say that," continued Uncle Lawrence, "for it's not charity to call the scoundrels by softer names, as some folks, I hear, do in these times. Nobody but a villain would rob the widow and the orphan. Especially a soldier's widow. It could only have been the refugees."

"But have you no clue to them?" said Major Gordon.

"No what?"

"Can you guess who did it?"

"Oh! ay! can I guess? I think I can. It's Ned Arrison, I'm a'most certain."

"Who is Ned Arrison?"

"He's a vagabond well known about these parts, Major, and likely to git his desarts if he's ever caught by the folks. He used to be a hanger-on of young Aylesford; he was ostler, I believe, at Sweetwater, for awhile; and as Master Charles, as they called him, was always in the stables, the two got pretty thick. Arrison's ten years the oldest, however, and wasn't born in this country either, but had to leave Ireland when he was about nineteen, I've no doubt for gittin' into some scrape or other there. He taught the young fellow to drink, and play cards, and worse, if all accounts are true. Long before Katie's father died, however, the tricks of Arrison were found out, and he was turned off."

"What makes you think he had to leave Ireland for committing some crime?"

"Why, you see, Major, the rogue has had some eddication, and it stands to reason that such a man couldn't have been brought up an ostler, or forced to fly his country without being in a scrape. To do young Mr. Aylesford justice, he'd never have been so thick with Arrison, if the fellow hadn't had some eddication. But this, and his cunning, and his always being ready to lick Master Charles' shoes, or go down on his knees to sarve him, which pleased the lad's high notions, made him the right-hand man of the young fellow."

"But all this does not prove that Arrison had anything to do with yesterday's affair."

"Not so fast, Major. It helps, as you'll see by-'m-bye. Arter being turned off, Arrison went away, and I heerd was living in Philadelphy. I've no doubt at all that Master Charles and he were as thick as ever, there, when the lad went up to town to school. I've heerd that a poor girl, whom it's said the youngster ruined, was arterwards made to marry Arrison, in order to hush it up; and that Arrison took the wife for the money that was put down, and then spent the money and broke his wife's heart, that is if it wasn't nigh broke before: but of this I ain't sartain, as what happens away off in Philadelphy, isn't easy to be got at here; and I never liked to ask outright, when I've been in town, and, besides, didn't know rightly who to ask.

"When the war broke out, and the time came, before Washington re-crossed the Delaware, that 'most everybody feared the king was going to win, who should come down here but Arrison, and as Katie's father was now dead, Master Charles was living at the big house, and took Arrison into his employment at once. There was deviltry enough went on, in a few weeks then, to ruin the souls of a hundred men. However, before long, the tables turned, and this young Mr. Aylesford, who, as I've said, is as cunning as he is hot tempered, began to be afeerd for himself, if he allowed such a tory to live with him. At this Arrison went away agin. But not long after he was seen, with some other precious scoundrels, hanging about the British camp; and by-'m-bye he came back to our parts, where he took to a reg'lar refugee life. Some of us, at this, turned out and tried to hunt him off. But we couldn't find him, till one day, he robbed a house down near the Banks. John Sanders was away when it happened, but coming home at night, and hearing from the women all about it, and how Arrison had sworn at 'em, and struck his old mother because she tried to hide some silver tea-spoons under her apron, he swore an oath, that he'd have revenge. He guessed that the refugees wouldn't go far that night, for they'd come in a boat, and as the wind was agin them, they'd naturally wait for the next tide: besides there were few men left in these parts at that time, and so they'd nothing to fear. On this, he struck through the woods, coming out on the shore of the river, t'other side of the big bend, some dozen miles below this. He'd taken his axe with him, and what does he do now," and Uncle Lawrence laughed a low laugh, "but cut a path through the brush, alongside the river, leavin' just bushes enough between him and the water to hide him. He made his path a couple of hundred feet long, and when he'd finished it, lay down at its lower end, after having double-loaded his gun with buckshot, to watch for the refugee boat. It was a bright starlight night, and I've often heerd Sanders tell, that as he lay there, he could see the dark tide, as it rolled by, rippling past the pint, and twinkling as if a swarm of fire-flies was settling close over it. It was as still, too, as a grave-yard. He could hear the water *lip-lapping* agin an old tree trunk, that lay in the stream right in front of him; and the whip-poor-wills, he said, never wailed so loud; while, whenever an owl *hoo-hooed*, away off in the swamp, it a'most skeered him, it seemed so near. At last, arter he'd waited a long while, he heerd the sound of oars, soft-like, as if a boat was being rowed only just enough to give her steerage way. He peeped out, his heart a-beatin', and sure enough there they were, dropping down the river with the tide. He knew Arrison, who had the tiller; and thought he knew one of the others too. There were five of 'em. So he kneeled down, resting his gun lest his hand should shake, for he wanted to be cock-sure, and when the boat came directly opposite, blazed away. He jumped up at once, but not before he'd time to see that Arrison clapped his hand to his side, as if hurt, and that the fellow next to him, who was pulling the stroke oar, tumbled over dead like. Then he ran, let me tell you, for dear life. The men who weren't hurt, fired right off. But," and again Uncle Lawrence laughed his low chuckle, "Sanders, by this time, was two hundred feet off, one way, while the tide had carried them a couple of hundred in another; so that their buckshot only stripped a few leaves off the bushes, and cut down a huckleberry branch or two. Sanders got home safe before daylight, and we heerd no more of Arrison for a long while, till it was told that he'd been laid up, for months, with a wound, and had arterwards gone over to Maurice river to carry on his deviltries there, thinking that these parts was too hot for him."

"Now that's just the kind of rogue," continued Uncle Lawrence, "that would rob a poor widow. And what makes me think, above all, that it was he burned widow Bates' house, was that, when Arrison was living at Sweetwater last, he insulted the widow, one day, when he was drunk, for which her husband, who was alive then, gave him a sound thrashing. He's the very man to remember such a thing, and take out his revenge in this cowardly way."

"Your conclusions seem accurate," said Major Gordon, "for it is scarcely credible that there can be two men, in all this district, who could commit so mean an outrage. You wish me, I suppose, to put my men on his track. If that is it, I will do it cheerfully. Though how we are to succeed in running him down, if you, who have better woodcraft, failed when he was last here, I don't see."

"There's nothing like trying," answered Uncle Lawrence, "and there's the more need of it, because there's worse mischief a-brewin', you may depend on't. This varmint wouldn't have dared to come back, especially when he knew there were soldiers at the Forks, unless he'd a good many men at his back, or there were other reasons for thinking he could snap his fingers at us. I can't tell what it is, but there's something, I'll stake my life on that."

"I'll go out this very hour with my whole force. Will you help?"

"That's what I came over for. I'm a pretty good guide through these woods, though I say it that should not say it, and can track a man a'most as good as an Ingin can. I'm agin shedding human blood, too, when it can be helped," added the old man; but slapping his gun, he went on, "yet if I draw sight on Arrison, he's a dead man, for I've loaded her with as many buckshot as she can carry, and I'd no more mind shooting him, than I would a mad dog."

As he spoke these words he came in sight of the Forks, where we will leave them for the present.

CHAPTER XXI
AYLESFORD AND MRS. WARREN

For on his brow the throbbing vein
Throbb'd as if back upon his brain
The hot blood ebb'd and flowed again. — *Byron.*

I am burned up with inflaming wrath;
A rage, whose heat hath this condition,
That nothing can allay, nothing but blood. — *Shakespeare.*

It would be impossible to convey, in words, an adequate idea of the state of Aylesford's mind, after his separation from Major Gordon. Rage, shame and jealousy possessed him by turns. But to one sentiment he was constant through all; he was resolved yet to have the life of our hero; to consummate the revenge of which he believed he had been baulked at the very moment of success.

Uncle Lawrence's description of him had not exaggerated the reality. On the contrary, it had fallen short of the truth in many particulars; for the patriarch was ignorant of some of the worst passages in the young man's life. Aylesford had long since squandered his entire patrimony, in the wildest excesses, and had now no prospect of retaining his position in life unless by marrying his cousin. Relying on the family understanding to that effect, he had never allowed himself to doubt Kate's assent; but had looked forward to her return to America as the period which was to set him afloat anew on the tide of fortune.

Expecting, however, that Kate would not only land at New York, but remain there until the colonies, as he hoped and believed, would be subdued, he had made every preparation to meet her at that port; but not supposing that she would arrive as soon as she did, he had delayed, until the last moment, entering within the royal lines, a step which he knew would prevent his return to Sweetwater or to Philadelphia. He was at the former place, accordingly, when his aunt and cousin, arriving from the wreck, brought the first intelligence alike of their having sailed earlier than they had designed, and of the catastrophe which had terminated their voyage.

At first he saw nothing in the somewhat reserved manners of Kate, but the coyness natural to her sex and age; in fact, for awhile he attributed it to secret admiration of himself. But time gradually undeceived him. Kate's reserve changed occasionally to marked aversion. He resembled, indeed, so little the cousin she remembered when a boy, that, when his attentions became particular, she shrank from him with feelings almost of disgust. As whatever was worst in his past career was concealed from her, this growing dislike must have arisen from the fine instinct of her sex.

Aylesford, like men of his class, looked everywhere but to himself for the cause of this aversion. He could find no explanation so plausible as in a romantic fancy, on the part of his cousin, for the handsome young officer who was said to have been the principal cause of saving her life. Giving way to his unbridled passions, he secretly swore to avenge himself on this rival. But, meantime, resolving to lose no opportunity of ingratiating himself with his mistress, he offered to visit Philadelphia, in order to attend in person to those commissions which the damaged wardrobe of the ladies rendered necessary.

Arriving at Sweetwater, after an absence unavoidably protracted, his first inquiry was for Kate; and his rage was only equalled by his astonishment, when he learned she had gone out on horseback with Major Gordon. Once, before his departure, he had offered to accompany her himself; but she had declined in terms that left no opening for repeating the request. A few questions, angrily put, extracted from the frightened servant, that Kate had been riding out daily for a fortnight with the man he already considered his rival. He was almost white with passion, therefore, when Mrs. Warren appeared.

His aunt, like all weak-minded persons, loved him none the less, perhaps, for his wild life, or his ungovernable temper. He had been her pet before she left for Europe, the more probably because his uncle so often frowned upon him, and now that she had returned, he seemed to her to be the same frank and good-hearted lad she had always persisted in believing him, only somewhat older in years, handsomer in person, and more finished in manner. To do her justice, Aylesford did all he could to deceive the simple dame. He was punctilious in attending to her wants, flattered her whims, and paraded his royalist sympathies freely in her presence. Accordingly, such was the hold he obtained over her, before leaving Sweetwater, that when, once or twice, her maid began to gossip about his antecedents, she sternly bade the girl to be silent, and resolutely refused to believe anything to his disadvantage.

"What is this I hear?" said Aylesford, with a lowering brow, when they had entered the parlor. "How could you allow this paltry rebel officer to establish himself here?"

Poor Mrs. Warren knew not what to say. She felt like a culprit. At last, not daring to look in his face, but fumbling, like a truant girl, the little, round pin-cushion, which, in common with all dames of her day, she wore at her side, she stammered—

"Indeed, Charles, I couldn't help it—"

He answered angrily—

"Why didn't you say that her horse was too wild? That you were afraid of the unsettled condition of the country? That it wasn't proper for Kate to be seen with an American officer?"

Bewildered by so many questions, Mrs. Warren could only reply to that which came last.

"Oh! Charles, how could I be so rude?" she answered, "Major Gordon, you should remember, saved our lives—"

"That's the very difficulty," broke in her nephew. "I wish the intermeddler had been at the bottom of the ocean."

"But we should have been drowned then," and Mrs. Warren held up her hands. "You don't mean what you say, Charles."

"Well, then, I wish I'd been there—"

"I wish so, too, from the bottom of my heart," said Mrs. Warren, beginning to cry, for his impetuosity had quite unnerved her.

"There, aunt," he said, curbing his passion, "don't. I'm sure I never intended to hurt your feelings." And he approached and kissed her.

"Nor have you, my dear boy," sobbed Mrs. Warren, throwing herself on his neck, and crying for a while hysterically. "But I'm sure nobody can blame me. I always knew there'd be trouble. I felt it from the first. I was satisfied you wouldn't approve of such an acquaintance, any more than our cousin, Lord Danville, would."

"Confound the old fool!" muttered Aylesford to himself. Then, giving up to his impatience, he said aloud. "It's not as an acquaintance I care about him. But," and he forgot himself so much as to utter a savage oath, "the fellow will be having Kate in love with him."

Mrs. Warren sank into a chair, holding up both her hands.

"In love with him? Deary me! deary me! I never thought of that! But it can't be, Charles," she said, eagerly, "you're joking with me. Kate would never throw herself away on such a person."

"How do you know?" abruptly said he. "There's nothing Kate won't do, if she takes a mind to it. The man saved her life, too, or she thinks he did; and she's as romantic as the devil!"

"So he did. So she is!" said Mrs. Warren, confusedly. "Oh! I see it all now. Why did I not do it before? But I never suspected such a thing. A rebel too, and worse, a rebel officer! We're disgraced forever. What would Cousin Danville say? What will the King say when he hears of it?"

"Well, if this isn't a precious partner I've got," said Aylesford to himself, "to help me in my difficulty. I might as well have a crazy person." But after a turn about the room, seeing that the handkerchief was still at her eyes, he said— "I'm not finding fault, aunt. But why the deuce," he cried "didn't you say that Arab was too wild for Kate?"

"I did, my dear boy, I did," was the eager reply. "I was going to tell you so, only you frightened me. I told her so again and again. But your cousin's as headstrong as her father, poor, dear man—I don't mean to abuse him, now that he's in his grave, but he'd always have his way; or for that matter so would your father, too, Charles, when we were children—I remember once seeing him, when he wasn't ten years old, jump on an unbroken colt, that the grooms were afraid to ride, in spite of all they could say, and though I screamed as if I'd go into fits—and so she would ride Arab, when the Major had tried him and pronounced him safe, and though I begged him not to favor the child's whim, and said to him, says I, 'she'll kill herself yet'—but he no more minded me than if I hadn't spoke, for I see now that he wanted to have a *tete-a-tete* with her—and so they've been riding together nearly every day—and it's all over with the marriage between you two, on which I've always set my heart"—and here the good dame, after this marvellously lucid narrative, burst into a perfect passion of sobbing, for she really could see no end to the troubles that threatened her.

Aylesford, with another oath, muttered— "Cold comfort this for a man. But what else can be expected from a whimpering old dunce? If she'd had sense and courage, she'd have got rid of this militia Major civilly, after the first interview. However," he continued, "I mustn't let her see what I think. She can be of service to me yet, and I must keep her in temper. I really believe she loves me as if I was her son." So, again going up to her, and embracing her, not without something even of affection, he said— "There, aunt, compose yourself. What's done can't be helped. But, now that I've come back, I'll take this matter into my own hands; and the first thing is to get rid of this rebel visitor. How long have Kate and he been out?"

He looked at the clock as he spoke, his frown deepening, for the hour was even later than he had thought.

"Deary me," exclaimed Mrs. Warren, in reply, her face displaying visible consternation, "it's almost noon. I wonder if anything has happened. I'm sure something has," And she began to wring her hands. "I've felt all the morning that it would."

Aylesford wheeled on his heel to conceal his impatience. But immediately he returned.

"Have they been absent two hours? Three? How many?"

"Deary me, don't be so cross?" replied his aunt, his very impatience frustrating his object. "You frighten me, Charles. I'm sure I've done nothing to deserve this—"

"For heaven's sake," cried her nephew, losing control of himself, "cut this short, and tell me how long they've been gone, and what road they took."

Aylesford at last extracted the unwelcome intelligence that Kate and his rival had been absent since eight o'clock.

"Time enough to make a dozen proposals," muttered he, "and talk down the scruples of twenty heiresses, especially when a beggar of an officer is the suitor, who has had the good luck to help her off from a wreck. But I'll put a stop to the fellow's insolent pretensions. If the mischief be not done already, I'll take good care he gets no more such opportunities; and if he has practiced on my cousin's susceptibility, of whom I'm the natural protector, as being her nearest male relative, I'll run him through."

With these words he stepped to the window, ordered a horse to be saddled, and having ascertained the direction in which the equestrians had ridden, set off in search of them. Fortune conducted him immediately to them, as we have already seen.

CHAPTER XXII
AYLESFORD AND KATE

Helen I love thee; by my life I do:
I swear by that which I will love for thee,
To prove him false that says I love thee not. —Shakespeare.

I cannot love him,
He might have took his answer long ago. —Shakespeare.

I'll have my bond, I will not hear thee speak.
I'll have my bond. —Shakespeare.

Though Kate could not think, without aversion, of ratifying the family contract to marry her cousin, yet she commiserated his disappointment, and was consequently more tender to his feelings than she would otherwise have been.

These sentiments had governed her during the interview at the bridge. No true woman takes pleasure in the suffering of an unfortunate lover. Kate had, on that occasion, thought more of her cousin's disappointment than of Major Gordon. But, when she had reached Sweetwater, and was left to solitary thought in the privacy of her chamber, she saw that, in trying to save the feelings of Aylesford, she had hurt those of her preserver. Her momentary anger at the latter's coldness gradually subsided, and when she met him, on the following day, she returned his bow, as we have seen, with all her old cordiality.

Kate was sitting alone in the parlor, to which we have already introduced the reader, on Monday morning, when her cousin entered the apartment. Something in his manner betrayed to her that he sought a private interview. Her heart began to beat fast.

Aylesford, for a minute or two, did not speak. He walked, in an embarrassed way, to the window; looked out a moment, glanced at Kate, and then tattooed on the panes with his fingers; and, finally, turning abruptly towards her, said—

"How is it, Kate, that you have compromised the family, by permitting this Major Gordon to visit here so frequently? His rebel commission surely ought to shut your doors against him."

Kate's color, which had been heightened ever since Aylesford entered, flushed to a still deeper crimson at these words. But, having determined, while remaining firm to her purpose, to do everything else to conciliate her cousin, she paused awhile before replying, in order to command voice and judgment alike.

"I do not see, Charles," she said, finally, "that I have compromised the family. Major Gordon, though not a royalist, is a gentleman, and entitled to the civilities due to all such. In addition," she added, with another blush, "he deserves particular attention at our hands; you yourself must admit this."

"I don't admit any such thing," answered her cousin, nettled alike by her quiet manner and by her words. "He helped to save your life, I know; but so would any other person in his place. I myself," he added, with an outburst of really natural feeling, "would have given my right hand to have been there, and risked my life also for you."

Kate was touched.

"I believe you," she said, with a voice full of feeling.

To do him justice, Aylesford loved her with all the passion of his illy regulated nature, and when he heard this reply, and saw Kate's emotion, what was good in him awoke responsive to it. He fell upon his knee, by a sudden impulse, and seizing her hand, said—

"Then why won't you believe still more, dear Kate? Why won't you believe that I am the most sincere and devoted lover ever woman had? That I have been taught, from my youth up, to look upon you as my future wife? That all my associations of home and happiness have centred around you? Oh! Kate," he cried, as she withdrew her hand and shook her head sadly, "have pity on me. Don't let your heart be estranged from your own blood and kin, merely because a stranger has done that which I would have died a thousand times to do."

Kate shook her head again mournfully. "It is not that," she faltered.

"Then what is it? I implore you to tell me. By the memory of our fathers, who loved each other so well, what is it that makes you cold to me, and to me only?"

Kate had been struggling for composure to reply. Deeply moved, she said—

"Rise, Charles. This is no attitude for you to assume, nor for me to allow."

Her manner was firm, though gentle, and Aylesford rose and stood before her.

"I cannot listen to such language," she began. "I must be truthful, even if I speak words that may seem harsh; and I do not love you, Charles—"

He clasped his forehead violently with both hands.

"Yet what have I done," he cried, after a moment, like one beside himself, "to win this hatred? Oh! never man loved as I love you, Kate."

"I do not hate you, Charles," was Kate's mild reply. "You are my cousin, and the last male representative of our family, and therefore have a double claim on me. I like you as a relative, though I see much," she added, hesitatingly, "to condemn. But to be your wife is impossible. It would bring happiness to neither of us. And knowing that it would not bring happiness," she added, in a firmer tone, "it would be a sin in us to contract it. Otherwise, perhaps," and here her voice trembled, "I might have ratified the wishes of our parents; which, but for this incompatibility between us, I should feel bound to obey."

Aylesford, whose angry sense of humiliation had been gradually rising, was subdued again by these last words, for he thought Kate was relenting. He, therefore, answered eagerly—

"There is no incompatibility. Or," for she shook her head, "there shall be none. Only try me. I will be anything you wish. We have been apart so long, that perhaps we do differ in some things; but I place myself in your hands; mould me as you will."

His impassioned manner left no doubt on his hearer's mind that he was sincere, at least for the time; but Kate well knew that natures like his were past reforming; and she could not, therefore, permit herself to be misled by these earnest protestations. The interview was becoming too painful, and she rose to terminate it.

"Don't talk in that way, Charles," she said, with tears in her eyes. "Please don't," she added, placing her hand restrainingly on his arm, as she saw he was about to renew his pleadings. "My decision is final. The heart cannot be forced."

There was no mistaking the sincerity of this avowal. It left no room for hope. Her manner also confirmed her words. As Aylesford seized her dress to detain her, when she would now have left the room, she gently but resolutely removed his hold.

The ill-regulated nature of her cousin passed, in a moment, from entreaty to rage. He was like one of those volcanic countries, where suddenly, on a clear day, the heavens are filled with smoke and the solid ground shaken with earthquakes.

"Then you love this Major Gordon," he cried, livid with suppressed passion. "You have lost your heart, like a romantic fool, to a rebel beggar, merely because he happened to be present when you escaped from shipwreck. Yes! go," he added, bitterly, as Kate, with dignity, was proceeding towards the door, "but know that I will go to him, and force down his throat a disavowal of his suit to you."

This threat checked Kate's steps. The scandal of an encounter between her cousin and her preserver, apart from her well-founded dread of the former's skill at fence, induced her to stop, with the hope of preventing this mad threat from being executed.

"You will do no such thing," she said, fronting Aylesford with decision, yet with something of entreaty too in her manner. "You will not, you cannot, so disgrace her whom, but a moment ago, you professed to love. Nay, Charles," she continued, as he was turning away, and advancing quickly she caught him by the arm, "you must promise me this. I demand it as a woman, as a relative," and seeing he was still unmoved, she added, with spirit— "the honor of our family is concerned, that a gentleman who preserved my life should not be so grossly insulted; and I call on you, as my nearest male connexion, to sustain that honor."

But Aylesford still turned from her with gloomy rage. As she still continued to hold fast to him, he finally shook her off roughly, saying—

"It is you who dishonor the family, by loving this base-born adventurer."

"Oh! Charles," she cried, reproachfully, with a burst of feeling, "I had not expected this of you."

He turned on the instant. Again he thought she might be induced to relent.

"Promise me," he said, eagerly, "that you will listen to my suit. Only promise me a probation, I ask nothing more. I will then do anything you wish."

She shook her head sadly, but firmly.

"Then it's no use deceiving me," was the angry answer, as he flung off the hand which he had taken.

"You love this low fellow, this cowardly traitor—"

"Stop," said Kate, with an air of command, her person seeming actually to dilate before her companion's eyes. "I will not hear a gentleman maligned to whom we all owe so much. Nay!" she continued, almost sternly, as Aylesford attempted to speak, "I will be heard, and once for all. You forget yourself, and trespass on even the privileges of a relation, when you charge me with loving Major Gordon. You grossly insult me, when you say that I could love any man merely because he saved my life. Moreover," she added, with something of haughty scorn in her manner, "if you will seek this gentleman's blood, you may find to your cost that he is anything but a coward. As for me," and her eyes sparkled with determination, "I shall take good care that Major Gordon knows that I have no share in this dishonorable requital."

With these words she swept from the room like an empress, not condescending to pursue the altercation further.

Aylesford, with an oath, saw the door close after her, when, hastily arming himself, he ordered his horse saddled and went forth to provoke the duel which we have seen so opportunely interrupted.

CHAPTER XXIII
THE REFUGEE'S HUT

Oh! Buckingham, beware of yonder dog;
Look, when he fawns he bites. —*Shakespeare.*

Few men dare show their thoughts of worst or best;
Dissimulation always sets apart
A corner for herself. —*Byron.*

Deep in the forest, that stretches, a pathless wilderness, to the south and west of Sweetwater, there stood, at the period of our story, a solitary log-cabin, with about two acres of cleared land surrounding it. On nearly every side it was surrounded with swamps, so that approach to it was almost impossible. Here, an hour or two after the rencontre between Aylesford and Major Gordon, the former drew up his horse.

It was a wild scene, characteristic of the region. Huge pines surrounded the clearing, and towering high into air, almost shut out the light. In the small fields about the house the stumps were still standing. A rude stable, or rather shed, built of logs with the bark left on, stood a few rods from the house, while between the two was a well, with a high swinging pole hung in the crotchet of a young sapling. The atmosphere, even on that sultry morning, was damp and cool from the evaporation; the clearing being situated on a small knoll, which rose like an island in the midst of vast swamps, miles from any village, or even farmhouse. It was a haunt fit for outlaws.

As Aylesford approached, a huge bloodhound started up in front of the house, at whose outcry a short, thick-set man came forth, with a countenance which had never been pleasing, but was now embruited by intemperance and other vices. A dirty red beard, which had not felt a razor for a week, increased the repulsiveness of his appearance.

"What a hole you have, Arrison," said the visitor, with an oath. "It's the devil's own retreat. I was half an hour in finding the blind path, and twice came near being swamped before I succeeded. And now, in the fiend's name, tell us what's brought you into these parts, and what you want with me."

"As many questions as would take a week to answer," replied the man, coolly, "and asked in a temper that would get anything but a civil return from most persons. You needn't frown. You know I dont't care a curse for such things. What's the matter with you? Out with it, or it will choke you."

Aylesford looked, for a moment, as if he would have liked to run his sword through the speaker, as well as through Major Gordon. But the man met his angry gaze with cool indifference, turning a quid leisurely in his mouth, and waiting for an answer.

"I came here to question," said Aylesford, haughtily, "not to be questioned. Again I say," he added, as he dismounted, "what, in the devil's name, has brought you here."

"Let me tie the horse. It's my trade, you know," said the other, with a sardonic grin. "Or shall I put him up? No, you must return, that there may be no suspicion! Well, then, come in, and I'll tell you all about it."

They entered the cabin, and took seats by a table, on which Arrison immediately placed some peach brandy. No one else appeared to be present about the premises, though, at first, Aylesford thought he heard a light step moving in the interior room, for the house had two apartments. After taking a long draught, Arrison spoke.

"You were surprised, I suppose, to get the word I sent? You thought I was completely driven out of these parts? But there's a good time coming, let me tell you," and he rubbed his hands, "for his Majesty, God bless him! is going to send an expedition against the Neck, burn the vessels there, and reduce the whole district about the mouth of the river. Before a week we'll have the pick of all the booty here, live and dead, that can be had. The pretty girls, I suppose," he added with a leer and chuckle, "are not all gone yet."

For a moment Aylesford sat in mute surprise.

"You amaze me," he cried, finally. "I have heard nothing of this."

"How should you?" answered Arrison, with a laugh. "'Gad, if the rebels caught you acting the spy, they'd string you up to one of the buttonwoods, at the Forks, before you could say Jack Robinson. They'd not stop a minute for your laced coat. It would be a short shrift and a dance on nothing, as they say in the old country."

"Then you play the spy on the rebels, and in return get at the royal General's secrets—is that it?" said Aylesford.

Arrison nodded.

"And you are sure of your news?"

"As sure as I sit here. The expedition has sailed before this, and its arrival can be delayed only by head-winds. It may be playing the devil among the rebel privateers and their prizes even now."

"This is news," answered Aylesford, joyfully, filling his glass. "Let us drink to his most sacred Majesty, and confusion to all traitors."

"With my whole heart. The toast is good and the liquor better."

"It is this which has brought you back? Under the shelter of the royal wing you think you can safely resume your former pranks?"

"Yes, if nothing better turns up. I've some old scores to wipe off, and began them yesterday."

And he narrated his outrage at the widow Bates' farm, describing, with boisterous glee, the rueful face which the widow must have worn when she returned home and saw but the smoking ashes of her late dwelling.

"But," said Aylesford, "the people will know your mark, and hunt you down at once. I shouldn't be surprised if old Herman was already on your trail."

"They'll have enough to do to take care of themselves," was the cool reply. "Before another week, I'll burn old Herman himself out, like a rat in his hole. There is not many men left in these parts anyhow, and the attack on the Neck will take away what few there are. I owe a debt to another, Jack Sanders, whom I'll not let off so easily. I carry two of his buckshot still in me; and I've sworn to have a life for each one; himself and his wife, if possible; if not, others of his family."

"And now, what's the matter with you?" resumed Arrison. "Even this good news can't make you look pleased more than a minute. Come, drown care in a cup." And filling his glass again, he handed the bottle to his guest. "What, not drink? It must be something very serious, then."

"I have to return to Sweetwater, you know. My cousin and aunt are there."

"I'd forgot. And it wouldn't do, so early in the day, to show signs of a debauch." He interlarded this and all his other speeches profusely with oaths. "And how are the good ladies?" he added. "Miss Kate must be grown up into a beauty, if all I hear is true. Ah! you change color. You frown. I have it at last," he continued, slapping his hand on the table and bursting into a laugh, "it's about her that you're so cursedly cross."

"Come," answered Aylesford, in a heat, rising from the table, "I've had enough of this. Remember, I was once your master. Have you forgotten, sirrah, how to be respectful?"

"I cry your pardon," answered Arrison, with a profound obeisance, though with a slight tone of mockery. "Sit down again, Mr. Aylesford. I do forget myself sometimes, in talking to you, but it's because you've always allowed me to be familiar. There, don't let us quarrel; I may want your countenance yet; and in return might be of use even in this affair, if you'd tell me what's the matter."

Aylesford allowed himself to be persuaded to take a seat again; but, had he seen the cat-like glance of Arrison, he would have felt far less confidence in the outlaw's professions.

"You have been a faithful fellow," said Aylesford. "I'll not deny that. But this is an affair above your surgery. However, you've a quick wit, and may hit on something; and I want somebody to advise with. I'm desperately in love with my cousin, who's more beautiful even than report allows, and she won't have me."

Arrison felt very much inclined to make a jest of Aylesford at this confession. But he saw that his guest was in no mood for banter. So he answered—

"She must be a prude of the worst kind, then."

"No, she's in love with a rebel officer, who is stationed at the Forks, a Major Gordon," and he ended with a hearty curse on his rival.

"Are you sure of this?"

"She has refused me, and that's enough," replied Aylesford, passionately, drinking off a bumper, and setting the glass down with such force as to dash it to splinters. "Besides, this fellow has saved her life, or she thinks he has, which is the same. The ship, in which she came over, was wrecked off the mouth of the river, and he had a hand, somehow or other, in getting her ashore. I had my sword at the rascal's throat this morning, and was on the high road to revenge, when we were interrupted." And he proceeded to narrate the rencontre, which Uncle Lawrence had so opportunely broken off.

"That old, canting scoundrel again," answered Arrison. "Well, he hasn't long to run. He's about hunted to the end of his track, I take it; and I'll put a bullet through him, or a knife into him, before the moon's a week older; and so have my revenge for the harm he did me with your uncle, and for his stopping your slitting this Major's windpipe. But, to come back to your own affairs," continued the villain, "I don't see that they're half as desperate as you think they are. You remember the old proverb, 'out of sight, out of mind,' don't you?"

"What of it?"

"Only," answered Arrison, with a laugh," get rid of this Major."

"But how?"

"If 'twas me I'd go out quietly, some fine morning, and take a good position in the brush, near by where I was sure he would pass, and when he came along, I'd pull trigger on him, and so have done with his interference forever. All things are fair in love as in war, you know."

But Aylesford had sufficient honor left to decline such a proposal, involving deliberate assassination, though he would have eagerly seized any opportunity to take the life of his rival in a less cold-blooded way.

"Well, then," said the villain, "since you won't take that course, we must try and get him picked off in a fight. He'll probably, if he's not a coward, go down to the Neck the moment he hears the vessels there are in danger. It would be a possible thing, though not an easy one, to shoot him there."

But Aylesford shook his head.

"Too much uncertainty about it, you think? Well, maybe you're right," said the outlaw. "I would wish to make a sure thing of it, if I was yon, that's a fact. But my invention is almost at an end. I really don't know what to advise," he concluded, with a puzzled air.

"If she had only reached New York, there would have been none of this," said Aylesford, gloomily. "I wish to heaven she was there now."

"Nothing easier than to get her there," answered the refugee, "if that will suit your purpose. By the Lord, I've hit it at last," cried he, with sudden energy, emphasizing his words by striking the table till the bottle danced again. "I can put her in New York in a week's time, if you'll trust to me; and you shall, moreover, do what will make a set-off to this Gordon's rescue of her; in short, if you place yourself in my hands, she'll be yours, or else you're a fool, which no one yet ever took you to be."

Aylesford gazed at the speaker with undisguised astonishment. But there was evidently no jest in what Arrison said. His plan, whatever it was, he clearly considered feasible.

"I give you my word," reaching over and taking the outlaw's hand, "which I never broke to any man yet—"

"We'll say nothing of woman," interrupted Arrison, with a coarse laugh.

"Which I never broke to any man yet," repeated Aylesford, "that I'll pay you a thousand pounds if you succeed. On the day I marry my cousin, the money is yours."

"I'll put her in New York for half the sum—is it a bargain?"

"It is," answered Aylesford. "Now for the scheme."

But we must reserve this for another chapter.

CHAPTER XXIV
THE PLOT

Foul whisperings are abroad; and unnat'ral deeds. —Shakespeare.

I follow you.
To do I know not what. —Shakespeare.

"Does Miss Aylesford ride on horseback as she did before she went abroad?" said Arrison.

"Yes! This militia Major has been riding with her every morning."

"But don't she ever ride alone?"

"Sometimes, I suppose. He can't be for ever dangling after her. At any rate, now that I've come back, I'll take good care that he don't." And he finished with an oath.

"Then, without having yourself suspected, get her to ride unattended to-morrow or next day. Yon must also find out which way she is going. I will be on the lookout, with three or four trusty fellows of my gang, and on a sudden, we will rush out and make her our prisoner. You needn't start and look in that fashion," said Arrison, with a laugh at his hearer's glance of alarm, "we'll not hurt a hair of her head. We shan't even gag her, as we would anybody else, for the road will be a lonely one most likely, and there'll be no occasion for rough usage."

"What next?" said Aylesford, seeing that Arrison paused. And he proceeded contemptuously— "I can't see any such pretty scheme in this project of kidnapping."

"Then you haven't the sense I give you credit for," answered Arrison. "Don't you see? I and my followers are to seize her, and you are to rescue her. That'll be an ace to play on this Major Gordon's king, and a trump card at that."

Aylesford's countenance brightened, the look of suspicion disappearing totally.

"I am dull," he said. "This infernal affair has driven me half mad, I believe, and benumbed my senses."

"Of course," answered Arrison, "it won't do to rescue her right away. For then, you know, you'd have no good excuse for carrying her within the royal lines, a step which must be taken if you wish to get her to New York. Though, for my part," added the outlaw, "I don't see why you should trouble yourself to make so long a journey. Now, in the old country, and especially in the parts where I lived when a boy, it was a common practice, when a gentleman wished to get a wife, for him to call together a party of his friends, waylay the girl, make her a prisoner, carry her off to the mountains, and never let her go back till the priest had made them man and wife. Many's the Squire's lady that was won in that way; and they say girls of spirit like it better than more formal wooing. Now, if you say so, we'll play the part of your friends, instead of acting more naturally as refugees; and though a priest may not be so easy to come at, you're not what you once were, if you can't find a way to make the lady eager enough to marry you, after she gets out of the swamp."

The cool, matter-of-fact manner in which this atrocious proposition was made, showed how business-like the villain considered it. But Aylesford, though he would not have hesitated, as Arrison knew from the past, if the victim had been some poor and friendless girl, revolted at such an outrage on Kate. His face flushed with anger, and he partially rose from his seat. But recollecting immediately that Arrison was not in love like himself, and that the customs of his country had accustomed the refugee to look on such abductions leniently, he resumed his place, while the red tint of passion faded from his brow. But he shook his head.

"No, we'll stick to the other plan," he said. "I won't woo Kate in that fashion, if I never get her, so help me God," he added, earnestly.

"Just as you say. But I meant no offence," answered Arrison.

"I believe you" replied Aylesford. "But, apart from every other consideration, my cousin is not the girl to be won in that fashion. She would, I am convinced, kill herself sooner than yield; and even if she was prevented, by force, from injuring herself, she'd hate me to her dying day. No, it would be madness."

"I think you're mistaken," answered Arrison. "I know women better than you do, if you have such notions of them. Their bark is worse than their bite. There'd doubtless be a great tearing of hair, any amount of screeching, vows to starve herself to death, to stab herself, to kill you, perhaps even to turn informer; but she'll be at last, as they always are in Ireland, as gentle as a lamb, and would crawl to your knees, if necessary, to beg you to make an honest woman of her by marrying—"

He was not allowed to finish the sentence. There was still enough that was good left in Aylesford, or, if not this, love had temporarily bestowed it on him, to make his blood boil at the cool deliberation with which this hardened villain spoke. He sprang from his chair, half drew his sword, and exclaimed—

"Are you man or devil? Another word like that, and I'll run you through. Miss Aylesford," he added, haughtily, "is not to be spoken of, sirrah, in this diabolical way."

Arrison, on seeing him rise, had sprang also to his feet, knocking down the chair behind him and retreating a few paces, while at the same time he whipped out a knife, whose blade gleamed as he held it ready to strike. For awhile, the two men stood regarding each other, without a word being uttered. At last the outlaw spoke—

"Put back your sword, Mr. Aylesford, and I'll sheathe my knife. You really are not yourself any longer. I don't know how to talk to you. Every word seems to anger you to-day. We've often spoke of women—well, well," he continued, observing Aylesford's quick frown, "enough of that. I only seek your good. I'll say nothing more about the lady, except to tell you my original plan, and to swear by all that's good, that I never thought to insult you or her."

Had Aylesford been less accustomed to his present associate, or even perhaps had he been less eager to secure Arrison's co-operation, he would have broken off the interview. But he allowed himself again to be soothed, and, replacing his sword, took his seat.

"I have said," resumed Arrison, "that it won't do for you to rescue Miss Aylesford at once: for then you'll have no excuse for not taking her back to Sweetwater. I'll put her in a boat and carry her down the river, making her believe my intention is to throw pursuit off our trail. In this way I'll conduct her to the vicinity of the Neck, if not past it; the exact point will depend on yourself. You'll of course be on the watch. Having gone ahead, you'll know where to look for me, for you'll have found out how far his Majesty's pickets extend; and you'll naturally wish to attack me before I get within the lines, as otherwise the lady might see that I was really taking her to the British, instead of to the woods, and was your confederate."

Aylesford nodded approvingly, as Arrison paused for an opinion, on which the latter proceeded.

"It will be easy for you to get together a half dozen stout fellows, followers of the royal forces, with which you'll put yourself in communication at once. I'll time my arrival so as to reach your neighborhood about dusk. You'll know my boat by seeing me in the stern sheets. You must shoot out from under the bank of the meadow, where you've been hid, and, with a cheer, dash right on us. We'll have our cue, and pretend to be taken by surprise. You'll board us, after a few guns are fired, which we'll take care, on both sides, shall be without shot. To seize your cousin, transfer her to your boat, and sweep away as fast as the tide and four oars can take you, needn't be but the work of a moment. Some of us will, meantime, have leaped overboard, the better to carry out the farce; for we can easily swim back to our boat, or make the shore, where our comrades will pick us up. By this little bit of stratagem," he continued, with a hearty laugh at his own cunning, "you'll get the credit of having saved your cousin from blood-thirsty villains; and if that don't trump this Major Gordon's claims, call me a fool. Curse me," he added, as he filled his glass, and laughed till the tears ran out of his eyes, "I ought to have been a writer of plays, as I might have been, I suppose, if I'd stayed in Dublin; I think I can fix off a plot as well as old Shakespeare himself."

"It's certainly a capital plan," answered Aylesford, even his disgust now gone, so certain seemed the result. "If it succeeds, I'll make you a gentleman for life."

"Succeed? It *must* succeed. Come, cheer up, sir. Faint heart never won fair lady. Gad, I'm bound to have it succeed, if only to make me a gentleman again; a thing I was born for, but missed by my cursed stupidity."

"You've often hinted at that," said Aylesford, "and it's easy to see you've had a good education. How did you ever come to seek your fortune as an ostler in the colonies?"

"Some other time, maybe, I'll tell you," answered Arrison, his gayety giving way to gloom. "It's enough for to-day, that I became an ostler because I knew more about horses than anything else."

And gleams of dignity broke through even his imbruted face, and exhibited themselves in his manner as he spoke.

"Of course," resumed Aylesford, in an ironical tone, "I'll find it impossible to carry Kate anywhere else than down the river, right into the heart of the British squadron, where the royal commander, also of course, will retain us. My cousin, as an heiress, will be too valuable a prize to be parted with, and her desire to return, if she urges it, will be civilly, but resolutely resisted by his Majesty's officer. Besides, we will tell her that it would be madness, after her narrow escape, for her to go back to so disturbed a region, and one also which is about to become the theatre of incessant skirmishes. It's a capital plan, most capital," said Aylesford, gleefully. "You have a genius for scheming, Arrison. I'll do my part, and engage that, to-morrow, Kate shall ride out alone. Let me see. She'll take the road through the cedar-swamp, towards Herman's. I think I can manage that. You know the way, don't you. Be there early. If, by any accident, she fails you to-morrow, then be there every day till she passes."

"I'll wait near the spring," said Arrison, rising, as he perceived Aylesford prepare to go. "In going down the bank of the river, I'll take the other side. You'll be ready below, will you?"

"Yes," answered Aylesford, as he proceeded to mount his horse. "But it's nearly noon, and I must be at Sweetwater by dinner-time."

With these words, he put spurs to his horse and disappeared in the forest.

CHAPTER XXV
TREACHERY

Thus do all traitors;
If their purgation did consist in words,
They are as innocent as grace itself. —*Shakespeare.*

Thou art a traitor and a miscreant;
Too good to be so, and too bad to live. —*Shakespeare.*

Circumstances favored the wishes of Aylesford even more than he had dared to hope, for that evening, at the teatable, Kate announced her intention of riding over, on the following morning, to Uncle Lawrence's. She had heard of the destruction of Widow Bates' dwelling, and understanding that the houseless family was sheltered at Mr. Herman's for the present, desired to ascertain in what way she could best assist them.

Aylesford had been watching for an opportunity, the whole afternoon, to fulfill his promise to the outlaw; but none had offered. He, therefore, heard this announcement with pleasure. But, in order to prevent suspicion from afterwards resting on himself, he ventured to suggest that it was scarcely safe for Kate to venture out.

"Surely," were his words, as he looked at Mrs. Warren rather than at his cousin, "if the refugees are so daring as to burn houses on Sunday, they will not be afraid to rob, and perhaps insult, a defenceless lady on Tuesday."

"Suppose you go with me, Charles," said Kate looking up.

To understand this frank offer, it is necessary to recall the fact that, as but one person, beside the actors, had witnessed the rencontre between Aylesford and Major Gordon, and as Uncle Lawrence had wisely kept his own counsel, Kate was ignorant of the affair. She naturally concluded, therefore, that her cousin's threat had been an idle one. In his calmer moments he had, she reasoned, repented of his angry violence. She accordingly resolved to exhibit, by a conciliatory manner, her appreciation of this conduct.

Aylesford, for a moment, was embarrassed, but less by the offer than by the tone in which it was made. He attributed it, however, to its true cause.

"She would be very far from being so affable," he moodily thought, "if she knew all."

"I am sorry," he said, "that I cannot accompany you," addressing his cousin. "But I leave, as early as possible, for the mouth of the river." And as he spoke, he looked around to see that none of the servants were within hearing.

"For the mouth of the river," exclaimed Mrs. Warren and Kate in the same breath. "Deary me, what now's the matter?" added the aunt.

Aylesford made no direct reply, but began whistling the Jacobite air, "Over the water to Charlie."

"What does he mean?" said Mrs. Warren, looking in alarm at Kate.

"I suppose he is going to join his Majesty's troops," answered our heroine. "But surely," she added, addressing her cousin, "you choose a roundabout path."

It must be confessed that Kate's heart beat high even at the suspicion that Aylesford was going within the royal lines; for in that case he had concluded, she reasoned, to abandon his pretensions to her hand. She waited, therefore, for his reply with deep interest.

"What if his most gracious Majesty's forces," said her cousin, speaking low, and again glancing cautiously around, "were coming half way to meet me? What if there was a royal expedition at this moment lying in the bay below?"

"I hope not," answered Kate, turning pale. "I sincerely hope not."

"And why not?" asked Aylesford. "Is my fair cousin so much of a rebel to her king as to wish for the defeat of his Majesty's cause."

"Deary me!" said Mrs. Warren, lifting her hands, "Kate a rebel. How can it be? Who told you so?" she added, confusedly, looking from one to the other. "It isn't so, Kate, is it?"

"I never said it was," answered our heroine composedly. "I merely expressed regret at the possible arrival of a royal expedition against the bay, because it would lead to bloodshed, and bring the horrors of war almost to our very doors, and lo! Charles," she added, with something of haughty contempt, "cries out that I am a rebel."

"I knew Kate wasn't a rebel," said Mrs. Warren, looking appealingly to Aylesford. "You don't really mean to say she is one, nephew? You were only jesting?"

"I cry Kate's pardon," answered Aylesford, whose object was not to irritate, and who had now hastened to repair his error. "As you say, aunt, I was only jesting. But, in serious earnest, a royal expedition has probably anchored in the bay by this time; and, as I am tired of an aimless life," he glanced meaningly at Kate as he spoke, "I intend seizing the opportunity to offer my sword to his Majesty."

"Oh! my dear boy, don't think of it," cried his aunt in alarm. "You'll be killed, I know you will; and then what will become of us."

"Never fear for me, aunt," replied Aylesford. "I am no more unfortunate than others, at least in war," he added, significantly looking at Kate. "The chances are ten to one that I'll escape even a wound. And then, you know, I'll naturally rise in the service; all officers who serve faithfully do; so that, by the time these revolted colonies are subdued, I'll probably be a Colonel. Let us hope, some day, to attend a levee of his Majesty, I accompanying you in the uniform of that rank. Besides, aunt, I'm but doing my duty. No Aylesford should refuse to draw sword for his king. I've no doubt Cousin Danville has often wondered why I did not serve."

This last allusion, adroitly introduced, calmed the good lady's fears, and reconciled her to the scheme more than anything which had gone before. She still, however, looked undecided.

"What do you think of it, Kate?" she said, in perplexity. "It does look odd, doesn't it, that none of our family are in arms for the King?"

Kate, during the time Aylesford was speaking, had been carefully counting the grounds in her tea-cup. She was persuaded that this sudden scheme of her cousin's had its origin entirely in her refusal. She could not but feel a pang at being the cause of his exile, yet her reason told her that it was the best for both him and her; and therefore, on being thus appealed to, she looked up and said—

"If Charles thinks he ought to go, under all the circumstances," and she emphasized these last words, "it is not for us to thwart him. There is certainly both honor and wealth to be had in the service of King George; while here there is nothing at all to engage a man of spirit. And if any Aylesford joins the royal standard," she added, laughingly, striving, for her aunt's sake, to give a gayer tone to the conversation, "it must be Charles, unless you choose, aunt, to enlist, *a la* Joan of Arc, or I go a soldiering, like a vivandiere in the French army."

"Well, you two children will have it your own way," said Mrs. Warren, with a sigh. "All I hope is that we shall soon see you back again, Charles, with a royal army. Who knows but his Majesty may make you Governor of New Jersey, when the war's over?" she added, abandoning herself to her favorite castle-building.

"Who knows?" answered Aylesford.

"But Kate said nothing. She was again studying the contents of her cup. After awhile she looked up.

"You really go to-morrow, Charles?" she said.

"Really and positively. I shall only wait to see you in the saddle, that is if you still persist in your determination."

"I see no reason," answered Kate, frankly, "why I should not. The very fact that a royal expedition is down the river will make it all the safer here; for the refugees will flock there like vultures to a feast. They are but carrion warriors at best," she added, contemptuously, "and only devour generally the prey that stronger and braver ones have pulled down."

Aylesford thought that he had remonstrated enough for his purpose, so he said no more, not wishing to hazard Kate's undertaking, by arousing his aunt's fears.

"I will attend you as far as the church," he said; "for my way will lie down that side of the river." He deemed it best to do this, in order to be sure, before he finally left Sweetwater, that Kate would fall into the ambush prepared for her. "But," he added, lowering his voice and looking across to Kate, as his aunt turned for a moment, "a word from you will change all my plans."

"It cannot be, Charles," answered Kate, in the same low tone. But her eyes thanked him for his forbearance.

Aylesford was not so degraded but that he felt a pang of shame. It was not too late, he reflected for a moment, to retreat. But the thought passed as instantaneously as it came. Before he could reply, Mrs. Warren again turned and spoke; and directly afterwards they all rose from the table.

"Why here is Aunt Chloe!" cried Kate, approaching the window. "She has come to see you, cousin; for it was but the other day she was asking when you would come home." And she ran out into the porch.

"How is yer, honey?" said the old nurse. "'Pears to me yer gets more beautiful ebbery day, 'deed yer does." Kate blushed, as she answered—

"Ah, aunty, you know how to flatter. But you've heard, I suppose, that Cousin Charles has returned. And here he comes."

"Glad to see yer, Marse Charles," was the old creature's greeting. "It does yer old mammy's eyes good, 'deed it does. I heerd yesterday dat yer was come; but dis ole rheumatiz kept me at home. Dey do say dat dar is sometin' dey sell at de Forks dat'll cure it, sartin sure. Yer hasn't got a dollar, Marse Charles, or haf a crown, has yer, for poor ole aunty?"

Aylesford laughingly handed her the gratuity. After a few kind words from Kate, Aunt Chloe kept on to the kitchen, where, seated in the high-backed settle, within the ample fire-place, and with her short clay-pipe in her mouth, she prepared to have a gossip with the magnates of that apartment, about the fire in the woods, the new preacher, the return of Aylesford, and other current topics of interest.

CHAPTER XXVI
POMP'S ADVENTURE

Did you ever see the devil,
With his iron-wooden shovel,
A scratching up the gravel.
With his night-cap on?

Did you ever, ever, ever,
Ever, ever, ever, ever,
Ever, ever, ever, ever,
Catch a whale by the tail! —*Comic Song.*

The indigenous negro, as he used to exist in New Jersey, has long since disappeared before the inundation of new comers of the same race. Aunt Chloe, and her kitchen friends, belonged to the good old stock, however, such as our elder readers may remember to have met with in their youth. They had all, at one time, been slaves in the family, and, though now free, still regarded the Aylesfords as belonging to them, in a sense at least. Hence they freely canvassed the conduct of all, from Mrs. Warren down; and on this occasion, we may be sure, their criticisms were not withheld.

In this conversation Aunt Chloe maintained the principal part. Her auditors were the cook, a good-looking mulatto about forty years old, whose stout and comely person bespoke the excellent living at Sweetwater. A Madras handkerchief, tastefully wrapped about her head, and a new dress, gave Dinah quite an imposing air this evening. Her husband, who was at once overseer, gardener, and head ostler, a Guinea coast African, as black as midnight, sat in front of the fire; while her son, Pomp, a lad of eighteen, who officiated as stable boy, squatted on the floor in the background. Two other servants hovered in the distance, eager listeners, but not daring to join in the conversation with their superiors, especially with Aunt Chloe.

After the fire had been discussed, the return of Aylesford was brought up, and its effect on Major Gordon duly canvassed. Servants are more observant than is always thought, and the kitchen at Sweetwater had discovered the condition of our hero's affections long before the parlor, or even himself, had suspected it. Aunt Chloe, in spite of having known Aylesford when an infant, leaned to the side of the Major, chiefly, it must be confessed, in consequence of the douceur the latter had bestowed upon her. For a similar reason, Pomp, who as stable-boy, had often received small gratuities, secretly favored the same cause. But, on the other hand, Dinah, as well as her husband, neither of whom had been in the way to be favored by our hero, were warm advocates of Aylesford.

For a time the discussion waxed quite animated, but finally it died away, and the new minister came up for scrutiny in turn. On this subject Aunt Chloe spoke authoritatively, laying down the law to her gaping listeners. It is well known that illiterate negroes are somewhat peculiar in their religious notions. The imagination has a powerful influence over them, and they are exceedingly susceptible to nervous excitements, as any one, who has ever been at a camp-meeting, must have observed. Frequently, indeed, they seem to actually realize mere dreams. Hence it is a common thing to hear them tell, with the greatest gravity, stories of personal interviews with the Arch Enemy. Sometimes, however, these are not delusions, but deliberate romances, invented to increase the importance of the narrator.

"It did dis chile good," said Aunt Chloe, "to hear dat preacher dis morning. I bless my hebbenly master dat dar are left some who speak de plain trufe. It 'most made me feel as I did when I fast got religion. Ah! dat was a happy time. It was long ago, Pomp, before you was born, at a woods meeting over by Waldo. 'Peared as if I was light as a bird, and could fly right up to hebben. I nebber saw de stars shine as dey did dat night, when I walked home; and nebber 'spect to till I get over Jordan, and into de New Jerusalem—dat is if de ole debbil, dat roarin' lion, who goes about seekin' whom he may devour, don't git dis chile yet."

Pomp, at this mention of the ubiquitous character of the enemy, mindful, perhaps, of some late improper acts, looked fearfully over his shoulder, as if expecting to see him lurking in the dark shadows at the further end of the kitchen; for it was now after sunset, and the only light in the room was that of the smouldering fire.

"Ah! dat debbil," groaned Pomp's sire, rolling up the whites of his eyes. "We must watch and pray, Aunt Chloe, or he'll git de best of us in spite of all. He 'most had dis chile once. He was near to me, 'deed he was, as Pomp dis minnit."

Pomp started as if he had been shot, and began to edge away from his parent, at this renewed assault upon his nerves.

"You don't say dat?" cried Aunt Chloe, lifting up both hands. "You're makin' fun."

"'Deed I isn't, aunty. I seed de debbil, dat ole dragon, only dis last spring, sure sartin."

"How?" and Aunt Chloe, stuffing more tobacco into her pipe, began to smoke anew, looking the speaker eagerly in the face.

"I was out in de cornfield, one day, hoein'," said he, "when, stoppin' to rest a minnit, and looking up, I saw dat of a sudden de woods at de odder end had clean gone away, and de field had stretched hisself away out," and he extended his arm as he spoke, with the palm of the hand inclined downwards, "just so, slopin' like, as de roof of a barn does, yer know, only it went slopin' down, down, till it cum to de end of de world. But it didn't 'pear to be de end of de world eider. For over again de field dar was a hill, which sloped up 'most as high on de odder side," all this time going through an active pantomine, "and between de two, and kind o' under de one I was on, was de bottomless pit, 'deed dere was, wid de brimstone flames and smoke a-shootin' up, ebbery now and den, like fire out of de stack of Waldo furnace. And standin' dar between de two hills," continued the narrator, leaning forward, "and right ober dis pit, I saw de debbil hisself, 'deed I did, aunty. He had great horns on his head, and eyes like red-hot iron, and held a big pitchfork in his hand, and 'peared to be a watchin' me, as near as I could tell, for you see de smoke kept rollin' up and hidin' him 'bout half de time. 'Oh! Lor' Amighty!' I said, 'dis chile done for now; de debbil will hab him, and no mistake.' Wid dat, of a sudden, my knees guv way, I fell, and as I fell I begun a slidin' down de hill. De debbil he saw me a-comin', and made a grab at me wid his pitchfork; but he couldn't reach me yet. I tried to cotch hold of somethin' to stop me, but de field 'peared to be nuffin but loose sand, widout a cornstalk left, or a blackberry bush, or even a root. De debbil he now made anoder grab at me, but he wasn't near enough yet. By dis time de sand of de field began to slide, like shelled corn pourin' out of a half-bushel, slippin', slippin', and de debbil reachin', reachin', to get my poor ole soul. By'm bye, I saw dat de next time he would fotch me sure. I was away down, yer see, just at de bottom of de hill, and could hear de roarin' of de flames, and Dives a lookin' up and cryin' for a drop of water. De debbil he kind of braced hisself, seein' me so close, and lifted his pitchfork to hab it ready; and I went slidin', slidin', and de hill wid me, faster dan a streak of lightnin', right down—"

"Datll do," cried Aunt Chloe, rising authoritatively. "Lord a massy, how you can lie, ole nig." And as she spoke, the expression of her countenance, which had been one of incredulity almost from the first, settled into disgust.

"I'll not stay," she continued, "to hear sich tales. I wonder you ain't ashamed, and before Pomp too."

The abashed romancer could not utter a word. Dinah in vain interposed to persuade Aunt Chloe to remain. At last the offender, eager to purchase his peace, said that, if Aunt Chloe must go, at least she must permit Pomp to accompany her home. "Dar was nuffin so ungenteel," he said, "dan fur company, 'specially ladies, to be 'lowed to go home alone."

Pomp, whose ever active fears had been unpleasantly excited already, would fain have declined, but did not dare; and Aunt Chloe, somewhat mollified by this civility, set off with her attendant. The distance was about a mile, which was soon passed, too soon for Pomp, indeed, who, all the time, had been dreading the lonely walk back.

There was no help for it, however, and so, after leaving Aunt Chloe at her gate, the lad, whistling to keep his courage up, set his face homewards. As long as he remained within sight of the cabin, he managed to keep down his fears; but when he had fairly plunged into the forest, his teeth began to chatter, his knees to shake, and his heart to palpitate. The night was starless, as well as moonless, so that, even in the open country, it was quite dark, while in the narrow wood road the gloom seemed almost palpable. Pomp could not see a dozen feet ahead. He began to recall, not only the story his father had related, and which he firmly believed in spite of Aunt Chloe's skepticism, but all the supernatural narratives he had listened to during his whole lifetime. Tales of the Arch Enemy, assuming the shape of a wild beast, and pouncing on lonely travellers from some dark covert; tales of the dead coming forth; tales of whole legions of devils carrying off benighted wayfarers; these, which he had often heard beside the kitchen fire, recurred to him now, till his hair stood on end, and he started at every sound.

His road lead near the grave-yard, and as he approached it, his terror redoubled.

All at once, and when at the very darkest part of the road, what seemed a groan made him come to a halt. He immediately rallied, however, and tried to persuade himself that it was only the wind in the tree-tops, which had again momentarily startled him. But as he listened, it came once more, an awful, unearthly sound, that chilled his very marrow. His limbs now refused to support him, and he sank nerveless and shaking to the ground. But when a moment had elapsed, and the sound was not repeated, he began to gather a little courage, thinking that, perhaps, it was only the distant hooting of an owl. Reassured somewhat, by this idea, he rose feebly to his feet. But he had not advanced a step before the sound was heard again, and indisputably close at hand, so close indeed, that he seemed to feel the hot breath from the invisible presence that uttered it. He fell at once flat on his face, half dead with horror, and expecting the next instant to be clutched and borne off.

He was almost too frightened to pray, a duty in which, he now remembered, he had lately been remiss: but he managed, with rattling teeth, and nearly paralyzed jaws, to articulate at last.

"Oh! Marse Lord," he cried, "don't let de debbil git dis poor chile, not dis time anyhow. 'Twasn't Pomp, dat was in de watermelon patch dis mornin', when he ought to have been at meetin'. Dar's some mistake, deed dar is. It's Sam Jonsing dat you want, Marse Debbil. Tink what my ole mammy will do if you—"

But he never finished his adjuration, for at this crisis two glowing eyes emerged out of the darkness, and stood staring over him, two enormous horns followed, a bellow was heard that seemed to shake the woods for miles, and Pomp felt himself lifted bodily from the sand. It was more than nature could endure. He fainted outright.

When he came to himself, he was lying at the side of the road, stiff with bruises. At first he could not believe that he was still alive. But gradually, though not till after he had pinched himself frequently, he became assured that he was yet in mortal guise; and that his unearthly enemy had disappeared. He now feebly struggled to his feet, and began to feel his limbs; but none were broken, though he found his breeches torn nearly off. Gathering courage, by degrees, he crept away, moving fearfully and cautiously, however, till he had fairly emerged from the woods and passed the grave-yard, when he broke into a run and fled homewards as fast as his limbs would carry him.

Here, to a gaping audience, he recounted breathlessly his narrow escape.

"You darn fool," said his sire, when Pomp had finished his narration, incredulous of others, because conscious of his own habit of romancing, "do you tink your ole farder'll believe dat pack of lies? You neber saw anything, but made it all up."

"De chile didn't," said Dinah. "Dar! What you say to dis?"

She exposed to view, as she spoke, the damaged seat of Pomp's breeches, which afforded unmistakable proof of his having come into contact with an enemy of some kind, even if not a supernatural one. But the sire was still incredulous.

"He's gone done tore it a purpose," was all the stubborn skeptic said.

But the next day he professed to solve the enigma. He came in from the barn, where he had been giving Arab an early feed, and, laughing, said—

"De black bull was loose all night, and went way up de road, past de meetin'-house, 'zactly whar dis darn fool of a Pomp says he met de debbil. It's lucky his breeches tore, or de critter might have killed him, deed he might. I told you de chile was lyin'. Lor' Amighty, to get skeered dat way, at nuffin at all!" and he laughed till the tears ran out of his eyes.

But Dinah as well as her son persisted in their original version of the story, and thereafter two distinct accounts of interviews with the Arch Enemy were told in the kitchen at Sweetwater, neither party, however, believing a word that the other said.

CHAPTER XXVII
THE ABDUCTION

And many an old man's sigh, and many a widow's,
And many an orphan's water-standing eye—
Men for their sons', wives for their husbands' fate,
And orphans for their parents' timeless death—
Shall rue the hour that ever thou wert born. —Shakespeare.

Infamous wretch!
So much beneath my scorn. —Dryden.

Kate came down to breakfast in her riding habit, and when the meal was concluded, mounted almost gayly; while Mrs. Warren, nearly weeping, awaited the departure of her and Aylesford.

She watched the equestrians till they reached the bend of the pond, when Aylesford, with a low bow and a wave of the hand, parted from Kate; and immediately after both were lost to sight in the forest, he keeping on over the bridge, and she turning to the left.

Kate rode on, with a light heart, talking to Arab, in the exuberance of her feelings, as if he had been a human friend, patting him caressingly, with her right hand, as she spoke. The intelligent beast pricked up his ears, and looked around as if he actually understood her words.

"Let us have a gallop," she said. "Here is the road where you beat Selim. You remember it—don't you, old fellow?"

She gave her horse his head, at these words, striking him smartly, and away they went at full gallop.

Her fate hung, at that crisis, on a single thread. If Arab had maintained, for a quarter of an hour, the pace at which he was going, Kate would have passed the ambush prepared for her, at a speed which would have prevented her detection. Could but a warning voice have whispered to her the peril, could but one of those strange presentiments have come which often occur, she would have escaped the danger. But, suspecting no peril, she drew in her horse, as she approached the spring, where the road became rougher, and reduced his pace to a walk.

"Well done," she said, leaning over him and patting him again, "good Arab."

Suddenly she felt her bridle seized, and instantaneously the road was filled with strange faces, to the number of at least half a dozen. They were all alike coarse and ruffian-looking. The person who had seized her bridle was the only one who struck Kate as not unfamiliar; but his countenance was artificially blackened; and she could not, therefore, discover when or where she had seen him.

At first she had uttered a slight scream. But this had been occasioned rather by the startling suddenness of the attack, than by the assault itself. In an instant she had recovered her self-possession, when her first act was to strike her spur violently into Arab, and simultaneously to give him his rein, in hopes to shake off the grasp of the stranger.

But the ruffian's hold was too firm to be loosened. Arab sprung forward like an arrow, with a snort of rage and terror, lifting the villain almost from his feet and dragging him several paces forward. But it was in vain. The gripe now fixed on the bridle was one evidently accustomed to such work, and though the horse plunged, reared, sprang aside, and resorted to other means to get rid of his mistress' assailant, the effort was to no purpose.

"So ho, so ho," said the man, in a deep, gruff voice of authority. "Won't you be still, sir?" Gradually the restive animal subsided into quiet, and stood trembling all over, the sweat oozing out from every pore, till his satin-like coat glistened like glass.

Meantime his mistress, who had continued spurring him till she saw it was useless, sat in her seat as if she had been part of the animal, till even the coarse ruffians about her audibly cried out at her skill. "It's no use, miss," said the voice of the disguised leader. "I've held worse colts than this, and when once I get my grip on a horse, he's bound to stand till I let him go."

The man's voice, she thought, was one she had often heard. His evident familiarity with horses was another proof of his identity. She looked again at the burly figure, and at once remembered who he was. "James Arrison!" she said, in surprise.

The ruffian made no distinct reply, but muttered an oath between his teeth.

"What do you mean by this rudeness?" she said, with a dignity amounting to sternness. "Let go my bridle, sir."

The villain had now, however, recovered from his momentary discomposure at the detection of his disguise. He looked boldly up, and said ironically—

"Not if you please, miss. We haven't come so far or waited so long, to give up our booty in this fashion."

Kate's heart, stout as it was, sunk within her. Though she had heard nothing of Arrison's proceedings since his return to the vicinity of Sweetwater, and did not therefore identify him with the burning of widow Bates' house, yet she knew enough of his former deeds to satisfy herself that she had fallen into the hands of refugees. The utter disregard of law, both human and divine, exhibited by these outlaws, was well known to her. She was aware that they valued even human life lightly, when it stood in the way of their plans. It was but a few months ago, if report spoke correctly, that a gang of them had attacked a lone farmhouse at midnight, in a neighboring county, murdered the owner and his wife, and sought even the blood of the innocent daughter, who, however, luckily escaped to a neighboring wood. It was within a period, scarcely less remote, that a band, fifty or sixty strong, had assailed the dwelling of Major Huddy, at what is now Colt's Neck, and carried off the proprietor as their prisoner, after a protracted defence, which was only terminated by the outlaws setting fire to the house. It was less than a twelvemonth since an armed launch, managed by twenty similar ruffians, had cruized off the mouth of a neighboring river, and even ravaged its shores. Innumerable were the tales authenticated of the ruffianly character of these desperadoes. Old age had been assassinated by them in cold blood; and women, it was said, had been not unfrequently violated. Their brutal ferocity had passed into a proverb. At the name of refugee the very children turned pale, and crept closer to their mother's side. Yet into the hands of a gang of these ruffians Kate saw that she had fallen, and fallen moreover in consequence of a premeditated ambush.

Most persons of her sex would have lost all presence of mind, at realizing her situation. But Kate's courageous heart rose with the occasion. Others of her sex also, even if they had retained their presence of mind, would have resorted to tears and supplications. She, however, saw that these would be wasted on the hardened ruffians into whose hands she had fallen. She resolved, accordingly, to appeal to their self-interest, supposing that ransom was their real purpose.

She turned to the refugees, saying—

"Name your price, and, if it is within our means, it shall be paid when and where you please. You all know who I am, I presume. The word of an Aylesford is as good as a bond."

The men looked at each other, and then at their leader but none of them answered, evidently leaving it to him to be their spokesman.

"And how much do you think you could raise at Sweetwater?" asked Arrison, sneeringly. "If we had known it was such a bank of England, that it could pay down golden guineas for your ransom, maybe we'd have sacked it first, and then carried you off afterwards. Now how much will your ladyship give?"

The tone in which he spoke, coupled with his enigmatical words, gave Kate her first suspicion that the ruffians' motive was not wholly mercenary in waylaying her. Her cheek, in spite of herself, was a shade paler, and her voice trembled as she replied—

"In heaven's name, Arrison, state your terms, and let me go. We have but little gold on hand, as you ought to know, in these times; but we can get it; and I pledge you my honor, the honor of my father's daughter, that your price shall be paid."

"Without treachery?"

"Without treachery."

"If I name a day and place, will you send a trusty servant with the gold, and let no one know of it?"

"I will."

"Will you swear it?"

"I will swear it."

The particularity with which he proceeded gave Kate hope, which was increased by his next words.

"Will a hundred guineas be too much?"

"I will promise you a hundred guineas," she said promptly. "It is a large sum, a very large sum, for these times, and you must give me leisure to procure it." She would have added, "The more as my cousin, Mr. Aylesford, is absent." But, remembering that this betrayal of her defenceless condition might stimulate the cupidity of the refugees, she corrected herself, and said— "It will require at least a fortnight."

Anxiously, as she spoke, she studied the faces of her hearers, especially that of their leader, to notice the effect of her words. The affected interest with which Arrison had conducted the conversation, now suddenly gave place to a look of sardonic triumph, which betrayed to Kate that he had been amusing himself at her expense, as the tiger is said to play with his victim before he laps his blood.

"It won't do, my pretty miss," said the villain. "I'm too old a bird to be caught with such chaff. Your promises wouldn't be worth a farthing, when once you were out of my sight. No, no, my cunning she-fox, you're not so smart as you think you are. I have a plan of my own which you shall know in good time, by which I expect to make a better thing than a hundred guineas out of you. But, for the present, we will listen to no talk of ransom. You go with us, and if you can make up your mind to go quietly, it will be to your interest. But if not, we'll find a way to make you."

Kate trembled secretly at the dark hints of the ruffian. Oh! how she longed, at that moment, for the sight of even her cousin. The thought of Major Gordon also, and his stout arm, and of Uncle Lawrence and his brave spirit, rushed across her; and she glanced eagerly up and down the road, in the wild hope of beholding one or both.

"Come," said her captor, brutally, "make up your mind quick. You needn't count on help, for we're strong enough for twice as many as would be likely to pass by; and now that we've got you we mean to keep you, even if we have to slit the throats of a dozen rebel officers or canting old scoundrels." And as Kate's countenance betrayed that he had divined her thoughts correctly, he continued— "You see I know what you're hoping for; but they'll not come, if you wait till to-morrow; since they've both gone down the river to fight King George, like two fools, leaving the coast clear for us." And he laughed again mockingly.

With this announcement, that the only persons to whom she could have looked for aid were absent, her last hope departed. She now recognized fully to what a deliberate and carefully-executed plan she had fallen a victim. As Arrison had intended, she believed herself to be a prey to a lawless gang, who, as they seemed to be above the temptation of lucre, must have designs upon her at which she shuddered even to glance.

But she saw that not only expostulations but even promises were useless, and from this moment, therefore, she was haughtily silent. She resolved that, at present, she would make no further efforts at resistance, since they would only be fruitless; but that, yielding to necessity, she would accompany her captors; determining to reserve all her strength for a crisis, which she now deemed not improbable, when death might probably be her only resource from dishonor.

"If you don't try to escape," said Arrison, seeing she did not speak, "we'll not disturb you, except to lead your horse; and in that case you may ride. But if you give us trouble, we'll make you dismount and walk; and if you refuse to do this, I'll blow your brains out."

The ruffian; as he spoke, drew a pistol from his breast, while he laid his hand emphatically upon her arm. Kate knew that he would keep his promise, both from his past reputation and his present determined look.

"Don't touch me, sir," she said, sternly, shrinking back by an impulse she was unable to control, "I will go quietly, since go I must."

The man answered by a brutal laugh, but removed his hand and put up his pistol. Turning to two of his gang, whom he called by name, he directed them to take Arab by the bridle, close to the bit, one on either side, and so lead the animal.

"And now, miss," he said, "we'll be off; for we must put many good miles of land and water between us and Sweetwater before night; because, in matters of this kind," and he sneered in his cold-blooded way again, "it's just as well, you know, to clinch the nail. There's nothing like making even a sure thing surer."

Without further word the party set forth, in something like military order. Two of the gang went a hundred yards in advance; then came the two who were leading Arab; and, a hundred yards behind, the remaining two brought up the rear. Arrison, at first, walked beside Kate, but as they progressed, he shifted his position frequently, now going ahead even of those in advance, and now dropping to the extreme rear, always on the watch against surprise. Occasionally he addressed our heroine, but as she adhered firmly to her purpose of not answering, and scarcely made an effort to conceal her scorn, he finally relapsed into silence.

Their way led through old and half-overgrown wood-roads, through most of which a vehicle would have found it impossible to pass. Familiar as Kate considered herself with the by-ways of this description in the neighborhood of Sweetwater, most of these they now followed were quite strange to her. She soon lost all knowledge of their whereabouts, in consequence.

Her suspicion that they were following the river towards its mouth became a certainty, as the day wore on, when they emerged suddenly on the banks of a deep, and comparatively wide stream, the shores of which she recognized immediately. A boat lay concealed, under the shadow of overhanging trees and bushes, as if awaiting them.

"You'll dismount here," said Arrison, breaking silence for the first time for several hours. "Remember my threat, which, if you scream or resist," he added, with an oath, and a meaning tap of his breast, "I'll keep."

Kate haughtily waved him away, as he approached to assist her, and leaping from the saddle, gathered up the skirts of her riding-dress and walked to the boat, whither his look had directed her.

But even in that perilous moment, when she knew not but that the crisis, which she had feared all day, was close at hand, she could not part from Arab without a pang. As she took her seat in the boat, her eyes still followed her horse; and she was comforted to see that a lad, who appeared all at once, was hoisted into her saddle, as if to ride the animal to a place of safety.

Directly that Arab had disappeared, after turning his head sadly, and as if reproachfully, towards her, the refugees entered the boat, the men assumed the oars, and Arrison taking the rudder, in a moment more they pushed off.

CHAPTER XXVIII
THE VOLUNTEERS

"Why have they dared to march
So many miles upon her peaceful bosom;
Frighting her pale-faced villages with war." —*Shakespeare.*

"Front to front,
Bring thou this fiend of Scotland, and myself;
Within my sword's length set him." —*Shakespeare.*

We must now return to Major Gordon and his companion, whom we left, long ago, proceeding to the Forks.

The Forks, as its name imported, was situated at the head of navigation, at the junction of two small branches of the river, on whose shores the events we have been narrating occurred. It was a settlement comprising about twenty-five houses, whose inhabitants were exclusively engaged in the trade, which the unloading of prizes at this point had created. Springing up in an incredibly short time, its prosperity was as evanescent as things of rapid growth often are; and long since every vestige of it has departed, except a solitary domicile, and a few grand old buttonwoods.

At the time of which we write, however, the Forks was in the full career of success. The western shore of the narrow but deep river in front, was lined for a considerable distance with vessels, which either had discharged valuable cargoes, or were about to do so. Many a fat merchantman, which had been originally laden with goods for the markets of Jamaica, was there contributing unwillingly to the wealth of the American patriots; and many a proud West Indiaman, which had been freighted at Kingston with sugar, rum, or molasses for London, was now unloading at the Forks for the benefit of Philadelphia. The place, in fact, was the head-quarters for the spoils, ravaged by American privateers from his Majesty's mercantile marine.

As such it presented a scene of comparative liveliness. Teamsters were there, swearing at their horses, drinking in the tavern, or wrangling about their load; brokers were there, in behalf of the merchants of the capital, bartering for desirable goods; and sailors, watermen, laborers, and occasionally a small farmer or two were there also; while a few soldiers, constituting the small command of Major Gordon, lounged about and completed the diversity of the scene.

Scarcely had Major Gordon arrived at the Forks with his companion, when he was called aside, and informed that an express rider had just reached the place and was anxiously inquiring for him. It was added that the man, though he refused to divulge his errand, was evidently from Washington's head-quarters.

"Send him in," said the Major, leading the way to his bed-chamber, the only private apartment he could command. And turning to Uncle Lawrence, he asked the latter to excuse him for a few minutes.

The express rider was soon ushered into the presence of the young officer.

"His excellency, the commander-in-chief," said the emissary, "has received news that the British are about fitting out an expedition against the lower settlements on this river, with the intention to burn the prizes collected below, and perhaps even to penetrate up to this point. So much I was told to carry by word of mouth, in case any accident happened to my despatches. But I was to preserve them, if possible, and hand them to you." With these words he drew out a packet, which he delivered to Major Gordon.

The official document confirmed what the messenger had stated, but went much more into detail. It informed our hero that General Washington had ascertained, from reliable informants in New York, that the British commander-in-chief, enraged at the serious damage done by the privateers harboring in the river, had resolved to despatch the Vesta man-of-war, with a sufficient number of auxiliary vessels and a force of nearly a thousand men, to break up the American settlements, capture the armed ships, and burn or bring off the prizes. "In a word," concluded the despatch, "it is the royal General's intention to devastate the whole region. No hope is left for the inhabitants but in rallying promptly to resist the aggressors. Had the enemy been able to surprise the district, as he confidently expected, his bloody designs would incontestably have been carried out. But the commander-in-chief is in hopes that the timely warning he sends, will allow the inhabitants to make such preparations for defence, as will frustrate the plans of the invaders. He advises that all private armed vessels be conveyed immediately to a place of security; that defences be thrown up at the points most likely to become the objects of attack; and that those persons who are well affected to the Congress be summoned, from the surrounding neighborhoods, to defend the soil from aggression. He will despatch a body of dragoons, under the Count Pulaski, as soon as possible, to assist the militia; meantime, Major Gordon is instructed to hasten at once to the Neck, which is one of the spots certain to be assailed first, and remain in command there until relieved by the Count."

Major Gordon, having hastily perused this missive, turned to the express rider.

"Are you too tired to go on with the news?" he said. "if not, you are the most suitable person."

"I'm all ready," answered the messenger. "I sort of thought you'd wish to send me forrard, and so I took a bite while waiting for you, not knowing," and he touched his cap, and smiled, "when I'd get another."

"You are a veteran already in one thing," answered Major Gordon, gayly, "even though young in years. Mount then, at once, and make the best speed you can to the Neck. Once there, despatch messengers across the country and along shore to rouse the people. Let the rendezvous be at the Neck. I will march, with all the forces I can collect, within an hour or two; but as my progress will necessarily be slow, as compared with yours, I trust to find, by the time I arrive, a goodly number of armed citizens assembled to meet me."

Having dismissed the express rider with these words, Major Gordon called Uncle Lawrence aside, and communicated the intelligence he had received. He concluded by saying, "So it will be impossible for me, as you see, to give you any assistance at present in tracking the refugees. The object of their return here, however, is now apparent. They all keep up communications with the royal forces, and having heard of this expedition, have swarmed here to plunder at will if the enemy should succeed. Under these circumstances, the shortest way to drive the vermin from the region, is to strike at the royal forces; for if we defeat them, the refugees can afterwards be easily mastered in detail. Even, however, if my judgment continued in favor of your proposal, my orders would forbid my entering on any such enterprise at this juncture."

Uncle Lawrence answered promptly,

"You are right. My old blood warms, too, at the news of this expedition. What! the tories coming to attack us, in our own river, and to burn down our very houses. God helping me," he said, glancing reverently upwards, and then striking his gun emphatically, "I'll march myself against the invaders. You'll take, me, Major, I spose?"

"Gladly," replied our hero, seizing the old man's hand, and shaking it warmly. "It is what I would have desired, above all things else; but could not have presumed to ask, considering your years. Your example will be worth fifty good men to me. When such as you march, who can hold back?"

"Strike while the iron's hot, then," pithily said Uncle Lawrence. "Call for volunteers right off, Major. There's a dozen idle fellows here that might go as well as not; and will, maybe, if you tell the news straight out, and say, too, that every man's wanted."

Taking the old man's hint, the Major stepped out in front of the house, just as everybody was crowding, full of curiosity, to see the express rider depart; and having waited till the messenger dashed off, he proceeded to impart the contents of the despatch, after which, in a short, but stirring speech, he called for volunteers.

No sooner had he finished than Uncle Lawrence, who had stood leaning on his gun, as if idly listening, stepped forward, and taking off his cap, remained a moment gazing at the crowd in silence, the wind waving his long, thin, silvery locks.

The action drew every eye upon him. All saw that he had something to say, and waited for it respectfully.

"Neighbors," he said, looking around with simple dignity, "here stands the first volunteer."

At this unexpected declaration—unexpected, however, only because of the veteran's age, for otherwise it was in keeping with his whole life—the audience, after a pause of silent admiration, broke forth into an enthusiastic cheer.

The old man's eyes brightened. "And now," he continued, "who'll go with me to fight for our homes, our wives, our darters, and our babies? Liberty or death!" And he waved his cap around his head. "Huzza!"

"I'll go—and I—and I," cried almost every voice, as the speakers rushing forward, grasped first his hand and then that of Major Gordon; for the effect of his appeal was electric. "Liberty or death! Liberty or death!" And the welkin rung with the reiterated shout.

"That's what I expected," said the Major, when silence had been procured again. "That's what I expected—after such an example—from such brave fellows and such good friends to their country. The right way, my lads, when an enemy is about, is to march boldly to meet him, and not wait to be smoked out like a fox in his hole. One more huzza for liberty or death," he continued, leading off the shout; "and now every man arm himself, taking plenty of powder and ball; and be ready to set out within an hour. We must reach the Neck by nightfall, or earlier, if we can."

The crowd dispersed at this, though not till they had given nine cheers, three for Uncle Lawrence, three for Major Gordon, and three for General Washington.

In little more than an hour, nearly the whole available male population of the Forks had rendezvoused in front of Major Gordon's lodgings; and boats having been provided, as affording the speediest method of reaching the Neck, they pushed off, with a round of huzzas to cheer the hearts of their wives and sweethearts left behind.

Uncle Lawrence had not even returned home to acquaint his family with his intentions. He had, however, despatched a lad to perform this duty, for which he had not time himself. The youngster passed directly in front of the mansion at Sweetwater, in the execution of this task; but as the inhabitants were regarded as being tories at heart, he forbore to communicate his news.

Meantime, Major Gordon, and his veteran companion, little imagined the peril that threatened Miss Aylesford. The idea of so daring an outrage as the abduction of Kate would never have suggested itself to them under any circumstances; but in fact, they were both so engrossed by the news of the threatened invasion, that they thought of nothing but repulsing it. It was long after the Forks had faded in the distance, before even Major Gordon, hero as he was, remembered our heroine; and though, after this, her image often recurred to him, it was with no suspicion that she was less secure from harm than the queen on her throne.

As they descended the river, the Americans stopped at the various farmhouses on the shore, to give notice of the British expedition. At the principal settlement, Major Gordon landed in person, and directed that sentinels should be posted to watch ascending and descending boats.

"There are more or less disaffected persons above," he said, "who may seek to join the enemy or carry information to him, so that it is important that a strict watch be kept and every boat stopped. This is so necessary that we shall leave a few men with you till your neighbors can rally. If more than a dozen come in, however, send on the balance to the Neck, where every musket will be wanted."

CHAPTER XXIX
CHESTNUT NECK

*"The sky
Is overcast, and musters muttering thunder."* —*Byron.*

*"I heard the wrack,
As earth and sky would mingle."* —*Milton.*

The Neck was a tongue of land, which, jutting out into the tide, and surrounded on two sides by salt marshes, formed the last piece of solid ground as the voyager descended the river. As the crow flies, this point was but a few miles from the bay. But the navigator, after leaving the Neck, practically had to conquer many a weary league before he reached the Atlantic, the stream winding, in sinuous turns, in and out among the low meadows, before it finally attained its destination.

On this bit of fast land a few scattering houses had been built, the principal one being about a hundred yards from the water's edge. Cornfields extended for some distance inland, where they were met by dense woods, which stretched on both sides, wherever there was solid ground, as far as the eye could see. A few fine old chestnut trees, growing in a clump near the extreme end of the point, made the spot a land-mark, visible for miles up and down the stream.

The neck of land formed, on its upper side, a little bay, in which were now disposed about thirty dismantled merchant vessels. Bales of goods were piled upon the shore, as if just unloaded; while others were being hurried into the neighboring store-houses. At least five hundred men were already collected, when Major Gordon reached the rendezvous. They were all busy, for those who were not engaged in securing the cargos of the prizes, were occupied in throwing up a rude earthen breastwork for the defence of the place.

Among the first to welcome our hero was the old waterman, Mullen, whom the reader will recollect as having been with him, when Kate was rescued from the wreck. Charley Newell was also there, but came forward more coyly, and blushed like any girl when the Major complimented him for his conduct on that occasion.

From these old comrades our hero learned that the express rider had preceded him several hours; that intelligence had already reached the settlements on both sides of the river; and that the privateers had made good their escape. Nothing, as yet, had been seen of the British. Meantime, the whole country was rising, and Mullen predicted that, before four and twenty hours, a thousand men would rendezvous at the Neck.

"There's no danger of surprise?" said Major Gordon, interrogatively.

"We know the cut of every sail on the river," said Mullen, "and can tell a strange one miles off. There isn't a child even, hereabouts, who can't say whether a craft is ours or not, a'most as soon as he can pint out a gray-back or a millet. The river makes a wide sweep, as maybe you may remember, just below here, so that what's but a mile right across the mash hereaway, is a matter of three miles as the water runs. You can see a sail an hour or more before she can reach the Neck."

Satisfied on this point, and having posted sentinels at every proper point, so as to provide against being surprised in the darkness, Major Gordon dismissed his command to their quarters soon after nightfall; and directly hundreds of men, fatigued by a hurried march, or a day of severe labor in storing goods, were fast asleep, bivouacking around him. Slumber was not, however, for his eyes. Though he scarcely expected an attack before the following day, even if then, the anxiety natural to his position kept him awake. He paced slowly up and down, hour after hour, under the shadows of the chestnut trees, now listening to the sentry's cry of "all's well," and now to the low plash of the tide as it swept past the point. Or he stood, with folded arms, cooling his heated brow in the night air, or gazing dreamily over the vast and silent expanse of salt meadows between him and the ocean, as they were vaguely seen in the starlight. Occasionally he went the rounds personally. At other times, he leaned against one of the old chestnuts, and gave himself up to reflection, Kate dividing his thoughts nearly equally with the responsibilities of his command.

The morning dawned, close and misty. The fog hung low and thick over the marshes, or lay packed, like aerial fleeces, upon the stream. Now and then a faint breeze would wave it gently, as when a light curtain is stirred by the wind; and here and there it eddied and undulated, apparently without cause. The atmosphere was warm, almost stifling.

"An enemy might steal on us now, like a thief in the night," was Uncle Lawrence's morning salutation to Major Gordon. "The fog's so thick it looks as if one might cut it with a knife."

"It's a'most as bad as the fogs off Newfoundland," put in Mullen, coming up, "where the Marblehead fishermen have a saying they can make steps in 'em, as if they were rock. Ha! ha!"

"When I was at Newport," remarked Major Gordon, joining in the humor of the moment, "in the beginning of the war—and Newport's famous for its fogs, you know—they told me the girls used to hang their heads out of the windows, whenever there was a fog, to bleach their complexions; and certainly the ladies there look almost like wax-work." And thus speaking, he laughingly passed on.

"Like wax-work!" said Mullen, contemptuously. "Give me an honest tan on the face. A woman ain't good for much that can't dig potatoes, or maybe hold a plough a bit, while her husband's out a fishin'. In these parts, at any rate, a man don't want a wife that he has to keep in a glass case."

"Every one to his taste," interposed Uncle Lawrence. "Now there's Miss Aylesford would stand but a poor chance digging potatoes with them white little hands of hern, yet she's a brave gal for all that, as you know, Mr. Mullen."

"Ay, ay, that do I. Lord A'mighty, how beautiful she looked, when she ran for'ard on that ere wreck to cast off the cable. What a pictur she'd a made. There's nothing in my old woman's family Bible as fine."

As the day wore on, the fog lifted, and Major Gordon's anxiety was relieved by discovering no signs of the foe. Aware of his as yet insufficient means of defence, he wished to postpone the struggle as long as possible. For though he had several hundred men under his command, and though the number was hourly being augmented, they were wholly undisciplined, and the breastwork, which might have aided him materially, was still unfinished.

Meantime, he urged forward the construction of the fortification, often personally assisting the laborers. He hoped, by another day, to have the defences finished, in which case he thought he could make good his post, even if Pulaski should fail to come up. Nevertheless, he was not over-sanguine. For the thousand disciplined soldiers, marines, and sailors, whom the British were despatching against him, were not to be despised by a brave and prudent commander. Two-thirds of his men had never seen fire; and though their patriotism was unquestionable, no leader, he well knew, could count certainly on such troops.

When, at last, noon arrived, and the fortifications were pronounced half-finished, and when, having swept the river below with his glass, no enemy was seen, Major Gordon went to his meal with something like relief.

Clouds had been hovering all day, however, around the horizon, portending rain; and more than once low growls of thunder had come up faintly from the distance. While the men were at dinner, the threatening vapors culminated, and a storm, as sudden as it was violent, broke upon the little camp. The Major was seated at his meal, in the "best parlor" of the principal dwelling, when his attention was aroused by the unexpected darkness that fell across the room. Almost immediately there came a rush of wind, which dashed the sand against the window-pane like showers of fine shot, while the enormous chestnuts were heard swaying and moaning as if twisted and tortured almost beyond their powers of endurance. Rushing to the casement he saw the air filled with a ghastly dust, through which the light looked lurid, as if the Judgment Day had come. The young saplings were bending like reeds; while some cattle, which had been driven into the camp to be slaughtered, had broken loose, and now ran wildly about, tearing up the loose soil and bellowing in affright: and overhead, the birds, scared from their noontide shelter, flew hither and thither blindly.

All at once a dead silence fell upon the scene. The wind ceased as if by the command of some fell magician. This quiet was, however, even more awful than the preceding turmoil. It was, indeed, as if all things had come to their last gasp, and earth wanted but the word to dissolve forever. Suddenly this ominous stillness was broken by a terrific clap of thunder bursting almost overhead. Simultaneously a vivid streak of lightning, that filled the whole room with dazzling light, and blinded Major Gordon for a moment, shot to the ground just in front of the garden fence; the earth opened, ploughed up for yards on either side by the red bolt, and then, while a dense smoke rose, or seemed to the dizzy eyesight to rise from the spot, the house apparently rocked to its foundations, and the firmament shook, while peal on peal reverberated into the distance, as if thousands of artillery wagons were jolting at full gallop down the pavement of heaven.

Involuntarily Major Gordon sprang back from the window, while the servant girl, who had been waiting on him, ran screaming from the room, crying that the end of the world had come. Then a rushing sound was heard, and a burst of rain followed, as if the windows of the sky had been opened, the rain dancing on the road in huge drops, and hissing as though it fell on a furnace. Hail was soon mixed with the descending water, which now poured down in sheeted cataracts, and with the roar of an avalanche. The icy particles, as big as hazel-nuts, rattled on the roof like buckshot, cracked the frail glass of the window-panes, and heaped themselves up in the ruts, like pebbles left by a mountain torrent. The trees once more bent in the driving gale, and the rain, swept almost horizontally along, smoked over the fast land and vanished in clouds of gray mist across the distant marshes.

For more than an hour, the rain continued to fall. The fury of the tempest, however, began to subside long before that period had elapsed. At last Major Gordon ventured out. The storm had crossed the country diagonally, and was now moving towards the Atlantic, its gloomy mass extending along the eastern horizon and far up towards the zenith, black as a funeral hearse and procession. No sable pall could have descended more wall-like, over the salt marshes and river below the Neck, than did the ebon clouds of the tempest. Continually, down this inky curtain, crinkled the zig-zag lightning, its white-heat blaze irradiating all around for an instant, and then leaving it seemingly duskier than before. Wherever the storm came down, in this way, on the river, a murky glare fringed its lower edge, diffusing a ghostly reflection on the troubled waves in front of it. Every few minutes the thunder boomed from out of this black ominous mass, sounding fainter as the storm receded, however, until at last it subsided into a low, sullen growl, as when a baffled lion retires reluctantly into the night before the hunters.

Suddenly, around the nearest bend of the river, a fleet of boats was seen advancing towards the Neck. The rowers were evidently men-of-wars men; while intermingled among them were the red coats of British soldiers and the caps of British marines. The whole number of the boats was not less than thirty, and Major Gordon, at a hasty glance, estimated the entire force of the assailants at nearly a thousand.

The enemy had approached undetected, under cover of the tempest, and in consequence of having no sails; and was now within a quarter of a mile. Not a minute was to be lost in preparing for defence. Our hero, therefore, hurriedly ordered the alarm to be sounded, and began to marshal his men, eager to do the best he could to avert the consequences of this surprise.

CHAPTER XXX
THE PURSUIT

"White as a white sail on a dusky sea,
When half the horizon's clouded and half free,
Fluttering between the dim wave and the sky,
Is hope's last gleam in man's extremity." —*Byron.*

"Hope, for a time,
Suns the young floweret in its gladsome light,
And it looks flourishing—a little while—
Til passed." —*Miss London.*

It will be remembered that we left Kate a few chapters back, about to be embarked on the river.

Clouds had been hovering, all the latter part of the morning, around the horizon; and about noon these had collected into the thunder-storm, which we have seen pass over Chestnut Neck. Kate and her captors, however, escaped the tempest, it being almost an hour in advance of them.

With rapid strokes the refugees urged their boat along, as if desirous to gain their destination, whatever it was, before nightfall. For nearly an hour they continued to advance in this way, between shores still overgrown with forest, with here and there a small clearing peeping out on the river. At last, on turning a sudden bend in the stream, they came in sight of a considerable settlement. A small field piece was mounted near the bank; and quite a number of armed men lounged about; while a couple of sentinels marched to and fro behind the cannon. On a flag-staff, in front of one of the houses, floated the stars and stripes of the confederated states.

Kate had noticed, that, as this settlement opened to view, the refugees had kept away, as close as possible to the other side of the river: but scarcely had they rounded the point and came fairly in view of the sentinels, when a hail sounded across the water.

To pass this armed party was almost impossible, for the boat had still a considerable distance to go before it would be in front of the dwellings: and even if it should safely reach and pass that point, it would be within range of their muskets for a long distance below, to say nothing of the field piece. The heart of our heroine beat high with hope. Here, when she least expected it, was succor. For she resolved, the instant the boat came to, to declare herself and claim protection, even if Arrison had his pistol at her heart.

The refugees appeared as disconcerted as she was overjoyed. They looked at each other and at their leader in dismay; but continued pulling lustily, still hugging the opposite shore. They were not allowed to go far, however, unchecked; for the sentinels, finding their summons disregarded, fired at the boat; and the ball of one of them passing close to Arrison, he suddenly ordered a halt.

"This is the devil's own work," he said, savagely. "Keep still, Miss, or I'll put my knife into you," he added, as Kate seized the opportunity to waive her handkerchief; and he snatched the handkerchief from her. "They are getting ready to fire their field-piece. We shall never be able to pass them. Who'd have thought that the rebel knaves would have rallied so quickly."

"We'd better turn back," said one of the men, who seemed the leading person after Arrison. "It's been slack water for some time, and the tide will begin to run up directly; it's making up, in fact, already, along shore. Before we could get by, with no wind and a head tide, they'd smash our boat to pieces with their cursed gun."

"Back let it be then," said Arrison, after a minute's angry reflection. "We'll lose the bounty, lads; but," he continued, as if by a sudden thought, "we'll have the prize; and gad! I'll find a way to make that pay you better than if we had gone on."

A burst of brutal merriment from the man was the answer to this sally, which, though partly enigmatical to Kate, had yet sufficient meaning to her to terrify her beyond description. For the words seemed to imply that the return of the ruffians would involve her in a more dreadful peril than even that which she had escaped.

The sentinels had remained quiet, watching the boat during this pause, because evidently expecting obedience to their summons. But when the refugees turned her head up the stream, and began vigorously propelling her in that direction, there was a general stir on shore, and several persons, hastily running to the bank, fired their muskets at the retreating boat. The balls came whistling by, and one even struck the gunwale not far from Kate. Simultaneously the field piece was trained after the fugitives, while a man ran to the nearest house as if for fire to discharge it.

"Pull, pull for your lives, my boys," shouted Arrison, leaning forward and assisting the man who pulled the stroke oar. "If we once get round the point again, we are safe."

Kate saw, from the velocity with which they moved, that this object would soon be gained. She feared also that the patriots had not seen her, and would probably not pursue the boat. With the quick decision and boldness of her character she rose suddenly from her seat, and screamed for help, making gestures of appeal to those on shore.

But, almost instantaneously, Arrison, who had seen her rise, struck her a violent blow, which felled her nearly senseless into the sternsheets. Here she lay, comparatively helpless for a while, stifling the moan which pain extracted from her.

Meantime, however, her scream had been heard on shore. The firing of the field piece was stopped. But, in its place, a boat, which lay near the bank, was instantly manned by several of the men, and a pursuit begun. The refugees had, indeed, a considerable start; but so energetically did the patriots row, that, before the former had got half a mile beyond the bend, the latter were seen rounding it gallantly in full chase.

The struggle soon became one of thrilling interest. The refugees had the lightest boat, but were fatigued with their day's toil, and with their exertions at the oars in descending the river; while the patriots were entirely fresh. In a short while, consequently, it became apparent that the former were losing ground.

Arrison, at this, broke into a torrent of oaths, and urged his crew afresh.

"Pull, pull," he cried; "do you want to taste cold hemp, you rascals?"

The stimulus of these words produced a perceptible influence on the speed of the boat. The refugees, stripped to their shirts, and with their chests and arms bared, toiled at the oars till the big drops of perspiration gathered like beads upon them. The stout ashen blades, with which they propelled their craft, bent until they seemed about to snap in two. The boat itself fairly leaped along, the water surging under her bows, or whirling in roaring eddies from the rudder.

"We hold our own now," cried Arrison, swaying to the strokes of the oarsmen. "Pull, pull, and we'll gain on them. There, we made something at the short bend. No," he added, suddenly, his inflamed face reddening still more, "they cut across after us. Pull, pull, I say," he shouted, "or we are taken."

As he spoke, he glanced over his shoulder continually and in perceptible anxiety. The men knew that the chase was for life and death; and rallying all their strength, they struggled on.

Meantime the exertions of the other crew were not a whit behind those of the refugees. Their helmsman could be seen stimulating them by pointing to Kate; and continually one or more of them glanced over his shoulder to see how the chase went on. The water flashed and glittered in the fading sunlight, as it fell showered from the blades of their oars; while the cataract of foam that rolled under the bows of their craft, proved with what velocity they were driving her along.

"Give way, stronger and longer," shouted Arrison, looking over his shoulders for the thirtieth time during the last half hour, "they gain again on us. Give way, or we are lost."

They had just crossed from one side to another of the river, in order to take the shortest cut up the next reach, and Arrison had confidently expected to see their pursuers follow in his track. But the patriots, by selecting a somewhat different course, had apparently secured more of the current, for they were now rapidly coming up, lessening the distance between the two boats astonishingly.

The refugees, like hounds incited by a fresh blast of the hunter's horn, sprang anew to their task; and for awhile their boat perceptibly increased her swiftness. But the pursuers, observing how much they had gained by their helmsman's dexterity, cheered lustily, and stretched to their strong blades, like thorough-breds coming down the last quarter. Gaining steadily now at every stroke, they rapidly approached, huzza following huzza, in the confidence of approaching victory.

Much of this advantage was evidently owing to their helmsman, who, by still continuing his adroit manoeuvres, constantly cut off more or less of the distance, or availed himself of more powerful currents of the tide. He plainly knew the river even better than Arrison.

The countenance of the refugees had been darkening with sullen despair for some time, when at last Arrison's lieutenant broke the silence, by addressing their leader.

"They gain on us, captain," he said.

"Yes," was Arrison's curt reply.

"That fellow knows how to steer."

"Yes! curse him."

Nothing could exceed the intense bitterness with which this was pronounced.

"Couldn't you manage to put a ball through him?" continued the lieutenant.

Arrison half started from his seat as if he had himself been shot.

"By the Lord," he cried, a gleam of savage delight breaking over his face, "it's the very thing. Why didn't I think of it?"

He seized a loaded musket as he spoke, turned, took rapid but sure aim, and fired.

It was all done so quickly, that Kate, who had sprung up as soon as she comprehended the plan, in order to knock down the refugee's gun, had not time to effect her purpose, before the report sounded heavily on the evening air.

"He's hit," cried Arrison, with a hurrah, not seeming to notice Kate, and leaving his lieutenant, who pulled the stroke oar, to drag her down again. "See, they stop."

As he spoke, the crew of the pursuing boat ceased rowing, and the two nearest rushed aft, for the coxswain had fallen across the seat, as if dead. When they lifted him up he had every appearance of being lifeless.

For the first time, on that agitating day, Kate burst into tears. The hopes of rescue, but a moment before, had amounted almost to a certainty; but now it would be impossible, she knew, for the pursuers to overtake the refugees.

The patriots apparently had come to the same conclusion, for one of them suddenly took up a musket, as if their only hope was in disabling the refugees in turn; but just as he was about to fire, a companion knocked the gun down, pointing vehemently, as if at Kate.

"Oh! if they would but disregard me and fire," she cried to herself.

But her agonized exclamation was in vain. After a few moments, apparently employed in eager consultation, the patriots turned the head of their boat down stream, and reluctantly gave up the chase.

All this time the refugees had been rapidly increasing the distance between them and their pursuers. But at this sight, they burst into a huzza.

"Now you can take it more easily, lads," cried Arrison. "These fellows have had pepper enough for their supper."

The men laughed at his coarse wit, and relaxing their exertions, rowed slowly up the river, wiping the perspiration from their heated brows; and in the general hilarity, Kate's daring attempt at interference was either pardoned or forgotten.

Faint from physical exhaustion, from the blow she had received, and from the utter destruction of her lately awakened hopes, Kate lay, or rather reclined in the sternsheets, where she had been thrust down by the lieutenant. More than once, in her despair, she was tempted to throw herself overboard and seek refuge in death. Perhaps Arrison suspected her of such a purpose, for he kept his eye almost constantly on her, so that, even if she had made the attempt, he would have been able instantly to frustrate it.

The night now began to fall. Yet, for nearly an hour, the refugees continued to urge forward their boat. At last, landing on the southern bank of the river, they rudely bade Kate arise. Resistance was in vain. While Arrison proceeded to cut off the superfluous part of her riding-skirt, so that she might walk, one of the gang took her by either arm. In this way they led, or rather dragged her, over rough wood-paths, and by circuitous ways, deep into the forest.

After a journey that appeared to her to extend to hours, they reached a house, surrounded on all sides by swamps. A savage bloodhound came forth baying to welcome them, eyeing Kate curiously, and by no means in a friendly spirit.

"Down, sir, down," said Arrison, addressing the dog: and entering the house he said to his prisoner, "we have but two rooms here. You will occupy that," and he pointed to an inner one.

With these words, he pushed her unceremoniously in.

CHAPTER XXXI
THE REFUGEE REVEL

"Beyond the infinite and boundless reach
Of mercy, if thou didst this deed of death,
Art thou damned." —*Shakespeare.*

"I'll lay a scene of blood,
Shall make this dwelling horrible to nature." — *Otway.*

Our heroine was so completely prostrated by physical fatigue and mental excitement, that she sank into the first chair which presented itself, when the door closed; and covering her face with her hands, remained in a sort of stupor, till she was aroused by some person endeavoring to effect an entrance. Starting to her feet, she was only in time to see Arrison enter, bearing some food, which having deposited he was about to address her, when voices were heard calling him from without, on which he abruptly departed.

Those few minutes of rest had, however, partially refreshed Kate, and, alive now to her unprotected situation, she looked about her to see if there was any prospect of escape, and failing in this, if she could preserve her apartment from intrusion. Though she had eaten nothing since breakfast, the instinct of safety predominated over that of hunger, and therefore she left the coarse, and by no means tempting food, untasted for the present.

Her chamber was comparatively small, quite one half of it being taken up by the bed, which, to her surprise, was neatly arranged, as if female hands had been occupied about it. Opposite its foot, and where the light from the solitary window fell strongest, stood a dressing-table, made of common pine, but cushioned on top, and covered with spotless dimity, another proof that some person of her own sex, and one not without germs of refinement at least, occupied the apartment generally. This discovery cheered Kate's spirits wonderfully. Her naturally sanguine character whispered to her that, with a woman by, she could not be foully wronged.

But this bright coloring to her thoughts was not destined to be of long duration. An examination of the room satisfied her that escape was impossible. There were no outlets but the window and the door, and while the former was secured without, the latter led, as we have seen, into the common apartment. There was but one consolatory feature, which was that the door opened inwards, so that by barricading it, ingress would be effectually prevented, except with considerable difficulty.

The refugees, meantime, appeared to be preparing for a debauch. They had called for something to eat, as soon as they arrived, and Kate now thought that she heard a woman's step, moving about as if preparing a meal. She listened in vain, however, to detect a female voice amid the increasing din of jokes, laughter, snatches of coarse songs, and noisy conversation. The uproar, however, served her purpose, since in consequence of it, she was enabled to move the bedstead unheard, and barricade the door with that comparatively heavy article of furniture. After this, reflecting that she would need all her strength, she forced herself to partake of some of the food which had been brought by Arrison.

The clink of glasses, and the increasing boisterousness of the mirth, showed that the refugees, in the contiguous apartment, had now finished their meal and were beginning their debauch in earnest. It was impossible for Kate, in such close vicinity to the revellers, not to hear much that was said. Her attention was soon arrested by her own name being mentioned in connexion with that of her cousin: and listening with awakened curiosity, she gradually made out that she had been betrayed into the hands of her captors by Aylesford himself. She had not dreamed that such baseness and perfidy could exist in the world. With ashen lips she asked herself, "if this was the conduct of her own relative, who was a gentleman by birth and education, what had she to expect from a ruffian like Arrison?"

Breathless with interest she listened to what should come next. At last, after much had passed, but little of which, however, she could distinguish, in the uproar, though that little confirmed the connexion of Aylesford with the murderers, the conversation took a new turn, and now consisted principally of boasts of their exploits, on the part of the ruffians, alternated with jests at each other's courage. The narratives of their several butcheries, though loathsome to Kate as a woman, were yet terribly fascinating to her as a prisoner in the unrestrained power of such villains. On their own showing her captors had nothing of human mercy left in their hearts. The gratification of all unbridled passions was the acknowledged object of their lives; and they appeared to have been collected together from all parts of the state, lured to this comparatively remote quarter, by the prospect of increased booty under the leadership of Arrison.

"You should have seen how Steve Ball prayed and begged for his life," said one, with a mocking laugh, alluding to one of his exploits, "when we hung him at Bergen Point. He wouldn't believe we were in earnest for a good while; for he had brought provisions to sell under a promise of a safe return, but when the time was up, and he saw the tree and cord, he bellowed like a bull. If we'd only give him an hour, he cried, or a half, or a quarter. Ha! ha! 'twas better than a play. But we told him we'd no time to lose, and that if he wanted a parson, one of us was ready to serve him in that line. When we turned him off, I put a pistol into his hand, telling him it should never be said we sent him into the other world without arms."

There was a roar of general laughter, at the end of which Arrison said, "why didn't you tell him, that when he met the devil, he might cry to Old Nick to stand and deliver."

"Be Jabers," cried another, whose brogue betrayed his birth-place, "you'd have seen the rare sport, if you'd been with me, and some other of the boys, when we picked Major Dennis' feathers for him, down here jist, by Manasquan river. The Major wasn't at home, the more's the pity, for we'd have strung him up in no time, and done the job nately too; but the old woman was, and though one cried out to let the rebel go, the rest of us determined that she should hang, bad cess to her. And we took her own dirty old bed cord, and tied her up by the neck to a cedar; och! you should have seen dancing there, as merry as at a fair!"

"But I've heard she got off after all," interposed the lieutenant. "You were so busy filling your pockets you forgot her; the rope slipped, and she made off to the swamp with only a fright."

"It's the true word you say," answered the narrator, not a whit abashed. "But now we'll have the fun of hanging her agin, which couldn't have been if she hadn't got off."

Another burst of laughter followed this. Then one of the company said,

"What's become of Jack Stetson? as jolly a blade as ever lived. I thought, captain, I'd meet him here, sure. He went over to Maurice river with you, didn't he?"

"Yes," answered Arrison, "but he was in that affair with Riggins. If I'd been there it would have ended differently."

"With Riggins? I haven't heard of it."

"Why, Jack and a lot of others, without my knowledge, made up their minds to attack a shallop belonging to a whig named Riggins. Now I'd have let Riggins alone, if he had let' me alone in turn, for he's as big as an ox and as strong. But Jack thought he'd frighten the whigs by making a bold dash, so he attempts to board the shallop, as she was going down the river. Gad! though all of Riggins' men jumped overboard, or skulked into the cabin, except one man, the old pine-knot stood to it; fired twice, and then clubbing his gun, knocked our lads in the head as fast as they attempted to board. He settled poor Jack with one blow. They say too that he thinks more of having smashed his gun than of cracking so many skulls. Some of these days I'd like to draw a sight on him."

"Well, if Jack is gone," was the answer, "and here's to him, I'm glad to say that Parson Caldwell, the canting scoundrel, went to the devil before him." And he proceeded, amid shouts of approving laughter, to recapitulate a tragedy, with which the whole country was ringing, of which the Rev. James Caldwell, one of the best patriots, purest clergymen, and most upright men of his day, was the victim.

"He was always preachin' agin the King, and agin us in particular," said another. "He act'lly used his meetin' house for a hospital. He oughter ha' been shot when his wife was."

"Gad," said Arrison, his eye gleaming with tiger-like ferocity, "I'd liked to have been the fellow that finished her. She was as bad as him, if not worse. She was praying, wasn't she?" he added, laughing sardonically. "Praying with her young whelp, Smith, when she was shot by one of your fellows through a window."

"Yes," replied the outlaw appealed to, "and arterwards we threw her body into the road, where it lay all day in the sun, before we'd allow 'em to take it away. If a few more were sarved in the same fashion, it would be better for all of us, as well as for the King."

"They ought to have their throats cut, the whole spawn of them, women and children too," said another savagely, striking the table with his clenched fist. "There'll never be peace till there is."

"Nor booty for us," cried another, with a laugh.

With a shudder of horror, Kate reflected that the men who applauded these atrocities, had her now in their power; and that to their natural ferocity the stimulus of intoxication was rapidly being added. Involuntarily she began to grope about the room, hoping to find a knife, or other weapon of defence. "But you haven't told us," said the lieutenant, after awhile, addressing Arrison, "what you're going to do, to make up the plunder we were to get by taking this gal down the river. Will you put her to ransom?"

"Better than that," was the answer. "I intend to marry her."

"Marry her? But where's the parson?"

"I'm parson enough."

"Whew! that will be playing, high, low, Jack and the game. But you ought to double the pay," he continued, "if we help you to such an heiress."

"And such a devilish fine bit of woman flesh," put in another. "What an ankle she has! If the captain hadn't began the affair, I'd say we ought to toss up for her; and maybe we ought as it is."

"Hold your tongue," said Arrison, with a frown that knit his forbidding brows into dark, red knots. "She's mine, and there's an end of it. But I'll come down handsomely, lads" he added, seeing signs of discontent. "I was a fool ever to think of carrying her off for Aylesford. In my country, many's the rich heiress that's married in this way by gentlemen; and gad! as I too was born a gentleman, I mean to do the same."

"The captain's a broth of a boy," interrupted the Milesian. "I'll help to do the thing nately, and play praist if he says it."

"You'll find her a restive filly, though," laughed the lieutenant, brutally, "if she is often like she was in the boat."

"I know a way to tame her," was Arrison's reply. "I'm used to breaking in her sex; and have bitted and spurred worse fillies than she is. She'll be glad enough to marry me, before I've done with her." And he burst into a roar of drunken derision, in which his hearers joined.

The reader can but faintly imagine the feelings of our heroine as she listened to this conversation. More than once she started to her feet in wild alarm, as the uproar occasionally deepened, thinking for the moment, that the imbruted wretch was about to force his way into her chamber.

"Oh, God!" she cried, clasping her hands and raising her eyes above, "is there no help?"

CHAPTER XXXII
THE ATTACK

"It was a dread, yet spirit-stirring sight!
The billows foamed beneath a thousand oars." —Scott.

"Though few the numbers—there's the strife,
That neither spares, nor speaks for life." —Byron.

The British advanced in the most gallant manner to the attack of Major Gordon's position, each boat keeping its place as carefully in the line as soldiers on parade. In a few minutes the fleet turned the point of the river, and came dashing up to the landing, the water rolling under the bows and the oars keeping steady time. The sunshine, which now began to stream from the west, glanced from the muskets; was reflected from the bright buttons of the soldiers; and flashed back from the millions of drops showered from the ashen blades, till the river seemed alive with diamonds, sparkling as they fell.

Major Gordon, by this time, had arranged his men behind the half-finished breastwork, which, being within a short distance of the river, was intended to command the landing.

"Look to your priming carefully," were his last words. "Let nobody fire till I give the word; then every other man. When I give command again, let those who have reserved, fire. Everything depends on steadiness. Remember Bunker Hill."

He had scarcely finished passing along the line, repeating these orders, when the boats dashed up to the landing, their crews giving three cheers; and immediately the British, numbering several hundred, began to marshal themselves on dry ground, as coolly as if Major Gordon and his little force were a thousand miles away. Our hero saw that not a moment was to be lost. Springing upon the rampart, where he could be seen by all, he waved his sword and gave the command to fire.

Instantaneously a volley of musketry rattled on the air; a stream of fire ran down the line; and the rampart was covered with light blue smoke, which the breeze wafted slowly away. Other muskets followed in irregular succession, when the firing ceased.

At first the enemy had staggered: but the stern voice of the British commander, crying, "close up, close up," they moved steadily forward, with fixed bayonets, giving a gallant cheer. This was the moment for which Major Gordon had reserved his second fire. He knew that if the enemy reached the rampart, there would be but little prospect of a successful defence.

Again, therefore, leaping up on the breastwork, he waived his sword and shouted to fire.

But no volley, as he had expected, answered his command. Only a few dropping shots were heard. His men, in the ardor common to raw troops, had been unable to retain their fire before, and being flurried by the novelty of their position had scarcely taken aim at all. Fifty good muskets, in fact, would have done more execution than the hundreds which had been discharged ineffectually, leaving scarcely a score serviceable now.

The British discovered immediately the advantage which they possessed. Their leader, springing in front, raised his blade, and pointing to the Americans, called on his men, in words distinctly heard behind the breastwork, to "drive the rebels to the woods."

At the same instant a heavy launch, which, armed with a swivel, had pulled around on the flank of the fortification, began to open a galling fire on the defenders.

"Stand to your post," shouted Major Gordon, observing that some of his men began to waver under this unexpected assault. "Load and fire as quick as you can. Beat them back with the butts of your muskets. Liberty or death!"

The stirring cry; the gallantry with which our hero exposed himself; and the firmness which a few exhibited, headed by Uncle Lawrence and Mullen, stayed the rout for awhile. The men hurriedly loaded and fired, each one for himself. But in the excitement of their novel position in presence of an enemy for the first time, they generally wasted their powder; and in fact it was no uncommon thing for many a gun to be discharged before the ball had been placed in it, while a few actually fired off their ramrods.

Major Gordon saw all this with feelings it is impossible to describe. As long, however, as there was the remotest prospect of success, he omitted no effort to repulse the foe. He rushed to and fro along the line, encouraging, ordering, and appealing; now snatching a musket from a hesitating defender and discharging it himself; and now heading a hand to hand struggle, at an opening in the defences, where the British were endeavoring to enter.

It was here that the crisis of the conflict took place. In less time than we have taken to describe it, the enemy had reached the foot of the ramparts, when the cry became general that all was over, and most of the militiamen sought safety in flight. Up to this point they had fought courageously, even if with comparative inefficiency, but when they saw the glittering bayonets, levelled in a serried line directly under them, they recoiled in dismay. Not once in a hundred times, indeed, can raw troops stand a bayonet charge. It is scarcely an imputation on those undisciplined defenders of the Neck, that, finding themselves without this weapon, they abandoned the breastwork, leaving the position to its fate.

Not such, however, was the conduct of Major Gordon and the few heroic followers, who, either attached to him personally or gifted with more than ordinary courage, rallied to the defence of the spot we have described. Here, for the space of nearly thirty feet, the ramparts were unfinished: and assailants and defenders consequently met on equal terms. At the near approach of the enemy, the Major had flown to this spot, aware of its weakness: and hither also had followed Uncle Lawrence, Mullen, Charley Newell, and about a score of others, equally indomitable in courage.

"Never give up the gate," cried Major Gordon, manfully opposing himself to the glittering line of bayonets. "Stand fast about me. Liberty or death!"

"Liberty or death!" shouted Uncle Lawrence, swinging in the air his heavy musket, which he had taken by the muzzle, and placing himself at the side of our hero.

"Liberty or death!" echoed the brave Mullen, holding his loaded piece ready, with his finger on the trigger, and only waiting for a suitable foe to fire.

"Liberty or death!" repeated Charley Newell, as he pressed forward to the side of the latter; and "Liberty or death!" cried every man of that devoted band, rushing to this new Thermopylae.

It was a sight that might well make the bravest pause, that little company of heroes, thus declaring their readiness to make a rampart with their bodies. Foremost of all stood Major Gordon, conspicuous in his blue and buff uniform. His brow was knit; his eyes flashed; his mouth was rigid with indomitable resolution. The next most striking figure was that of Uncle Lawrence, who, having lost his hat in the melee, now stood with his bare locks streaming in the wind; while his eye blazed with all the fire of youth, and the usual wintry russet of his cheek was flushed to vivid crimson.

At the aspect of this little band, the serried line of bayonets came to a halt, and for a moment the two parties stood breathlessly regarding each other. The British, up to this crisis, confident of an easy victory, recoiled at the expression in the faces and attitudes of the patriots before them, as a party of hunters may be supposed to start back, when, having followed the lion's cubs to their den, they suddenly hear the growl of the parent lioness, and discover her eyes gleaming at them from the entrance.

It was only for a moment, however, that they hesitated. An officer, who was but a few paces distant, rushed to the spot, exclaiming that the Americans were in full flight everywhere else, and that it needed only a bold push to carry the works.

"Forward, forward," he cried, throwing himself into the very brunt of the conflict. "Come on, the day's our own."

But, at that instant, and before Major Gordon could measure swords with him, Mullen discharged his gun, and the chivalric officer tumbled headlong at the very feet of our hero. His example, however, had not been lost upon his men; and the sight of his fallen body stimulated them to madness. With a wild, angry cry, they dashed forwards, bearing everything before them for an instant.

"Break in on their line," shouted Uncle Lawrence, as with a blow of his tremendous gun, he struck down the bayonet of the soldier opposed to him. "Liberty or death!" And with the words, he grasped his opponent in mortal struggle.

"Close in, close in," cried Major Gordon, availing himself of the disorder caused by Uncle Lawrence's blow, to grapple with a soldier likewise. "Liberty or death!"

In an instant all was confusion. Nearly everywhere the patriots succeeded in breaking the steel rampart before them, and in engaging hand to hand with the enemy, though it was often at the cost of the lives of those who attempted it. Foe soon became intermixed with friend. The cries of "Liberty or death" were mingled with those of "God save the King." The shouts of the living rose to heaven simultaneously with the groans of the wounded and the expiring gasp of the dying. Such was the fury of the fight, that the combatants disappeared on either side like grass before the scythe. Yet Uncle Lawrence and our hero still remained unhurt, as if bearing charmed lives, and still led the terrible strife. Each had long since overcome his first antagonist, and was striking right and left in aid of others of the defenders unequally matched or overpowered by numbers. Wherever the former rushed, with his uplifted musket, it seemed as if a new Artimesius, with his flail, had come; for his opponents went down before him like oxen in the slaughterer's stall. His voice was faint with shouting the war-cry of his little band, "Liberty or death!" but his arms appeared as nervous as ever, and his blows fell with crushing rapidity and force.

But the defenders were now reduced to a dozen men, and what could that number effect against hundreds? Already the British had cleared the works everywhere else, and now assailing Major Gordon and his party, in flank, rear and front at once, soon left no hope of retreat, if retreat had been even now the aim of our hero. But such was not his purpose. Unappalled by the overpowering odds, he continued battling stoutly, with Uncle Lawrence at his side, until a bayonet thrust pinned him to the earth, and the assailants rushed in over his body.

CHAPTER XXXIII
THE SACK OF CHESTNUT NECK

"Alas! poor country,
Almost afraid to know thyself." —*Shakespeare.*

"But things like that, you know, must be
After a famous victory." —*Southey.*

The British, being thus masters of the field, proceeded to their work of destruction. Their wounded had first to be removed indeed, and their dead buried; but as there were few of the former and still fewer of the latter—the chief defence having been by Major Gordon's band—little time was occupied in this duty.

The sun was still an hour high, therefore, when the first torch was applied to the store-houses and dwellings. Very soon the whole number were in flames, with all their valuable contents. The combustible character of the edifices, for they were built altogether of wood, and the inflammable materials collected within the warehouses, rendered the heat rapidly so intense that the troops were compelled to withdraw to some distance, where they stood for a while watching the scene of ruin, giving an occasional hurrah whenever a roof fell in. No other persons were in sight, except a few women who watched, afar off, from the edge of the wood, the destruction of their humble houses, and the total loss of their scanty, but hard-earned household goods.

There had been comparatively little breeze when the first torch was applied; but before long the wind was roaring around the burning edifices, in almost a gale. Swiftly the various store-houses succumbed to the conflagration. One, which had been overlooked when the others were fired, and to which no torch had been applied, resisted for some time the contagion, standing up black and weather-beaten in the centre of the burning circle, like some dark rock at sea amid the angry surges. The shingled roof could be seen smoking for a long while, though without any sign of fire within; but at last it flashed all at once into flames, as when a train is touched; and, quick as thought, the whole was in a blaze. Directly after, forked tongues of fire shot out from under the eaves, and though they were gone in a moment, they reappeared almost instantaneously. Next, the fire showed itself at the windows, and then between the clap-boards; until finally it burst out from the doorway, and curling upwards, covered the whole edifice to the very top.

The conflagration had now swept over nearly the entire settlement, sparing only a few dwellings, which either stood too far off to be reached by the fire, or were too inconsiderable to call down the vengeance of the invaders. Thick masses of pitchy-black smoke rose in puffs, and collecting overhead, afforded a canopy, impervious to the sunshine, against which the lurid reflection from below shone with a dull red glare. The leaves of the chestnuts, close by, were blackened and shrivelled up by the heat; and at one time it seemed as if the old trees would actually burst into a blaze. The spectacle had an almost human interest added to it, by a few tamed pigeons, who, having been harbored in the loft of the last store-house, were now seen flying wildly to and fro, refusing to leave the vicinity of their old home, circling around and around, crossing and re-crossing, until they dropped one by one into the conflagration. It was pitiful, amid the cheers of the British and the deep roar of the flames, to hear occasionally the flapping of their wings as they ventured near to a spectator, only however to fly immediately from their human enemy back to their burning homes.

To increase the terror of the scene, the dismantled ships, which had been fired soon after the warehouses, speedily began to irradiate the river. The flames mastered the vessels even more rapidly than they had the buildings. The fire, once fairly started, shot up the masts, till it soared above the round-top, licking up whatever bits of rigging had been left, and rising, like the pointed spire of a Gothic cathedral, needle-like into the sky. A thousand tongues of fire, hissing and flashing, came and went; and then, darting into light, again hissed and flashed once more for a moment or two, in as many different points; after which an unbroken sheet of flame wrapped the entire vessels above the bulwarks from sight. Continually bits of fire, whirling off from one ship, alighted on another; while millions of sparks rose in showers and floated to leeward, in startling relief against the deep sable canopy, which now covered the sky above both sea and land. Up the river, at a cable's length from the burning fleet, the smoke had settled down upon the stream like a fog, obscuring the sun, and rendering the outlines of sky and water undistinguishable. Occasionally fragments of wood, swept away by the tide, were seen drifting into the gloom, like meteors of unknown and terrible aspect floating through the darkness of space.

By nightfall most of the warehouses were reduced to heaps of smouldering ruins, glowing all over with fiery chinks as lava when it is half cooled. Every few moments, however, one of these heaps would belch upward a huge column of bituminous-looking smoke, after which flames would leap out at the spot and the conflagration renew itself there for a while. The air was heavy, almost choking, and impregnated with a pungent, stifling odour indescribable.

The hulls of the vessels, however, continued to burn brightly, though the masts and rigging, where such had been left standing, had long since disappeared in charred fragments that strewed the decks or dropped sullenly into the stream. The wind, no longer nourished by the powerful conflagration, which compels currents of air to its centre as into the mouth of a furnace, had now almost entirely died away. What little was left, drew up the stream; and in that direction, as we have seen, the smoke lay packed close on the water, and reaching across the river, excluded from sight both shores towards the west. But the northern bank, opposite the Neck, was still dimly visible through the twilight; while, down the river, the prospect was comparatively clear. It had a strange and weird effect to see the stars, that shone so clear and lustrous on the eastern horizon, grow dim and ghostly through the smoke overhead, and then gradually vanish in the west, devoured by the pitchy darkness that lay in wait there like a second chaos.

The British, though they had accomplished their purpose, showed no disposition however to retire. The few Americans, who hovered in the neighboring woods, and stole occasionally to the edge of the fields to make observations, noticed that picquets were posted as if it was the intention to remain for the night. The two or three houses, which had been spared in the otherwise general conflagration, were hastily prepared for the accommodation of the principal royal officers; the cattle which had been brought in for the use of the Americans, and had become part of the spoils of victory, were slaughtered for the conquerors; and a succession of camp fires, lighted to cook the food of the soldiers, soon twinkled, like a continuous chain of beacons, along the whole extent of the British line. As the evening wore on, sounds of merriment rose from the encampment, and floated dimly to the woods where the ejected women and children cowered in darkness and terror. Snatches of lewd songs; ballads coarsely ridiculing the Americans; oaths of blasphemous exultation over their fallen foes; shouts of drunken laughter; boasts of how many rebels had been killed that day; all these, and other noises as horrible, were wafted to the ears of the weeping mothers, who clasped their houseless babes as they crouched on the cold earth. Or the ribald songs and rejoicings were heard, with half smothered oaths, by the fathers who were forced to look on all this, yet were impotent to redress it.

Towards midnight, however, the reveling in the British bivouac ceased. The camp-fires died down; the songs were hushed; the merriment gave way to sleep; and the low hum, which by day always attends any large body of men, was distinguishable no longer. The royal force lay in profound repose. The conflagration had exhausted itself long before, even among the shipping, only a few skeleton-like hulls burning redly, here and there, through the now ashen-gray smoke. A deep silence brooded over the scene, broken only by the breeze soughing gently through the trees, the tide lapping against the shore as it came lazily in, or the wail of a solitary whip-poor-will, which, slowly sailing in the obscure distance, seemed to be the spirit of some slaughtered patriot come back to bewail his ravaged life, the dishonor to his country's flag, and the fresh perils which the morrow would probably bring forth.

But, notwithstanding this stillness, it was evident that the British slept on their arms, and that, at the slightest intimation of an attack, they would be up in a moment and ready for the foe. The dark forms of the sentries could be seen constantly going the rounds, and the warning cry of "all's well" periodically passed around the bivouac.

CHAPTER XXXIV
THE REPULSE

"Hear me, for I will speak;
Must I give way?" —Shakespeare.

"By his closed eye unheeded and unfelt,
While sets that sun, and dews of ev'ning melt." —Byron.

The story-teller is like the weaver of an elaborate pattern in tapestry. To a spectator he seems continually to be dropping threads without necessity, and as often taking up new ones which are uncalled for; but it must be remembered that he has the completed picture before him, and that he knows best what is necessary to do.

Aylesford, whom we last saw parting with Kate, reached the lower part of the river in safety, about noon; and proceeded immediately to procure the assistants, necessary to carry out his plot against Kate. He was not able, indeed, to gain the British camp, and had therefore, to hire a boat's crew at random. But there were men of idle habits and royalist sympathies to be found, all through the war of independence, in every district of New Jersey, but particularly in those bordering on the sea-coast, where many circumstances contributed to render patriotism at a discount and open the field for venal services to either side. Aylesford, by his course of life, had become cognizant of one of these persons, to whom he now applied. This man was acquainted with others; and so, after only a few hours' delay, he was enabled to set out to meet Arrison.

But the best laid plans of villains, as Burns says of mice and men, "aft gang agee." We have seen how Arrison's scheme to deliver Kate, by collusion, into the hands of Aylesford, had miscarried: and this failure necessarily involved the disappointment of the plans of Aylesford also. The boat of the latter was actually in sight of the refugees, when Arrison turned and fled up the river, though no one of the outlaws, nor even Kate, saw it, all having their attention concentrated on the patriots on shore, and subsequently on the pursuing craft. But Aylesford, seeing his prey ravished from him almost in the moment of seizing it, became nearly beside himself with rage. He had, in fact, arrived at the bend of the river below the settlement, quite half an hour previous, when, observing to his surprise that the inhabitants were keeping watch, he had laid by, under the bank, intending to wait for Arrison. He did this, because the latter would have to pass the armed party on shore but once, whereas if he should keep on his way, the risk would be run in both going and returning. He never doubted, meantime, that Arrison would push on at any cost.

When, therefore, he saw the refugees face about, he lost, as we have said, all control of himself. Starting up, he exclaimed —

"Cast off, board, give way. I'll double your reward if we catch them."

The men obeyed, though not without some signs of reluctance, until they had gained a position nearly opposite to the settlement. This was a little later in point of time than when the patriots had put off in pursuit of the refugees. During the whole of this period, Aylesford, who officiated as coxswain, had not ceased to stimulate his men to row faster, alternating promises of reward and urgent appeals, with passionate ejaculations against the poltroonery and treachery of Arrison.

"Pull, pull with a will," he cried. "We'll catch them yet, huzza! The double-dyed traitor. Yes!" he added, between his teeth, "he has intended it all along. I see it now, dupe that I am. Curses on my mad folly in trusting him! Why do you stop?"

This last sentence was spoken aloud and angrily, for the men suddenly ceased rowing.

But the reason was apparent as soon as he looked ashore. The sentinel at the settlement had presented his musket, and now followed it up by crying,

"Boat ahoy!"

The men looked at each other and then at Aylesford.

"Never mind him. Pull away," cried the latter.

The report of the musket was heard, and the ball whistled close past; while at the same time some of the patriots ran to the field-piece. Instantly, as if by one impulse, Aylesford's crew pulled their boat around and began to urge her down the stream.

At this, Aylesford, his whole countenance distorted with rage, reached forward and laid his hand on the stroke oar.

"How dare you?" he cried, his face white with rage.

The man, who pulled the oar, was far more powerful than his employer, and he wrenched the blade from Aylesford almost immediately, saying sternly,

"None of that, if you don't want to be pitched overboard. We're not going to get a skin full of shot in us, or be sent to the devil by grape, just to please you."

Even through his passion, Aylesford had the sense to see that he could do nothing against the majority by compulsion, but that his only hope was in appealing to the selfish interests of the men.

"I'll give each of you twenty guineas, twenty guineas in gold," he said, eagerly, "if you'll keep on and overtake the boat."

But, by this time, the field-piece on shore was ready to fire. The match was being whirled around to keep it burning, while a patriot sighted the gun for the last time; and the men saw this with a terror against which even the large bribe could not prevail.

"We've come too far already," said the spokesman. "Steer the boat while we pull, or I'll blow your brains out. What good would your guineas be to men who wouldn't live to get them?"

At these words, the four oarsmen gave way lustily, as men only row when the race is for life or death.

"God! there it comes," suddenly cried the stroke-oarsman, ducking his head involuntarily.

At the moment, a jet of flame shot out from the cannon, followed by a puff of dense, whitish smoke. Instantaneously a hurtling noise was heard through the air, the water was ploughed up astern of the boat, and Aylesford, with a sharp groan, suddenly dropped the tiller, and tumbled headlong forward into the stern sheets.

"He's hit," cried the oarsman, and without looking around, he continued, "is anybody else hurt?" For the others had ceased rowing.

No one answered. All the rest had fortunately escaped.

"Then pull like devils," cried the spokesman, when he saw this. "If they get another chance they'll sink us. We must put the bend of the river between us and them, before we even stop to see how much he is hurt. Once in the next reach and we'll be safe." And, suiting the action to the word, he pulled till his strong blade bent like a whip-stalk.

The remainder of the crew made corresponding exertions, so that in a few minutes the boat shot around the turn, interposing a wooded point between it and the settlement. The men now rested on their oars, when two of them, the spokesman being one, proceeded to examine into the condition of their fallen employer.

He was not dead, as they had begun to believe from his silence and his not even stirring, but badly wounded in the side by a slug, the gun having been apparently loaded with that description of missiles. On being moved, he opened his eyes with a groan, stared vacantly around, and then closed them in a swoon.

"He's booked for Davy Jones' locker," said the spokesman, "unless we can get a doctor for him soon; booked for it whether or no. Lay him down easy, Bill; put his head here—that's all we can do for him."

With these words they resumed their oars, and pulling steadily down the river with a long, regular, man-of-war's stroke, soon left the vicinity of the settlement behind them. The men, thus unexpectedly burdened with a wounded employer, were as yet uncertain where to find a physician soonest in the disturbed state of the region, and were debating it among themselves, when suddenly the noise of firing, as of volleys of musketry, was heard in the distance ahead.

"The King's men hare attacked the Neck," cried the man who had been the principal speaker all day. "Hark! there it is again."

There was no mistaking the sounds of battle, which now grew momentarily stormier, filling the air and booming along the water. As the boat struggled onward against the tide, the noise of the strife continued to stimulate the rowers, who, though comparatively near, yet made such slow headway as to be uncertain, for what seemed an age, which way the victory would incline. At last the curve in the river disclosed to sight the group of tall chestnuts, and immediately afterwards the British flag floating over the works.

Aylesford had now recovered from his swoon, and was sensible of what was going on, though as yet he had not spoken.

"We'd better land him there," said the spokesman. "There's always plenty of doctors with his Majesty's troops. Besides, they'll make us come to, any how."

"Yes! land me at once," said Aylesford, feebly. "I'll see that you're protected."

Accordingly the man directed the boat to the landing, where they disembarked just as the evening was closing in.

CHAPTER XXXV
THE DEATH-BED

"Ah, what a sign it is of evil life,
When death's approach is seen so terrible." —Shakespeare.

"Black it stood as night,
Fierce as ten furies." —Milton.

"To die, I own
Is a dread passage." —Thomson

It was several hours later in the evening. In a small room, in one of the dwellings which the conflagration at the Neck had spared, Aylesford lay extended on a bed, his life ebbing fast away.

On landing, he had desired to see some of the principal officers, to whom he had disclosed the name of his family, which he found not unknown; and having besought that the men who had accompanied him should not be considered prisoners, desired next the services of a surgeon as soon as one could be spared. Fallen, as he was, in many particulars, his sense of honor made him thus provide for the safety of his companions before looking after his wound.

The surgeon attended immediately, accompanied by the leader of the expedition, for the latter, aware of the vast estates of the Aylesfords, in the colonies, as well as of their noble connexions in England, and hearing that the male representative of the name had been brought in wounded, naturally concluded that the hurt was received while he was hastening to join the royal standard. On discovering the precarious condition of his guest, this officer directed that the utmost attention should be paid to him, and left with reluctance to attend to the urgent calls of his command.

The surgeon was not long in discovering that the wound of his patient was mortal; that human skill could even do but little to prolong life; and that all which was left for him was to alleviate the sufferings of the dying man. Aylesford read his doom in the countenance of the physician. He had, however, suspected it from the first. As we have seen, on former occasions, he was not deficient in courage, and he asked in a voice quite calm if his suspicions were not correct.

"Don't be afraid to speak out, Doctor," he said, resolutely, though in a feeble voice. "It's false kindness to conceal the truth, when a man's within an hour of death."

"You have been bred a gentleman," answered the practitioner, replying in a spirit more common then, when caste was thought to make one man superior to another, than now, "and can therefore summon courage to face anything, I suppose. I am sorry I cannot hold out hope. If you have any arrangements to make, it would be wise to lose no time. Can I be of service to you otherwise than professionally?"

Aylesford turned uneasily in his bed, and did not reply for a moment. At last he spoke.

"No, thank you, Doctor. I have no affairs to settle, such as you mean."

He seemed, however, as if there was something on his mind, so that the surgeon, lingering as he arranged his instruments, was induced to speak again.

"Perhaps you would like to see a parson," he said. "Fortunately we have a chaplain with us."

"It is not that," answered Aylesford. "But you may send him, nevertheless." He spoke, all this while, with difficulty. Then, as the surgeon went out, he murmured to himself, turning uneasily again, "Oh! Kate, Kate, what have I brought on you!"

We have failed to convey a true idea of Aylesford, if the reader considers him a remorseless villain. He was, indeed, deeply stained with vices, but they were mostly those, which, while violating the moral code quite as much as more brutal ones, yet do not degrade the entire nature. He was a spendthrift, a gambler, licentious, passionate and haughty. He was even capable of treachery, as we have seen, under the double temptation of interest and love. But this last crime had been the first of its kind he had ever been engaged in; his conscience was not yet seared to such atrocities; and now, when he found death approaching, the idea that Kate was in the hands of Arrison, and that she had been brought there by his own act, woke a thousand serpent-stings of remorse at his heart.

He lay there, but could not rest. He tossed from side to side, in spite of the entreaties of his attendant, a surgeon's assistant, who declared that he was shortening his life. Deep groans continually broke from him, not because of pain, but in consequence, as the attendant saw, of mental anguish. The youth hoped that when the clergyman came, his patient would obtain peace of mind; but neither the presence of the chaplain, nor the prayers he read, nor the soothing words he addressed to the invalid, had any effect in composing Aylesford.

It was at this point of time that the present chapter opens. The clergyman had risen from his knees, and was sitting at the head of the bed; the surgeon's assistant stood looking down on the invalid with folded arms; and three or four other persons, who had crowded into the room in the confusion, gazed with serious, awe-struck faces, now on the dying man, and now on his medical and spiritual advisers. A single tallow candle, placed on a little old-fashioned stand, on which were also several phials, threw a dim and yellow light on the disturbed countenance among the pillows and on the dark dress of the chaplain, leaving the remainder of the room in deep shadow, out of which the anxious, earnest faces of the spectators looked forth like the dark heads in old and time-stained pictures.

For sometime there was silence in the apartment. The invalid, at a pause in the clergyman's exhortations, had suddenly turned his back on the speaker, with a deep groan that seemed wrung from his inmost heart; and now appeared to be dozing. The priest knew not what to do. He was a sincerely good man, far different from many among chaplains of that day, but his services, he saw, had produced no impression, and he was not sure that they were not positively rejected. Still he was willing to remain, in hopes that a better frame of mind might arise in the patient; but for this he thought it best to wait in silence.

"Will he wake again?" said he, at last, rising and whispering to the assistant. "This looks like the stupor of death."

Perhaps it was the rustling of the silk canonicals which roused the invalid, perhaps his doze had come to an end of itself; but at this Aylesford turned quickly around, and half raising himself on his arm, fixed his eyes on the priest. A wild gleam shot from his haggard eyes.

"You can do me no good," he said, in a hollow voice, "but, but," he struggled for words, "stay by me to the last. I thank you."

"I know, my son," mildly answered the clergyman, "that I can do you no good; but there is one who can; and to Him I exhort you to turn your eyes."

But the sick man, shaking his head, interrupted the minister of heaven.

"It is too late, too late," he said, "even if your religion is true." The venerable man lifted his hands in horror, and raised his eyes in a mute petition above. "But enough of this," continued Aylesford. "I don't wish to hurt your feelings, sir; you mean well, and I thank you: but that is a subject on which we shall never agree, and my time is too precious to waste."

Aylesford was, like most fashionable profligates of that day, an atheist at heart. It was an age, when the French Encyclopaediasts had exhausted every resource of sophistry and satire to shake the belief in a divine revelation; when young men thought it smart to laugh at the Bible, as a collection of old legends only fit for women; and when Voltaire, Helvetius, D'Alembert, and other mere analytical thinkers were ignorantly ranked, by men of little learning and less wisdom, above the great synthetical minds who have, throughout the generations, held fast to Christianity, not only as a revelation historically established on irrefragable grounds of proof, but as a religion whose divinity is proved, apart from this, by its wonderful adaptation to all the wants of the human soul, to its sorrows as well as to its joys, and especially to its longings after immortality. So firmly established was Aylesford's atheism, that it left him with few or no doubts, even in this dread hour. Perhaps—for who can tell?—men may commit the unpardonable sin, so awfully denounced in Scripture, by obdurate unbelief: and it is certain that this thought flashed across the mind of the clergyman, who put up a mental petition that it might not be so in this instance.

"A little while longer, O Lord, forbear," he prayed. "Spare the barren fig-tree yet a space."

"It's another thing I want to speak about," said Aylesford, after a pause for breath. "I had resolved to die without revealing it; but I feel as if it must out. If there's a hell at all," he suddenly added, while he glared, almost like a wild beast, at the clergyman, while he struck his breast with his clenched hand, "it's here now, here at my heart, where it's been gnawing, gnawing—"

"My son, oh! my son," cried the white-haired clergyman, deeply impressed, and with tears in his eyes, making a last effort to benefit the dying man, "there's a worm that never dies, that gnaws forever."

"Away with your idle tales," fiercely interrupted Aylesford, flinging himself away from the chaplain. But immediately he turned again. "I can't waste time, sir," he resumed, "and maybe by speaking, I may avert foul wrong. But no! no! that is impossible," he almost shrieked, as he spoke these words, gazing hopelessly from the assistant to the minister, like one drowning out at sea may be supposed to turn his frantic eyes towards the unattainable shore.

"She is past rescue."

"She?" said the clergyman. "My son," he added solemnly, "if, as your words imply, there is a wrong to be remedied, speak out without delay. Next to repentance comes reparation, and it may be," he added, as if speaking to himself, "that God, in His infinite mercy, will consider one to include both."

Aylesford looked eagerly into the chaplain's face, and, without further parley, proceeded to narrate, though in broken sentences and with rapidly failing words, his scheme to carry off his cousin, its failure, and the great probability there was that she was now in the power of a licentious, brutal, and reckless outlaw.

The narrative, indeed, was not consecutive. Whether the mind of the dying man began to wander, or whether remorse made his thoughts incoherent, he was not able to give an entirely connected story; but from his bitter denunciations of Arrison, his curses on his own folly for being duped, and his apostrophes to Kate, his hearers had no difficulty in arriving at a tolerably correct idea of our heroine's peril.

"Alas!" said the clergyman, when Aylesford had concluded, "this is a wrong done which is beyond remedy, I fear."

But Aylesford, at this, sprang up in bed.

"I tell you it is not beyond remedy," he cried, shaking his damp hair like an angry lion rousing in his lair; and while his eyes gleamed with the fires of partial delirium, he continued, almost with a howl, "I'll go myself to her rescue. Don't you hear her reproaching me? Unhand me, I say." And he struggled to get out of bed.

"We will send word to the enemy's camp through a flag, that they may do all that can be done," said the clergyman soothingly, as he and the assistant held down the frenzied man. "There, my son, lie back on your pillow again. There is no one calling you, that you need glare into that dark corner. God help you!"

Gradually the delusion passed from the mind of the invalid. His eye assumed its natural expression. He looked inquiringly around, like one awaking from a dream, and with an attempt at a wan smile, suffered himself to be placed in bed again.

"Thank you," he said feebly, as the clergyman stooped and gently wiped the big drops from his hair. "I've been talking wildly, I fear. The fever's in my head. But did not some one," and he glanced around, "say that they'd send pursuers out after her?"

"I said I would send word to the enemy's camp," answered the chaplain; and looking around the room, he singled out an individual who had been a spectator hitherto. "You have heard what has been said," he continued. "Will you undertake to see that this is done?"

The person addressed nodded his head, and departed immediately, Aylesford watching his retreating figure eagerly till it disappeared through the doorway, when he closed his eyes with a deep sigh, and remained motionless and silent so long afterwards that the clergyman began to think life had departed with that profound expiration.

He, therefore, whispered to the assistant.

"Does he still breathe?"

"Yes!" was the reply, after the speaker had leaned over the invalid for a moment. "He dozes again. That burst of emotion exhausted him terribly, however, and it may be that he'll never come to again."

The clergyman made no answer, but clasping his hands, appeared engaged in silent prayer.

In about ten minutes the dying man stirred again. His eyes were still closed, but he murmured incoherently. At first his words were low and disconnected, but gradually he spoke louder; and finally the listeners distinguished parts of sentences. But whether he was referring to the tragedy he had just detailed, or to some other, or whether what he said was purely the effect of delirium, the hearers could not ascertain.

"The pitiless villain," were his words. "No mercy, no mercy. Oh! that I had run him through when he proposed it. I broke her heart. Mary! Mary! blessed saint," he exclaimed piteously, "don't look at me so reproachfully."

"He thinks she is already dead," whispered the clergyman to the assistant.

"Or perhaps there is still another," was the low reply.

Tossing from side to side on the bed, working his fingers on the counterpane, every lineament of his face betraying the terrible mental agonies he was undergoing, Aylesford lay, a picture of remorse which had come too late. As his broken ejaculations went on it became evident that another person, as the surgeon had hinted, now mingled in his thoughts with Miss Aylesford.

"Forgive me, Mary, forgive me," he cried, clasping his hands, "I have indeed deserted our child; but if I had known—if I had—"

Here his words sunk into indistinct babblings, all that could be distinguished being the single phrase, "they call her his niece, you know."

He lay still for nearly a minute. Suddenly he sprang up again, glaring wildly at the opposite part of the bed.

"Take him away," he shrieked, in a voice that made the hair of his hearers stand on end with horror, and was heard far away out across the silence of the night; "his fingers almost touch me."

He clung to the clergyman, as a child, when woke from a dream in which it has seen horrible shapes, clings to its mother; his eyeballs starting from their sockets, his features convulsed with agony, and the perspiration exuding, like huge rain drops, over his clammy forehead.

It was a scene, which those who were present, could never shake off. The terrified countenance of the dying man, the despairing clutch with which he held on to the chaplain, and the fixed, stony gaze of horror which he fastened, as if on some object right across the bed, and almost within reach; the whole rendered, for an instant, visible with more than ordinary distinctness, as a burning deck of one of the ships that was consuming, fell in, shooting a quick, intense glare into the room.

"Oh! my God," he cried, "they come; there is a hell."

The piercing tone, almost amounting to a shriek; the awful look; the gesture of horrible fear with which he shrank closer yet to the clergyman; these no pen can adequately paint.

But in a moment, a convulsion passed over him; a deep breath was heard, which was nearly stertorous; and he fell back into the chaplain's arms, stone dead.

CHAPTER XXXVI
THE ESCAPE

This night methinks is but the daylight sick,
It looks a little paler; 'tis a day,
Such as the day is when the sun is hid. —Shakespeare.

The whole air whitens with a boundless tide,
Of silver radiance, trembling round the world. —Thomson.

We must now return to Kate, whom we left a prisoner with the outlaws, and momentarily in dread that she would be compelled to sacrifice life in order to avert dishonor.

The debauch of the refugees at last came to an end. Not being a witness of the scene, Kate could judge as to the manner of its termination, only from the laugh of derision with which it was said successively that another "was under the table." Gradually the voices of the speakers became so thick as to be undistinguishable; the revelers apparently grew fewer and fewer, and finally a heavy fall was heard, as of the last boon companion, followed by silence.

For a long while Kate listened, dreading lest she should hear some one stir, for she dared not hope that sleep had overpowered the whole gang. But five minutes passed without any one moving, then ten, and then finally a half an hour. When this latter period had elapsed she began to breathe freely again. The thought of escape flashed upon her. She reasoned that if she could pass the sleepers undetected, and gain the forest, she might find some place of refuge, perhaps, before the outlaws would awake. Ignorant as she was of the exact locality of the hut, she yet had a general idea of the direction in which the Forks lay, and she determined to make the attempt to reach that post.

But she resolved not to essay escape as yet. The night without was pitch dark, so that it would have been impossible to find her way through the woods; and as she knew the moon would rise in about an hour, she determined to wait for that event; and accordingly threw herself on the bed to watch for the propitious time.

Fatigued by physical exhaustion as well as by mental excitement, however, she unwittingly fell asleep, and when at last she opened her eyes, the moon was shining full in at the window, having attained a considerable elevation above the horizon. For a moment she did not recollect where she was. She started up, at first, with a look of bewilderment, which changed to one of affright, however, and then of despair, as the past came up again to her memory.

"What precious hours I have lost," she mentally exclaimed. "Perhaps now it is too late. Oh! how could I sleep!" And she wrung her hands.

But directly she recovered the energy natural to her. In truth, her slumbers had vastly recruited her strength and spirits; and of this she began soon to be sensible. She sprang to her feel, saying to herself with decision,

"But why do I waste precious moments? There may yet be hope—they seem to sleep as soundly as ever—at the most I can but fail."

As she pronounced these words, she began, though with hands trembling with eagerness, to move the bedstead from the door sufficiently to allow egress. With what intense anxiety she listened, during this proceeding, lest the fabric should, by creaking, awaken the refugees! Even if one should be aroused it would be fatal to her; and the slightest noise might produce this result. She was almost breathless with suspense, until the bedstead had been removed enough to allow her to pass. But when this was effected, her heart was fluttering so wildly, that she had to pause an instant, pressing her hand on it to still its throbbings, for while it palpitated to such a degree she was too weak to proceed.

She now ventured to lift the latch, which at first resisted her efforts, and which, when at last it yielded, gave forth a sudden, sharp click, that, for a moment, made her fear it had awakened one or more of the outlaws. She waited, therefore, to assure herself that no one was stirring, before she ventured to draw the door towards her. In the unnaturally excited state of her nerves, the almost imperceptible sound of the hinges smote on her ear with alarming distinctness, so that she felt confident that now at least some one of the outlaws must awake. In fact a burly ruffian, in whom, to her horror, she recognized Arrison, and who lay directly across the doorway, not a foot from her, actually stirred, muttering incoherently, as if about to arouse from sleep; and at this sight Kate, brave as she was, felt all her courage and strength desert her, and was compelled to lean against the wall, in order to support herself from falling.

The ruffian, however, proved to have been only dreaming. After mumbling a few broken sentences, and tossing his arm over his head, as if to relieve it by a change of posture, he sunk into slumber again. Never was sound sweeter to Kate's ears than the loud, almost stertorous breathing of the inebriated sleeper. Reassured of this, the violent beating of her heart ceased, and she recovered strength to renew her attempt at escape.

The door of the outer apartment was fortunately open, and the moonlight, streaming in, lit up a scene, such as the Flemish masters loved to paint. Down the centre of the apartment ran a table, covered with overturned drinking glasses, and empty bottles, amid which a huge black jug, with a cornstalk cork, stood, like a grim, giant warrior, of old, in the centre of a troop of modern pigmies. A few square bits of wood, in each of which a hole had been bored to insert a candle, were scattered about the table; but the candles had long since guttered down, the melted tallow flowing over and adhering to the board. On one side of the table had been a row of split-bottomed chairs, but these were now either pushed back against the wall, or had been kicked over; while on the other side was a rude bench, made of the first plank that is cut from a log, the convex part, to which the bark still adhered, being downward. A broken clay pipe, black with smoke, lay on one end of this bench, and by it slept its owner, a brawny, unshaven savage. Two of his companions were stretched on the floor, on either side; another was directly under the table; a fourth filled a shadowy corner, looking an unsightly, mis-shapen mass in the obscurity; while a fifth, still sitting in his chair, slept with his head leaning on his hands crossed before him on the table. Across this central figure the moonlight poured in a flood of intense brilliancy, and shot onwards to where Arrison lay at the feet of Kate, leaving the rest of the room in comparative darkness, as in a painting by Rembrandt.

Kate saw that it would require the utmost caution to pass the sleepers without awakening them, for the room was so narrow, and they lay in such positions, that it was almost impossible to reach the door without treading upon more than one of them. Arrison himself lay close to the door of her room, as if his last thought, before he succumbed to the effects of his copious libations, had been to place himself there on purpose to keep guard. She could not advance a single step, indeed, without passing over his body; and if, in making the attempt, even her skirt should brush him, all would be over. Perhaps, she reflected, he would be aroused even by her shadow crossing him; she herself could easily be woke in that way. These suggestions of an active brain would have paralyzed many a female in Kate's situation; but they only had the effect of quickening her pulses, and increasing her caution.

Holding her breath, and gathering up her skirts firmly, she stepped rapidly across Arrison's body, and not pausing to look behind, advanced stealthily but swiftly towards the door, keeping as much as possible in the shadow. She was but a few seconds in crossing the apartment, but it seemed to her almost an age. Every instant she expected to hear Arrison spring to his feet, or to see one of the ruffians in front rise to intercept her. At every footstep she trembled with nervous apprehension. As she approached the door, she was compelled to almost brush one of the outlaws extended on the floor: he stirred at that crisis; and she thought that she was discovered. Instantaneously she stopped and shrank into the shadow. The man was only turning in his sleep, however, and the next moment was snoring as heavily as before. Inexpressibly relieved, Kate drew her garments close to her figure, and gliding lightly past him, gained the door in safety.

It was a magnificent night without; and what a contrast to the scene within! Not a cloud was in the sky, not even a speck of fleecy vapor; only the blue, starless heavens were seen above, and in their eastern depths the silver moon. A vague, awe-struck feeling came over Kate as she looked up, and saw the solemn pine-trees standing, dark and weird, against the silent sky, and above them the calm, cold planet, looking down on her as pitilessly as it had gazed on the suffering Job on the plains of Mesopotamia, ages before. Not a breath of air stirred even the topmost tassel of the tallest fir; not a sound broke the deep stillness: it seemed, indeed, as if to breathe was to break some potent spell and bring down ruin on her head.

The little clearing was everywhere as light as day, except where the shadows of the rude fences checkered the ground, or where the gloom, cast by the forest, fell like an ominous pall across the eastern edge. Before our heroine was the little, tumble-down barn, which we have once before described. One side of this, including the roof, was flooded with the moonlight, while the other was black and vague, the deep shadows effectually concealing its outline. Right opposite the glorious planet, and therefore dazzlingly lit up by her radiance, a road opened into the forest, which soon, however closed about it, sombre and awful, as some unfathomable cave swallows up the ray of sunlight that streams through a chink in the roof. It reminded Kate of a pathway into some land of enchantment, at first beautiful to the eye, and light almost as day, but soon darkening into the gloom of death, amid bogs, and torrents, and labyrinths without end. A shudder came over her as she gazed, as if a shadow of impending evil fell across her; but shaking off the feeling as childish, she advanced into the open space, and directed her steps to the road.

But scarcely had she emerged fairly into the moonlight, when a low, deep growl startled her, proceeding apparently from the barn. Looking eagerly in that direction, her heart sank, for she saw the ferocious bloodhound, which she had observed on her arrival, slowly rising to his feet from out of the shadow. His huge form, as he stalked into the light, seemed, to the excited nerves of our heroine, to be of even more colossal stature than it was in reality; and with a stifled groan, clasping her hands, she stood transfixed in speechless horror.

CHAPTER XXXVII
INTERCEPTED

A violet by a mossy stone,
Half hidden from the eye,
Fair as a star, when only one
Is shining in the sky. —Wordsworth.

Suddenly a figure glided forth into the moonlight, which, for one moment, Kate almost fancied was a spirit. It was clothed in white, and bore the semblance of a young girl, not more than ten years old; but so sylph-like were its movements, so noiseless its tread, and so pure and innocent was the expression of the face, that it could not, Kate thought, be there, yet be earthly. This transient illusion, however, was instantly dissipated, by a childish voice calling out to the dog, in low tones, as if fearful of awaking the sleepers.

The bloodhound apparently recognized the accents as those of one who had shown him acts of kindness, for he ceased growling immediately, and going up to the young girl, lifted his head as if to be caressed. The child patted the ferocious animal, whispering soothingly to him, on which he crouched down at her feet, like the lion before Una.

Our heroine fully expected that the alarm given by the dog would have aroused the sleepers; and she even fancied, for an instant, that she heard the refugees stirring. She turned, therefore, eagerly to fly, but at the first step the young girl advanced, laying her hand on Kate's arm and shaking her head in the negative.

Kate glanced affrightedly over her shoulder, sure that she would behold Arrison; but her excited fancy had run ahead of the reality. She drew a deep sigh of relief, and turning to the young girl, said, breathlessly.

"You will not stop me—you will save me from these dreadful men, by letting me go before they awake."

The child shook her head again.

"I dare not," she said, but in a low, sweet voice.

"And why not? Oh! surely they would not harm you."

"He would kill me," replied the child, glancing in terror towards the house.

"Who?"

"Uncle."

"And who is uncle?"

"Don't you know?"

"What! Arrison?"

"Yes."

Kate looked at the child earnestly. There seemed to her something strangely familiar, in the large, eloquent eyes of the young creature before her. The whole countenance, indeed, reminded her of some one she had known, but she could not recall whom, though she endeavored, again and again, to remember. The likeness, after all, however, was a confused one, with gleams of that which was familiar mingled with others which were foreign; and these latter it was which appeared to Kate to give such an air of innocence and even holiness to the face. After a moment's scrutiny, she recalled her perilous condition, and as every instant was precious, endeavored again to persuade the child to allow her departure.

"You must be mistaken," she said, "your uncle surely would not hurt you."

"You don't know him," answered the child, "Oh! I am sure he would kill me if I let you go," she continued, clasping her little hands.

"But I *must* go," replied Kate, with an endeavor to overawe the child. "You cannot help it."

The child laid her hand significantly on the bloodhound, which had risen from his reclining posture and now stood at her side, watching alternately her countenance and that of Kate. This gesture he seemed to interpret as it was intended, for he bristled up and uttered a low growl.

Kate shudderingly looked over her shoulder in the direction of the house.

"Don't—don't," she cried, in an eager whisper, imploringly glancing down into the child's face, and laying her hand on the girl's shoulder.

The child looked up, with her sad, earnest eyes, at the same time patting the bloodhound, who became quiet at once.

"Oh! if I could let you go," she said, and her little face was eloquent in every feature with sincerity. "I haven't slept a wink all night, thinking of you. That was before I saw you," she added, naively, "before I knew you were beautiful, or looked so good."

"Does nobody live here but you?" Kate said, wondering to find the child in such a place. "I mean nobody but you and Arrison."

"He hasn't lived here always," she replied. "He did once, and then went away, and only came back a week ago."

"But you didn't live here alone?"

"No, Granny Jones lived with me. But she's cross too. Oh!" she suddenly added, with passionate earnestness, "if mother hadn't died."

Kate was silent. The child was then an orphan. She said kindly, after a moment.

"You remember your mother?"

"Oh! yes. She was so beautiful," and the tears glistened in the child's eyes. "Not beautiful like you, not proud looking and grand, but so sweet and pretty. She never scolded me in all her life, never, never." And the child burst into low, half-stifled sobs, which, in her effort to suppress them, shook her little frame.

Kate was again silent; tears sympathetically dimmed her eyes. The child saw it, and hushing her sobs, said,

"But Granny Jones was sent away, when uncle came back."

"And when he's away, you're alone?" The child nodded.

"All alone, except with Lion," she said, glancing at the bloodhound. "He's such a good fellow," she added, her eyes brightening. "We play together, when we've time! Don't we, Lion?" and she caressed him.

Kate sighed to think of this lovely child, brought up by an outlaw, yet retaining so much of heaven's purity, living here in the forest with no companion but this ferocious dog. She longed to question the little outcast respecting her mother, about whom there seemed some strange mystery. But she refrained out of respect to the girl, who evidently suffered at allusions to her parent's name.

"Why won't you go with me?" said Kate, winningly. "Help me to get away from this place, and I'll take you home with me, where you shall have everything you like, and be my little sister."

The child looked up at her, with eyes dilated to their utmost size in wonder, evidently unable to credit what she heard.

"I am rich," said Kate; "you never need work any more. Look in my face and you'll see I speak truth."

The child gave a long, earnest gaze, and answered. "I believe what you say. I know you are good."

"Then come," said Kate. But the child drew back.

"No," she said, "it wouldn't be right. Mother told me to stay with uncle till I grew to be a woman; that he was a hard man, but my only friend, and I promised I would do it."

"But your mother did not know that I would make you my sister. If she had known that you could go away to a fine house, have plenty of clothes, have books to read, and have a sister to love you, don't you think she would have been willing?"

The child looked puzzled. She fixed her large eyes, in doubt and inquiry, on Kate, as if she could interrogate our heroine's very soul.

"Maybe she would," she answered frankly, at last. "She was always afraid of uncle, and often cried after he'd been to see us. But I promised her I'd stay with him. Is it right to break promises? Wouldn't that be to tell a lie?"

Kate felt her eyes shrink before the gaze of the innocent child. She was no adept in casuistry, and if she had been, the inquiry of the little girl, thus put, would have silenced her. Even the strong instinct to escape could not induce her to mislead one so young and pure.

"God help me!" was her answer, wringing her hands. "I must then stay here. Oh! if I were dead."

The child looked at her earnestly for a moment, and then said, pulling her by her sleeve,

"Don't, don't. They won't hurt you—will they? Uncle told me he was going to marry you, and that I must give up my room to you, and go and sleep in the barn, for tonight, anyhow. If you don't like uncle, you needn't marry him, need you? I thought people only married when they liked each other."

"You cannot understand it all, my child," answered Kate, placing her hand on the girl's shoulder. "But listen! I don't want to marry your uncle. I never will marry him. They brought me here by force, or I'd never have come. If you don't let me go, I'll not live till night; and you'll see me dead here, before your eyes."

The child started back with a sudden shriek, which she stifled as hastily, looking in terror towards the house; and then, taking Kate's hand, she drew her away within the shadow of the barn. Here, pausing, she said,

"You don't mean it. They'll not kill you?"

"As sure as there is a good God above us," answered Kate, solemnly, "if you don't let me go, I'll not be alive to-morrow. There is no help for it. While, if you do let me go," she continued, eager to take advantage of the favorable chance, "nobody will know you helped me. In fact, you won't help me; you'll only keep Lion quiet; and if they were to know you helped me, they couldn't harm you, innocent child that you are. If your mother was alive, she'd wish you to let me go. You know I wouldn't tell a lie, darling, or I'd have tried still to get you to go with me, in spite of your promise to your mother. Every minute is precious. It will soon be daybreak. Only keep Lion quiet, leave me to myself, and go back to your bed in the barn."

"You *shall* go," suddenly said the child. "I'll go inside, and take Lion with me."

"God bless you!" cried Kate, seizing her in her arms and kissing her again and again. "If I escape, and you ever want a friend, you'll always have one, if you ask for Miss Aylesford, of Sweetwater."

"Good-bye," said the child, timidly returning the kisses. "Take the road in front, and keep straight ahead. Only," she added, "when you come to the big cedar, past the log bridge, a mile off, you must turn to the right."

"I will, I will," breathlessly said Kate, but, in her hurry and excitement, paying less heed to the direction than she ought. "Again God bless you!"

With tears in her eyes she gave the child a last embrace, and first glancing towards the house to see that no one was in motion, ran swiftly across the open space, entered the road, nor slackened her speed until not only the turn concealed her from sight, but a considerable distance intervened between her and the clearing. Then, almost out of breath, she subsided into a quick walk, occasionally stopping to hear if the steps or shouts of pursuers were following in the distance.

As for the child, she remained in the shadow, caressing the dog to keep him quiet, and watching the retreating figure of our heroine, until Kate had wholly disappeared. Then, suddenly bursting into tears, she turned, and entered the dilapidated barn, leading the bloodhound, whom, the instant they were alone together on the hay, she clasped to her arms, in a mute eloquence that said he was now again the only friend she had in the world.

CHAPTER XXXVIII
THE FLIGHT

Whence is that knocking!
How is it with me, when every noise appals me. —*Shakespeare.*

Like one, that on a lonesome road
Doth walk in fear and dread.
* * * * * *
Because he knows a frightful fiend
Doth close behind him tread. —*Coleridge.*

The precious moments which Kate had lost, first by falling asleep, and afterwards through the watchfulness of the hound, stimulated her now to the utmost speed of which she was capable. Running until she was forced to pause for breath, then pausing an instant to listen, now walking at her utmost pace, then running again as soon as she had recovered herself, she reached the bridge of which the child had spoken, in a period of time incredibly short, and only to be accounted for by the terror with which the fear of death or dishonor winged her feet.

At this point she was compelled to come to a full stop, and remain for awhile in perplexed thought, uncertain which way to go. In vain she tried to remember which road the child had told her to take. As she stood there, hesitating, her fears received fresh stimulants. Every noise was magnified into the sound of pursuers. Even the soft sighing of the wind in the distance seemed to her excited fancy the remote baying of the hound; while the sudden dropping of a pine-cone near her made her start, with a half uttered scream, as if her foes were already upon her. To have seen her then, as she stood glancing fearfully across her shoulder, her hand pressed to her palpitating heart, her lips parted in terror, and her cheek lividly pale, one would have compared her only to some beautiful, milk-white doe, suddenly startled by the hunter's cry, and feeling in imagination the fangs of the enormous stag-hounds already at her throat.

To no purpose either was her scrutiny as to the condition of the two roads, in order to ascertain which of them presented the appearance of being most frequently travelled. It had plainly been many days, if not weeks, since a vehicle had passed over either. At last Kate selected the road to the right as the one which seemed to be the principal one. Yet, at this point, it flashed across her that, perhaps, the most travelled path was really the one she should avoid; for it probably led into the great highway, connecting Philadelphia with the sea-shore. She was but little acquainted with the country on this side of Sweetwater, forests extending almost unbrokenly across from one river to the other; but what little she knew satisfied her that this great highway might be traversed for hours without reaching succor. Within twenty years of the present time, the writer has passed over a space of twelve miles at a time, without seeing more than one house; and at the period of our story, the village at the end of that desolate stage was not even projected. Kate, indeed, might have walked all day along that highway, without meeting enough persons to protect her from the refugees. It was, therefore, almost certain recapture for her to take the path communicating with that road.

She paused, therefore, again. But the more she thought the more perplexed she became. Time, meanwhile, was passing; precious moments, big with destiny. She could not rely on the outlaws remaining ignorant of her flight a moment after daybreak; and already the night was waning fast. Drawing forth her watch, of which she had not been despoiled, most strangely as she thought, she discovered that the dawn was only an hour distant. What was an hour's start, however, to one like her, wearied by the excessive fatigue of the preceding day, unused to travelling far on foot, and deprived of sleep for the last twenty-four hours, except for the slight interval at the hut. How could she expect to gain the Forks, even if she struck the right road, in less than two hours?

"If I hesitate longer," she cried, in despair, "they will overtake me, long before I can reach any place of safety I am acquainted with. I must decide in some way. This right hand road, I fear, leads into the King's highway: I will take the one on the left: God help me if I am wrong!"

Accordingly she turned in that direction, and having rested herself partially by the pause, ran forward again until she was quite out of breath. For half an hour, she continued alternately running, walking, and running again, occasionally pausing to listen: and in that time, as she calculated, had traversed between two and three miles. The forest still continued as wild as ever; but this did not alarm her; for she was aware that the wilderness extended to the very doors, as it were, of the settlement at the Forks. She therefore pushed forward, her excitement enabling her to disregard fatigue, and to forget that she had eaten little for a day. For another half an hour, consequently, she hurried on, and as the distance between her and the outlaws was increased, her hopes gradually rose.

Day was now beginning to break. The moon continued to shine as lustrously as ever; indeed, being now nearly at the zenith, her light seemed even more effulgent than when Kate left the hut; but there was a cold, gray hue over the eastern sky which heralded the morning. Gradually the white light of day stole over the orient heavens, when that of the moon assumed a partially sickly cast. The birds too now began to twitter in the underbrush and smaller growth around.

At this point Kate reached an opening in the woods, where the trees had been cut off a year or two ago. On the eastern side of this was a tract of pine land, where a fire had passed, leaving the tall firs standing stripped of their foliage, like a forest of black, charred masts against the heavens. Through this, in the distance, was seen a reddened sky, a proof that the sun, though still below the horizon, was close upon it. The route of Kate lying in the direction of this burnt district, it was not long before she saw the upper edge of his disc emerge, shooting long lines of light towards her, that came glancing between the black trunks of the pines, or bathed the greener space more directly in front with showers of golden radiance. The whole forest around was now alive with twittering birds. Meantime the moon, as if suddenly struck pale by an enchanter's hand, seemed all at once to have lost its late glorious effulgence, and was now seen, a faint, waning orb, apparently powerless in the zenith. To the right and left, however, in the recesses of the woods, where the sunshine had not yet penetrated, the moonlight still lay, cold and beautiful, though even there less lustrous than it had been.

In a few minutes it grew dim also even in these secluded aisles, fading perceptibly to the eye as in a dissolving view. The sun had now risen completely above the horizon. The exhalations of the night still partially obscured him, however, so that he loomed large and inflamed on the vision. But directly he surmounted the region of these vapors; and at once the whole landscape was flooded with dazzling light. The black, charred pines; the verdant tract of low brush oak; and the arcades that ran before the eye into the forest on every side, glowed with the excess of effulgence: the leaves, that rustled slightly in the wind, flashed in the bright rays: and the moon became a pale, uncertain circle, the affrighted shadow of herself.

For another hour Kate pursued her way, without stopping longer than a few moments at a time, and then only to listen if she was pursued. At the end of that period she began to think that she ought to be in the neighborhood of the Forks. She pressed on, however, till the sun was nearly two hours high, yet without reaching her destination. She now became alarmed. At the pace at which she had been advancing, she ought, she knew, to have arrived at the Forks before this; besides, the road was becoming a mere wood-path; while the forest around was changing its character and assuming that of an impenetrable swamp. She now bethought her to compare the position of the sun with what it would be if she was advancing in the right direction. To her dismay she found that luminary over her left shoulder and behind, instead of in front, and on the right, as it should have been. At this discovery she came to a halt, overcome with the sudden faintness of despair.

During her progress, she had frequently passed other roads, opening into the one she was traversing, but as they were either evidently paths used only by the wood-cutters, or led off at right angles, she had carefully avoided them. Studiously had she kept to what appeared to be the most direct and beaten way, nor until this moment had she thought of testing it by the heavens. Thus she had unconsciously turned her face in the wrong direction, by following its tortuous course.

A moment's reflection, however, suggested to her that the deviation of the road might be only temporary, though the fact that she had not reached the Forks, as she ought, told against this supposition. Drowning people, it is said, catch at straws, however, and nerving herself with this hope, she started afresh. But after walking for a considerable period longer, and carefully noting the position of the sun all the while, she became convinced that she was receding from the point of her destination, instead of advancing towards it.

When this discovery forced itself on her, nature at last gave way. Overtasked though she had been, hope and energy had kept her up; but now both succumbed together; and her strength departed with them. Sinking tremblingly and powerless on the huge root of a mossy tree, she covered her face with her hands, and burst into sobs like a child.

But, when she had wept for a while, a reaction took place. She started suddenly to her feet.

"Why do I give way thus?" she cried. "Is not anything better than falling again into the hands of those ruffians? Better to drop down and die from sheer exhaustion, than to sit here trembling, like a hunted hare, till I am seized."

As she spoke, she resumed her flight, running till she panted, and then walking rapidly on with desperate, but alas! purposeless energy. For the further she advanced, the more remote became the Forks, as she saw by the position of the sun; yet she dared not turn back, as that would be to run into the jaws of her hunters. The first cross-path that she met, and which led in the right direction, she entered, however. But after following this for awhile, it also went astray, and now she was in greater perplexity and dismay than ever.

In fact she was evidently advancing into one of those almost pathless swamps, which abounded in that region, and which had engulphed many a lost traveller as effectually as the sea swallows up a foundered crew. The soil beneath her was no longer solid, though sandy; but was a soft, black vegetable mould, in which she often sank to the ankles. The path, for it was now scarcely a road, was almost overgrown with bushes; and occasionally it was really difficult to tell where it was, the wheel-tracks, if they had ever existed, having long ago been obliterated.

Yet she struggled on. Despair gave her now the energy which hope had formerly supplied; and though almost exhausted with physical weakness, her brave soul still upheld her flagging frame, and still urged her forward. Thus she staggered on, all that morning, dragging her heavy limbs along, and continually rallying herself to a swifter pace, when she mistook the wind among the trees for the hurrying tread of pursuers, or the distant bay of a hound.

The sun was now high in the heavens. Kate had been on her feet since two hours before the dawn. She could no longer advance at a faster pace than a walk, and that a slow and painful one. She saw also that she was moving almost in a circle, the sun being now before her, now on her right, now behind her, and now to the left. But, though hopelessly lost in the swamp, though sometimes almost miring in the oozy soil, she did not, for one moment, entertain the thought of turning back.

"Oh! no, no," she said wildly, "certain death, death in any shape, is better than falling again into those merciless hands."

Even the idea of lingering for days, in a state of starvation, was less terrible to her than being retaken. She had heard of persons, lost in swamps, who had perished miserably for the want of food, and whose bleached skeletons, found long years after, had been the only clue their friends ever had to their fate; and she had formerly shuddered at such tales. But she did not shudder now. She felt that, if she could purchase immunity from the outlaws in no other way, she would gladly accept even this horrible alternative.

"God," she said, "tempers the wind to the shorn lamb. He will give me strength to face such a death."

Noon was now at hand. The path had long since dwindled into a mere blind track, formed rather by the natural space between the trees than by the footsteps of man or beast. Frequently tall bushes, interlaced into an impenetrable net-work, guarded the sides like a hedge; and again the path swelled into natural openings, half an acre or so in extent. Lofty trees, whose sombre verdure threw an almost funereal gloom around, towered high into the sky, with here and there a blasted pine, shooting, arrowy-like, high over all, and adding to the desolate aspect of the landscape.

CHAPTER XXXIX
THE BLOODHOUND

But I, in none of these,
Find place or refuge. —Milton.

What miracle
Can work me into hope! —Lee.

Then, as the headmost foes appeared,
With one brave bound the copse he cleared. —Scott.

Suddenly the distant cry of a hound seemed borne upon the air. Often before, during the morning, as we have said, Kate had fancied she heard such a noise; and as often had she been happily disappointed. But this time there was no mistaking it. No sighing of the wind among the pines, no murmur of distant water, could produce that peculiar cry, which was plainly the hoarse, deep bay of a bloodhound heated with the chase.

Kate gazed in terror around, vainly seeking a hiding-place. If the earth had opened, at that moment, and swallowed her up, she would have welcomed it as a relief. The worst that she had feared, that recapture which was more horrible than death, was now about to befall her. Help there was none. The nearest human creature, possessed of the sympathies of our common nature, was probably miles away; and as for pleading for mercy at the hands of the outlaws, she knew she might as well petition to the winds.

Meantime the bay of the hound sounded louder and louder, fiercer and fiercer, nearer and nearer. Occasionally he would appear to lose the scent for a moment or two, for the deep cry would die away through the wilderness; and Kate, at such times, would listen breathlessly, fluctuating between hope and despair. But the hoarse bay broke forth invariably again, at intervals greater or less; and always with a startling ferocity that sent the blood back in torrents to her heart. After thus recovering the scent, the cry of the hound would be heard almost incessantly, till the forest resounded with a hundred echoes, and the very heavens seemed to give back the sound. Though the pursuers now drew near, and then receded a space, as if following a somewhat circuitous path, the terrible bay of the hound plainly approached closer, with the lapse of every quarter of an hour.

There was but one hope now left for our heroine, which was that death would put an end to her miseries, before she could be dragged back to the outlaw's hut. Her efforts to escape had so completely exhausted her, that her heroic spirit would have been unable to force the weary limbs onward much further, even though the refugees had failed to track her. She felt satisfied that she could not retrace her steps to the cabin, and that she would perish on the way if the attempt was made to compel her.

But, hopeless as was her condition, Kate still remained true to herself. The fate which she could not avert, she resolved should be met with dignity at least. She abandoned, therefore, all further thought of flight, determining to face her inevitable destiny where she then stood. Like a Roman virgin, stout-hearted to the last, as became the daughter of illustrious heroes, she drew her garments decorously and proudly about her, and stood up to face the foe.

It was not only on herself that she relied, however, in this most terrible of all extremities. The reader is already familiar with the fact that Kate was sincere and earnest in her piety; and now, when she considered death as imminent, she looked up to the Almighty for support in that dreadful hour. She had been educated in the liturgy of the Established Church, as her fathers had been since the days of the saintly Latimer, and though she worshiped with other sects as fervently as with her own, when the ministry of her church was impossible, her thoughts naturally turned, in this extremity, to the solemn words of that litany which she had learned first at her mother's knee.

As she stood, therefore, facing the foe, and bravely supporting her weak frame by leaning against a tree, her eyes were raised to heaven, and her lips moved in earnest supplications. We have seen somewhere a picture of a Christian virgin, bound to an oak by Pagan enemies, and about to suffer martyrdom by being transfixed with arrows as a target. So Kate looked now. Her hands were clasped downwards before her; and her uplifted countenance glowed with a fervent enthusiasm that proved the mortal part above the fear of death. Thus she stood, while the bay of the ferocious hound drew nearer, and shouts, mingling with the hoarse cry, showed that her pitiless hunters were now close at hand; yet not an eyelid quivered, not a muscle about her mouth twitched, not a shade of color rose into her composed, though pallid face.

"Remember not, Lord, our offences," she prayed, "nor the offences of our forefathers; neither take thou vengeance of our sins; spare us, good Lord, spare thy people, whom thou hast redeemed with thy most precious blood."

Again the hoarse cries of the bloodhound, nearer at hand than ever, woke the echoes of the wilderness, mingled with the exulting shouts of the outlaws; for the pursuers knew, from the rapidity and power of the dog's cries, that they were now almost up with their prey.

"By the mystery of thy holy Incarnation, by thy holy Nativity and Circumcision; by thy Baptism, Fasting and Temptation."

Again the ferocious bay of the bloodhound rose to the sky, and reverberated through the forests.

"By thine Agony and Bloody Sweat; by thy Cross and Passion; by thy precious Death and Burial; by thy glorious Resurrection and Ascension; and by the coming of the Holy Ghost."

Still a third time the cry of the excited hound rung across the silence.

"In all time of our tribulation; in all time of our prosperity; in the hour of death, and in the day of judgment."

Still rose, as if in answer, that deep, hoarse bay of the bloodhound, which seemed almost to deny the justice of heaven.

But now the victim began to pray for others, and for her enemies even, as the litany of the Church teaches.

"That it may please thee to have mercy upon all men."

The bay of the hound replied almost beside her.

"That it may please thee to forgive our enemies, persecutors and slanderers, and to turn their hearts."

A burst from the bloodhound, at her very side, was the answer; and immediately the terrible animal broke from the undergrowth.

His reddish coat seemed more inflamed in color than ever; his open mouth, with its blood-colored tongue, was white with foam; and his eyes blazed with such fury, that they seemed to emit phosphoric light. He paused an instant, erecting his tall form, his hairs bristling with rage, for he did not immediately perceive his prey. His glance soon rested on her, however, when, with a yell that rung far and near through the forest, and startled the beasts of the chase from the noon-day coverts they had sought, he sprang at the throat of our heroine.

But, at that very instant, just as the hound was half way towards his victim, darting through the air with distended jaws and eager fangs, a quick, sharp report was heard, a whizzing sound smote on Kate's unnaturally excited ear, and the dog, as if struck suddenly by a bolt from heaven, rolled over on the ground, nearly at the feet of his intended prey, his head shattered to pieces by a double load of buckshot.

For a moment, our heroine knew not whether to hail this as a welcome relief, or only as a respite to a more miserable doom. Her first thought was that Arrison, finding that the hound had outrun him, had fired to save her from the fangs of the excited animal. This impression was fortified, by seeing the refugee himself dash upon the scene, almost before the single convulsive movement of the dog was over, after he had fallen.

But this belief was removed by the very first words of the outlaw. Without even looking at Kate, he rushed up to the hound, and first gazing hurriedly on his mutilated form, glanced angrily around the little open space where these scenes were being enacted. Discovering nobody, however, he seemed for a moment perplexed; but instantly suspecting it was some one who had outstripped him, he cried, with every feature working with passion,

"Who fired that shot? Who dared kill my dog?" And he concluded with a blasphemous oath.

An answer came sooner than he expected, for while he still scowled around, the bushes parted directly in front of him, and Uncle Lawrence appeared, his finger on the trigger of his gun, and the piece held ready for instant service.

"I fired it, you villain," coolly replied the veteran, placing himself before Kate, but without looking at her, while all the time he watched the outlaw as warily as one would eye a panther about to spring.

"Keep still—don't touch me," he whispered to our heroine immediately, in a tone so low as to be heard only by Kate. "Help is near, if we can gain time. I'll die with you, my child, if I can't save you."

As he spoke, he still kept his eyes on Arrison, his finger on the trigger, his piece ready for instant use.

CHAPTER XL
POMP AGAIN

His hand did quake,
And tremble like a leaf of aspen green. —Spenser.

Still as he fled his eye was backward cast,
As if his fear still followed him behind,
As flew his steed as if his bands had brast,
And with his winged heels did tread the wind. —Spenser.

The adventure of Pomp with the black bull, or, as his mother persisted in declaring, "wid dat ole enemy Satan," had no little influence on the events of this story, for it was partly in consequence that Kate received no succor sooner from either Sweetwater or the Forks.

Up to within an hour of dinner, Mrs. Warren felt no uneasiness at her niece's absence, but when the time for that meal came, without the return of Kate, the good dame began to be seriously alarmed. Our heroine had not only said that she would not be gone for more than two hours, but had never before protracted her stay to dinner time.

Another circumstance contributed to the fears of Mrs. Warren. During the course of the morning the quiet of Sweetwater had been suddenly disturbed, by the appearance of a body of cavalry, which, emerging from the woods in the direction of Mr. Herman's, had paused for awhile to water their horses at the head of the pond. Lying about under the trees, in a temporary bivouac, while their chargers cooled off, the dismounted horsemen had not, at the time, affected the good dame with any other feeling than that of admiration of their picturesque appearance. But when the trumpet had summoned them to the saddle; when they had wound slowly past the bridge, with their arms glittering in the sun; and when, two hours after, dinner was ready to be served, without Kate having returned, Mrs. Warren began, not only to be alarmed at her niece's disappearance, but to connect that disappearance with the advent of the cavalry.

"Deary me," she cried, wringing her hands, as she walked the parlor, "how could Charles leave us so unprotected. These rebel horsemen have carried off Kate, there isn't a doubt of it." For Mrs. Warren, with the prejudices of too many of her class, persisted in believing that the patriots were little better than highwaymen. "Oh! my poor niece! My poor niece!"

She burst into tears, and in this condition Pomp found her, when, some time later, he made his appearance to ask her whether dinner should be served immediately, or whether she would wait for Miss Aylesford.

"I couldn't eat," she answered. "Tell Dinah to keep the dinner waiting till my niece returns: that is, poor dear! if she ever returns. I've a presentiment she won't, though. I felt so dreadful, when she went away this morning, that I know something terrible would happen." And again she gave way to loud weeping.

Pomp, in consternation, summoned his mother, who, in turn, called in the assistance of the lady's maid. Opportunely, at this crisis, Pomp's other parent appeared, and he, as the only male present, proceeded to take the reins of authority into his own hands.

"Look a here, yer lazy, good-for-nuffin wagabond," he cried, turning to Pomp and cuffing him soundly, "how dare yer stand dar a-gapin', when yer know yer ought to be off a-lookin' up young Missus? Yer'll come to the gallous, some day, deed yer will."

Pomp ran to a corner, defending his ears with his hands, and protesting, in a whining tone, that he did not know where to go.

"Yer lie, yer young scape-grace," interrupted the irate parent. "Young Missus took der road to Uncle Lawrence's, and dar yer'll find her, if nuffin has happened. Go right off, not a word," and he menacingly followed the unwillingly retreating messenger, adding, "go, or I'll skin yer, deed I will. Maybe she's at Aunt Chloe's, or maybe her bridle's broke. Take der colt, and ride for dear life," he cried, elevating his voice louder and louder, as Pomp increased his distance.

Mrs. Warren, who had become quite hysterical, was gradually soothed by assurances that Kate had not met with any serious misadventure, and that the American cavalry, at least, had not interfered with her.

"I axed one ob de men," said Dinah, "who was de handsum officer a ridin' at de head; and he told me dat it was a grand furren count."

"Do you remember his name?" said Mrs. Warren, eagerly, her face brightening. "A nobleman wouldn't do any harm to a gentlewoman. You're sure you're not mistaken."

"De blessed Lord knows I'se telling de truf," answered Dinah. "I wouldn't for de whole world lose my poor ole soul, by telling a lie."

"You don't recollect his name? Was it Pulaski? The Count Pulaski, I believe, commands a regiment of cavalry in the American army."

"Dat's de name. Count Poorlackey," cried Dinah.

"Pulaski," said Mrs. Warren, correcting her, and smiling through her tears.

"Well, Poorlackey or Puleskaski; it's all one, I spose," replied Dinah, with an air of offended dignity. But, relenting immediately, she added, "Now, Missus, ef yer'll just eat a little bit of somethin', say de wing of dat boiled chicken, dat's a spoilin' wid waitin,' you'll feel like anodder person; deed yer will."

The eloquence of Dinah, who continued expatiating on this subject for some time, finally induced Mrs. Warren to consent to her wishes. Buoyed up with the persuasion that Pomp would soon return, bringing intelligence of Kate, she ate with appetite, and indeed forgot for a season her niece, in the delicacies before her.

Meantime, Pomp had saddled the colt and set forth, but with reluctant steps, for his thoughts reverted to his adventure of the preceding evening, and his teeth shook in anticipation, when he remembered that his road would lie directly past the spot where he had been set upon, as he conscientiously believed, by the Arch Enemy. As he approached the head of the pond, he drew the colt into a walk, and began to soliloquize thus with himself:

"Yer's in a fix now, Pomp, ef ebber yer was. Ef yer go after young Missus, de debbil will cotch you sure; and ef yer don't go, yer daddy'll skin you."

He had now reached the point where the two roads met, that to the right leading past the church and across the bridge, and that to the left conducting to Aunt Chloe's and Mr. Herman's. He came to a dead halt.

"Yer'll be a darn fool, Pomp," he soliloquized again, and his teeth began to chatter with the thought, "to run right into de jaws of de debbil, arter havin' got off once. He's a lyin' dar, like a roarin' lion, ready to jump out on yer."

As he thus reflected, he slowly turned the colt's head to the right.

"Pears to me," he resumed, glancing affrightedly over his shoulder towards the haunted road, "dat poor young Missus has been a took off by dis ole Satan; and dat it wouldn't do no good, sartin it wouldn't, to go arter her. It would ony be givin' yerself, Pomp, to de debbil, deed it would."

The colt's head was now turned even more to the bridge, and Pomp had actually permitted it to walk a few paces in its direction, when suddenly he checked the animal.

"Pomp," he said, "what yer doin'? Yer'll get skinned alive, sartin sure. Yer ole daddy never said he'd do it, dat he didn't. Lor' Almighty, how he licked yer, Pomp, dat last time; and de more yer cried 'murder,' the more he said he'd giv' yer 'somethin' to cry murder fur,' deed he did." And Pomp rubbed sympathetically that portion of his person which had felt most keenly his sire's wrath.

It would have moved even the most serious to mirth to have seen Pomp's countenance, as he thus alternated in his fears. Twice he turned the colt's head towards the fatal road, and twice altered his mind, the whimsical contortions of his face, all the time, exceeding anything that Hogarth ever painted. At last there arose, out of the heart of the forest on the left, one of those low, long wails, which, on a summer day, is often the precursor of a coming storm. Pomp's already excited imagination needed only the smallest circumstance to decide him. The moan of the rising wind was to him irresistible proof of the presence of the Arch Enemy. He dug his heels into the flanks of the colt instinctively, and sped over the bridge, as yet with no fixed determination where to go, but only to escape as well from parental vengeance at Sweetwater, as from the supernatural foe: and as he galloped off, his eyes were dilated to the size of saucers, his dark visage positively paled, and his teeth chattered, as if they would drop out of his jaws.

When Mrs. Warren found that Pomp did not return, all her old fears came back. It was night before she and her attendants finally abandoned the hope of seeing him, and then it was too late to take further action. Besides, her servants were, by this time, nearly as incapacitated as herself. This was especially true of Dinah, who filled the house with her lamentations, declaring that Pomp had been carried off by Satan himself, "deed he had."

All that night Mrs. Warren walked her room, wringing her hands and sobbing, and occasionally falling into fits of hysterics.

CHAPTER XLI
THE PRISONERS

Be just, and fear not!
Let all the ends thou aim'st at be thy country's,
Thy God's and truth's, then if thou fall'st, O Cromwell!
Thou fall'st a blessed martyr. —Shakespeare.

Seek not to know to-morrow's doom,
That is not ours which is to come. —Congreve.

Though Major Gordon had been pinned to the earth by a bayonet, in the breach of the fortification, he was fortunately not killed. For a moment, indeed, he believed his last hour had come. He would, in fact, have perished, had it not been for Uncle Lawrence. When he saw all hope of victory gone, he dexterously threw himself down, across the prostrate body of our hero; by this stratagem, both covering his friend, and inducing the belief that he also was dead.

In the hurry and confusion of the melee it was not difficult to carry out this deception. The eager soldiery, fired with emulation of their comrades, hurried to be within the works as soon as possible, and consequently did not care to stop, in order to examine in whom of their fallen enemies life yet remained. It was enough for the victors that the way was now clear before them, and accordingly they rushed forward, pell-mell, with loud shouts, over the prostrate heap of wounded and slain.

In this way our hero escaped with only a bayonet thrust in his left arm, while Uncle Lawrence received only a few bruises, the result of being trodden upon. Others, however, of the brave band were less fortunate. Charley Newell lay stark and stiff, with a bullet through his heart, having fallen in the early part of the conflict; while Mullen was seriously injured by a wound in the side, from a bayonet. Three others also paid the forfeit of their lives for their gallant defence.

When the fight was over, and all danger of being murdered in hot blood had passed away, Uncle Lawrence rose, surrendered himself a prisoner, and besought for a surgeon to examine his friend's wound. The rank of

Major Gordon obtained for him immediate attention. His hurt was found, however, not to be dangerous, though it would incapacitate his arm for awhile.

"All the inconvenience you will be subject to," said the doctor, "will be the having to carry your arm in a sling. Perhaps a little fever may set in, but we can soon reduce that: I will look you up, later in the day, and give you some medicine, if necessary."

For the present the prisoners were placed in a barn, Major Gordon being accommodated, as an officer, with a place by himself. This was a small apartment, partly shut off from the rest of the building, in which meal had been kept. A few armsful of sweet, salt hay, thrown upon the floor, rendered the accommodations a palace comparatively, at least to one who had experienced the hardships of Valley Forge. Uncle Lawrence was permitted to remain with our hero at his own request.

Here, as evening closed in, the two friends sat, conversing in low tones. Major Gordon was regretting that Uncle Lawrence had not availed himself of a chance to retreat, instead of remaining to save the speaker's life.

"I have no family," said the Major, "no ties on earth whatever. I have lost this post. Life is comparatively of little value to me."

"Don't say that, Major," interrupted the veteran. "It's agin religion, if not agin natur. No man knows what the Lord may have in store for him. You'll not be long a prisoner, maybe, and you've friends, and warm ones, where you least suspect, perhaps."

"No, my good, kind Herman; I will not affect to misunderstand you; I know to whom you allude; but it is not so. Your partiality has misled you. That lovely creature, whom I shall never cease to reverence, through my whole life, is too far separated from me by fortune, social position, and difference of political opinion, for me ever to hope to be honored with her love. I talk to you as to a father, you see, frankly and unreservedly. She can never be mine. It was folly in me to think otherwise, even for a moment."

"You are low-speerited, Major," said the honest old patriarch. "You're worn out, body and soul, just as I've been sometimes after hunting all day. The loss of this post sticks in you too, I see; though a braver fight was never made than you made, and so everybody, even the tories, will say. Cheer up! It's always darker, you know, just afore the dawn."

"Ah!" answered the Major, "it's less for myself than for you I am cast down. For my sake you are a prisoner. And do you know," he said, looking earnestly at his companion, "what that means?"

In the uncertain twilight of the place, the countenance of the speakers could still be faintly discerned; yet Major Gordon saw no perceptible change in the face of the old man, as the latter replied.

"It means a prison-ship, the fever, and maybe death," he said, "but I am in the Lord's hands, and his will be done. I'd do it over agin, Major, this minit," he said, earnestly, "if I had the chance; for it was duty; and my notion is that a man's got to do that, if wife, and children, and life too, all go for it."

The veteran's voice quivered at this thought of his family. But he resumed almost immediately, and in a firm voice.

"Howsomever, as I said afore, the Lord's will be done. He took Daniel out of the lion's den, and saved Shadrach, Meschid and Abednego in the fiery furnace; and if his ends are to be sarved by it, he'll open my prison doors as he did those of Peter."

"Alas! I don't wish to say anything to shake your beautiful faith," answered Major Gordon, "but the days of miracles are over. It's because I see no way in which you are to be restored to your family, that I blame myself so; for I was—say what you will—the instrument of bringing you to this pass."

Uncle Lawrence paused a moment, when he replied, in a voice slightly husky, but which he evidently tried to deprive of every evidence of emotion.

"If you please, Major, we'll say no more about the wife and boys at home. It's not the wisest plan, I take it, when a man's never to see 'em agin, perhaps, to aggervate it by telling him of 'em."

"Forgive me," said the Major, deeply touched, and grasping his hand; feeling more poignantly than ever the evil he had unconsciously done.

"Well, we'll say nothing about it," continued Uncle Lawrence, "but there's nothing to forgive."

There was a moment's silence; and then the old man spoke again.

"You're mistaken, though, Major," he said, "in what you say of Miss Katie. She's no more a tory than you and me."

"Not a royalist!" exclaimed Major Gordon, surprised out of his depression. And he added, after a pause for reflection. "Indeed, you must be mistaken. What grounds have you for your opinion?"

"Did you ever hear her say she was for the King?"

The Major thought awhile. He could, to his surprise, recall no such circumstance.

"Never!" he said at last.

"Haven't you heerd her say that she was a patriot?"

Again Major Gordon reflected.

"I have," he said, "but only in jest."

"Only in a joke, you mean, I suppose," answered Uncle Lawrence. "And don't you know Miss Katie well enough to know, that she says many a true thing in that gay, joking way of hers? Have you ever heerd her make fun of the poor fellers in General Washington's army, the Lord bless him! as she makes fun of the red coats and their dandy officers?"

Major Gordon was compelled to acknowledge, greatly to his own astonishment, that he never had. In fact a light began to break in upon him. He suspected that he had been in error all along, simply for having started with a fixed impression that Kate was a royalist, and having consequently viewed her acts and weighed her words under that delusion. Uncle Lawrence confirmed his opinion.

"I'll tell you what it is," said the veteran, with a triumphant chuckle, "you're like what I was once, when I put on the preacher's green spectacles, which he wore for his eyes; everything was sort of colored by the glasses; the sand looked as green as a meadow in spring, and the sky all over sickish-like, as if it had been on a spree, as they used to call it when I was a wild youngster. You've thought Miss Katie was a tory because her aunt was, and her cousin; but she's as good a whig as Lady Washington herself; and what's more, she'd as soon marry a monkey as one of them red coated captains," and the old man snapped his fingers with a gesture of sovereign contempt.

"There's her cousin," Major Gordon ventured to say; for since the conversation had became so familiar, he no longer avoided questions, which, at an earlier period of his acquaintance with Uncle Lawrence, he would have omitted from motives of delicacy to Kate.

"Her cousin!" and the veteran snapped his fingers even more scornfully than before. "If there wasn't another man on airth, she'd never marry Charles Aylesford. I tell you, Major," he added decisively, "she'd never marry where she don't love; and there's one man she loves already, or my name ain't Lawrence Herman."

His hearer's heart leaped into his throat, but he dared not ask who the man was.

The veteran saw, by the faint light the conflagration cast through the chinks, the emotion of our hero; and his gratification was evinced by another silent chuckle. He waited awhile, but receiving no answer, went on.

"You don't ask who the lucky man is," he said. "Now what if I was to tell you it was yourself?"

"You can't mean it!" cried Major Gordon, half starting to his feet; a glow of happiness, such as he had never experienced, shooting through his frame.

Uncle Lawrence was about to answer, when the door opened, and a stranger stooped to enter. He carried a lantern, which, though it threw a vivid glare on the two prisoners, did not at first reveal the face of the intruder. But, when the door was closed, this person raised the light so as to show his countenance, and held out his hand to the Major, whom he called by name.

"Captain Powell!" exclaimed our hero in astonishment, rising and grasping the proffered hand. "It is—isn't it?"

"It is Captain Powell," was the reply. "The last person, no doubt, you expected to see. But I owe you a heavy debt, and I have come to pay it, by setting you free."

"The Lord's hand is in it," cried Uncle Lawrence, lifting up his eyes reverently. "Did I not say, 'trust in the Lord,' Major?"

CHAPTER XLII
THE RELEASE

Oh! give me liberty. —Dryden.

Thus doth the ever-changing course of things
Run a perpetual circle. —Daniels.

'Tis not the many oaths, that make the truth;
But the plain single vow, that is vow'd true. —Shakespeare.

Captain Powell was one of those who had been a listener at Aylesford's bedside, during the confession of the latter. Arriving in New York, after the loss of his ship, without employment, or the chance of any, he had volunteered on the expedition against the Neck, and hence his presence. He it was, also, who had been commissioned by the chaplain to quiet Aylesford, by carrying a message to the American camp.

Accordingly, Captain Powell had left the room, but with other ulterior designs. He had already ascertained that Major Gordon had been made prisoner, and having heard his name mentioned by Aylesford more than once, a suspicion of the truth had flashed upon him. Indeed, often since his rescue from the wreck, had he speculated on an attachment springing up between our hero and Kate; for though he had seen little of the officer, he had observed enough, during those hours of terrible peril, to be convinced that he and Miss Aylesford were eminently fitted for each other. He resolved, accordingly, to see Major Gordon, in this crisis, satisfied, that if it was as he suspected, the best course would be to secretly liberate the prisoner.

"This is my friend," said our hero, turning to Uncle Lawrence, on observing that Captain Powell seemed surprised at not finding him alone. "He has, this day, saved my life, and whatever debt you may think you owe to me, I transfer to him."

The captain looked at Uncle Lawrence, at these words, with increased interest. But he was a judge of character, and the simple dignity with which the veteran rose and returned the salutation of the visitor, at once convinced the latter that the old man was no common person. The delicate subject, however, on which he had come to see Major Gordon, made him hesitate. Our hero, discovering this from his manner, said,

"You can speak, Captain, before Mr. Herman, as frankly as if he was myself."

Still, Captain Powell knew not how to open his mission, and paused in embarrassment. At last he bethought him to mention the fact, that "a young gentleman, named Aylesford, had come into camp desperately wounded, and was now at the point of death."

The surprise of Major Gordon, the horror of Uncle Lawrence, and the interest of both, produced immediately a torrent of questions, which led the conversation to the point that the visitor desired.

We will not attempt to paint the excitement of the hearers, when Captain Powell informed them that Kate was in the hands of Arrison. The emotion of Uncle Lawrence was almost as great as that of Major Gordon. The former, in fact, was more thoroughly acquainted with the refugee's character, and had consequently a keener sense, if possible, of Kate's peril. It was fortunate it was so: fortunate that the Major could scarcely believe in depravity so great as Arrison's; for otherwise he must have gone mad with suspense.

As it was, he could not keep still for an instant. He had started to his feet again, on the first intimation of Kate's danger; and had heard the conclusion of the narrative, striding up and down the narrow apartment, like a chafed lion in a cage.

"Oh! if I had been there, instead of here," he cried, clenching his hands. "Just heaven! such villainy."

"Calm yourself, my dear Major," answered Captain Powell. "You will be overheard." For this, as well as the former conversation between the prisoners, had been conducted in low tones, to prevent the other occupants of the building from hearing, whereas the Major, under the excitement of his feelings, had uttered these exclamations aloud.

"Calm yourself," continued Captain Powell. "It is to set you free, remember, that I am here."

The words were scarcely uttered before Major Gordon stopped in his walk, and seizing the speaker's hand, wrung it with energetic gratitude. His heart, however, was too full to allow him utterance.

"I need not say," resumed Captain Powell, "that there is not a minute to be lost."

But suddenly a shade of deep concern extinguished the light in Major Gordon's countenance. For the instant he had forgotten his fellow prisoner. But it had been only for an instant. Much as he desired freedom, in order to rescue Kate, or die in the attempt, he could not abandon Uncle Lawrence. He paused, and fixed his eyes on the old man, who stood silent and motionless, though every feature of his face was working with intense emotion; emotion not on his own account; not because the Major was to be freed, and himself remain a prisoner, but because his darling was in the hands of such a ruffian as Arrison.

"I cannot go," said Major Gordon, turning frankly to Captain Powell, "at least alone. My friend must accompany me. He has a family, and his life is precious to them; let him be released in my stead."

Captain Powell looked perplexed. But Uncle Lawrence spoke up.

"No," said he, addressing Captain Powell, "I am an old man, and my time is nearly out, while the Major is young, and can yet be of service to his country."

"But the young lady, consider her, sir," urged Captain Powell, speaking to Major Gordon. "Time is precious, and succor ought to be sent at once. For God's sake, Major, don't stand on scruples, which would honor you at another time, but are only periling Miss Aylesford's life at this crisis."

A sharp pang of agony shot visibly across his hearer's face. But the Major was inexorable. He resembled Uncle Lawrence, indeed, in the inflexibility with which he walked in the path of duty, when that duty became plain. No martyr, condemned to pass barefoot over burning plough-shares, could have executed his task more unflinchingly.

"Mr. Herman," he replied, "is the more suitable person then to be released, for he knows every acre of the forests about Sweetwater; and can do more, in an hour, in tracking these ruffians to their den, than I could in a day."

Captain Powell was evidently struck with this remark. He looked inquiringly at Uncle Lawrence, feeling, by that instinct which is called insight into character, that the veteran would speak the truth in reply, irrespective of conventional reserve on the one hand, or of self-interest on the other.

"I'll not deny," said the patriarch, mildly, "but what the Major speaks truth, in that partic'lar. I've hunted a'most every inch of the woods, for a dozen miles about, on every side, these forty years nigh. And I'd give," he added, earnestly, "half of the years I may have to live, if the Lord allowed me the right to do it, that I might be free. I'd burn the rascal out, like a fox from his hole, I'll warrant, afore to-morrow's sun was many hours high."

Captain Powell looked from one to the other, in perplexity, for a full minute, before he spoke again. At last he said, with sudden impulse,

"You shall both be free. Nay! no thanks," he continued, as the Major sprang forward again, and grasped his hand, "but listen. I have a pass for the Major. You, my venerable sir, are luckily about my height. You must exchange hats and coats with me," removing the articles as he spoke, and proffering them to Uncle Lawrence. "Go boldly out, for I left the pass with the sentinel, as if you were myself. The breeze was beginning to blow freely up the river, when I came in. You'll find a boat, with her sail ready, lying near the outside of the camp. The sentinel there will let you pass, on giving the watchword, 'loyalty.' Make the best of your way, in God's name, up the stream; and may success crown your efforts!"

He pressed the hands of both his hearers, as he ceased speaking, and the change of garments having been effected, fairly pushed them out of the place, first giving the lantern in charge to Uncle Lawrence, and whispering, as a parting admonition, "I brought it in with me, and they'll naturally expect to see me carry it out—be sure to lose not a minute, for the trick must soon be found out."

We will not detain the reader with the obstacles which the fugitives met on their way to the boat. To avoid being seen they were forced to skulk along in the shadows; but twice even this failed; though fortunately the knowledge of the pass-word secured their safety. At last they reached the skiff, and were almost instantly sweeping up the river, carrying what was a wholesale breeze, when we consider the size of their craft.

She was, indeed, but a mere cockle-shell, one of those small, decked, gunning skiffs, such as are still used in those waters, intended for only one person, but capable on emergency of carrying two; and she sank under the weight of her passengers, quite to the gunwale. There is, in these light and buoyant craft, which a strong man may easily carry on his shoulder, a small hole cut in the deck, where the sportsman sits, covered with sedge, and so paddles himself unperceived upon the wild fowl. Into this aperture, Uncle Lawrence directed Major Gordon to insert himself, while the old man, sitting flat on the stern, took both the tiller and sheet in his hand.

"Now, all I'll ask," said the veteran, "is that you'll trim boat as I tell you, and that this 'ere wind will hold all night. There's one or two reaches, where we'll have to row, probably."

Kate Aylesford | 229

"But I must first land and seek my late command," interposed Major Gordon. "If Count Pulaski has come up, I will then attend you; but if not," and he sighed audibly, "you will have to proceed alone."

Uncle Lawrence did not reply immediately. But a little reflection convinced him that his companion had decided aright, and therefore he said nothing to change the Major's opinion, though his heart ached.

"We had better come to here," he said, at last. "There's a road, somewhere near, that'll take us where we'll be pretty sure to find the Count, if he's on the ground."

CHAPTER XLIII
PULASKI

The storms of heaven
Beat on him; gaping hinds stare at his woe. —*Joanna Baillie.*

Deserted is my own good hall,
Its hearth is desolate; Wild weeds are gathering on the wall,
My dog howls at the gate. —*Byron.*

An exile, ill in heart and frame,—
A wanderer, weary of the way. —*Mrs. Osgood.*

Fastening the skiff to the overhanging bough of a tree, Uncle Lawrence stepped ashore, followed by Major Gordon. For about ten minutes, the two advanced along a narrow woodland path, until suddenly they were stopped by the challenge of a sentry.

Yielding themselves prisoners immediately, they were conducted to a woodland bivouac, where several volunteers recognized both Major Gordon and his companion. The horses picketed about, with the dismounted cavalry soldiers, imparted to the Major the glad intelligence that Count Pulaski had arrived.

"Say to the Count," he said, addressing his captor, "that I desire an interview, as soon as possible." For he was now all impatience to be gone.

In a few minutes he was ushered into the presence of his successor, whom we must take this opportunity to describe.

The Count Pulaski, who served so gallantly in the war of independence, until he fell at the storming of Savannah, must not be confounded with his relative, who achieved the daring feat of carrying off Stanislaus, King of Poland, from the heart of his capital. Nevertheless he was scarcely inferior in daring to that adventurous conspirator. Driven from his native land, in consequence of his connexion with the patriotic party, the Pulaski to whom we now introduce the reader, had, like Kosciusko, offered his sword to the struggling colonies of England, and now held the rank of Brigadier General, with the command of the entire American cavalry.

A more consummate horseman, perhaps, never lived. When in the saddle he seemed to be a part of the charger he bestrode. The traditions told of his skill appear really fabulous. He could pick up a pistol when galloping at speed; dismount and mount again in full career; and make his horse execute the most difficult feats apparently without moving hand or limb. Seventy-five years ago, equestrianism, as an art, was carried to a perfection unknown at the present time; and to say that Pulaski was considered the most perfect rider of his day, is, therefore, to assert that he would have been regarded as a miracle now.

Those who were intimate with the exile spoke enthusiastically of his lofty honor and the steadfastness of his friendship. But the number of these were few. Though courageous in his deportment, he was reserved, and this, added to his ignorance of the language, circumscribed the number of his associates. When alone he was the victim of a settled melancholy; for he remembered then, in all its force, that he was an exile, and what exile meant. As an officer he was diligent, sober and intrepid, never permitting himself to be disheartened by difficulties, but prosecuting the vexatious duty of organizing the cavalry force amid a thousand discouragements. The legionary corps which he established, and which he so chivalrously led till he fell at the siege of Savannah, was the model of one subsequently raised by Major Henry Lee, and which won immortal laurels under Greene, in the southern campaign.

Major Gordon was among the few who enjoyed the friendship of Pulaski. The gallant Pole was standing with folded arms, looking sadly up to the sky, thinking that the stars, which shone down on him, shone also on his native land, when the Major was announced. At once the melancholy faded from the Count's face, and he eagerly embraced our hero in the Polish fashion.

"Mon ami," he cried, in excellent French, "this is, indeed, a surprise. I heard you had been taken prisoner, or killed, the accounts did not agree as to which. How did you manage to escape?"

In a few hurried words, Major Gordon explained the cause and manner of his deliverance. The Count listened breathlessly. When, at last, the Major paused, Pulaski said, earnestly,

"Much as I wish to have a friend's companionship tonight, for I am in one of my dark moods, I beg you, dear Major, to be gone at once. Miss Aylesford must be rescued, or avenged, no matter at what cost. I shall count it one of the few fortunate events of my life, that I arrived here in time to release you from your command, especially if you succeed in recovering this fair girl from the hands of the refugees."

The Count accompanied Major Gordon to the river side, where, with many a "God-speed" from Pulaski, our hero and his companion embarked again. The little lateen sail was given to the wind, and the boat went dancing up the stream, until it vanished from the eyes of the spectators like the white wing of a gull disappearing in the distant gloom of the seaboard.

For some time there was silence on board the skiff. But at last Uncle Lawrence spoke.

"We'll be able, I suppose," said he, "to find a few men at the Forks; and we'd better strike into the woods there, instead of following the track of the varmints from the river. I've a notion I know pretty well where to find the rogues. If Arrison was alone, you might have to hunt him here, and there, and everywhere; but when a lady's in the case, he's sure to take to some roof; and there's a clearing, a matter of six miles or so, sou'east of Sweetwater, and right in the heart of the swamp, where a little gal lives, that I've heerd was a niece of Arrison's. I once stopped there for a drink of water; but though it's the only time I was ever there, seein' I don't gin'raly hunt on that side of Sweetwater, I can go to the place as straight as my gun would carry buckshot; it's a pity," he added, with a sigh, "that I've lost the old piece."

The fugitives did not, however, continue their route without pausing at the post where the refugees were fired on. They did this in the faint hope that the patriot boat, which Aylesford had seen set forth in pursuit, had overtaken the refugees.

Neither Major Gordon nor Uncle Lawrence knew how much each had secretly nourished this expectation, until it was destroyed by the intelligence they received at the post. But one good result followed the narrative they hurriedly gave in return. The sentry, who proved to be an old acquaintance of Uncle Lawrence, when he learned who the lady was, and into whose hands she had fallen, promised to follow, within half an hour, with four other able woodsmen. "We shan't be wanted below now, since the Neck's burnt," he said, "unless the British advance up the river; which they'll not try, I reckon, since Pulaski's come."

The sun was but an hour high, when every arrangement had been completed, and a party of a dozen determined men, all experienced shots, and all well armed, set out from the Forks, under the guidance of Uncle Lawrence and the leadership of Major Gordon. To hunt down the refugees, if it took days instead of hours; to rescue Kate unharmed, and to avenge her, at any cost:—these were the solemn vows of every member of the party.

While Uncle Lawrence had been marshaling the expedition, Major Gordon had thrown himself on Selim, and galloped to Sweetwater, with the faint hope that Kate might have been released, or made good her escape. Early as it was, he found Mrs. Warren already up. The good lady, as we have seen, had not slept a wink; and, just before the Major's arrival, she had been summoned to interrogate Pomp, who, to the amazement of all, had suddenly appeared, leading Arab captive.

The lad, of course, suppressed his fright, but said, that not hearing anything of Kate on the road to Mr. Herman's, but observing the tracks of what he thought her horse, he had followed down the river, by unfrequented paths, till about nightfall, when, passing a small cabin, he had been surprised to hear Arab whinny, from a shed that was apparently used for a cow-stable.

"When I hears dat," said he, "I goes up to de door, and axes ef dey wouldn't let me stay all night, telling 'em I'd lost my way, and was afeerd of de refugees. Dey said I might, ef I'd sleep in de barn; and guv me some cold pork. De minnit I goes in de stable, Arab he knew me, and lays his nose agin me, as ef he'd been a kitten, deed he did. I got in among de salt hay, and begun to snore dre'ful loud; but I wasn't asleep for all dat. By'm bye, when de moon rose, I gits up, saddles de colt, takes Arab by de halter, and here I is." And he looked around, not a little proud of his exploit, while Dinah, hugging him in her arms, sobbed over her recovered boy.

It was at this juncture that Major Gordon arrived. Mrs. Warren, in dishabille, her hair all dishevelled, no sooner saw him, than she rushed forward, frantically asking if he had brought back Kate. The Major, who had hoped, as we have seen, to find Miss Aylesford at Sweetwater, was not less disappointed than the anxious aunt; but he controlled his feelings better, and considerately forbore informing Mrs. Warren either of the terrible situation of her niece, or of Aylesford's death. A fit of hysterics almost immediately seized the now heart-broken woman, in which condition, time being precious, the Major was compelled to leave her, in order to reach the rendezvous.

Uncle Lawrence was waiting for him on his return. The little party set forth immediately, the veteran leading the way to the refugee's hut, almost in a straight line.

CHAPTER XLIV
THE PURSUIT

A stony adversary, an inhuman wretch
Incapable of pity, void and empty
From ev'ry drachm of mercy. —Shakespeare.

Spare not the babe,
Whose dimpled smiles from fools exhaust their mercy. —
Shakespeare.

The astonishment of Arrison, when he discovered the escape of Kate, was only equaled by his rage. He was not the first, however, to detect her flight. Having resisted the influence of the last night's potations longer than the rest, he slept sounder than some of the others, and was still lost in a deep stupefying slumber, when one of the gang waking, and looking around, as he sat up on the floor, started to observe the door of the inner chamber open.

"Hello!" he cried, rubbing his eyes, to be sure that he beheld aright. "The bird's flown."

With the words, he sprang to his feet, and advancing hastily to the chamber, leaned over Arrison's recumbent body, and looked in. His suspicions were immediately verified. Their prisoner was gone. The discovery struck him in so ludicrous a light, that he burst into uproarious laughter.

This loud mirth roused all the sleepers, Arrison among the rest.

"What do you mean?" cried the latter, leaping to his feet, and collaring the laugher. "What are you doing here?"

Arrison, still confused in intellect, and not yet comprehending the truth, had seized his comrade, by instinct, on finding the refugee so near Kate's chamber.

"Ha! ha!" continued the youth, unable to restrain his merriment, "to think she's flown, after I nailed fast her window too."

"Who's flown?" angrily cried Arrison, shaking the youth violently; while, with an oath, he added, as he now first observed the open door, "You don't mean to say Miss Aylesford's gone."

The youth stopped laughing, and breaking loose by a sudden effort, answered, with a flushed and angry face,

"Take care who you collar, Captain; I'm not a nigger." And as Arrison rushed into the chamber, he muttered, sulkily, "I'm not sorry she's gone; for he was goin' to make all for himself there was to be made; takin' the oyster and leaving us the shell."

A rapid glance satisfied Arrison that his prey had really escaped, and he came back, perfectly white with rage, just in time to hear the concluding murmurs of the youth, though without being able to make out what was being said.

"What's that you're muttering, you mutinous rascal?" he shouted, darting on the speaker. "I believe you had a hand in it. She couldn't have got off alone."

The youth sprang nimbly to one side, just in time to elude the grasp of his enraged leader, and interposing the table between himself and Arrison, drew his knife.

"Keep off," he cried, "or I'll drive this into you, Captain or no Captain. Say that again, if you dare. It was your own stupidity, in getting drunk, not drawing the bolt on this side, and sleeping like a log of wood, that let the girl off."

He flourished his weapon as he spoke, and glared at Arrison with such savageness, that the latter, heated as he was with passion, paused. Before either could make any new movement, and while they watched each other like two angry tigers, the lieutenant, whom we have seen so active the preceding day, rushed between them.

"Captain, you're too quick," he cried; "Bill, put up your knife; the Captain's hardly awake. If the gal's really gone," he continued, more composedly, "the best thing to do is to put after her; she can't have got far; and with that hound of yours," and he turned to Arrison, "we ought to be able to track her to hell itself."

"I meant no offence," said Bill, who was easily mollified, as men of his disposition usually are. "But when I found she'd got off, by walking right through this 'ere room, I couldn't help thinking it a good joke. She's a gal of mettle, anyhow." And he laughed again, in spite of Arrison's scowling brow, and the lieutenant's significant winks.

Arrison, now that he had time to reflect, saw that Bill spoke the truth, and though the youth's laughter galled him, he could not resent it further.

The ties which held his followers to him, were wholly voluntary, and he feared, if he persisted in wreaking his vengeance on Bill, that a real mutiny might arise; for the lad was a general favorite, as he always told the merriest tale, was continually joking to beguile the time, and generally was the life of the gang, socially. So the chief answered, smothering his rage, "I was but half awake, that's a fact. The jade's had no one to help her but herself; and Bill must forget what I said." He held out his hand as he concluded, which the youth took and shook in token of restored amity.

"That's all I ask, Captain," replied Bill. "I don't wonder you're a little riled, for if she'd been mine, as she was yourn, I'd have fell on the first feller I saw, when I woke and found her gone, so infernally rampaging mad would I have been. She'll be lucky if she gets away; for them ere swamps ain't so easy for a stranger."

But the wrath which Arrison could not discharge on Bill, found vent on the helpless child, his reputed niece. It suggested itself to him, at this point, that the bloodhound must have been roused by Kate's escape; that the child must have interposed to quiet the dog; and that thus his prey had succeeded in escaping. Scarcely had the speaker ceased, therefore, before Arrison rushed out, and entering the barn, where the child still lay asleep, grasped her rudely by the arm, and jerked her to her feet.

Terrified, and as yet but half awake, the poor thing began to tremble violently; and seeing Arrison's face distorted with rage, burst into tears, exclaiming,

"Oh! don't—please don't—"

But the ruffian, shaking her violently, she could not proceed; and so remained sobbing and choaking, piteously supplicating him with her eyes.

"You jade," he cried, "I'll shake the breath out of you to some purpose. You little liar, don't dare to say you didn't do it."

"I didn't say it," gasped the child. "Please don't, ple-e-ase—"

But again he shook her, till it seemed that her little limbs would be rent apart; and her touching words of pleading ended in inarticulate murmurings. When he had fairly exhausted himself by this brutal exhibition of passion, he stopped, and holding her before him, as in a vice, said,

"Tell the truth, or I'll break every bone in your body. You kept the dog quiet while she went off."

"Oh! please, don't. You hurt me so," answered the child, endeavoring, with one of her little hands, to remove his iron grasp, which was bruising her arm.

"Answer me," yelled the monster, purple with rage, and shaking the friendless orphan again.

The child would not reply falsely; she, therefore, said nothing.

"What! You won't speak?" he cried, perfectly beside himself and; he struck her a blow over the head, which brought the blood gushing from her ears and nose. She fell, as if dead, at his feet.

His comrades had witnessed this scene, and though hardened to most descriptions of crime, could not longer endure his brutality. Indeed, Bill and another would have interfered before, if the lieutenant had not held them back, telling them it was Arrison's niece, and that "he had a right to do as he pleased with her." But now even this personage overcame his scruples.

"Come, come, Captain," he said, picking up the child, "we'd better be off. What's done can't be helped. She's but a poor, weak thing, anyhow; and who knows that the dog gave the alarm at all?"

At first Arrison scowled at this interference, but the faces of his followers showed him that the lieutenant had spoken the will of the majority. So, resolving to punish her to his heart's content at a future period, he bade her "go and wash her face, and stop crying, or he'd give her something to cry for," and turned away.

It took but a few minutes longer to complete the preparations for the pursuit. The refugees hastily swallowed some food, and drained each a deep draught of Jamaica, after which, with the bloodhound for their guide, they began the search. The dog struck the trail immediately, and went off in full chorus: and in a little while the pursuers were out of sight.

The child remained where she had been left, sobbing as if her heart would break, and with her face buried in her hands; every bone in her body aching from the violence she had suffered.

"Oh! I wish I was dead! I wish I was dead!" she cried, rocking her little body to and fro. "Mother, mother, let me come to you;" and she looked up piteously to the skies.

Gradually, however, the passion of her tears ceased. She had often endured equally brutal treatment before; and she was, in a measure, hardened to it. So her sobs grew less frequent; her thoughts dwelt less on her own sufferings; and she began to recollect Kate.

"I hope she'll get off," she cried, jumping up and clapping her hands. "If she only took the right road."

But scarcely had she spoken, when she reflected that, if his prey wholly escaped, Arrison would return more violently enraged than ever. Experience warned her that, in such a case, he would wreak double vengeance on her. She burst into tears again, in almost speechless terror at the idea.

She could think of nothing in this extremity, but the little prayers her mother had taught her, and which she still murmured nightly before retiring, for lack of others more suited to her years. So she fell on her knees, and, with her hands clasped before her, prayed. But, with the almost infantile words went up earnest heart-petitions, which, more eloquent than the most burning language, reached—who shall doubt it?—the ear of the Father of all.

When Uncle Lawrence reached the hut, an hour or two later, the child, who had heard the approach of the party, was nowhere to be seen; for she had hidden herself in terror in the barn, thinking her persecutor was coming back. But she was not long suffered to remain concealed. Alarmed at the evidences of the debauch, Uncle Lawrence decided to search every spot about; and thus the child was soon discovered. On finding that the intruders were friends of Kate, the poor thing lost her terror, however, and answered their questions eagerly, giving what information she could as to the route the pursuers had taken.

The woodcraft of Uncle Lawrence now came into full play. No Indian could have tracked the refugees more surely than he did. Occasionally, a few moments were lost in hesitancy, but he invariably selected the right crossing at last. Such minutes of delay, however, were almost intolerable, especially to Major Gordon; for, now that the crisis of Kate's fate approached, he felt the agony of suspense increase tenfold. His incessant cry to himself was, "we shall be too late." This terrible conviction deepened, as the hours wore on without conducting them to our heroine, or apparently bringing them nearer to the refugees, the bay of whose bloodhound they listened for in vain.

But when the way became more difficult, they began, though as yet ignorant of it, to gain rapidly on Arrison; for, as the path had grown more intricate, the bloodhound had been often at fault, and thus had lost much time.

At last the cry of the hound was heard. What a thrill of joy it sent through Major Gordon's frame! Every nerve tingled, as he cried,

"She is yet safe. On, on, for the love of God—we may not be too late after all."

The pace of the pursuers was now accelerated to a run. Suddenly Uncle Lawrence said,

"That dog is nearly up with her; I know it by the quick way in which he cries. Follow the track as fast as you can. I'll take a short cut through the swamp; I think I can make something by it, though none of the rest can. The cry of the hound will lead me to the right spot."

He had never ceased running as he spoke; and it was wonderful to see how he could run, with the weight of sixty winters on him; and he now vanished from sight, the bushes crackling as he dashed right into the undergrowth.

Following the trails made by the wild animals, and occasionally breaking through a thicket; now wading in black, slimy water up to his knees, and now plunging into blacker mud ankle-deep; and guiding himself, partly by the cry of the hound, and partly by a woodman's instinct of the course which he knew Kate must have taken, he reached our heroine, as we have seen, just in time to save her life by shooting the bloodhound that was springing at her throat. Then pausing to reload, with a veteran hunter's precaution, he leaped into the open space, and confronted Arrison.

Everything now depended on the length of time it would take Major Gordon to come up with his companions. Minutes, at present, were worth hours at any other crisis.

CHAPTER XLV
THE DEATH-SHOT

With wild surprise,
As if to marble struck devoid of sense. —*Thomson.*

Amaz'd,
Astonished stood, and blank, while horror chill
Ran through his veins. —*Milton.*

Arrison was thunderstruck by the sudden apparition of Uncle Lawrence. His first movement was to start back, as if he saw a spirit; for the old man was the last person he had expected to confront him. But in a moment he recovered his usual presence of mind. When he perceived that he was opposed by veritable flesh and blood, and that too in the person of one he hated for his goodness, he secretly exulted; for having no suspicion that Uncle Lawrence had friends at hand, he considered that his long threatened vengeance was certain.

Yet he was in no hurry to assail the old man. Aware that his followers must be close behind him, and that a few moments at furthest would enable them to arrive, he determined to keep the contest confined to words, if possible, until they came up. Old as Uncle Lawrence was, he bore a reputation for bravery, skill and strength, which made Arrison quite willing to avoid a hand to hand struggle with the patriarch.

"You!" cried Arrison. "Take a word of advice then, old man, and don't mix yourself up with a business that's none of your concern."

"But suppose I think it does consarn me," coolly answered Uncle Lawrence. "Miss Katie here is an old pet of mine, so stand aside and let us pass."

"Not so fast. Again, I say, go your ways and save your life."

"I do not go without her. Stand aside, villain."

"Never," exclaimed Arrison, chafed at these words. "I warn you not to try my patience too far."

"I'm not afeerd of you, James Arrison," answered the old man, in a tone of contempt, "and you know it. Keep your warning for some one else."

"Will you go?"

"No!"

Scarcely had the veteran spoken, when the refugee pulled trigger. But, quick as he had been, the old man was quicker. Resolving to save his fire if possible, in order to be better prepared for self-defence, if the refugees arrived before Major Gordon, he suddenly and dexterously thrust forward the barrel of his piece in such a manner as to knock up the gun of the outlaw. The movement was so swift that Arrison had time neither to counteract it, nor to prevent his load from going off; and the consequence was that his ball whistled harmlessly over Uncle Lawrence's head, burying itself in the tree against which Kate leaned, a few inches above her. A savage oath broke from the refugee at this failure, and his eyes flashed lightning as it were. He shortened his gun instantly, as if to club it; then hesitated whether he had not better throw it away and rush in on his antagonist; and finally stood irresolute, his face purple with rage and baffled hate.

Had it suited Uncle Lawrence's purpose that second would have been the last of the ruffian's existence. A younger man would have been unable, in the sudden heat of the affray, to have restrained himself, even from motives of the clearest policy. But the veteran was as cool and wary now as when sitting by his own hearth. Nothing could induce him to waste his fire; for, in that case, he might not have time to reload before the other refugees came up.

"Throw down your gun," he said, however. "You are at my mercy."

What answer Arrison would have made, if no succor had arrived, we cannot say. But, at this crisis, his sharpened ear heard the crackling of the undergrowth, as his followers came running up at full speed, their pace accelerated by the two shots which had been fired in such quick succession; for though it has required a considerable time to describe all this, the whole period between the death of the bloodhound and the useless discharge of Arrison's gun, had scarcely occupied more than a minute.

Aware that an overwhelming force was now at hand, the outlaw sprang forwards towards Kate, endeavoring to elude his antagonist, and crying out,

"Shoot the old man; but spare the girl. Shoot quick!"

But he did not finish the sentence. Uncle Lawrence, who faced the intruders, had the advantage of observing what Arrison could not; and saw that the new comers, so far from being refugees entirely, were partly Major Gordon and his follows.

In fact, the speed of the patriots had been also accelerated by the shots; they had rushed forward at full run, fearing that Uncle Lawrence was overpowered; and had arrived at the scene simultaneously with the outlaws, the latter only discovering the presence of foes at the very moment that Arrison cried out; for, on their part, they had been so entirely absorbed in what was going on ahead, that they had neither looked behind, nor heard the steps of their pursuers. Instead, therefore, of being able to assist their leader, the outlaws found their own hands full; for the patriots dashed upon them at once, like hunters that have run down a wolf, which has long been the terror of the district.

All this Uncle Lawrence took in with one rapid glance, and seeing that the ruffian's time had come, he leveled his gun at Arrison's heart and pulled the trigger, just as the wretch was darting past to lay his sacrilegious hands on Kate.

"To die the death of a dog at last," he mentally ejaculated. "I knew it years ago."

As he thus soliloquized, the burly person of the ruffian, spinning half round, while the arms were suddenly thrown up, tumbled headlong to the ground, where it fell directly across the body of the dead hound. Life was gone, even before the form touched the earth.

Meantime the pursuers had closed with the refugees, discharging their guns, each at an antagonist, and following this up by closing with such as were either not injured, or only wounded. Some, dropping their fire-arms, drew their swords, and engaged in a hand to hand conflict; others clubbed their pieces, using them like maces; and some grappled with the refugees to prevent the latter employing their guns, few of which had been discharged in consequence of the surprise.

The onslaught had been so unexpected, and was kept up in so rapid a manner, that the refugees did not hold out long. Two were killed at the first assault; others soon lay on the ground desperately wounded; and finally the survivors, seeing that all was over, broke desperately from their antagonists, and rushing madly into the next thicket, disappeared from sight. Only two succeeded, however, in making good their escape in this way, and one of them at least was seriously wounded, for the bushes were stained with blood as he passed.

The victory was complete, and, owing to the surprise, comparatively without cost. The patriots did not lose a man, and had but two seriously wounded, the rest receiving only slight scratches, scarcely requiring surgical aid. As one of the conquerors was accustomed to say, in rehearsing the transaction afterwards,—he was an inveterate duck-shooter whose language always drew its metaphors from his favorite pursuit— "We stole up onparceived, you understand, and killed and wounded five, whom we got, besides two that scattered that we didn't get."

Uncle Lawrence had not joined in the fray after his decisive shot. In fact, the conflict was over before he could have taken any further part in it, even if he had wished; but knowing that a chance shot might strike Kate, he chivalrously threw himself before her; and thus protected her at the risk of his own life.

Major Gordon, ignorant whom he was assailing, had engaged Arrison's lieutenant. The latter had been the first to discover the pursuers, and had turned immediately and fired at our hero; but in the hurry of the act had fortunately missed his mark. The Major, having no gun, had rushed in with his sword, and though incommoded by his wounded arm, which he still carried in a sling, had run his antagonist through, after an ineffectual attempt on the part of the refugee to avert the lunge. Disregarding every other consideration, our hero had sprung to Kate's side immediately, which he attained just as the combat was finished, and the last of the outlaws took to flight.

The cold formalities of conventional life were forgotten, in that moment of joyous excitement, as if they had never existed. Even those considerations of superior fortune and presumed difference of political opinion, which had so tormented our hero before, were overlooked. Clasping Kate's hand, he pressed it with a fervor, which brought the eloquent blood over her pallid countenance. On her part, the behavior of Kate was equally impulsive. It is fair to presume that she did not know what she was doing; for she returned the pressure almost convulsively. Giving one long, grateful look, in which her whole soul went forth, as her eyes met those of her lover, she essayed to speak. But though the sweet lips half parted, no words followed, for a faintness suddenly overcame her; and feeling everything swimming around, she involuntarily staggered towards the Major for support, who clasped her in his arms just as she was falling to the ground.

When next Kate opened her eyes, her head was lying against her lover's shoulder, while Uncle Lawrence, kneeling beside her as tenderly as one of her own sex, was bathing her temples.

For an instant she did not recognize where she was. She even shuddered at first, with a vague notion that she was still in the power of the outlaws; but when she saw Major Gordon's face, which was looking anxiously down on her, she closed her eyes with a smile. If, simultaneously, she nestled closer to that manly shoulder, it was only for an instant; for, while she was still half unconscious of what she did; for immediately after she opened her eyes again with a deep blush, and made an effort to rise.

But Uncle Lawrence prevented this. He gently pressed her back, while bathing her forehead, saying, soothingly,

"Hush, darling, and lie still a bit longer. You'll be fainting right off again, if you get up awhile yet: and you mustn't think you hurt the Major, for it's the other arm that's wounded."

To his dying day, Major Gordon was accustomed to say that a sly look, almost imperceptible, accompanied these last words. But, if so, Kate saw nothing of this, having grown faint again, from the exertion she had made. Her head now swam around to such a degree, that she was compelled, at this crisis, to close her eyes, and even to repose once more on the Major's shoulder.

Strange to say, the turn of Uncle Lawrence came next. When Kate was, at last, sufficiently restored to be able to sit up unsupported, she observed a slight stream of blood trickling down the hand of the good old man. With a faint scream she called Uncle Lawrence's attention to it, who, stripping up his sleeve, found, to his surprise, that a ball had struck him just above the wrist; evidently one of those discharged in the melee, and which would have hit Kate, if he had not interposed his body, in the true spirit of ancient knighthood.

"It's nothing, my child," he said, as, indeed, Kate immediately perceived.

But even while he spoke he fainted dead away, for Uncle Lawrence, brave as he was, both morally and physically, had that strange peculiarity common to some of the most courageous men that ever lived, to swoon at sight of his own blood.

It was now Kate's turn, and, weak as she was, she would allow no one else to bathe the old man's brow and bind up his wound. Uncle Lawrence's swoon soon passed away, however. When he opened his eyes, it was with a smile of gratefulness inexpressibly sweet.

"The Lord bless you, darling," he said, tenderly, as his gaze lingered on Kate's countenance. Then he added, looking around on the anxious faces, "Pretty doings, to get sick in this way, like a narvous, sterricky woman. You'd drum such a cowardly fellow out of the army, Major—wouldn't you?"

"If we had a few thousand heroes like you," answered Major Gordon, pressing his hand, while sudden tears dimmed his eyes, "we'd have had our country free long ago."

CHAPTER XLVI
SWEETWATER AGAIN

Such is the power of that sweet passion,
That it all sordid baseness doth expel,
And the refined mind doth newly fashion
Unto a fairer form, which now doth dwell
In his high thoughts, that would itself excel,
Which he, beholding still with constant sight,
Admires the mirror of so heavenly light. —Spenser.

But now lead on;
In me is no delay; with thee to go
Is to stay here; with thee here to stay
Is to go hence unwilling; thou to me
Art all things under heaven. —Milton.

It was some time before Kate was able to undertake the fatigues of a return. At last, however, she set forth, supported by Major Gordon, who had, notwithstanding his wound, an arm uninjured to offer to her. When they had emerged from the denser part of the swamp, it was proposed to construct a litter for her, the road now allowing of her being transported in this way; but she declined the proffer, insisting that she was able to walk to the hut, at least.

For, as the way led back to within a mile of that place, Uncle Lawrence decided that it would be advisable to go there at once, because Kate could then obtain some repose, while a messenger, despatched to Sweetwater, might bring a carriage to transport her home, later in the day. As by this plan Mrs. Warren would obtain intelligence of her safety sooner than if they all pursued their way to the family mansion immediately, Kate pronounced in favor of it. Moreover, by this scheme, she would be able to bring away with her the orphan child, who had been so instrumental in her escape, and who, now that the reputed uncle was no more, would be willing, Kate reasoned, to accompany her to Sweetwater. To this desolate little girl our heroine felt her heart strangely drawn, even apart from the gratitude which filled her heart towards the child as the preserver of her life.

Accordingly, when they reached the main road, where Kate had taken the wrong turn, two of the patriots left the party, and hastened with all their speed to Sweetwater; while the remainder, striking into the byway that led to the cabin, advanced at a slower pace, accommodated to our heroine's fatigue.

When the latter reached the clearing on the knoll of the swamp, they found that the child, already forced by circumstances to be a housekeeper, had removed the evidences of the last night's debauch, and restored everything to order and comparative neatness. The table was set away; the chairs replaced in their positions; the floor swept and subsequently sanded, as was then the fashion. The child was sitting, trying to read with difficulty, when the party came up; and the book falling from her hands in her surprise, Uncle Lawrence took it up, and discovered, as he had suspected, that it was a Testament.

When she recognized Kate, the orphan stole immediately to her side, and, clasping the hands of our heroine between both her own little palms, said, gently,

"I'm so glad you've come back. Oh! how I wished, all the morning, that these good people would find you."

"I've come back to take you away with me," said Kate, stooping, and kissing the child. "You musn't shake your head sadly. There's nothing now to keep you here. That bad man, who called himself your uncle, is dead and gone."

The orphan looked wonderingly at Kate; then at Uncle Lawrence; and, finally, around the entire group. Reading a confirmation of this truth in every eye, her little face assumed an awe-struck expression, and she burst into tears.

Kate tried to soothe her.

"He wasn't your uncle at all, dear," she said, taking the child in her lap, for they had now entered the house. "These gentlemen," turning to Major Gordon and Uncle Lawrence, "say they know all about you. So you musn't think of him, except as a bad, bad man, who has brought death on himself by his own wickedness."

"It's that that makes me cry," said the child, looking up through her tears.

Uncle Lawrence, laying his hand on her head in his fatherly manner, said to the orphan,

"I've no doubt, my little one, that this lady here is nearer related to you than maybe you or she thinks. But more of that bye and bye," he continued. "It's to her house you're to go, and you ought to thank the Lord, my child, that he's given you such a friend."

"Now," said Kate, kissing her, "you can't help being my little sister."

"I'll be so glad," murmured the child, hiding her face on Kate's shoulder, and closely entwining her arms around our heroine, who looked up, smiling through her tears, at Major Gordon and Uncle Lawrence.

Nearly four hours elapsed before the expected vehicle arrived from Sweetwater. During this interval, Kate was urged to snatch some repose, for it will be recollected that excepting the short period she slept by accident the night before, she had not closed her eyes for thirty-six hours, while, meantime, she had undergone the greatest fatigue of body and mind. But her nerves were still too excited from the agitating events which had followed her first capture, to permit her to compose herself to sleep; and besides, she shrank from re-entering the chamber where she had passed a night of such agonizing suspense.

Mrs. Warren's joyful consternation, when she heard of Kate's safety, it is almost impossible to describe. The effect of the news was completely paralyzing to her, as much so, for awhile, indeed, as if it had been intelligence the most disastrous.

For quite a minute the servants thought she was dying, and being, to use one of their own expressions, "a'most as flustered as herself," they did all sorts of absurd things in the effort to help her. Pomp's father seized a flower-vase, which Kate had arranged the preceding morning, and threw its contents into her face, plants and water alike. Dinah, his wife, attempted to cut the good lady's stays with the back of a bread-knife, with which she had rushed in from the kitchen, being engaged in slicing a loaf when she heard the uproar. The maid screamed at the top of her lungs, and ran out of the room, with a vague design of seeking a vinaigrette bottle in one of the chambers; but she finally captured a phial of patent medicine, which Mrs. Warren patronized, as many excellent old dowagers will, and unconscious of her error, rushed back again, screaming as fast as ever, and popped the horrible compound under the dame's nose. Between the application of Jim, and this of the maid, Mrs. Warren soon came to; and it was fortunate for her she did; for, as one of the news-bearers said, in rehearsing the tale afterwards,— "they'd have killed her next, seein' that we was so frightened by the infernal screechin' of that Frenchified gal, with the physic-bottle, that we thought the old 'oman had gone for sartain."

When Kate at length arrived at Sweetwater, the good dame had recovered her usual equanimity. Having improved the interval to repair the disorder of her attire, she now appeared in all her ordinary pomp of costume; her voluminous furbelowed gown sweeping half the room; her high, red-heeled shoes pattering, as she rushed down the porch; and the powder flying like snow from her tower-like head-dress, and perfuming the air around her, as if the wind blew from a spice-garden.

Extending her arms, into which Kate threw herself, she said,

"Bless us, my child, what trouble you've given me, and all from riding alone. I knew something terrible would happen from the first. But don't think I blame you. I'm too glad to see you for that."

In fact, Mrs. Warren, having discharged her conscience in the way of reproof, began to kiss her niece passionately, at the same time bursting into tears. Uncle Lawrence afterwards remarked, that he thought, that "next to fallin' into the clutches of a baar, the most dangerous thing was bein' hugged by Mrs. Warren, for she nigh a'most squeezed Katie to death."

It was a long time before Kate recovered from the effects of that terrible day and night. Though she had borne up so heroically while the peril continued, she broke down completely after she found herself safely at home; and for nearly a week she was unable even to leave her chamber. By the end of that time, however, she appeared in the parlor, where, though still pale, she seemed to Major Gordon lovelier than ever.

Our hero, who had called daily to inquire after her progress, was almost transported beyond himself, when, one morning, on being shown as usual into the parlor, he saw Kate sitting there instead of her formal aunt. The young heiress rose immediately, and frankly advanced, extending her hand.

"This is, indeed, a surprise," cried Major Gordon, taking the delicate little palm between his two hands. "I had not hoped so much, after what Mrs. Warren said yesterday."

"My good aunt," replied Kate, with a smile and a blush, "always takes the worst view of things, you know."

"Has she done censuring you for being the sole cause of your late peril, by riding out alone?" asked the Major, smiling also, as he led her to the sofa.

"She has it over a dozen times a day, and always ends by declaring she 'knew something dreadful would happen;' that's her pet phrase. But come, we musn't laugh at aunt's foibles in this way; she's an excellent creature; and, you know, you and she are to be the best of friends."

From this opening of the conversation, and from the tone of the speakers, it was evident that they had come already to a perfect understanding. Major Gordon, in fact, had written a letter to Kate, when he found that she could not leave her chamber; for he deemed it due to both herself and him, that an explicit avowal of his feelings should be in her hands without delay. This letter was really the best medicine Kate could have had; for, by assuring her of his love, it removed what otherwise would have been a source of secret agitation to her.

The reader, indeed, must long since have suspected that Kate was as much in love with Major Gordon as he with her. The interview at the bridge, with our hero's conduct afterwards, had first opened her eyes to the state of her heart. The letter of our hero afforded her at last an opportunity, consistent with maidenly propriety, to acknowledge her affection; and as she was too true-hearted and sincere to trifle with her correspondent, she wrote immediately such an answer as made the recipient nearly wild with joy, though the note itself was quite simple and even laconic.

We leave them together, on this first meeting since their betrothal, to exchange those questions as to when each first began to love, and renew those protestations, which made the pair happy beyond words, as such things have made many another pair, but which would be insipid enough if printed.

CHAPTER XLVII
THE ORPHAN CHILD

Is there, in human form, that bears a heart—
A wretch! a villain! lost to love and truth?
That can with studied, shy, ensnaring art,
Betray sweet Jenny's unsuspecting truth?
Curse on his perjur'd arts! —Burns.

Naught so ill
As the betrayer's sin! salvationless
Almost. —Bailey.

The intelligence of Aylesford's death deeply affected both Kate and her aunt. The latter, who had lavished so much of her affection on him, was almost inconsolable. In charity to the dead, and from respect to Mrs. Warren's feelings, Aylesford's connection with Kate's capture was concealed from her.

"Why tear open the wounds of the past?" said Major Gordon, when Uncle Lawrence, from what he thought justice to Kate, would have told the whole story. "He has gone to his account, bitterly repenting, before he died, this act at least. His aunt is childless, and had lavished the chief stock of her love upon him; and to destroy her idol now, will go near to breaking her heart. At least, wait until Miss Aylesford recovers, and can be consulted."

These arguments prevailed. When Kate's opinion was asked, she pronounced at once against informing her aunt. "It can do no good to the living, and can but harm the good name of the dead. I freely forgive him. Aunt would go pining all the rest of her days, if forced to believe the truth of my poor cousin."

But this abnegation on the part of our heroine, cost her many a complaint from Mrs. Warren, who, ignorant of the true cause of Kate's capture, continued to insist that her niece's temerity, in riding out unattended, had led to all the perils which had followed. It is probable that the good dame, if she had known that Aylesford was in chase of the refugee boat, when shot, would have secretly laid his death at the door of her niece.

It was long before Mrs. Warren became reconciled to her nephew's loss. She openly bewailed his death, as the extinction of the family name, "for," said she, "when you marry, Kate, you know you'll be an Aylesford no longer." The cup out of which her "child," as she now called him, had drunk at his last breakfast; the knife and fork which he had used; and a pair of gloves he had accidentally left on the hall table, were carefully preserved by the old lady, and were annually drawn from their receptacle, on the anniversary of his death, and regarded with tears. Let us not ridicule the fond illusion of the poor creature. She worshipped, in this sacred way, a visionary memory it is true; but the image was a reality in her eyes and therefore dear to her.

They were so careful of her feelings that they spared her even the knowledge of the parentage of the little girl, whom Kate had brought home and now publicly adopted as a sister. That the child had been instrumental in preserving our heroine's life was the avowed reason of this adoption; and it satisfied Mrs. Warren, though she could not help saying, that "Kate was an odd girl, and often over, paid her debts." But those, who knew the true history of the orphan, were aware that other considerations also had led to this solemn act.

The Testament, which Uncle Lawrence picked up, and which was subsequently handed to Kate by Mrs. Herman, contained the inscription, "Margaret Rowan, her book, A. D., 1769," written in Aylesford's handwriting. The volume was evidently, therefore, the gift of Kate's cousin to the child's mother, about the time when his acquaintance with the latter commenced, and before he had, by deserting her and her babe, brought on that broken heart of which she died. The book, as was frequently the fashion then, was carefully covered with cloth, between which and the original sheepskin binding Kate found a paper, the purport of which was that "Charles Aylesford and Margaret Rowan" were lawfully married "on the 10th of December, A. D., 1769." On the back of this certificate was written, however, in a tremulous, unformed female hand, "I have proof that the within named clergyman was an impostor," the words being signed, "Margaret Rowan, 1773." The whole book, inside and out, was much thumbed and blotted with tears. It revealed to Kate, already possessed of other facts in relation to this early aberration of her cousin, a tale of youthful passion, deliberate perjury, and subsequent abandonment, which made her heart yearn to the innocent orphan more than ever.

From chance references made to her mother by the child, from what Kate had heard formerly, and from the results of inquiries she set on foot now, our heroine succeeded in finally filling up the outlines of this humble tragedy, which, if it could have had a Shakespeare to narrate it, might have moved nations and generations, instead of making but a faint echo in its little circle, and then dying away forever. Aylesford, when still a youth comparatively, had met and loved the reduced and orphan daughter of a British officer, who, dying in America, towards the close of the old French war, had left his child and wife penniless strangers in a foreign land. The mother had soon followed the father, and the daughter being left destitute, had sunk into a subordinate position. When Aylesford first met her she was only sixteen, innocent in every thought, and a mere child in her knowledge of life. Occupying the place of a seamstress, in the house of a wealthy female connexion of the Aylesfords, she was thrown in the way of the young man, and readily bestowed her affections on one so much superior in outward bearing to other persons of his age and sex whom she had met. Aylesford had but little difficulty in persuading her to give him a right to elevate her from her dependent position; but he brought forward the prejudices of his family as a reason for having the marriage secretly performed. He chose this method of betraying his victim, because he knew that a false priest could easily be procured, and because he was aware that in no other way could he carry out his base designs on this friendless girl. Accordingly Arrison, who had been the Mephistopheles of this tragedy all along, procured a tool to play the part of a clergyman; and the unsuspecting Margaret became a victim, where she fondly believed she was to be a wife.

More than a year, however, elapsed before she discovered the perfidy to which she had been sacrificed. But when, after the birth of her child, Aylesford's passion began to cool, Arrison surprised her by insulting proposals, which, on her indignantly rejecting them, and adding that she would expose him to her husband, led to an avowal from the ruffian of the true position in which she stood. She lost no time in charging Aylesford with the deed; a violent altercation ensued, and the sated young man, not sorry for an excuse to quarrel, parted from her forever.

We draw a veil over years that followed. The deserted, heart-broken creature, whom common rumor said had consented to marry Arrison, would not even see that person, but hiding herself from all eyes, sought to earn a humble livelihood by her needle. But the blow, which had ruined all her bright hopes, had undermined her health forever. She was not fitted, either physically or otherwise, to struggle with adversity. From the hour that she learned she was not a wife, she faded slowly but surely. After a few years of severe toil, rendered necessary to obtain food for herself and child, she found herself on the bed of death.

At this crisis, the pride, which had made her reject pecuniary assistance from Aylesford, gave way in view of the approaching destitution of her child. She penned a letter to her betrayer, which would have moved a heart of stone, and which induced him, though he had long since forgotten her, and though he had sworn, when she first declined his money, never to give her or her babe a farthing, to propose supporting the orphan. He would not consent, however, even to do this, unless the child should pass for Arrison's niece. An annual stipend, promised to his uncle's former servant, secured the co-operation of the latter. To these cruel terms the dying mother was compelled to accede. Deserted by all the world, she was fain to charge her child to remain with Arrison.

But trembling for the influences the orphan would be brought under, she besought the little one to remember what she had taught of God, and to read, at least once a day, the Testament, her only legacy, which she placed in the daughter's hands. Perhaps the dying mother would have declined the proffered aid altogether, if it had not been for a secret hope that when Aylesford knew the child he would become interested in it. But this expectation was never realized. Aylesford studiously avoided seeing the friendless orphan, and only remembered her existence when called on to pay her annual stipend.

With these facts before her, no wonder that Kate loved that orphan so much. The mother's wrongs, not less than the child's sufferings, appealed to our heroine's heart. "Little Maggy," as she called her protege, repaid these feelings with a fervor that was beautiful to see. Never having had any one to love since she lost her mother, the child fairly worshipped our heroine.

Kate took pleasure in instructing the orphan, and in watching the rapid unfolding of this youthful intellect, which promised to be one of rare and precocious power. Yet often a sigh rose to our heroine's lips, as she thought of the future destiny of her protege, for in that day, even more than in this, such children suffered for the parent's sin; and Kate foresaw that the cruel sneer, the whispered remark, the cold avoidance, would be almost death to the sensitive nature of little Maggy.

Meanwhile the family at Sweetwater went into mourning for Aylesford, and the marriage of Kate, which otherwise would have taken place immediately, was postponed until the spring. There was a town house in Philadelphia, belonging to the family, and thither it was resolved that they should remove for the winter, partly because Kate wished her protege to have the benefit of teachers, who could not be obtained at Sweetwater, and partly for reasons connected with her large property.

In one particular, the arrangement was fortunate for the lovers, for, about this time, Major Gordon received an appointment in the metropolis.

While these events had been transacting, the British expedition, which burned the Neck, having found itself thwarted in the further measures it proposed, had returned to New York. Count Pulaski, though arriving too late to prevent the destruction of the prizes, succeeded in intimidating the enemy, who abandoned the field, being able to pluck no more laurels except the surprising of a picket, about thirty in number, whom they slaughtered in cold blood. In retiring, the man-of-war which accompanied the expedition grounded in the inlet, when the British, finding they could not get her off, set fire to her, lest she should fall into the hands of the Americans. It was amid the derisive cheers of the patriots, and the echoes of her guns, which went off as they became heated, that the royal troops finally stood out to sea, and took their way, crest-fallen, towards Sandy Hook. They had, indeed, burned a few store-houses, given some thirty dismantled prizes to the torch, and ravaged one or two inconsiderable patriot settlements; but they had failed of the great object of their undertaking, the seizure of the privateers, and had lost the most valuable ship of their flotilla. Taught by the result of this enterprise, they never again vexed the neighborhood, though it continued to be a thorn in their side to the very last month of the war.

This is the proper place to mention that one of the refugees who had escaped into the swamp, was captured the day subsequent to his flight, on his coming forth to seek some food; and that, it being proved that he had committed many atrocities, which brought him within the pale of the law, he was condemned to be hung. The sentence was executed at the Forks, and to this day, as a superstitious tradition goes, his ghost haunts the spot where he expiated his crimes.

CHAPTER XLVIII
THE AYLESFORD MANSION

Hark! through the dim woods sighing,
With a moan;
Faintly the winds are crying,
Summer's gone. —*Mrs. Norton.*

Farewell! I will omit no opportunity
That may convey my greetings, love, to thee. —*Shakespeare.*

When the leaves had fallen, the November rains set in, and the winds begun to rave and sob, alternately, around the mansion at Sweetwater, the family departed for Philadelphia.

The old church, amid its now verdureless grove of oaks, seemed, as they drove past, to look sadly on their departure; while the stream in its rear audibly lamented, and the ancient cedars sighed mournfully in the wind. Kate gazed at the dear objects, and then turned, just as the carriage was about to enter the forest, for a last glance down the pond, in the direction of the house. At that instant the sun, which had been obscured by the leaden-colored clouds, suddenly burst forth, kindling the whole landscape into life: the white mansion flashed out; the ruffled lake sparkled like silver; and a glory was flung over the whole western heaven, where the clouds lay piled like peaks and ridges in a mountain region.

When the travellers reached the cross-road, which led towards Uncle Lawrence's farm, the old man was there waiting for them. He stood leaning on his gun, silently enjoying the beauty of the autumn-tinted sky, and inhaling the soft air, as one quaffs delicious wine. So profound was his abstraction, that he did not hear the approaching vehicle, until it was close at hand.

"Good morning, Uncle Lawrence," said Kate, merrily. "Confess now that we have taken you by surprise; and surrender a prisoner at discretion. In other words, jump in and go to town; for we have a spare seat."

The veteran smiled kindly.

"I own that I was off my guard," he said, "but it was the sweet air and beautiful skies that made me forget myself. I was thinking, my child," he continued, his eye kindling, and looking at Kate as if he knew she would appreciate him, "that the New Jerusalem must be as much more splendid than the clouds yonder, as they are than the common things of earth; and I said to myself, that if looking at 'em made me so happy here, what would I be should I get to the heavenly Canaan; and so I prayed to the Lord to keep me steadfast to the end."

Kate gazed at him almost reverently.

"But I've not been idle, either," he said. "I've no doubt I was up before you, after all; for I had shot a deer two hours ago; he hangs out yonder, a mile away, where I left him for the boys to bring home. Remember, you're to tell the Major that I'll look out for him about the time he promised; and that we'll have as great a hunt as ever was known in these parts. Now will you be honest in telling him?" he asked, with a sly twinkle, "for, if you won't, I'll get sister Maggy to do my errand instead."

"Oh! I'll tell him," replied Kate, with a blush and a gay smile, answering in something of her old rattling style. "He'll be getting tiresome, I've no doubt, before Christmas, so that it will be a happy deliverance to me to have him go away for awhile. But, meanwhile," she added, "why not come to town with us, as I have proposed? You don't know," she continued, seriously, "how I shall miss you all."

"It's onpossible just now," replied Uncle Lawrence, shaking his head. "But I reckon I'll be there next spring," he added, with a significant smile, "that is, if I'm alive, even though I have to walk all the way."

Kate blushed crimson at the allusion, but rallying, answered promptly, while she extended her hand for a parting farewell,

"I shall be sure to expect you, and will take care that a carriage is sent for you. You must bring my old friend, Mrs. Herman."

"Mother's too much of a home body, to come," replied the veteran. "Besides she'd be flustered so, she wouldn't know what she was doin', when she found herself among all the grand folk I spose will be there. I shouldn't wonder now," he added "if General Washington himself was to be present."

"Oh! you must come and see," laughed Kate.

"And that you'll be married by your own preacher. I've heerd they wear black gowns, like we see in pictures. I reckon that'll be more cur'us to me than a'most anything else."

"You shall see all," said Kate, "only come; and there'll be no one more welcome."

"Well, you may depend on me, as I said before; that is if I'm alive. The Lord bless you, my child," he concluded, with great seriousness, "and make you as happy as you are good and beautiful."

"Farewell," said Kate, the tears coming into her eyes; and the carriage drove on.

The veteran remained standing, with his hat off, and his thin gray hairs stirring in the autumn breeze, until the coach had disappeared; when he turned to seek his dwelling, feeling as if he had parted with one of his own flesh and blood; and that night, when he led the family devotions, he prayed as fervently for Kate as for any member of his own household.

The Aylesford mansion, in Philadelphia, was an imposing, aristocratic looking edifice, standing back from the street, amid venerable trees, and surrounded by a spacious garden. Thirty years ago, more than one such stately relic of the ante-revolutionary times was still to be seen in our midst; but they have all been long since demolished, or have been so shorn of their surroundings, as to have lost most of their ancient dignity. The town-house of the Aylesfords was among the proudest of these old colonial mansions. It had been, in the preceding generation, the head-quarters of fashion in the city. In the grand, wainscotted room, every person of distinction, who had visited the metropolis, during a period of nearly twenty years, had been entertained. There beauty had rustled its silks, dazzled with its diamonds, conquered by the graceful use of the fan, and awed by the haughty carriage of its plumed and scornful head. There Washington, then a young man, had visited, on that memorable tour in which he lost his heart to the beautiful tory of New York. There royal governors and titled nobles, courted heiresses and worshiped belles, officers and statesmen, the proud Virginia planters and the wealthy Boston merchants, the chivalrous Carolinian and the princely manorial lords of the Hudson, had assembled to drink the rare wines of the host, dance the minuet, or exchange the stately courtesies of the time.

But for many years the mansion had been shut up. A solitary servant had been its sole tenant during all this time. The boys had been allowed, unchecked, to club down the English walnuts from the trees in the yard, and the towns-people had come to consider its desolate look as one of the characteristics of the street where it stood.

Consequently, when the shutters were seen thrown open, one fine November day, and the servant was observed to be carefully scrubbing the gray stone steps in front, everybody was agog with curiosity. The arrival of a travelling carriage, towards evening, collected quite a crowd, and when a tall and graceful girl alighted, followed by a child, and subsequently by a stately, dowager-like lady, the spectators spread the intelligence that the Aylesfords had actually come to town as if to stay, a fact which set half the teatables in the place speculating as to whether the family could be as great tories as rumor had said, or whether it was really true, as had begun to be whispered by those who ought to know, that the heiress was going to marry a patriot officer, high in the esteem of General Washington.

When Kate, the morning after her arrival, walked through the desolate-looking garden, she almost despaired of ever being able to restore it to order. The once clipped boxwood had grown into all sorts of fantastic shapes; the gravel walks were covered with grass; rank weeds had overrun the flower beds; and the grotto at the foot, which, in her childish days, she was accustomed to regard as the greatest wonder of the world, was damp with water, stripped of its shells, and covered with green, slimy moss.

Mrs. Warren, who, to do her justice, was as notable a housekeeper as she was a martinet in dress, walked through the mansion, meantime, absolutely beside herself with dismay. Panes of glass were cracked; spider-webs were everywhere; the wood work was almost black from damp and want of light; the roof leaked; and the whole place, she declared, smelt musty. The good dame exaggerated not a little; nevertheless, the house was in sad, almost dismal disarray, and as the instructions to have it renovated had been disregarded, maids were set to work immediately. For nearly a fortnight buckets and scrubbing brushes had it all their own way. Mrs. Warren, with the true spirit of an old-fashioned Philadelphia housekeeper, was so happy amid this turmoil, that she forgot to reflect on Kate for having ridden alone. Indeed, the excellent dame was never better pleased than when house-cleaning, unless, perhaps, when talking of her cousin, Lord Alvanley, or appearing in a new damask gown.

At last, however, the dowager pronounced "things fit to be seen;" and, ceasing to scold the maids, reassumed the great lady. To use her own phrase, she could now go about the house without "getting the fidgets." We may amuse ourselves in this harmless way, with smiling at the excellent creature's nervous abhorrence of illy-performed housework; but, perhaps, the dames of the present age would be none the worse if they imitated the habits of their great-grandmothers in personally supervising such labor more frequently than they do. The highest in the land, in the good old times, were not above ordering their households; and did not either delegate the duty to upper servants, or leave things to chance.

By the close of November, the Aylesford mansion was restored to all its pristine freshness, and to much of its former vivacity. There were no balls, it is true. But visitors came and went continually, for it was impossible for a family of such consideration to fix their abode in a city so small as the metropolis then was, without all the gentry calling upon them. A whisper of the approaching wedding, which, as we have seen, had got abroad, assisted to stimulate these civilities; for every one wished to be a guest at what, judging from the wealth and position of the bride, could not fail to be an unusually brilliant affair.

CHAPTER XLIX
MAGGY

I cannot speak, tears so obstruct my words
And choke me with unutterable joy. —*Olney.*

With goddess-like demeanor forth she went,
Not unattended, for on her as queen
A pomp of winning graces waited still. —*Milton.*

That what she wills to do or say
Seems wisest, virtuousest, discreetest, best. —*Milton.*

The venerable edifice of Christ Church, the oldest house of worship of its denomination in Philadelphia, still retains the outward appearance it wore five and seventy years ago. But its stately front and exquisite steeple, instead of rising within view of the fashionable quarter of the town, as it did then, now overlooks a wilderness of shops, while its pavement is encumbered on market days with the eggs, chickens, and vegetables of farmers, who chaffer for a cent. The interior of the ancient edifice, however, has undergone great changes, not the least of which is the substitution of comfortable modern sittings for the stiff, high-backed pews in which Lady Washington and the *elite* of that day used to worship.

The appearance of the Aylesfords in their family pew at Christ Church attracted universal attention. The worthy rector lost no time in paying his respects to them, and was charmed with little Maggy as well as with Kate. He became a frequent visitor. He often seemed lost in thought, as he gazed on the child. At last, when Kate and he were alone together one day, he said,

"I have long wished, my dear young lady, to broach a delicate subject to you. I hope you will not think I wish to interfere impertinently in your family matters; but permit me to ask whether that beautiful child, who has just left the room, is really, as report declares, your cousin."

"She is," answered Kate. "But why this question?"

"The daughter of Mistress Margaret Rowan, so called?"

Kate inclined her head in assent.

"From what I know of you then, my dear young lady, and from the kind countenance I see you bestowing on the child, you will rejoice to hear that the fraud, so basely attempted on her mother, utterly failed."

"What!" cried our heroine, with sparkling eyes, clasping her hands in joy. "Can it be possible?"

"Never was there wife, if that poor girl, whose father I knew in England, was not legally wedded to the late Charles Aylesford, Esquire."

"Thank God!" ejaculated Kate, fervently.

"Yes! we may well thank the Almighty one," reverently replied the clergyman; "for out of evil counsel he brought good. But I must explain. It happened in this way."

The rector then proceeded to state that, a few months before the Aylesfords arrived in Philadelphia, he had been summoned, one evening, to the bedside of a dying man in one of the miserable taverns then, and still existing, by the water-side. The invalid was undergoing the most terrible agonies of remorse, having, on his own confession, lived a life of the greatest depravity for many preceding years. He had been, he said, originally a clergyman of the Church of England, had been left a small fortune, and had graduated at Trinity College, Cambridge. But, having fallen into evil courses, through his fondness for company and wine, he had gradually been excluded from the society he was born for, and, finally, had been obliged to fly to America to escape the vengeance of the law. In the colonies he had met Arrison, had become a confederate in his villainies, and had consented to be the tool of Aylesford and him in the clandestine marriage of Miss Rowan. Neither of his employers, however, were aware of his true clerical character; but supposed his assumption of the robes was only a cleverly managed disguise. Nor was this all. Abandoned as he was, the fallen clergyman had still some conscience left, so that he secretly procured the documents necessary to render the marriage a valid one, in all respects. Subsequently he had left Philadelphia, and had remained absent for years, having only returned, in the last stage of a consumption, a few weeks before sending for the rector. A principal object of his coming back, he confessed, was the desire to make reparation for the great wrong he had done Mistress Rowan. Nothing in his whole career, though he acknowledged to being stained with the blackest crimes, had ever affected him, he said, like his share in that treacherous transaction. He had just succeeded in tracing the poor victim, in discovering that she had been abandoned by her husband, and in ascertaining that she died after a few years of toil and shame, when his disease assumed so violent a character that he was unable to prosecute further inquiries. What had become of the child, whether it was dead or living, he had been unable to ascertain. In this extremity, tormented by restless anguish, he had sent for the rector of Christ Church, and placing in the good clergyman's hands the proofs of the legality of the marriage, enjoined him to endeavor to discover the fate of the orphan. Having done this, he seemed more at ease, and expired the same night, shortly after the rector had departed.

"As soon as you came to town, and I saw your little cousin in your pew, I felt that the lost child was discovered," continued the clergyman. "But it was not until I had more certainly ascertained that she was really your blood-connection, that I ventured to take the present liberty."

It now became necessary to acquaint Mrs. Warren with Maggy's real parentage, and consequently with one of those transactions in her nephew's life which had been studiously concealed from her. It was, at first, a terrible shock to the poor creature. But after awhile she became more reconciled to it, finding those excuses which simple, loving hearts like hers always will. It had the beneficial effect, in the end, of making her almost worship little Maggy, whom heretofore she had treated, as we have seen, with comparative indifference. The orphan now came in for the love that had been lavished on Aylesford, and Mrs. Warren entered eagerly into all Kate's plans for the instruction of Maggy; but especially did the good lady interest herself in what she called the "domestic" education of the child, saying naively to her protege; "my dear, as every woman's proper destiny is to be a wife, and to be happy as a wife, it is indispensable that you should know how to prepare a good table for your husband, as all men like good eating, and can indeed be best kept in humor by tickling their palates." This remark was the nearest approach to wit which the dowager ever made; and was slyly quoted to Major Gordon by Kate, as a commentary on his sex.

No one could have progressed with greater rapidity in her studies than did Maggy. Perhaps it is a mistake, into which modern times have fallen, that they put children to school too soon; for, if the young intellect was left unvexed awhile longer, it would probably learn all the quicker when once it began. Certainly, little Maggy, who, at ten years old, could read with difficulty, made the most astonishing progress, so that, by the time she was fourteen, no young lady of her age could boast of so many acquirements. The superior education which Kate herself had received was doubtless of benefit to the child, because it enabled our heroine to impart much instruction not then taught in American schools. In music Maggy had an exquisite ear, while her voice was one of great promise. To hear her sing the simple ballads, then so popular, often brought tears into the eyes of the listeners. It is a strange sight to see such effects produced in our days; but it would be heretical nevertheless to say that we ought to give up opera music in parlors, and return to the artless, plaintive song; for of course we are wiser in this, as in other things, than our ancestors; and it is quite absurd to think that there can be music unless the windows shake, the piano shudders as if in an ague fit, and the dear, sweet performer, opens her month as if she was about to swallow music sheets, instruments and all.

Among those who shed tears, at hearing Maggy's ballads, were several French noblemen, officers in the army of his most Christian Majesty Louis the Sixteenth, at that time the good ally of the confederated States of America. These members of the most artificial and luxurious court in Europe, the principal part of whom had joined the expedition to reinforce Washington out of sheer ennui, having long ago exhausted every phase of life that even Paris presented, were delighted beyond measure at the artless singing of this innocent child of nature. It was not mere highbred courtesy either, which induced them to extol her simple ballads, though never were men more polished in manner than the French nobility of that day. But, as we have said, the unbidden tears started into their eyes as they listened, and there was an earnestness in their tones, that carried the conviction of truth with them, when they told Major Gordon that they had never heard such singing from the gay Marchionesses of Versailles, or even the stars of the opera.

For it was with Major Gordon that these visitors always came. Whenever a French officer brought letters of introduction to the city, our hero was one of the first he called upon; and the latter took his guest to the Aylesfords, as a matter of course. Indeed, had he not done so, he would have constantly been besieged for an introduction to our heroine, as the Duc de Lauzun, who had met her early in the winter, went back to camp enthusiastic in her praise. "La belle Americaine," as he called her, had, he said, the grace and refinement of a Marchioness, with a freshness and originality that was perfectly bewitching. It was said of him, by his intimates, that he had really lost his heart; and it is certain that, years after, when he had became le Duc de Biron, he would talk of the fair Philadelphian; and once he was heard to declare, with a sigh, that he had seen, in America, "the sprightliness and beauty of Marie Antoinette, combined with the innocence and truthfulness of St. Pierre's Virginia;" and it was to our heroine that he referred.

If Mrs. Warren worshipped Maggy, the orphan adored her cousin. It was beautiful, indeed, to see the constant evidences which the child gave of her affection for Kate. When the latter spoke even the most trivial words, Maggy listened eagerly, and seemed by her looks to appeal to others to hear also. On one occasion, when our heroine was sick for a few days with cold and fever, the orphan went almost distracted. She always waylaid Dr. Rush on his retiring, in order to receive the assurance from himself, that Kate was really only triflingly indisposed. When her cousin recovered sufficiently to come down again to dinner, Maggy was nearly beside herself for joy, dancing and skipping about the convalescent, bursting into snatches of song, and continually catching Kate's hand and kissing it.

This slight indisposition reminded our heroine of an unfulfilled intention regarding Maggy. Kate had early resolved to dower the orphan with a portion of her own wealth, and now, as soon as she had recovered, she sent for her attorney and directed him to make out a deed of gift, in favor of the child, as well as to prepare other law papers for her.

"If anything should happen to me," she said, "I wish my affianced husband to inherit the principal part of my estate; but I wish, as much, that Maggy shall not be unprovided for; and I desire also to leave a competence to my aunt."

These generous wishes were accordingly fulfilled. The Major, when he heard of the intentions of his betrothed with respect to himself, would have remonstrated; but Kate silenced him by the gravity of her reply, declaring that, "if he was not worthy to be entrusted with her fortune, in case of her decease, he surely was not with her happiness, if she lived."

Thus the winter passed on. March, with its blustering winds, succeeded; April, fickle as ever, followed; and May, blushing and beautiful, came in. The appointed time of the wedding had nearly arrived, and every body was on the *qui vive* for an event which promised to be so dazzling.

CHAPTER L
A WEDDING IN 1780

Her gentle spirit,
Commits itself to yours to be directed,
As from her lord, her governor, her king. —*Shakespeare.*

To cheer thy sickness, watch thy health,
Partake, but never waste thy wealth,
Or stand with smile unmurmuring by,
And lighten half thy poverty. —*Byron.*

She is mine own;
And I as rich in having such a jewel,
As twenty seas, if all their sand were pearl,
The water nectar, and the rocks pure gold. —*Shakespeare.*

Expectation was more than realized when the ceremony actually came off. All that was distinguished in rank, talent, wealth, beauty, fashion, or social position in Philadelphia, assembled on the eventful evening at the Aylesford mansion. The commander-in-chief, who happened to be in the metropolis, conferring with the Congress, honored the occasion by his presence, and gave away the bride; while the French ambassador, with a large number of officers of his most Christian Majesty's army, also attended; in fact, it was universally conceded that so brilliant a social assembly had never before been gathered together in Philadelphia.

That city, it must be remembered, was not only the political capital of the country at that period, but was also the first in the nation in respect to wealth, intelligence, scientific attainments, and social influence. A few years before, John Adams, on coming up to Philadelphia to attend the first Congress, had written home to his wife, in terms of amazement at what he styled the princely luxury in which the richer citizens lived, and to which, he declared, he had seen no parallel in Boston. Since that period there had been no decline, but rather an increase, in this splendid hospitality. There were fortunes, at that day, which, considering the difference in the value of money, would put even some of the colossal ones of a more modern period to the blush; while the example of the mother country, and the characteristic ostentation of the age, led to a far grander style of living than the taste of the present generation favors. The pompous coach and four; the crowd of liveried footmen; and the gold brocade dress, which a whole year's expenses of a modern toilet would scarcely purchase; these have long been things of the past.

The front of the Aylesford mansion was a blaze of light, on the evening in question. The uproar of carriages, arriving and depositing their precious freights, was almost deafening at times. Between lanes of servants the guests passed up to the imposing doorway, and entering the carved and wainscoted hall, which was now fairly dazzling with light, were shown up the wide staircase to the chambers set aside for dressing rooms. It was a splendid spectacle to see the proud dames, attended by their lovely daughters, come pouring down the ample, heavily balustraded steps, and flock towards the drawing rooms like stately birds. The rustle of stiff brocades, and the fluttering sound of fans, were mingled with a rich, low murmur of animated conversations, carried on in whispers, that was like a soft undertone to a gay piece of music. Nor were the cavaliers less aristocratic looking than the swan-like creatures, before whom they bowed, offering the tip of their gloved fingers to their partners, in the ceremonious but lofty gallantry of the time. The age of dark and sober hues had not yet wholly usurped that of gay colors and silken fabrics for gentlemen's wear; and the *petit maitre* of the day thought himself unfit for female society, if his ruffles were not of the choicest lace, his coat and waistcoat elaborately embroidered, and his white hands sparkling with jewels. All was a blaze of light and grandeur, therefore. Swords jingled; diamond shoe-buckles flashed; necklaces sparkled till they rivaled the fair wearer's eyes; and the air was fragrant everywhere with the exquisite perfumes of the powder shaken from dozens of lovely heads whenever they moved. From a military band, stationed close by in the garden, came bursts of proud music continually, that made many a charming little foot move impatiently, and stirred the blood even of the old.

It would be impossible for us to describe half the superb dresses that made their *debut* on that occasion; but our fair readers would never forgive us if we omitted those of Mrs. Warren and the bride. The former wore a petticoat of crimson satin, thick as a board, the very sight of which would drive a modern belle crazy with envy. Over this was a skirt of rich, gold-flowered brocade; the boddice being made of the same material; and sleeves that, reaching to the elbow, were trimmed with deep, yellow, old lace, of almost fabulous value. But the head dress of Mrs. Warren was the crowning triumph of the good lady's toilette. This coiffure was, in fact, the masterpiece of the French artist, whom Mrs. Warren had engaged three months before, and who had spent most of his leisure moments since in studying out this grand achievement of his genius. It rose nearly two feet in height, a perfect mass of interwoven ribbons, curls and jewels, almost rivaling that, which, a few years later, gave a European reputation to the celebrated Lemard, hair-dresser to Marie Antoinette, because he had consumed in it upwards of fourteen yards of gauze. It was, in short, a miniature tower of Babel, done in hair, pomatum and powder. The dowager was as proud of this *chef d'oeuvre* as her artist, and had but one drawback indeed on her satisfaction, which was that her cousin, Lord Alvanley, could not behold this miracle of art, taste and beauty.

The bride's dress followed the fashion of the hour less servilely, having been made subservient to her own excellent taste. Her hair was drawn back entirely from her face, as was the prevailing *mode*: a style that eminently suited her regular features; but instead of being raised into an enormous tower, it was simply combed over an ordinary cushion, a long curl or two being allowed to fall behind each ear. It was slightly powdered on this occasion, but with silver *mareschale*, which produced an indescribably brilliant effect against her fair complexion; and further ornamented by a wreath of delicate flowers placed on one side. On her snowy, swan-like neck, she wore a superb necklace of diamonds, which had belonged to her mother. Her petticoat was of rich white satin, the bottom being trimmed with wreaths of flowers; while her gown was of rose-colored brocade, wrought with silver flowers, and looped back from the under skirt with bunches of ribbons and flowers. Her stomacher was of costly lace, interspersed with diamonds. Her sleeves, like her aunt's, were tight to the elbow, where they were trimmed with a double ruffle of lace, whose fabric of frost-work set off the taper and rounded arm, heightening even its statuesque beauty. Her shoes were of white satin, pointed at the toes, and with high, red heels, a fashion which showed to the greatest advantage a lady's instep. She carried a Watteau fan, a gift from the French ambassador, worth almost its weight in gold.

Such was our heroine's costume, and amid all that splendid circle, with its furbelows and flounces, its silken net work over fair bosoms, its white shoulders, its powdered coiffures, its diamonds, and its scores of beautiful forms, she was, beyond rivalry, the loveliest. Nor was the bridegroom, who appeared simply in the uniform of his rank, less conspicuous among the array of magnificently clad gentlemen, who, in silk stockings, embroidered coats, broad-flapped vests descending to the hips, and lace frills and ruffles, moved proudly about the rooms. His air of command and of manly dignity had, indeed, but one rival there; and that was in Washington himself, who then, as ever, "towered pre-eminent." The grand, yet simple dignity of that heroic form; the quiet authority in the somewhat severe face; and the unaffected, yet awe-inspiring manner: ah! what pen can describe these, which contemporary painters confessed themselves unable to limn, and which the tongues of his most gifted compatriots fell short of depicting. But, though every eye turned first on the commander-in-chief, (even the eyes of those suspected of secretly wishing well to the royal arms,) the next object of admiration, at least among the ladies, was the bridegroom, as that of the gentlemen was the bride. Even the graceful, highbred, and splendidly clad French noblemen, who were present, altogether failed of attracting attention by the side of these.

The ceremony was impressively performed, the bridegroom making the responses in a firm voice, and the bride in one a little fluttered. After a proper interval had elapsed, the dancing began. But our fair readers must not suppose that those highbred dames permitted themselves, as their descendants do, to be taken familiarly about the waist by a comparative stranger, and whirled around the room in a schottish, or other waltz, as if the giddy pair were human spinning-tops. Nor must they imagine that the cavalier and his partner, with arms a-kimbo and faces alternately turned towards each other and averted, went stamping up and down the apartment, like wild Indians, in a polka. They must not even think that the gentlemen was at liberty to swing his partner till her wrists ached, whenever he approached her in a quadrille, for that now comparatively obsolete dance had not then yet come into fashion. The minuet was the only dance sufficiently courtly for that highbred age. It required something more than ordinary grace also to elicit admiration in that princely pastime; for it was performed in single couples, and with the eyes of the whole room watching for a blunder, or even for the slightest display of awkwardness. When the minuet, however, was danced to perfection, as it was more than once during this evening, it elicited that complete satisfaction in the beholder, which any finished work of art always produces. The gentleman, leading out his fair partner as ceremoniously as if she was a queen, bowed over her hand till he bent almost to her waist; while she curtsied in return, with lashes drooping on her cheek, the color rising into her face, and her damask-gown rustling as it sank to the floor; ah! this had a grace, a stateliness, and an air of chivalrous worship, such as, alas! we never see in a modern ball room. Then the exquisite ease with which the partners subsequently moved through the aristocratic dance, gliding to the slow, measured, stately music, the cavalier inclining his powdered head profoundly, with his hand on his heart, whenever he touched the hand of his companion, while she performed each evolution with a lightness of step, a tender coyness, and a formal grace, which seemed to be the poetical realization of that lordly and perhaps pompous, yet knightly age! When the bride executed the minuet, she carried off all plaudits, however, for notwithstanding others danced well, she danced surprisingly so.

Amid this brilliant assembly there was one personage who attracted no little attention. He was a man, apparently about sixty, dressed with great simplicity, yet with perfect neatness, in the plain garb of what was then called a yeoman. He was evidently unaccustomed to such assemblies, and consequently deficient in the conventional usages proper for the occasion; but no one could look upon his broad, square brow, or kindly eye, or observe his native ease of manner, without being satisfied that he was one of "nature's noblemen." The attention exhibited towards him by the Aylesford family, had already made the guests curious to know who he was; but when the commander-in-chief was observed to be conversing with him, eager inquiries began to pass around. When it was told that he had been an old field companion of the bride's father, and that he was the same person who had saved her life in a moment of great extremity, the romantic story of which was well known in town, everybody, especially the ladies, was crazy to be made acquainted with him. Franklin, in his plain costume, was not a greater favorite among the beauties of the French court, than was Uncle Lawrence on this occasion. Indeed, if it had been at all allowable so to distinguish any one but the bride, it is probable the enthusiasm of the fair creatures would have crowned the veteran with a chaplet, after the manner in which the ambassador and philosopher was honored about the same time at Versailles.

The conversation of Washington with the old man lasted for a considerable time. The unassuming character of Uncle Lawrence; his plain, homely sense; his sincere, yet unaffected piety; and the bravery which, as the General knew, had been proved at more than one crisis, were exactly such qualities as the great hero could fully appreciate. Few could so readily discern, and so thoroughly honor, true manhood, as the Father of his Country. In the course of their conversation, the General alluded to his companion's passion for the chase, which he declared he had once been as fond of as any man; asked several questions about the mode of hunting practised about Sweetwater; and on parting expressed his determination, if ever he visited that part of New Jersey, and had the leisure to spare from the cares of his office, to track a buck with the patriarch.

To say that Uncle Lawrence was not flattered by this mark of attention from the commander-in-chief, would be to misrepresent human nature. Yet he did not permit it to destroy his composure at the time, nor would his manner, a minute after, have betrayed the fact to an observer. He had too just an estimate of himself to be awed by the notice even of the General, though he looked up, and almost reverenced Washington, as possessor of a virtue nearly fabulous. He had also too strong a sense of the common brotherhood and inborn equality of all men, to feel dwarfed in the presence of any one, however high his rank or fortune.

"You have kept your promise. I am so glad," said the bride, beckoning Uncle Lawrence to her, as the General left him. "How are they all at dear Sweetwater?"

"Very well, darling," said the veteran, "or rather I should say," he added, with a sly twinkle of the eye, emphasizing the name, "Mrs. Gordon."

Kate blushed crimson. It was almost the first time she had been called by her new title. She understood the little touch of pleasantary on the part of the old man, however, and replied,

"No, call me darling still, I like it better from you. Though," she added, archly, "the other is a pretty name enough, at least 'my lord and master' thinks so, I suppose."

"He'll have his hands full," answered the old man, entering into this gay spirit, "if you begin in that fashion. I'm telling your bride, Major," he said, as the bridegroom approached, "that you must begin at once breaking her in, or she'll get the bit in her teeth, and runaway with you one of these days. When I was married, an old friend told me that the best way was to smash all the chaney, break the looking glass, and kick over the breakfast table, the very first day, and that arter that my wife would be so skeered that she'd never dare to have a will of her own."

"But you didn't do it," answered Kate, laughingly, quick as ever at repartee, "or else you wouldn't be afraid to go into the best room with your muddy boots on, which, you know, Uncle Lawrence," she added, saucily, "is your great cross in life."

"It's no use talking, when you're by," replied the veteran, "you'll have the last word always. If the Major here was to get druv half crazy, and drown you, as they did scolds in the old times, you'd snap your fingers at him, after your head was already under water."

The bride turned fondly to her husband, and putting her hand on his arm, looked at Uncle Lawrence, merrily challenging his misrepresentation. The Major laughed, Kate blushed, and the veteran, shaking his head, said,

"Well, if I'm not called in till you quarrel, I reckon I'll have an easy time of it."

CHAPTER LI
FAREWELL

A perfect woman, nobly plann'd,
To warn, to comfort, and command,
And yet a spirit still, and bright
With something of an angel light. —Wordsworth

A good man, and an angel! there between,
How thin the barrier! What divides their fate?
Perhaps a moment, or perhaps a year. —Young.

The lives of Kate and Major Gordon were as happy as might have been foretold, from their mutual affection, their firm principles, their good sense, and the adaptability of their characters. They were not exempt from the ordinary mutations of life, having their disappointments and griefs like other people; but these sorrows were never of their own making, but mysterious dispensations from an all-wise Providence.

They had the misfortune to lose their first-born, a beautiful little girl, in her early childhood, just as her budding intellect and grateful tenderness were making her dearer than ever to the heart of her parents. But with this great sorrow, came also many mercies. Other children, good and beautiful daughters, brave and conscientious sons, grew up around them, filling their household with happy faces, sweet laughter and dutiful affection. As years rolled by, and the parents verged to middle age, they had the gratification to see these daughters married to worthy men, the choice of their own hearts, and to know that these sons had found partners, who were not mere playthings of the hour, but companions competent for all the varied duties of life. One of the sons-in-law was an eminent Senator, and his wife an acknowledged leader of society in Washington, who is still remembered for her grace, her goodness and her rare talents. A son distinguished himself greatly at Tripoli, and another rose to be a foreign ambassador. Our heroine, in her mature middle age, and when still a beautiful woman, could say, with the British matron, that all her daughters were virtuous and all her sons brave.

At first, part of the year was spent at Sweetwater, and part in Philadelphia, but finally the residence of the family became fixed in the city, except for the summer months. This was in consequence of the professional calls on Major Gordon, and the unwillingness of Kate to be separated from her husband; for the Major, after the close of the war, had resumed the practice of the law, declaring that he could not be an idle man, even if his fortune was ten times as great. He brought up his sons, in imitation of his own example, each to some particular pursuit. "Every man, who wishes to be either happy, or useful," the Major was accustomed to say, "must have some business to follow; for otherwise the mind eats itself, and *ennui* and ill-health follow, even if idleness does not lead to evil courses." Thus it happened, that while other rich men's sons were bringing the gray hairs of their fathers prematurely to the grave, the children of our hero and heroine grew up to "honor their father and mother," and call their names "blessed."

But the Major, even to a late period in life, was always glad to escape to Sweetwater. Once a year, during the hunting season, he visited it for the purpose of bringing down a deer; and many an exciting day he and Uncle Lawrence had in the old forests round about. The veteran came at last to say that the "Major," as he still called our hero, "was nigh about as good a shot as himself;" and many a tale was he accustomed to rehearse, with a low, triumphant chuckle, of their mutual success. Even Mullen often received a visit from our hero. The waterman, though dangerously wounded at the fight on the Neck, subsequently recovered, and settled down, at the close of hostilities, in the harmless pursuit of a fisherman. He knew where all the best places to catch the finny tribe were to be found, and religiously kept the fact to himself, only admitting Major Gordon to the knowledge of it, and this under strict promise of secrecy. But, at last, our hero, profiting by this information, became so successful, that he often excelled his teacher and patron. Mullen, now grown to be a hardy, weather-beaten old man, with a face the color of mahogany, and a form as wiry as if made of steel, was accustomed, after such defeats, to shake his head, saying, half in jest and half in earnest, "That such treatment was too bad, he had a *despise* for it; it was *scandal-ous*."

Uncle Lawrence lived to a good old age. To the last he retained his fondness for the chase, as well as the physical vigor to endure its fatigues. In rain or shine he would set out, even when past the "three score and ten" allotted as the term of human life, with his gun on his shoulder, whistling as he went. At night his return would be announced by that low, monotonous whistle, long before his form could be discovered through the gloom or falling mist. His death was consistent with his life. One winter Sunday he walked to the old, dear church at Sweetwater; participated in the exercises with even more than his usual earnestness; answered the ordinary kind inquiries of his friends as to his health; and was told by the Major, who happened to be on a business visit to the place, that he had "never seen him looking better," on which he answered, "the Lord is merciful to me, and I have long since tried, as much as poor, human flesh can, to set my house in order." Returning home, he saw that the fire wanted some fresh wood, and his children being, by this time, grown up, and absent, he went out to get an arm-load. He had, however, scarcely laid it on the hand-irons, and was stretching out his palms to warm them, as the logs snapped and crackled into a merry blaze, when he suddenly fell over in his chair, and was dead before his wife could reach his side. The physician pronounced the cause of his sudden demise to be a disease of the heart. He was buried in the grave-yard at Sweetwater, in the spot he had mentioned to Major Gordon; and the leaves rustled, the birds sang, and the flowers blossomed over him, as he had desired. His farm passed long since into other hands. Lately it has been abandoned to the forest, which is growing up, wild and rank, on the fields where the patriarch tilled the soil, and close around the hearth where he offered his morning and evening prayers. Mother earth has claimed not only his own ashes, but even "the place that knew him." His memory, however, still lives, and he is yet traditionally known, in his native region, as a mighty hunter, who left no successor.

Mrs. Warren and Maggy are the only persons of whom it remains to speak. The former was characteristic to the last, and died at a good old age, about the period that Louis the Sixteenth, to use her own phrase, "suffered." In fact, the good lady never recovered from the blow, which the execution of that monarch inflicted on her heart. She had, originally, almost detested him, because he had taken sides against King George; for Mrs. Warren lived and died a tory. But when what she called "the *canaille*" obtained the ascendancy in Paris; when Lafayette carried the king and queen in triumph from Versailles; and when the monarchy itself fell on the fatal tenth of August, she became as violent a friend of the dethroned king as she had ever been his enemy. The trial and execution of the monarch smote her heart to its core. She could talk of nothing else. The bloody deed, in fact, brought second childhood upon her. And when, a few months after, Marie Antoinette herself was so brutally led to the scaffold, Mrs. Warren gave up the ghost, declaring that all order was lost, that birth was no more respected, and that the world was coming to an end; adding that "she had known it would happen all along, she had felt certain something dreadful would occur." In her will, she left what little she had saved to be equally divided between Maggy and "her cousin, Lord Alvanley," thus paying tithe of mint to affection and of cummin to rank.

Maggy grew up all that her friends could have desired, and finally made what everybody admitted was a brilliant match. It was, in truth, more lastingly brilliant than such unions generally are; for it was one of real esteem on both sides, and not a mere marriage of convenience. Her husband was a wealthy Virginia planter, who spent his time on his estates, devoting it to the improvement of his numerous servants: a man, who, though wealthy and well-born beyond most, considered it his duty to labor in his sphere for the interests of his race, and despise no man, however humble, poor, or degraded. In Maggy he found a help-meet, in the full sense of that good old Saxon word; a companion, a counsellor, and co-worker, who "smiled when he smiled, and wept when he wept." If we had not already reached the limits of our story, or if we should ever again take up the pen, we should be tempted to describe the married life of Maggy, in order to show that all romance does not cease when the nuptial knot is tied, and that there is a bliss of domestic life as perfect as the raptures of an Amanda Malvina or a Lord Mortimer.

The whole of that section of New Jersey in which the events of our story occurred, has greatly changed since the period of which we write. Sweetwater itself is in decay; the Forks is in ruins; and vast portions of the original forest have fallen before the woodman's axe. A railroad runs close to the place where the hut of the refugee stood; the scream of the locomotive is fast driving away the few deer left in the region. As we send these sheets to press, we notice that a land company is in operation in the neighborhood, and is issuing proposals to furnish "cheap homesteads," according to the approved fashion of these modern associations. All things have changed. If the author has succeeded in describing, however faintly, a region, a society, and a state of manners already nearly eradicated, he will be content to let the genius of improvement complete the work of destruction, and forever remove all traces of the ruder, but more picturesque past.